The Bitch Goddess Notebook

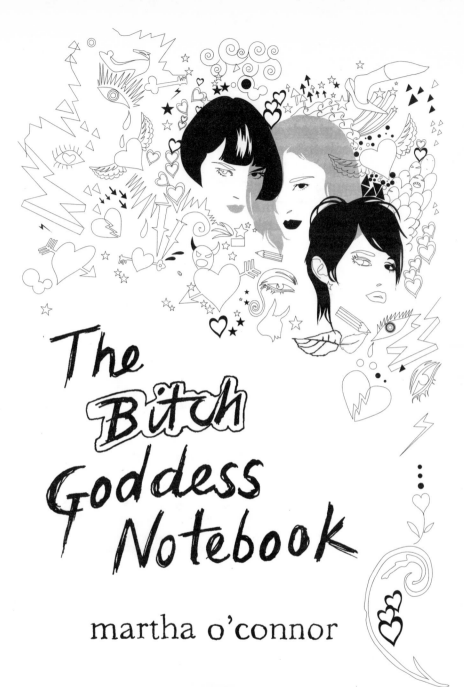

The Bitch Goddess Notebook

martha o'connor

ORION

First published in Great Britain in 2005 by Orion Books,
an imprint of the Orion Publishing Group,
5 Upper St Martin's Lane, London WC2H 9EA

1 3 5 7 9 10 8 6 4 2

Published in the United States by St Martin's Press as
The Bitch Posse.

CIP catalogue record for this book is
available from the British Library.

ISBN 0 75286 739 3

Typeset at The Spartan Press Ltd,
Lymington, Hants

Printed and bound in Great Britain by
Clays Ltd, St Ives plc

www.orionbooks.co.uk

Acknowledgements

I will always be indebted to my agent, Mary Evans, who not only believed in me from the get-go, but also understood my vision and coaxed from me the book you hold in your hands. I'm also thankful to Mary's assistant, Devin McIntyre, for his hard work from start to finish.

Many thanks to Kate Mills and the staff at Orion, and to Sarah Lutyens and Felicity Rubenstein; also to Jennifer Enderlin, Sally Richardson, George Witte, and Kim Cardascia, all at St Martin's Press.

I will forever be in awe of Deb Tomaszewski for her art and grace and friendship.

I owe so much to Jen Couture, the most loyal person in my universe: 'I do not wish to treat friendships daintily, but with the roughest courage. When they are real, they are not glass threads or frost-work, but the solidest thing we know.' – *Ralph Waldo Emerson*.

And my sincere gratitude to all the others who have been true friends on the long and crazy journey.

Last and most importantly, all my love to Phil and the children, who made everything possible.

for Phil
for listening, for believing
for being you

and for the children
for teaching me so much about love and life

I lock my door upon myself,
And bar them out; but who shall wall
Self from myself, most loathed of all?

Christina Rossetti, 'Who Shall Deliver Me?'

I am in blood
Stepp'd in so far that, should I wade no more,
Returning were as tedious as go o'er:
Strange things I have in head, that will to hand;
Which must be acted ere they may be scann'd.

William Shakespeare, *Macbeth*

Consumer Product Information

The Beverage You Are About To Enjoy Is Extremely Hot. Sip Carefully.

You have the right to remain silent. Anything you say can and will be used against you in a court of law.

Professional Driver on Closed Course. Do Not Attempt.

Parental Advisory: Explicit Lyrics.

You have the right to an attorney. If you cannot afford an attorney, one will be appointed for you.

Warning: You Have Now Entered a Chick-Lit-Free Zone.

Pass Icy. Chains Required.

Small Craft Advisory. Sustained Winds of 17–33 Knots.

Mind the Gap.

Want a beach book? Buy yourself some *Bridget Jones.*

Want to get off? Your local video store has a wide array of suitable titles. Or try the Internet.

If you want something simple, you're in the wrong place.

This is about revealing secrets, not tits and ass.

Well, not *just* tits and ass.

The truth, the whole truth, and nothing but the truth, so help you God.

Danger: Riptides and Undertow. Swim at Your Own Risk.

Haunted Forest, Witches Castle, 1 Mile. I'd Turn Back If I Were You!

Do Not Leave Child Unattended.

Say it aloud: *Screw fairy tales and chick-lit and all forms of lying.*

Gentles, do not reprehend.

If you pardon, we will mend.

Ah, just jump in. We dare ya.

1
Rennie

March, 2003
Mill Valley, California

Rennie's heart is pounding so hard her chest is going to burst in a minute. She floats her tongue over her lips as her student teacher, Bay, tosses aside the pillow. He knots his hands in her hair, dips down for a kiss, and they fall together onto the bed. Thighs aching, she spreads her legs and wraps her arms around his warm brown back. Each movement presses away her literary agent's critique of her novel chapters:

Don't open with a sex scene, Wren. Readers will lose sympathy for your heroine.

She tightens her legs around her lover, grabs his ass.

Fuck me.

The word 'cunt' in a novel aimed at women? Probably not a good idea.

Bay, Bayuni, Bayuni Henares, her pretty young lover, her student teacher from San Francisco State, her Bay. All hers, no one else's. He's working with Rennie this year at Tam High, learning from her. Ooh boy, all kinds of things.

And he swirls his tongue into her ear, just how she likes it.

Your heroine needs a gay best friend.

She needs better shoes.

Fuck me.

Other than the titillating little term the university uses, 'Master Teacher', there's nothing illicit whatsoever about her and Bay. She grabs his head and presses his mouth to her breasts and he nibbles and sucks and everything is perfect. This is the moment where her lips fall open and she breathes out an 'oh'.

Don't write about the Midwest, Wren, no one cares.

4

Fuck me.

She guides his hips and they've found a rhythm now; he's rocking into her, perfect, perfect.

She and Bay started like these things usually do. After a few weeks of exchanged glances, too-long planning conferences, phone calls at home about newspaper layouts, Rennie couldn't stand it. The same old pattern – it was like picking a scab, she couldn't help it.

When she's Rennie Taylor grabbing someone's ass to push him farther inside her, she's not Wren Taylor, who can't finish her second book. She doesn't have to hear Lisa's voice in her ears:

She needs to live in Manhattan.

San Francisco, can you at least do San Francisco?

Safe.

Safe.

Safe.

When she's screwing yet another student teacher here in her Mill Valley cottage, she doesn't have to think about Lisa, doesn't have to think about her empty, nonexistent novel, doesn't have to think about anything.

Not her past.

Not the Porter Place.

That wasn't real anyway.

No more yielding but a dream . . .

She washed all that away a long time ago. She has all kinds of tricks for doing that.

Fuck me.

Fuck me.

Fuck me.

The best thing about sex is the way it fills the emptiness.

Before Bay, it was Jason. Before Jason, it was Lee. Before Lee, it was Seamus. Before Seamus, it was KevinBenTroy-HectorJim. Then her student teachers blur into an endless string of Stanford undergrads including (if you count blow jobs as sex) that embarrassing little moment with a certain Stanford football player, whose real name she never did find out. When the quake hit in October of her sophomore year,

5

she was blasted on cheap sherry in the Maples Pavilion locker room, messing around with the star Cardinal quarterback and his best friend. Eight buildings on the Stanford campus were damaged that day, which just proves that disaster follows her wherever she goes.

An addict? It's crossed her mind but she's no addict. Addicts do it with random people in dark alleys, strangers they'll never see again, have sex partners into the hundreds.

She prefers to think of herself as a hobbyist.

Before Stanford, of course, it was Rob Schafer.

To blot away his face, the swatch of dark hair on his chin, she squeezes her eyes shut and presses against Bay, her breath quickening. A moan drifts from her lips, and she lets herself remember how it started with Bay, because that's the here and now.

That's the time and place she is fucking herself back into.

Late that night, as they were pulling student news items together, she watched him click away at layouts on the computer. Daring herself, she licked her finger, drew it across his neck. He turned, and she pressed her mouth on his. His lips parted and she dove right in, and his fingers tangled in her hair as he pulled her down on top of him. Clothes came off and they did it on the cold tiles, there at Tamalpais High School, after everyone had gone home.

Months later he's still coming to her little cottage in Mill Valley most afternoons after school. Of course their relationship isn't just about sex. They talk about teaching philosophy, learning styles, the war about to start in Iraq that Rennie's not really paying attention to because no one can change anything. What a fucking idiot, holding up signs in downtown Holland, Illinois. US OUT OF EL SALVADOR, what the hell difference did it make? Who in Holland gave a damn about El Salvador or could do anything?

If it weren't for the walls around Holland, everyone in the country would drown.

Holland makes her think of the Porter Place again, and her breath bursts out in hot waves. *Just fuck it out of me, take it away.*

6

He moves against her, faster now, and she needs to blur and blot out her memories, but at that moment a still-frame flashes in front of her, a wine glass suspended in mid-air, shards falling to the floor, each containing a feature of *his* face. The scream of a barn swallow tears through the silence. Cherry's eyes plead with Rennie through the car window, her lips forming the word that sealed her fate.

I'm such a bitch, I'm such a bitch, how could I let her do that? She presses against her lover, her fingernails biting into his back. *Oh, fuck me, just make it go away . . .* And it sort of works, better than anything else does, anyway. Maybe she and Bay will last a while, longer than the others. Her romances are dandelion puffs; one moment of a thrill and they're gone.

His fingers press her hair back from her face. But she aches for more, it's not enough, just sex is never enough, and despite her promises to herself she whispers, 'Bay . . . get it . . .'

Bay rolls off her. Rennie's fingers slips between her legs, and her gaze falls on her memory shelf. The red-stained jar holds the light like a garnet, reflected from the lamp on the bedside table. Bay's never asked about it. He respects her privacy or maybe there are things about her he doesn't want to know.

She keeps it because she can't get rid of it, but sometimes her glance flits in its direction, like tonight in the swell of sex in her room, in the womb of passion that still, somehow, contains *this*. A sinking spin flies through her stomach. Fifteen years ago, wasn't it? When the Bitch Posse girls took a straight razor blade, slashed it across their forearms, trickled the blood into three glass jars. That was before they'd pushed things too far, before that night in the middle of nowhere, before that night of blood for blood.

'Forever . . .' Cherry whispered in her ear, her breath blowing at Rennie's hair, then dyed pure black to match her crocheted see-through sweater, her shorter-than-short miniskirt, her Doc Martens. The jars had been Cherry's idea.

Oh, God, her girls, her lost sad girls . . .

That's the past, Rennie; you can't change it.

She presses her hands to her breasts, and now Bay's holding the knife just how she likes it. What she loves about Bay is that there's no hesitation; he wants only to please her, and he has never asked questions or judged. And she moves her fingers from her breasts to her eyes and lets the crish, crash rock her, not to sleep, but to that unworldly feeling, the one at the top of the roller coaster, the jumping out the window feeling, the second before gravity catches her and pulls her unabashedly toward earth. The moment wraps her up and spins her, and her body heats up, scalding, and she feels him get into bed with her, his skin smooth and sweaty against her belly.

That night fifteen years ago, things made sense. Amy held her hand over her eyes as the blood washed into the jars, but Rennie watched the whole thing. Cherry's fingers tangled around Amy's waist, her red hair whispering around her chin as Rennie clasped her arms around Cherry, in love with her friends, forever.

Forever.

Afterward they flopped across Cherry's bed, watched the blood trickle up and down the sides of the jars they turned this way and that, before falling asleep.

She leans to the bedside table and turns off the light.

'Now?' Bay slides the blade along her belly, gently, not cutting.

She can smell Cherry's incense, patchouli, or is it Bay's sweat, so sweet, so bitter? But she squeezes her eyes closed. Metal presses against flesh. 'Harder.'

He draws the knife across her belly again. This time the skin separates and she blinks her way back into the universe, watches the valley fold open, the blood seaming up along the cut and pressing out, blue to red in the air of this world, and as usual the pain springs her into the here and now.

But some blood will never wash away.

Forever.

How could they have known it would end the way it did? She's never talked about it, terrified, stricken, unable to

8

comprehend that she did such a thing, that it actually happened, that it materialized in the real world.

But the story plays itself over and over in her head when she's alone in bed at night, when guilt tugs her insides out and flings them into her face, when tears roll down her cheeks for no reason at all.

That's why being alone is so terrifying.

She lifts her body toward the knife, and Bay understands, slices again. She wonders sometimes if he likes this too much, because this time the cut is really deep, and she cries out, spreading her legs. He sets the knife aside and now, now, he presses into her again. They move together, the blood sticky between them. He's drawn her so close to the edge, so close, and she comes quickly, hard, heart beating in her ears as she scrapes her nails down his back.

When it's over embarrassment floods her, and they speak little as they attend to the business of daubing her belly, covering up with a bandage. The stage prop cigarettes are lit; smoke curls in the air. Shiny eyes blink in darkness, and Bay says comforting words: *You're so sexy, Rennie . . . My wild one . . . Did I do it right?* But of course that's not what she wants; she doesn't know what she wants. She felt good for a minute but now it's all she can do to keep from pulling the stained knife from the bedside table, slashing it across her wrists. Why is she so unhappy, with her pretty Bay, her great teaching job? She has only two preps this year, she lives near San Francisco just like she'd planned, out of Holland, Illinois for-fucking-ever. She's a published writer, an award-winner even. (Never mind that pesky second book that doesn't exist and maybe never will.) She and her younger lover are smoking in bed after terrific sex, and he'll stay over tonight, cook her pancakes, and they'll drive to school separately, surreptitiously. It's just naughty enough to be fun but not so naughty it could get her into trouble. Her life is all she's ever wanted.

Isn't it?

Some wounds will never heal.

From across the room the memory jar stares back at her.

It got too awkward to write to Cherry after a while, the letters pouring back in Cherry's rounded script, telling her way more than she wanted to know about where she was and why and how it felt. And Amy, of course, Amy pushed her away right after it happened.

Those girls are gone forever.

The Girl Genius is dead.

The tears that sting her eyes are easy to explain.

2
Cherry

March, 1988
Holland, Illinois

In case you were wondering, my mom's a total fuck-up.
Thank God for Rennie and Amy, the best friends I've ever
had. If I had Marian – she wants me to call her Marian – for a
female role model I'd have shot myself three years ago, when
I couldn't see far enough into the future to know there was a
sliver of hope in the distance, that I could transcend Marian
and become Cherry Diana Winters, Somebody.

Tonight's the perfect example. Here I stand in the kitchen,
dirty dishes scattered over the countertops. Do you think
Marian is helping wash, dry, stack, with some crappy,
unrealistic yet vaguely reassuring family sitcom on in the
background? Uh-uh. Marian's doing a couple lines in the
bathroom, all secretive like I don't know what she's up to.
Just a few seconds ago she was in here bitching about the
dishes, then she snarled at me about homework, like she
forgot what she was yelling about between the time her
sentence ended and the next one started. Maybe she was just
trying to do the responsible mom act, because when I said I
was starting the dishes she forgot about the homework and
took off to snort her coke.

If I didn't have Princess Di to look up to I'd probably kill
myself. I have her name, and part of me hopes that connects
me to her, that I could even be her, someday. That I don't
have to turn into Marian.

You do know I was born a princess, and the king and
queen just left me on Marian's doorstep, don't you? They'll
come back for me someday.

Yeah, right.

Should clue you in that she named me Cherry. Why do hippies saddle their children with wacko names like Peace, Rainbow, Moonchild? My best friend got stuck with 'Wren'. Only she goes by 'Rennie'. What am I supposed to be, 'Chair'? You know how many guys have made snappy remarks about my name, thinking they're oh-so-original? *What me to pop you? I'll break you* . . . Ha ha ha. Someday I'll go by Diana, but not while I'm playing the bad girl. When I'm grown up, when I'm good enough to be a princess.

The moments after the first couple lines Marian's usually okay, happy. Then her thoughts spin out of control, and her energy goes all over the room, and she says, *If I had a piano I'd play it till kingdom come* . . . but she doesn't so she takes out her cards and shuffles them, plays a game of solitaire, shuffles again, and plays faster and faster, and if it's a bad time she'll get depressed and nasty. And she cries.

I pull cat hair from the disposal, dreading her return. Did I mention we have fourteen cats in this tiny house? But I love them all: Pongo, Posey, Belinda, Baby, Bradbury, Bitch, Jezebel, Jaws, Jazzy, Juniper, Jelly, and the newest babies Skinny, Scream, and Shelly. Marian decided all of them were mine except Pongo and Posey, whom she never got fixed. Why else would someone own fourteen cats?

I flood the lasagna pan from two nights ago with soapy water and start scraping with a knife. Want to guess which one of the Winters women made the lasagna?

The abrasive, gentle rhythm of blade against glass is somehow comforting, and I flick on the radio with a soapy finger as Jelly or, no, I think it's Jezebel – they both have gray spots and both look exactly alike, but Jezebel's getting fatter, pregnant maybe? – jumps off the stove onto the floor and darts across the kitchen. When some asinine Bon Jovi song floats over the airwaves – what did I expect in Holland? – I pop in the Sisters of Mercy tape I shoplifted from the mall a few weeks ago. I felt bad ripping it off, but it wasn't like I had a choice, since I have no money, and I live in Holland, Illinois, where we vote Republican and till the fields, where Homecoming's big news, where practically the whole school's white and middle class and so fucking predictable, where noble farmers struggle their whole lives so the CEO of Archer Daniels Midland can buy his tenth Mercedes. Welcome to my hometown: Holland, Illinois, where cutting-edge radio is 'Livin' on a Prayer'.

I turn 'This Corrosion' up loud, way loud, to blast Jon-Bon-Fucking-Jovi out of my brain. Andrew Eldritch slashes thick and angry words into the air, words about bleeding until you can't bleed anymore, words that break my heart and words that make me hate and words that make me want to dance.

The lasagna pan needs more soaking, and I let it fall into the water, brushing my hair away from my face with the back of one hand. Marian appears out of nowhere, running her knuckles across her red, pasty nostrils. 'You're not going out in *that*.'

'That' is a super-tight black v-neck sweater, black mini-skirt, fishnets and combat boots. Sam likes it, but that's not why I wear it. My clothes are part of who I am. I wear this kind of outfit whenever I go out, so I don't see what her problem is. But this is part of her show. She'll let me wear the outfit. The only question will be how big a deal she makes of it. She dresses slutty herself, but that's not why she'll drop the subject. In a minute, if I'm lucky, her thought train will jump the track.

'Listen, Cherry.' She turns down my music, pulls a cigarette from the pack on the counter, and lights it. 'When I was your age, I dressed that way too. Do you see where it got me?' She offers me the pack. I shake my head – I've got a sinkful of dishes to do and I might have to make a quick getaway. 'A baby, no husband, and a fucking waitress job. Seventeen years later what do I have?'

'A seventeen-year-old, no husband, and a fucking waitress job.'

She blows out a thick stream of smoke. 'Do you want to be like me?'

'Like me' has nothing to do with her job or the fact that she was a teenaged mom or that my father's not part of our lives or even that she's a fucking cokehead. It has to do with who she is. I will never, ever, ever be like her.

I can't say that, though. I'm too cautious to stoke her fire, because I've seen her angry on coke, and it's worse than any other kind of angry I've ever seen. 'Yeah, Marian, you're right.' I don't mention the clothes again because she probably won't remember that the clothes were what got her started on the speech.

'I'm right?' Her eyes harden into pebbles. 'What's that supposed to mean?'

God, I can't say anything. 'Sorry.' I lift Bitch off the refrigerator and deposit her onto the floor. My heart beats in my ears as I dip my hands back into the sink. *Please, let her keep control.*

But she pulls a clean plate from the drainboard and hurls it at the wall, where it shatters. 'What do I have to do to get your attention? You're not going to be like me.' A shine of snot appears at the corner of her nostril, but she doesn't bother to wipe it away, just lets it glisten there. She yanks my arm out of the dishwater and squeezes it, hard. 'You don't want my life. Hell, I don't want my life. How the fuck did I end up here?'

I shake my arm away, just wanting to get the hell out.

'Don't pull away from your mother.' As if in slow motion, the open palm smacks across my face, and in spite of my prayers to stay strong I cry out, hands fluttering to my cheek. I back away from her, slowly; I don't want to upset her more. 'Someone needs to get your attention! Who do you think you are, going out dressed like a hooker?'

So she hasn't forgotten the clothes after all, or maybe it's just an excuse to blow up. Her eyes have that glassy look, the glazed-over TV set look, and I whisper, 'I'm sorry . . .' and hightail it toward the door before she hits me again.

Her face crumples. 'Cherry, I don't want you to end up like me. That's all.' Tears streak down her face, running her makeup so she looks like a clown in the rain. My cheek still smarts, but more than that my stomach burns, whirls. I just want out of here, forever.

14

'I'm sorry if I hurt you, honey. I love you,' she pleads, and now the sobs start, the wheedling voice, the gulps, the chokes, the cocaine-laced promises. I don't want to hear them. 'Wouldn't want to stay home tonight with your mom, would you?'

She's angling for something, probably wants a little company, someone to smoke some dope with when she gets too paranoid. Count me out. 'Me and Amy and Rennie are going to hang around the college awhile,' I say coldly. I'd far rather get drunk or stoned in the basement of the Psych Building with my two best friends in the world than toke up with Marian, who gets disgustingly chatty when high, and unpredictable when wired on coke. She's up for a bigger whaling tonight; I know she has it in her, and I'm sure as hell not going to be around when it happens.

I grab the keys from her purse — better that I have the truck tonight than Marian — and pull my leather jacket off the sofa. Before she can notice what I've done, I'm out the door.

What's on her agenda tonight? Is she going to space out in front of stupid sitcoms and mope about a life she'll never have? Or will I come home later to find her tangled on the sofa with a man I don't know, some bar pickup? Who gives a fuck, anyway?

Not me. I don't need a mom. I can take care of myself.

I pull my mittens on and walk toward the truck, and now's when the real fun's going to start; now's when the Bitch Posse's going out to raise some hell.

Oh, I'm the luckiest girl in the world to have the friends I do. They've freed me from Marian, made me into somebody. Rennie, who's way too beautiful to be a virgin, always acts like I'm doing her a huge favor by hanging around her, when really I was the one who ached for her attention and couldn't believe the smartest girl in class actually thought I was worth her time, said I was creative, told me she liked my poems, that I could be somebody. Cherry Diana Winters — Somebody. Of course, I'll never tell her how desperate I am for her friendship. It would totally shatter her image of me.

Part of why Rennie likes me is that I'm off the wall, wild, different, strong.

Maybe I am.

Maybe not.

And Amy – well, Amy's looking for fun, wherever it's to be had. She ditched the popular crowd to be with us because we accept her for who she is. Took a scissors to her fucking cheerleader uniform and threw it in the too-gorgeous face of her former best friend, Pammie McFadden. That was when we decided Amy was the Uber-Bitch-Goddess.

I let the truck run while I scrape the windows. Scoring Amy – Homecoming Queen Amy, Head Cheerleader Amy – gave me and Rennie credibility. We got together as best friends just before Christmas. First me and Rennie, then Amy. We christened ourselves the Bitch Posse. Figured that way we had license to do whatever the hell we wanted, since we were bitches anyway – we said so ourselves.

Tonight the Bitch Posse's going to find some trouble. I don't know what it is yet, but if you don't find trouble, trouble finds you. It's better to choose your own.

Besides, it's a hell of a lot more fun.

3
Amy

Amy presses her palm to her swelling belly and stares at the birthday cake on the gray marble countertop. Night blankets the four-bedroom Craftsman on the Saint Mary's River as a cold wind whistles outside, hard enough to blow her across to Ontario. Where the hell is Scotty? He promised he'd be home early tonight, that he'd cut short his trip to Hancock, where he's scoping out a second Toyota dealership he might buy.

Amy considers herself lucky. Most residents of the Soo aren't doing so well, so she has the best of both worlds: a painter's paradise of Lake Superior beaches, sunsets sparkling over the water, tall white pines, blueberry bushes, scrubby jack pines, the ground a blanket of needles; and of course, enough money to surround herself with the things that make her feel successful: hardwood floors, granite countertops, Viking appliances, Pottery Barn crockery, Martha Stewart copper cookware, embroidered dish towels, all bought online, stuff most of the permanent residents of the Soo could never afford.

But why, when she's alone at night, does she feel like a small ghost of a girl, about to blow away in the wind, disintegrate into ash? Didn't she do everything right, leave her old life behind her, change?

After all this time, why does it hurt so much to think of her old friends?

And why, after fifteen fucking years, do those four red letters still burn against her eyelids?

No. That girl at the Porter Place isn't a part of Amy

anymore. She was very careful to put that behind her, right after it happened. No letters to Cherry, not a word to Rennie, ever. The old Amy's dead. The new Amy's pregnant and well-to-do and happy.

Right?

This afternoon, she bundled up and walked to the Sault Harbor, just to pass the time. A tug and barge crunched their way through fairly thin ice past Mission Point at around one o'clock, bound for Detroit amid clouds of diesel smoke. Tonight, she heard on the late local news, they'll heave-to in the ice off Nine Mile Point, passing the hours till daylight when the Coast Guard icebreaker will help them the rest of the way along the lower Saint Mary's River. She feels a sense of kinship with the little tug, pulling Scotty along, hardly noticeable.

God, she hasn't painted in so long.

Her heart's not in it anymore.

The wind outside sings a familiar song, whose haunting notes she transposes in her mind to hopeful ones. Despite her anxiety, her annoyance at Scotty, and the cold loneliness that winter storms bring her, tonight's birthday is going to be special. No matter how late Scotty gets here, they'll have cake and milk (Amy wishes it was champagne, but she knows better than to drink while she's pregnant) and sing Happy Birthday. Later, much later in bed, they'll have that warm, wonderful sex that somehow seems so much better now that she's pregnant, his flat belly pressing against her rounded one, the skin over the baby so tight, so firm. For once she feels perfect. 'Your last birthday before you're a daddy,' she told him this morning, before he left. In three months they'll be joined by a little girl. Her baby was exquisite on the sonogram, each finger fully formed, the thumb of her left hand popped firmly in her mouth. Amy doesn't deserve this, does she, could she?

Scotty doesn't want to know if the baby's a boy or a girl. He covered his eyes during the sonogram, made a little joke of it even. But Amy's already bought some frilly outfits and folded them away in the dresser in the nursery that Scotty's painted yellow. She hasn't come up with a name yet. Bad luck, or superstition. After all this time, her life is coming together, but she can't quite believe it.

Oh, there are the small disturbances – tonight, for instance. Scotty promised he'd be home early to celebrate his thirty-fifth birthday with her. 'Can't promise I'll be back for dinner,' he said before grabbing his coffee and kissing her goodbye, 'but I'll be back for cake.' Now, she glances at the clock above the stove. Ten forty-five.

But the time, like all Amy's problems, seems small, unfair, compared to what most people have to deal with. Still, there's something not quite right; it's like that moment in the horror movie just before something awful bursts from behind the heroine. Inside her head lingers a niggling suspicion that life *won't* work out for her, because it shouldn't.

All this time she's thought her past was buried deep under layers of experiences and thoughts and her and Scotty's courtship, but somehow it keeps wearing away the wall she's built. She does a little patchwork now, mortaring over the crumbling bits with the good memories.

Oh, think of the U of M, think of the Angell Hall Psych lecture where we stared at each other week after week. His name, she knew, was Scotty. But neither exchanged a word until the last day of class, when he handed her a skinny paperback by a poet named Pablo Neruda. She read from it, not listening at all to the lecture, dipping at his phrases. *Ah los vasos del pecho! Oh the goblets of the breast! Ah los ojos de ausencia! Oh the eyes of absence!* Her breath quickened, and she stared at Scotty, her cheeks flushed, his eyes shining. *He ido marcando con cruces de fuego el atlas blanco de tu cuerpo. I have gone marking the white atlas of your body with crosses of fire.* Dizzy, half-drunk, her eyes scanned across *Quiero hacer contigo lo que la primavera hace con los cerezos. I want to do with you what spring does with the cherry trees.*

After class, he ducked out, but she said, 'Wait, wait,' and the 'wait' turned into a kiss, one that, in its lips and tongues and passions, reminded Amy of another gorgeous kiss, so long ago. The kiss turned frantic, and wordlessly they snuck to Harlan Hatcher Library for a tangle of giggles that turned into naughtiness in the deserted third-floor stacks. He leaned her against the wall, driving into her, kissing her neck. God, she'd no idea poetry could be so seductive. The best most exciting alive awake sex she's ever had, surrounded by books, words, thoughts and ideas folded up into themselves, undiscovered. As he cried out and she shivered into his arms and blinked him into focus, the first words he said to her were, 'I love you.'

She drowns herself in that memory awhile, letting the moments wash over her, anything to blur away the present, where Scotty's never home when he says he'll be, where all there is to do late at night is go online and drop a couple hundred on the latest Internet sale at J. Jill or Williams-Sonoma or the Gap or wherever, where she's alone in this cold house in this cold place, with memories that will never go away no matter how much money she spends.

She runs her nails across the perfect countertop.

Of course, she wasn't stupid enough to think sex would turn into love. When it happens this way most often the guy is a bastard; but odd, she and Scotty broke her own rule, in love already, must've been for a long time before the Neruda book. They stayed up night after night at his apartment talking, conversations turning into sex that was a poem itself, spinning tantalizing and seductive; Scotty always took his time with her. For the rest of the term they walked around holding hands, and by the end of summer she was wearing an engagement ring and her fairy tale had begun.

After their wedding came the move to the Upper Peninsula where Sarah and Ken Dionne welcomed her with open arms and a *So glad you're in the Soo, we promise not to call you a troll, eh?* Her in-laws, the parents she never had, initiated her into all the charming ways of the UP. Soon she too craved the strange meat and rutabaga pasties (which Amy quickly learned to call 'pass-ties' instead of 'pace-ties') and believed the best thing that could happen to 'Yooperland' would be the Mackinac Straits Bridge blowing up. She too called the Michiganders from 'below the Bridge' the 'trolls'; she too screamed her heart out at the I-500 snowmobile race. She even catches herself ending sentences with 'eh?' once in awhile. The Soo's not like the Midwest that she hates; it's more akin to Canada. Better yet, the UP should become its own country, secede from Michigan.

Deer hunting is the one Yooper tradition she still can't stomach, for obvious reasons.

Reasons she won't let herself think about.

Reasons she can never explain to Scotty.

She drowns that thought in the struggle to have a baby, the Pergonal injections and the second move and the wonderful day she heard she was pregnant.

That was a long time ago, those beautiful moments that threw warm earth on the boxed-up secrets of her past. But the past isn't gone at all. Yesterday, in one of the cartons she'd never unpacked from their move to the bigger house, she found it.

She felt the black cover, smelled the leather, ran her fingers along the crisp, unopened pages. The Bitch Goddess Notebook. Amy guessed she'd had it when it had all come down, when the Bitch Posse had been pulled apart, the girls separated, forever as it turned out.

She has nothing else of those days, not her blue beaded necklace, not her blood-stained glass jar, which she'd smashed soon after, well, never mind. As for the notebook, she didn't look at it yesterday, didn't dare. Why open the pages and send the past flying into the perfect present? Why let the voices and ghosts join her in her happiness? Instead she stashed it high on the kitchen cabinets, out of sight.

But something about Scotty being late tonight forces an ancient, visceral, female anger through her, one she hasn't felt for a long, long time. She pulls the notebook down from its place above the cupboard where she keeps spices and flour.

Biting her lip, she opens it.

Bitch Goddess Notebook Entry #1

Holland, Illinois
December 31, 1987
Ha ha ha New Year's Eve with the Bitch Posse!!!!

HAPPY BIRTHDAY AMY!!! You are the Uber-Bitch-Goddess! We are girls wrapped up in women, women bursting out of girls, eggs that came before chickens, bitches now and forever. We do what we want and God help anyone in our way. Fuck teachers, fuck the system, fuck everyone! We will make it till June and graduate, then goodbye Holland, for-fucking-ever. We don't even have to write this Credo because it's all in our heads.

The Bitch Posse girls. Cherry Winters, Rennie Taylor, Amy Linnet.

Amy traces her finger across the giant heart she drew fifteen years ago, skates over the pictures she sketched of the girls. Cherry, her red hair in a fuck-me bob. Just looking at her forces guilt and pain and love and heartbreak down Amy's throat. And Rennie, dyed black hair buzz-cut all over except for a crown of bangs and a few stray locks, here and there. Amy's own eyes are wide open, revealing mysteries, wispy blonde hair curving in tendrils around her face. Somehow, Amy looks the saddest of all. But pictures don't tell the future. Or do they?

She closes the notebook on the past and draws her fingers across the slick granite countertop of the present, then rests them on her swollen belly again. It feels fuller somehow. The pizza she ate after watching the boats was too spicy, or she ate too fast. That's what happens when you eat alone, you eat too fast.

Where the hell is Scotty?

You should be happy, Amy. Tears prickle her eyes. *You have everything that everyone your age wants.* The voice in her head doesn't comfort her, though. It sounds accusing, and her stomach ache is getting worse.

22

She pours herself a glass of milk and sits at the counter, staring at the cake, the white icing cresting in little snow-peaks over the center, thirty-five candles crammed into the pendulum. This afternoon she thought it'd be cute to make Scotty's cake in the shape of a clock. Then she'd have him unwrap the watch. It feels stupid now, a lame joke. As she gulps down the milk, each swallow makes her thirstier until she reaches the bottom. Droplets cling to her upper lip, a cold film over her warm skin, and she wipes them away, presses her chin in her hands, and stares at the cake, eye level, so closely she can see cracks in the icing, valleys and canyons in the mountainous snow country, places for climbers and skiers to fall into, to be buried by an avalanche. If she was there, she'd ski across that ridge – no, *that* one, and . . .

Pain shoots through her belly, stabbing, knives everywhere, and suddenly she's sitting in something wet and . . . Did she spill the milk? She glances down. Blood blooms through her skirt, blood's dripping over the edge of the stool, blood all over the place. Fear rips through her. *There's something wrong with the baby, oh God, there's something wrong with the baby . . .*

'Scotty!' She claws through the air, clutches at the phone. But a second name, stronger, firmer than Scotty's, pounds through her head. *Callie.* Even as blood trickles down her leg, puddles across the white tiled floor, and her abdomen cramps so much she doubles over in pain, she feels this all makes sense to her, that it's what she's anticipated all along.

That nothing good should happen to her.

She presses in the phone number of the auto dealer in Hancock, even though Scotty's surely on the road by now.

That she should pay.

'*Scotty!*'

4
Rennie

March, 1988
Holland High School

So here I am on stage, practicing my solo with Mr Schafer, and it's just as fantastically heart-pounding as I knew it'd be. After this I'm meeting the Bitch Posse, and I'm going to stay out late enough so Dad and Kelly and their precious little baby will be asleep when I get home. I don't know how Kelly wormed her way into Dad's life so soon after Mom took off, but the word 'slut' comes to mind. Now Kelly sets my curfew, criticizes my clothes, nags me about homework. (Not that she has to do that last one; I'm a study bug, it's a disease of some kind.) Yup, after two years with Dad, Kelly's decided she's now my mom. Um, I have a mom.

I try to see the good stuff about it. Mallory's a cutie, and having a baby around means Dad's decided I can fend for myself. Really the best part of Dad and Kelly's relationship is that Dad no longer thinks I'm his closest friend in the world. After Mom took off, things began to feel a little . . . weird. A little too close for comfort, that's all: his arm flung next to my breasts as we're watching TV, oh, not on them or anything, just too close. Now that Kelly's around there are no more too-long goodnight hugs, and funny he never walks in on me when I'm taking a shower anymore. Not that he ever tried anything. I don't think he would – after all he's my dad! But now he has someone else to snuggle up to, and that is the only, only thing I will ever thank Kelly for. Not out loud, of course.

As for Mom, I've turned her into a distant memory, in Texas now with her new man 'Devon'. What kind of creep is named Devon? I get birthday cards, usually about a week late, and I haven't visited since last summer. I'd love her if I could see her, but I can't so I don't. At least that's what I tell myself, and why am I even thinking about her when I'm alone with the sexiest man I've ever seen?

'One more time, Rennie, and then we'll try the new blocking. After that we'll call it a night.' Mr Schafer's teeth sparkle when he smiles, really sparkle, and I watch his lips too long until he nods a couple more times and I realize I'm supposed to be singing.

I push what's left of my hair behind my ears – my haircut's inspired by Liz on *DeGrassi*, buzzed all over, the rest choppy and chunky except for my bangs. Cherry did it over New Year's at Amy's eighteenth birthday party, dyed it black too. Of course Mr Schafer wasn't crazy about that, but what was he going to do? I start the number again. It's my signature song, 'There Are Worse Things I Could Do'.

Play practice is always, shall we say, interesting. Especially when I'm getting a little extra help like I am tonight. Darkness fell a long time ago, and I'll have to drive through McDonald's for my dinner if I'm going to meet my friends at the college when I'm supposed to. But it's not like I was going to say no to Mr Schafer. Oh, my God, if you could see this man. Fantastic dark curls shifting around his face, eyes you could drown in, strong jaw, blue-black razor stubble, great body, about thirty-five, maybe a little older. He looks more like the football coach than the drama teacher. A girl would be nuts to turn down a chance to be alone with him.

Last year I was in the chorus when we did *Carousel*, but something amazing happened to my voice this year and I landed the part of Rizzo in *Grease*. I have lots of lines and songs, too many. If I'd known how much work this was going to be, I would probably have said no, because my grades are starting to slip, and Rennie Taylor's grades don't slip. They just don't.

Of course, like all Broadway musicals, *Grease* has a happy ending; Rizzo's not pregnant, and everyone's friends again. But when she's singing 'There Are Worse Things I Could

Do', she's pretty sure Kenickie's knocked her up. It's a sexy song, but it's a sad song, too, and I'm having trouble reconciling the conflicting emotions in my voice. At least that's what Mr Schafer says, and why we're pretending to work on it night after night after the rest of the cast has gone home.

We both know what's really going on, even though neither of us has said it out loud.

'Good, Rennie. Let's walk through your marks.' He stands behind me and rests his fingers on my forearm, his lips so close to my ear I can feel his breath tremble through my hair. 'Cross to stage right . . .' As he guides me to the mark, he slides his fingers up my arm, so my skin tingles, bristles. But he's crossed this line before, and I don't care. 'Now stop.' I lean back into him, daring him to touch me more, just like I did last week, when I felt him pressing into my back and I was pretty sure I'd given him a hard-on. His hands lingered over my breasts, then he pulled away and ended the rehearsal soon after. But it was a good feeling, to be so drunk with power, to know I came close to making him lose control.

This time his hands move to my shoulders and now he's not directing me anymore. Maybe I should be scared, but I'm not. I know exactly what I'm doing, and it's a hell of a lot of fun. I've left last year's Rennie Taylor in the dust. It's bad enough I'm barely five feet tall, but I have such a boyish figure I could pass for twelve. And it doesn't help that they named me after a fucking bird, a little plain brown bird. My middle name's almost as stupid; don't ask.

Names. I have a bunch of them. Tiny Wren Taylor, Skinny Little Bitch, The Virgin Mary, Girl Genius. No wonder everyone hated me last year; I was fucking annoying, waving my grades all over the place. I still have straight As but I don't make announcements about it anymore. And I'm done being the good girl, everyone's baby sister, the virgin.

If I play my cards right with Mr Schafer I can turn all that around.

Rizzo's words drop out of my mouth, words I can't believe

I remember with so many thoughts bouncing around in my head. I let him pull me closer, and now his hands are slipping off my shoulders, toward my chest. I move forward so my breasts touch his fingertips, singing the number like nothing's happening. As the lyrics float into the air, his lips brush against my neck, and I cock my head so I'm closer and it's a real kiss, practically. Then he backs away and it's like I imagined it, fairy wings disappearing like they were part of a dream all along.

His wife's name is Dawn. She works at a law firm in Chicago and makes at least twice as much money as he does. Maybe he's jealous. Or bored. I don't really care because he's suiting my purposes very well at the moment.

As he presses against my back – and yes, Rennie Taylor, that *is* a hard-on – my heart catches in my throat. My bravado melts away, and the fear I refuse to feel creeps inside my lungs. My abdomen's empty. There's no air to push through, and my voice comes out like a whisper instead of my usual belt-it-out alto. The words tumble into the air, do fairy cartwheels across the stage, and disappear; I've forgotten the rest.

'Sensational, Rennie,' he whispers in my ear, and his razor stubble brushes against my bare neck. We've been this close before, but he's gotten scared and stopped things. This time, I bring my fingers to his and squeeze them, coaxing his touch tighter around my breasts.

'Is that better?' I whisper. Sick of the charade, I turn to him and lift my hands to the back of his head. I pull his mouth down on mine, pressing my fear away with his lips, and my heart pounds in my ears. He's surprised and stiffens against me, starts to push me away.

Now that it's finally happening I'm not going to let him stop it. I'm dizzy with it, the control I have over him, the thrill of ruining a decent man. I open my mouth and his tongue slides in.

That's when he pulls away. 'Rennie,' he says, holding me by the shoulders. 'Rennie, you're only seventeen.'

'So what are you waiting for?' I grab his wrists, snake my

27

fingers up his forearm, and pull him to me again. 'Corrupt me already. I won't kiss and tell.' I'm playing the confident hellcat, but despite my bravado I'm a little, well, scared. But I'm in too deep now, too far to go back.

My heart thumps in my ears, but as he circles my nipple through my black sweater, he presses away my doubts. I'm drunk with delight, and my fear, if I feel it, has melted into that heartbeat feeling. Fear's what's making me open my mouth, murmur as his tongue tangles with mine; fear's sending chills down my back as he tests me against his hips, pushes my skirt over my thighs, backs me up to the ladder near the wings and lifts me onto a rung. He slides my sweater over my shoulders, unhooks my bra, fills his hands with my breasts. Fear thumps in my chest and I'm dizzy.

'Mr Schafer . . .'

'Please, Rennie, call me Rob.'

Rob? It just doesn't sound right. I don't know him as Rob. 'I don't want to call you anything, I just want you to fuck me.' God, did that really come out of my mouth? What the hell am I saying?

He doesn't argue. And my boots and stockings have somehow ended up on the stage floor with his jeans and now it's happening, as I'm sitting on the ladder, my legs are spreading. 'Oh, God, Rennie, I can't believe I'm doing this . . .' He pushes into me – are we really fucking, right here on the ladder? God, it *hurts*, he's tearing me apart, bones are going to break, I know it! He hasn't even taken his sweater off, and he's too close to me now. Was it supposed to be like this? I suck in my breath, bracing myself. Was he supposed to be this close? His sweater is some kind of wooly material that's rubbing back and forth over my stomach, and he pushes in all the way, grabbing my ass and pressing me even closer. His face looks pained for a moment as inside me it burns, and something rips, and I know he's torn skin from my very flesh. I yelp and tears blink down my face. The wool scrapes across my belly a few more times until he finishes with a groan and pulls away. He rubs his eyelids, not looking at me, and slides up his briefs and jeans from the tangle around his ankles.

I'm sticky all over, and I slip my hand between my legs and bring it to my eyes. His semen mottles slickly over my fingers, dappled with my own blood.

That's it?

I feel ripped off, and disgusting. As I hop off the ladder, the rest of his semen trickles out of me. I need a shower, I'm meeting the girls later and . . .

'Are you all right?' he asks, pulling the 'Rydell High' banner off the ladder and bunching it into a pile. 'I didn't know you were a virgin. I wouldn't have . . .'

Tears come from somewhere and work their way into my throat, but I will never, never let them fall in front of him. I don't feel brave, or sexy, or any of that anymore. I feel like a stupid little girl. I don't have any words.

'Rennie?'

'I'm fine.' And suddenly it's very cold on the stage, and I snap on my bra and pull my sweater back over my shoulders and button it, the little peekaboo sweater that seemed sexy when I picked it up this morning, figuring I'd see him after school, the sweater that now seems slutty, uninspired, dirty.

'This is just between you and me, Rennie.' He leans close and kisses me. 'Our secret.'

My mind is a swirl. I pull on my underwear, and I know when I go to the bathroom later, when Cherry and Amy and I've been hanging around at the college downing the scotch or tequila or vodka or whatever Amy's swiped from her parents' liquor cabinet, there'll still be blood and semen clinging to the cotton panel, staining it, staining me.

'You're a very special woman, Rennie. You're absolutely beautiful. Perfection.'

I'm seventeen years old and now I am a woman. A very special one. Perfection.

I slide on my stockings, their feet damp with my own sweat. 'Do you have any smokes? I'm out.' The mundane request centers me somehow, and as I'm pulling on my Doc Martens, I notice my hands shaking. I do need a smoke.

He pulls a rumpled pack from his pocket and hands me one. Cupping his hand near my face, he lights mine first, then his. 'Did you like it, Rennie? You didn't, did you? It was too fast.'

I pull in some smoke and answer as I'm blowing it out. 'It was fine, great.' And a tiny part of me feels it *was* great, it's sexy to have an affair with a teacher. He's gorgeous; I'd be crazy not to want him as a lover. Tendrils of smoke curl over the stage, drifting into the auditorium. We smoke together quietly for a while, watching the empty audience; the show we've put on is over. My cigarette burns down to the filter, and I stub it out on the floor. 'I have to go. I'm meeting my friends.'

He bundles the banner in his arms. 'I need to take this to the laundromat.'

Because you can't wash it at home. Dawn might see. 'Whatever.'

'When can I see you again?'

'You see me every day, in Drama class.'

'That's not what I mean.'

I gather my backpack and my script from the corner of the stage. They seem the accoutrements of a grammar school girl, someone I'm not anymore. I don't know who I am now, who I want to be, what face I will show when I'm with my girl-friends later. Will they worm it out of me? Do I want them to? Do I want to have sex with Mr Schafer, Rob, Mr Schafer again?

I just open my mouth and let words fall out of it. 'Sure, we'll do it again. Maybe we can go to a hotel or something. Sex on stage is kind of weird.' And as the words come out of my mouth I feel that dizzying heat again, the buzzing in my ears, the excitement of our secret.

'It'll be better next time.'

Better. Next. Time. The words fall apart from each other in my head and don't mean anything at all.

I pull my leather coat around me. 'Goodbye, Mr Schafer.'

'Rob.'

I push open the metal auditorium door. The wind sweeps over me; I'm going to be blown away in it. 'Goodbye, Rob.'

I walk into the frigid air. It's started to snow, and the flakes are dry and papery. They swirl around me as I jog to my car without looking back.

5
Cherry

March, 2003
Freemont Psychiatric Hospital
Freemont, Illinois

Cherry folds the length of yarn in half and loops it over the warp thread, pulling the knot snugly, just like the woman from the Art Therapy program – Cherry can't remember her name, and it hardly matters – has explained numerous times. Soumak weaving, this is called. Cherry's taken this class before, years back, the first time she was here, after. The scars on her arms are the only remnants of those days. *What are the others doing now?* She laughs and passes the yarn under the warp thread and back through her loop. *Bet they're not in a fucking mental hospital.*

She was so naive then that she thought if she quit smoking and swearing they'd let her out. Back then Rennie wrote her letters – Amy never bothered, or was afraid to – and the memory of that night at the Porter Place was still so fresh in her mind she seized up in her dreams. Her eyes would pop open, and she'd be unable to see what was really there, because the screen in front of her eyes would play the old scene, and Cherry would be there again, drunk in the moment. Dr Baum talked to her about those dreams or nightmares or whatever they were. Where she thought they were coming from. Why she was having them. Who was making them. And apparently there was a point to all his questions, but Cherry never got it and took a different tack. Soon she became the model patient, obedient, cooperative, took her meds without a fuss. And then she fell in love, and at last they let her out.

And she lived her life for a little while, waitressing at

Friday's, paying rent, even (Jesus, it seems bizarre now) dating.

And then . . . was it that very day at Hillsdale Mall, or weeks, months before that, that she realized they hadn't made her well? That Dr Baum was a liar like the rest of them? She pulls her fingernail over her lower lip, the little buzz of sensations awakening her, letting her *feel*. No. It had been weeks before. She can pinpoint the date she knew everything was a lie. August 31, 1997. The day everything crashed and shattered and broke into pieces.

After Hillsdale, they labeled her a 'chronic case' and locked her up again.

She sighs. It feels so long ago. She tries not to care about anything now. She's let her hair go stringy, watches it grow gray near her earlobes, doesn't bother to dye it; she's becoming an old woman in here.

At least now she doesn't have to worry about money, paying bills, showing up for work, dating. Everything is scheduled; she doesn't forget to take her meds, and if she isn't 'somebody', at least she's doing good work. The tapestry she's working on is for a craft show to benefit the homeless of Chicago. She works across the row, tying a knot onto each warp thread. Making shapes on the tapestry is pretty simple, and the best part of Soumak weaving is there's no way to mess up. On her way back across the warp, she starts one thread away from her ending point and dizzies herself within the pattern, shutting out everything, the art teacher, her fellow patients, the whole fucking Occupational Therapy room.

Her fingers play against the yarn, knotting and weaving, building a pyramid with the wool. From time to time she takes the plastic comb and taps the row of knots, just to even things out. No one speaks, although Michael, the cute, mohawked college kid whose trembling hands are always clutching a cigarette (he's withdrawing from something, Cherry's pretty sure), sucks in his smoke quickly, puffs it out, sucks it in, fast fast fast. Cherry's breath quickens in her throat; even though she doesn't smoke anymore, he makes it look so damn good. His green eyes are pools of vulnerability, like Sam Sterling's, so long ago. Another project there for the taking, like Sam or Marian or her tapestry. Michael doesn't tap his ash, so the spent tobacco becomes a long, charcoal ghost, just ready to fall. Cherry wonders how she looks to him. Old, probably. The first time she was in here, she would have made a pass. God, it sucks to be thirty-two when you really still need to be seventeen.

As far as she can tell she's made no progress convincing them she's been cured. It isn't like the last time, when, even if they didn't exactly want to give her a chance, they were at least willing to watch her, to assess. Now it feels like a life sentence. It's been six years since she lost control in Hillsdale Mall, pressed the knife to the cashier's throat; she remembers hearing they locked up all sharp objects after that. Weirdly enough her 'episode,' as they called it, hit her right after her gorgeous flawed princess died in a car crash. Why did she care so much about a princess she'd never know? The grown-up, the Diana that Cherry would never become?

The police were called and then came the blur of the second trial, the same old same old with the attorney, the greasy-haired public defender who stared at her tits instead of listening to her. Except of course this time everything happened without the guidance counselor, without the school psychologist, without all those little safety people who made the first time feel important. Almost six years it's been since they threw her in here again.

Cherry Diana Winters – Chronic Case.

She still doesn't have off-unit dining privileges; the chicken breast and spinach she ate for lunch were delivered to the locked ward on a hard blue plastic tray. It isn't fair. She didn't hurt anyone at Hillsdale. Maybe it was because of the other . . .

And she can't think about that anymore.

The doctors, she's almost certain, still think she's a danger to herself, maybe to others too, still don't trust her to leave the unit, still don't dare send her for a walk outside all by herself. Dr Baum is gone. Now they're sending her to a woman, Dr Anders, some fiftysomething garbage brain who looks just like Marian and says things like *Yes, Cherry* and *I see, Cherry* and *I'd like to hear more about that, Cherry.*

Last time it didn't take long for her to smile her way to off-unit privileges, despite the charges (and after she was so sure she'd never be tried as an adult!), the court case, the evidence, and the whoosh of relief as it was this and not prison. Last time, it was so easy. It was only two years before she was pronounced 'cured'.

She twists another knot, tighter than ever. Squeezing the last bit of ease out of the yarn sends a rush through her, a whirlwind that starts in her stomach and twirls to a stop in her head.

Maybe it's the cutting. That's harder to quit than smoking. Through a half-lidded eye Cherry gazes at her sliced arm, red welts pulling up from skinny pale flesh, slowly healing. They took away all knives and sharp objects the first day, of course, just like they did before. And she'll never get her precious glass Bitch Posse jar back. They won't even let her have a can of Coke for fear she'll rip it up and use it to cut herself, and she still gets only a plastic knife with her meal. But she smashed her watch, used the crystal inside to slash at her arm, hid it in her pillow and lied and said she'd fallen down. No one believed her, of course, but it didn't matter. They turned her room upside down, shook out her sheets, all her clothing, her underwear strewn about the floor, to look for the knife or razor blade they were sure she had.

They haven't found it, after six years, and that accomplishment rolls waves of pleasure through her.

Her perfect princess was a cutter too. Afraid if Buckingham Palace found out, they'd take her children away, put her in an institution. So she and Cherry have more in common than just a name.

God, if she could bring herself to sleep with Dr Anders maybe it'd help. Dr Anders is so above-board, her red hair coiffed into a neat bun. It's not at all like those sessions with Dr Baum, when he told her he loved her, that she wasn't

35

crazy after all, that he'd get her out. And he kept his promise. Two short years and he got her out.

Of course, there were other promises he didn't keep.

'God fucking damn it.' Michael's cut his warp thread by mistake, and his whole project starts unraveling.

The art teacher leans over to knot it back together again. Josie looks up and meets Cherry's eyes – Josie, the waif-girl who looks like a teenaged Princess Di, or a combination of her two best friends, tiny Rennie, blonde and gorgeous Amy.

No, no. Never, never think of them.

Josie the heroin-junkie-turned-brownnoser glances worriedly at Cherry. Josie. She could be a project, too.

Cherry looks away. Lately she doesn't say much out loud. Words are massive efforts. Like moving boulders across football fields. Like creating Stonehenge.

'This project fucking sucks.'

Susan raises a disgustingly controlled eyebrow. Susan, the thirty-something-suicidal-housewife – Cherry feels like she should relate to her, but can't, because Susan had a young adulthood without courts, psychiatrists, drugs – Susan's problems are blissfully normal, a husband with an affair, a little Vicodin problem, a learning disabled daughter. Susan likes to egg Michael on, makes her feel powerful or something. 'This isn't high school, Michael.'

'Fuck you.' He slides the yarn over his fingers, and he's cut himself somehow – a drop of blood soaks from his skin into the wool.

Cherry's heart quickens. Her dry lips scrape together as she pushes out the whisper. 'If you don't swear so much, they might let you out faster.'

'Fuck you, too. Who the hell are you to tell me what to do?' His nose ring quivers and he rises to his feet. Here it comes. The Michael tantrum.

'Who the *fuck* do you *fucking* think you *fucking* are, you *fucking fuckhead*? *Fuck you!*' He pounds his fists on the table, his voice rising to a bloody, passionate, rolling-back-and-forth-on-the-bed, a fuck of the voice, a thump-thump-thump into the headboard, pushing her hands over her head and holding them together, teeth tearing into flesh.

Cherry's knees go weak under the table. Michael hurls his half-completed tapestry across the room and wrenches the table from the floor, topples it. The art teacher stands up, her face awash with terror as her supplies float around her, suspended in slow motion.

'Oh my God, oh my God,' whispers Josie.

The blur of the moment whirs through Cherry, pulling laughter from her stomach, her lungs, and she bursts into the silence with sobs of mirth.

The nurses call frantically for male staff, and Michael is gathered up and put into the quiet room.

Cherry can't stop laughing, even after Michael is put away into his little box. She's laughing so hard tears come from her eyes as she crosses her arms awkwardly, her just-grown-out nails biting into her wrists. As she breaks the skin she crests onto a high, like being on the top of the roller coaster at Great America, as high as she was that night at the Porter Place. She pushes her nails into her skin, flesh popping and wetness flowing, and glances at her red, sticky wrists. Suddenly she's choking on her laughter. She can't breathe, she's shaking, and she becomes aware of arms behind her back, seizing her wrists together, but they can't stop the blood from trickling down, licking her skin with warm wetness, ah yes, ah yes.

6

Amy

March, 1988
Holland Avenue, Stoplight

As I'm waiting at the stoplight in my dad's Mustang, snow flings itself onto my windshield. I press my cigarette to my lips, The Smiths' 'How Soon Is Now?' streaming from the car stereo. Morrissey wails, and I pull the smoke in hard, burning away the fight at home. It's not a part of me; it doesn't matter. I turn up the music because there's just something about Morrissey, how you know his heart is breaking, how you want to reach through the music and give him a hug. And I know just how he feels, aching to be loved and being disappointed. Every. Fucking. Time.

Tonight the Bitch Posse, Cherry and Rennie and I, are meeting at the college to hook up with some guys from the People's Think Tank who hang out late nights in the Student Union smoking, drinking coffee, and debating politics. A year ago I would've been cruising Greek Row with Pammie McFadden and Debbie Ridgeway, but last year I was fluffy and stupid. Or I pretended to be. Besides, unlike the Greeks, who in my experience subscribe to the bang-'em-and-forget-'em philosophy, the People's Think Tank guys actually call the next day. Sometimes they even want to hang out for coffee or go see college bands in the basement of the Psych Building. Of course, I'm no brain like Rennie, no debater like Cherry. The truth is that Brandon's uncomplicated and unneedy, and he looks good next to me, and I'm the kind of girl who needs someone next to her.

I pull into a parking spot. Man, it's icy. I push away the memory of swear words, screams, the constant and never-resolved fight over Callie. The scene's predictable, every movement choreographed. Dad suggests, for the millionth time, bringing Callie home. Mom, for the millionth time, says no and launches into a long list of reasons it's a bad idea. Dad pours a Scotch and soda that's mainly Scotch. Mom turns on the television and mixes a screwdriver. Dad tells Mom *Barb, you're being selfish.* Mom says *Fuck off, Rich.* The drinks pour again. The voices get louder. I put on my coat, swipe a bottle of anything from the liquor cabinet, grab my mittens, and get the hell out.

I wait for the song to finish and pull my backpack off the passenger seat. Cherry's truck is three spaces away, thank God. I hate being the first one here because usually the People's Think Tank guys want to know our opinions on world events. Rennie knows way more than me, and Cherry can bullshit her way around any subject, but I sit there like an open-mouthed fool. Which is fine if all three of us or even two of us are here – I can be the pretty, mysterious one – but last week I was alone for twenty fucking minutes before Cherry and Rennie showed up, and Brandon asked me my opinion of the situation in El Salvador. The only thing I could think of was a line from a Peter, Paul and Mary song that Mom likes, and I actually fucking blurted it out! Actually forced my lips around this hippie bullshit about the breezes blowing in El Salvador. Oh, my God! What an idiot! They thought I was making a joke. Brandon even said, 'You're damn cute, Amy.'

Yeah, it's weird, my parents. They used to be hippies, I guess. According to pictures. Mom always says, *Stand up for what you believe in, Amy.*

But I don't believe in anything. Not anymore.

At least that El Salvador thing turned out okay. Brandon and I had a pretty good time in the back of the Mustang later, the heater running full blast in the parking lot, Morrissey making love to me with his voice (yeah he's gay and depressed, but he wouldn't be either of those things if he knew *me*), the clicks of Brandon's kisses on my neck interrupting the music. I let him take my top off, and tonight, if he wants to, I'll let him do more. That's just the kind of girl I am.

I get out of the car. The icy wind whips around me, roars in my ears, scorches my cheeks.

I'm not sure, exactly, what I thought I'd change by hanging out with the Bitch Posse. I'm still the same old Amy, still cruising for guys, still hoping to get laid. They just have a different label: People's Think Tank instead of Sigma Nu, Doc Martens instead of the Gap. But at least my friends are true friends now.

I'm pretty sure.

The snow's a fucking mile high and someone's plowed a skinny pathway to the Student Union. I scoop up a fingerful of frosting with my mitten and let the flakes play over the yarn. As I toss the snow into the air, a bit sticks to my fingers, and like a little girl, I lick off the rest.

When I push open the door I see Cherry, chatting with Sam and Brandon and the guy with dark hair who never talks, just sits there staring. I think his name is Kent. She sees me and waves me over.

Sometimes I wonder what she and Rennie really think of me. In my old crowd, most of the girls hated each other's guts, spread rumors, backstabbed. I was probably the biggest bitch of them all. But my new friends are more complicated, or at least they show more of themselves to me. Rennie's virginal, perfect, holy almost, saving herself for marriage, pouring her passion into her poetry and her acting. And Cherry's hard, tough as nails. She's been around the block a few times, but the only guy she's let into her heart is Sam. They've been together since forever. They'll probably get married or something.

And then there's me, flighty Amy. Half the time I'm convinced they'll figure out who I really am and drop me.

They haven't yet.

I hurry toward their table. Cherry's probably high already since she has the coolest mom in the world. Her mom wants Cherry and us to call her Marian, and she doesn't care how long Cherry stays out as long as she's home by dawn. More than once she's joined us in Cherry's room to get stoned. And get this! Cherry doesn't even have to buy her own pot! Her mom buys it once a week and keeps it in this little box in the kitchen. Cherry can help herself. How cool is that?

'Hey, Cherry!' I call across the Union and join her and the guys. Brandon pushes his blond hair away from his face, and his gaze lingers on my breasts. If I was Cherry, I'd say something snappy like, 'I'm up here,' but I don't have the nerve. I don't care anyway.

Cherry blows a couple smoke rings, then whooshes out the rest and drops her cigarette into the ashtray that's surrounded by a flurry of papers advertising a rally about something I don't have the energy to try to understand. 'Hey, Aim. How's it going?'

I throw my backpack under the table and scoot a chair next to Brandon. 'Are you stoned?' I peer into her eyes.

'No, damn it. I don't even have any on me. Are you?'

'You disappoint me, Cherry. I'm not the one who has a pot dispenser in my kitchen. Brought some of this, though.' I unzip my backpack and show her the bottle of Smirnoff I've nabbed.

'Oh, Aim comes through again!'

Sam and Brandon are only twenty and I'm assuming Kent is too, so a bottle of vodka is much appreciated among them as well and they echo Cherry's delight. Cherry slides her pack of Marlboros toward me. I pull out a cigarette, lift it to my lips, and light it with Cherry's Zippo. The smell of lighter fluid opens my nostrils, and I have a strange impulse to push the flame closer to my face, to make it burn, just a little . . .

I snap the lighter shut and zip up the vodka for now. We'll head down to the basement of the Psych Building and drink it later. Security types hang out at the Student Union, and getting drunk or stoned there is asking for trouble.

In a way, Callie explains the numerous bottles of Scotch and vodka that go out in the trash each week. The drinking bothers me less than the fighting. Hell, I'm no angel when it comes to booze, and they know that, God do they ever. Callie's the angel. Her blonde hair curls around her face, catches the light from the window, falls around her shoulders. She's never had the chance to do anything wrong.

Callie. Why can't I stop thinking about her? Dad's words to Mom are knives, cutting, accusing. She throws words back at him like rocks. Callie. What's sad is if I had a sister, if I really *had* her, I could vent about them to her.

But I have Callie.

I swallow hard. What a baby! *Stop it, Amy.* I pull the cigarette to my lips, inhale hard, blow out fast.

Cherry untangles herself from Sam for a second and rests her fingers on my arm. 'Something's bugging you, isn't it?'

'Just the usual. They're fighting over Callie.'

I guess I should explain. Callie's my older sister. She's twenty-one years old and has what they call 'profound mental retardation' because when she was born there wasn't enough oxygen. She's in an institution – well, they call it Hemmler Memorial Foundation, 'a loving environment for children and young adults,' but it's an institution, make no mistake – near Chicago. When she was a little kid, she didn't go to school. They hadn't made those special day classes yet that they have now. Of course I was little then too, but I remember when Mom and Dad decided to move Callie to Hemmler. That's when the tears, the fights, all that started. No one would ever guess Dr Linnet, dentist of the strip mall, and Mrs Linnet, town librarian, had a drinking problem. Anyway, Mom still thinks Hemmler's the only option for Callie. I mean, she can't feed herself, can't get dressed on her own, can't talk.

Cherry leans close to me. 'Are you okay?'

I shrug. 'Whatever.'

Here's another thing. Callie's absolutely, utterly beautiful. I mean, she really is. Long, curly blonde hair, big blue eyes, rosy cheeks, full lips. She looks like a china doll, one of the ones I always wanted that closes her eyes when you tilt her backward. One of the ones Mom always said I'd break and I'd have to wait till I was a grown-up. One of those dolls that are too pretty to play with, that are really for collectors.

Me? I'm a cheap knockoff of Callie. I got the blonde hair, but it's stick straight and fine. I'm not exactly overweight, but I'm 'cheerleader chubby', and my nose is spattered with freckles. Maybe Mom and Dad were supposed to have just one child, some meshing of Callie and me, some perfect angel. And instead they got me, plain old ordinary Amy, and Callie, who's anything but.

Cherry's lips flatten. 'Shit. They shouldn't bring you into this.'

'Par for the course.'

The arguments about Callie have been a part of my life for almost as long as Callie has. Which is forever. Dad's always wanted to take Callie home. Mom says Callie 'loves' Hemmler, that the 'excursions' – Hemmler-ese for walks around the grounds of the institution – 'really enliven' her. She says Callie can't make it on her own, that she and Dad don't have the equipment to deal with her. She's not selfish exactly. At last I don't think so. It's just that seeing Callie always makes her cry. Daddy and I go and see her about every other week. Mom sees her less and less.

They argue about that, too.

Brandon reaches for my arm. 'I'm sorry, hon.'

His eyes are wide with concern, but I don't trust him. I don't trust anyone, really, when it comes to Callie. 'I'll be okay.' I don't need him for a confidant; our relationship doesn't run that deep, and that's fine by me. The only people my heart has room for are Rennie and Cherry. 'Can we talk about something else? Where's Rennie?'

Funny, when I was running with the crowd I ran with since junior high, I didn't mention Callie once. Not to anyone. Not even to Pammie. Pammie and I claimed we shared 'everything' with each other, but 'everything' meant juicy gossip, which girls were bitches, which were sluts, which were control freaks (um, that would be me and Pammie). Best friends who wanted to kill each other half the time. Pammie and I always competed to be prettier, more popular, sexier.

Having a sister like Callie is hardly sexy.

Sam's all over Cherry already. He's rubbing his fingers along her back, making her giggle. She leans back for a kiss and then answers me. 'Rennie's at play practice. She'll be here any minute. Are you sure you're okay?'

Brandon keeps staring at me. Kent hasn't said a word since I arrived, and now, sullenly, slowly, he stacks the flyers that are scattered all around the table and puts them in his satchel, sighing loudly like he's given up. Maybe me bringing Callie up put a damper on everything. The room echoes with silence, and fire floods my cheeks. 'Really, it's no big deal. I mean it's the usual crap. Forget it.'

When I was little, soon after she moved to Hemmler, I actually thought most people had family members in institutions. I like to think I'd trust Cherry and Rennie with my deepest secrets, but . . . They do know about Callie, have even looked at pictures of her with me, rubbing my back as I cried. Still, there are things about Callie I'll never tell them.

How I can't help blaming her, the silent angel, for all their fights.

How I'm jealous of how much time they spend discussing Callie. Callie this, Callie that. Hemmler la, group care da. Do you know what they said when I made Head Cheerleader after working my ass off for three years? *That's nice.* When I cut up the cheer uniform, do you think they fucking cared? Mom just said, *You'll have to pay the school for that out of your allowance.*

I don't tell my friends about the resentment that's a rock in my chest, that pulls me to the center of the earth, that's stronger than me.

I don't tell them how Callie makes me feel like such a small, stupid deal.

How I go to the Special Olympics, every year, by myself. Scoot next to some family with an athlete competing, and pretend they're my own. Cheer my heart out for their daughter or brother or cousin. 'Go DeAnn!' 'Go Sheila!'

How DeAnn or Sheila or whoever waves at the crowd as she runs or wheels or walks past, flashes a peace sign, stops to tie her shoe as runners trot by her.

It's never about winning of course.

'Woo-hoo!' I scream. 'You can do it, you're awesome!' How great I feel. How I could watch those Games every goddamn day of my life.

How in my head I hear, 'Go Callie!'

When I brought that up to Mom – that I wished Callie could do a race, so we could cheer for her – she said, *I don't think you have a realistic view of your sister's condition.*

And when I let thoughts like that cross my mind, the tears shimmer in my eyes, and now I'm blinking them out onto my nose and Cherry's putting her arms around me and Rennie's just arrived and swoops over and suddenly I'm bawling, and you know what the crappy part is?

No matter how much I dump on my friends (and it's too much, probably), they'll never know how it feels.

I push the tears away from my eyes. My mind's made up. I'm going to get laid tonight and forget Callie, just for a little while.

But I'm going to get good and drunk first. I lift my backpack over my shoulder, act tough. 'Let's go get wasted.'

7
Rennie

March, 2003
Mill Valley, California

Naked, Rennie sips coffee at the round kitchen table as Bay fries her pancakes in butter. Naked, he slides the spatula under one and turns it, and she swallows, watching his bare back all yellow sunshine and springtime. This has become their morning ritual, the coming out of darkness into light.

They'll make love again this morning, here in the kitchen, without the knife, their warmth matching the heady Marin County air outside. She'll forget the drama of last night, erase it all, blur away Lisa's latest e-mail (*Don't write about a writer, Wren, it's the kiss of death*), shatter the empty glaring computer screen that doesn't contain the imaginary novel she doubts she can ever bring into reality. She'll squash all that here with Bay, the end-of-rainy-season sun spilling through the window over the sink, slanting shadows across the kitchen table, perfect, rectangular shades.

Drawing lines. Making borders. The finite divided. Unconfusing. There'll be none of the choking, clotting darkness of last night.

And as Rennie bursts into orgasm, all of New York publishing will crumble to the ground.

Scribner.

Fuck me.

Warner Books.

Fuck me.

Penguin Putnam.

Oh, yes, fuck me, fuck me hard.

Bertelsmann owns almost everything these days.

Fuck me, fuck me, fuck me, Bertelsmann, oh, yes, yes, *yes*!

46

Then fall to pieces, brick by brick.

As Rennie wraps her legs tight around her gorgeous young lover, she will own everything.

In that pale brief moment before she feels empty again.

Rennie pulls some coffee into her mouth, warmth spreading over the inside of her cheeks – just a little sting, nothing much – and scribbles a few notes on Bay's student teacher evaluation forms for San Francisco State. For once the cottage feels like home. The warm, salty butter smell clings to everything, as if the air is a cheerful checked gingham curtain in an old farmhouse (*the farmhouse is burned to the ground, but the barn, that's where stuff happens . . .*)

She melts that thought with a gulp of coffee.

Her pen scurries across the paper. 'Bay, did you design student-centered lessons?' She doesn't wait for an answer before circling five out of five. 'Yes, you did. Did you ask open-ended, complex questions? Yes, you did.' At the bottom she scrawls, *Bayuni Henares is an extraordinarily gifted teacher. Almost instinctually he designs lessons that speak to all learning styles and abilities. The progress he's made in such a short time is incredible. To sum it up, he will be a sensational educator, and it's been a pleasure to observe him as my student teacher.* She reads it aloud to him. 'Do you like that, Bay? Is that good?'

His tight little ass shifts near the stove, his shoulder blades working like wings under his skin. Aching to touch him, she gets up from her coffee and evaluation and presses herself behind him, rubbing his hips, reaching for his cock, kissing his neck. 'I'll write whatever you want. Anything. You can even write it yourself, and I'll copy it out in my own handwriting.' She pulls her fingernails gently along his shoulders, over the little hills of his elbows, his wrists. He's motionless, won't look at her.

'What?' She's almost afraid to ask.

'You don't really think all that stuff, Rennie. That's just because . . .' He jerks his head toward the bedroom.

She can't deny it, really; she can't point to one specific lesson where he did an exceptional job, though he tries so hard, painstakingly outlines lesson plans and learning outcomes and times things to the minute. But his teaching's stagey, like she'd expect a student teacher's lessons to be – over-rehearsed, a little anxious, rushed.

She still hasn't answered, and now it's too late to sound genuine, because her hesitation has pierced the moment like a knife, deflated it, killed it.

She tries anyway. 'Teaching's hard. Keeping all the balls in the air at once, classroom management, student-centered lessons, progressive discipline, timing. You do a fine job.'

'But that's not what you said on the form.'

'Do you care?' She slides her fingers back up his arms again, nibbles his earlobe, and probably despite himself, he turns around, reaches for her breasts, oh God yes, things are all right again. She presses closer and whispers, 'Anyway, your seminar prof bases her grade on my comments. You'll get an A.'

He lets go of her breasts and glances at the clock, which crushes Rennie, as if not being late is more important than petting her. 'But do I deserve an A? Or a B? A C-plus? You don't even know, do you?'

He's hit it perfectly, of course. And before she knows it she's skipped a beat again, fucked it up. It'll never sound good now. God, he's too perfect, she can't spoil it.

So she lies. 'Bay, I'd never lie. Not to you. You're just what I said, sensational. There's an English opening at Tam next year. I'm pretty sure I can . . .'

His gaze flutters around the room like a butterfly, at the walls the windows the clock, everywhere but at her face. 'Don't say any more. Just fold up the damned thing and seal it. I don't want to know what you wrote.'

Nausea spins in her stomach, choppy waves rolling under a boat. Tears race through her and well up in her eyes, and she threads her fingers through his hair and pulls him toward her, as if by touching her he can become her, so she won't have to be herself. Into his ear she whispers, 'I'm sorry, Bay.'

He shakes his head. It's not okay but it's all right, and he's making his old sand circles on her back with his fingertips, comforting her. Maybe he does love her, after all.

She opens her lips. His mouth meets hers and the sickening spin turns into a happy, little-girl dizziness. She's on a carousel, the kitchen blurring around her, and she feels like laughing. As he hardens against her, she swirls her tongue into his, in this pure good fresh morning, yellow as dandelions, bright as daisies, clean clean clean of blood. The slice on her stomach has clotted over like blackberry jam. He wouldn't even have to notice it if he didn't want to. She lifts herself onto the table, opens her legs. And now she will fuck everything, and everything will be okay.

His eyes seem bruised, like a flimsy petal she's rubbed too much between her fingers, and she's pulled him too close, she knows that, even as he's fucking her one last time of the morning. *Goddamn it, I shouldn't have said that. I should have just written the evaluation and sealed it in the envelope like I was supposed to, oh God.* He pushes into her, farther, farther, why can't he fuck her harder, hurt her, make her bleed? She links her ankles behind his back to pull him in even more, and just as she's about to come she opens her eyes and notices the flames leaping from the pan. The pancakes are burning, and she yells 'Fuck!'

Bay pulls away and grabs the sprayer from the sink as she rushes over and turns off the pilot light. He douses everything with water, and now the nice morning smell is wrecked, the scorched butter hanging in the air like a refinery fire. All she can fill the awkward moment with is, 'Whoa, close one.' The sex is ruined of course, their heat burned into ash, and it's useless trying to start again.

She fills the sink with water and drops the smoking pan into it. It hisses for a moment, steams up, then sinks beneath the soapsuds. There's no time for breakfast, no time for anything.

'Should get going.' Bay grabs his lesson plan from the kitchen table, the beautiful gorgeous lesson plan that's perfectly typed and formatted. She did look at it, she *did*. He timed five minutes for warm-ups, ten for a freewrite, twenty for a group activity, and . . . Oh Lord, she drank too much last night. Her head hurts. A swallow of red wine beckons her from the bottle on the counter, and she lifts it to her lips, finishes it.

She splashes the coffee into the sink with the scorched pan. If she had time she'd light a candle and kill the ruined, petrified smell, but of course it's seven thirty already and traffic's fucked up by now. The mug clatters to the counter, and she follows Bay to the bedroom. From her dresser she pulls out her knit top and cardigan sweater and jeans for teaching, layers because it's always so cold in the morning and hot by afternoon.

Next to her Bay wordlessly pulls on his clothes. Neither of them looks at the knife that sits on the bedside table, stained with Rennie's blood.

8
Cherry

March, 1988
Holland, Illinois

There's a test in French, and I never study, so I cut and headed over to Sam's. Marian inhaled all her coke over the weekend which means she'll be a complete and utter bitch until she scores some at work tonight, so I'm sure as hell not staying home. Instead I'm lying on my back on Sam's living room floor, the bottle of Peppermint Schnapps inches from my fingertips as we debate Marx, physical labor versus intellectual labor. I get a charge out of debating because it makes me feel smart, smarter than Rennie, even. Sam and I are always on the opposite sides of things and sometimes things heat up so hot they scorch. It never scares me – Jesus, I live with Marian – and he rides me to the edge of the world; one breath and he could blow me into the universe. But we have to fight first. That's just how we work.

I'm about to logic-ize Sam under the table, which means I get to pick where in Sam's apartment we have sex and I get to boss him. I may not be Rennie Taylor, Girl Genius who reads the *New York Times* from first page to last every day, but my mind works quick, even when I'm fucked up, or should I say especially when I'm fucked up. Sam and I are so fucking predictable, but not as predictable as Marian. I half hope she *doesn't* score some coke at work, because when she brings it home she feels generous and wants me to do lines with her, presses it on me, pushes, pushes, just like ordinary moms probably fill your plate with lasagna despite your protests. Only I will never try cocaine, never never never never.

'Cherry, you don't even understand the most basic Marxist

51

concept. Let me say it very slowly. Value. Derives. From. Labor.'

He's being insulting, and half of me burns with hatred and half of me loves being given a reason to blow up, to fight, to release the tension that's built up in me. I vow to be a difficult bitch about the whole conversation because it makes things a hell of a lot more fun. 'Got. It. Sam.'

Sam always sweats when he drinks, and a few blond strands cling to his forehead, pulled together like snakes. 'So. Next concept. In *Das Kapital* Marx says, "More complicated labor counts as simple labor raised to a higher power." '

I know where he's going with this. He can be such an ass. 'What's your point?'

'That means I'm doing intellectual labor by writing my essays.'

See, he writes these fucking essays that no one but me and him reads, and he thinks that's going to, I don't know, start a revolution or something.

He takes the Schnapps bottle from me and gulps a few times. 'So you need to take care of physical labor like finishing those dishes in the sink and giving me a blow job.'

I burst out laughing. 'Show me someone who'll trade an essay for a blow job, and I'll show you a truly desperate individual.'

'Come on, Cherry. How much training does it take to do a blow job? Now, think about how many years of study I've put into understanding the works of Marx and Lenin and Trotsky. There's no comparison.'

'Who are you to say how many years I've put into doing blow jobs?' He's actually the first one, but I'll never admit that. I'm the girl who's been bad since the day she was born. 'Newsflash, here's how you get a blow job from me. Gimme some of this, then I'll give you some of that.'

His eyes flash as he drinks some more and wipes his mouth. 'So, are you going to write the definitive work about the transition from the first phase of communist society to its higher phase, and the complete withering away of the state?'

'The problem with your stupid argument, Sam, is that this society you describe has never existed anywhere in the world.' The fact that Sam can use Marxism to make me do the dishes or give him a blow job proves that there is something seriously wrong with that philosophy. 'Karl Marx can eat my sorry cunt.' Marx has a point, I guess, in that people are after money and power all the time, and the rich should share with the poor. But like most philosophies it doesn't stand up to reality. 'You want to move to the Soviet Union and stand in a bread line? Or would you consider Cuba a better example?'

'Old argument, Cherry. I don't think I have to explain that the dictatorship of the proletariat . . .' and he goes on, and on, and on, and I tune out and watch his face instead. Someday I'll reach way inside him and pull out that little boy I see in his eyes. Someday I'll make him care.

I half-listen but mainly I'm ticking away time until I can fall into bed with him. Really, what would solve things is if the Russians dropped a half dozen nukes on us and we'd have to start from scratch. When I saw *The Day After* I was only twelve and terrified out of my skull but if they show it again, I'll cheer. Better to blow up the whole sick planet than try to fix what's unfixable. It's just too late for stuff like Communism. I used to believe in anarchy, but to tell you the truth that idea scares me too – if there were no laws what would keep people from hurting each other. Anyway, anarchism's an 'ism' too.

Yeah, I know what I'm *against*, all right.

I just don't know what I'm *for*.

Probably, nobody does. 'Come on, Sam, the concept is dead.'

Animal hunger flashes in his eyes. This is the hot sexy moment when he's angry, when the hard cast to his gaze sends chills up and down my legs. Sam really thinks we're on the verge of revolution, that his essay matters, matters more than the papers he doesn't write for Psychology 203, Shakespeare, whatever classes he's cutting today, all the 'capitalist bullshit' he's supposed to be studying, and why he's on academic probation. But it's endearing in a way; hell, at least he thinks I'm worth discussing this with. I kick off my shoes, pull my sweater over my head, sit up and shrug off my bra. 'Give me the fucking Schnapps.'

'Where did those pretty tits come from?' He hands me the bottle, and I take a long swig. I just want to get so drunk that I forget how pissed off Sam makes me, that the dirty dishes lie unwashed in his sink. It's never that I buy into his bullshit philosophy but part of me feels sorry for him. Hell, his parents can't stand him; he doesn't have any-body either.

As peppermint's clearing my nostrils Rennie pops into my head. Something's worrying her. Her face was creased Friday night with some kind of frustration, and it's probably school because Rennie freaks out over a B-plus, a grade that would thrill me and most people I know. I vow to coax it out of her later and do some Cherry-therapy, which usually involves a great big ol' fatty in my room and some fuck-the-world music like the Dead Kennedys. I love that kind of music nobody likes, except lately it's occurred to me that even the Dead Kennedys have press people, a marketing campaign. I try not to think that way but I know in the end I'm just another consumer and it doesn't really matter which cassette I buy as long as I buy one. Which is why I try to shoplift as much as I can.

Yeah, I think I'll have the girls sleep over tonight. No one ever wants to go home, and even though I don't either, at least we can have the room to ourselves and Marian won't annoy us about getting so stoned we fall asleep.

Sam pinches my breasts, and I choke on the Schnapps. 'What the fuck's that about?'

'You're not paying attention.'

This is his challenge; we're just getting started now. 'You're such a dumb fuck.'

He grabs my wrists. 'Bitch.'

I sink my nails into the fleshy part of his forearms, slicing open the skin, and he squeezes my wrists harder. 'You bet I am.' He grabs my tits again and squeezes them so hard it feels like he's ripping them off me. And it feels good to hurt, to be hurt. I feel real.

My lips tremble, but I'm not scared. Just to prove it, I slap my open hand across his face. He looks a little surprised but grabs my hair and pulls the curls near my ears, hard. He presses my lips to his, and they're searing hot. I want to reach the top with him, to kill him, just for the high. 'Fuck you, Sam,' I whisper against his lips, and now he lets go to unzip his jeans. He grabs me by the waist of my skirt and yanks it, breaking the elastic. 'Asshole, I hate you.' This time I want to be the one to drag him to the bedroom kicking and screaming. I want to be the one to rape him. He's not much bigger than me, and I grab his hands and yank them behind his back, reaching for the set of handcuffs we keep in a little secret place behind the TV.

He bristles, pulls away. 'No.'

This is part of the game, so I slap him a little more. My handprints float across his back and his ass like butterflies. 'Kitchen table, now, you sonofabitch.'

A curtain of fire hangs in the air between us. 'No, Cherry. You this time.' I sting another slap across his face, and the flames light his eyes again.

He balls his hand into a fist and punches me in the face.

Goddamn, *fuck*! I put my hand to my nose and it comes away with blood. This is a line we just don't cross. The choke of sex flakes away to anger. 'What the hell'd you do that for?' I make a fist too and land one in his belly before he grabs my wrists and pushes them over my head. The cuffs snap shut.

'No one does that to me, Cherry, no one.' Even though I'm already bleeding, his fist lands on my cheek. But I'm strong and I kick him in the shin, hard. Tears are running down my cheeks. Am I supposed to be liking this? I'm a jumble of confusion and anxiety, and most of the sexy feelings have drained out of me. Somehow, I distance myself from the scene as he pulls me away from the kitchen table and tosses me onto the sofa, rolls on a condom and rides me. In my head my two best friends are holding my hands, and I watch

Cherry Winters cry out and beg him, *Fuck me, fuck me hard!* despite herself. Inside I'm saying, *I'm really pissed off at you, Cherry Winters, how could you be so weak?*

When it's all over Sam fixes my skirt with a safety pin. His I'm-sorry-it's-just-a-game kisses land all over my body, and he rubs my back, brings some tissues for my nose. When the bleeding stops I pull my makeup bag out of my purse, hand shaking as I brush mascara back across my eyelashes, smudge cover-up over my nose. Why did it happen? Is he losing control?

Or am I?

9
Amy

March, 2003
Chippewa County War Memorial Hospital
Sault Sainte Marie, Michigan

Scotty's still not back from wherever the hell he's been all night. The logical thoughts of why this might be the case float around Amy's mind, but she can't process anything right now.

What's going on behind the curtain? She hears the strain in the doctors' voices as they're cutting her baby out of her. Her abdomen must be a mountain of steaming blood. Of course they won't let her see anything. The whole show's going on behind the curtain, so all she can do is imagine.

Next to her left ear, the anesthesiologist says, 'I can give you something to make you sleep. If you don't want to be awake for this, it's perfectly understandable.' She wants to smack him; of course she wants to be awake for her daughter's birth. Only this isn't how she imagined it. She pictured a vaginal birth, at term, Scotty cutting the cord, the doctor (just one, her OB) placing the baby on her belly, letting them nuzzle, snuggle, bond right away, maybe even nurse.

Instead a hospital band's tight on Amy's wrist, the plastic cutting into her flesh, and for some bizarre reason that's all she can notice even though the rest of her is numbed from the neck down, from the spinal for the emergency C-section. She's watching it all like she's in a dream, the doctors' anxious voices rising around her. The ceiling is pure white, a sky of fog, and somehow, although she should be worried about the baby, all she can think about is the damned wrist band and how she'll get it off. Or maybe that's all she'll let herself think about, because if she doesn't fill her head with

57

thoughts, *CallieCallieCallieCallie*, the name of her dead sister, thumps through her brain.

Amy's next door neighbor Catey drove her here last night. They talked little in the car, Catey straining to see through the little patch of windshield she'd scraped clean.

It must be morning by now.

Bits and pieces come back. Amy hemorrhaging all over the car and crying. Catey stroking her hair as she drove. The blood warming the car even more than the heater. A Rorschach of blood against snow as Catey helped her to the emergency room. In an instant they hooked her up to monitors, and that was probably when they put this god-damn wrist band on her, and when they told her that the worst-case scenario was that the baby could be born not breathing and be put on a ventilator, have a hemorrhage in her skull causing brain damage or death, be blind, mentally retarded, handicapped for life. *CallieCallieCallieCallie*. Amy swallowed the words like pills, downed them by herself since Scotty wasn't there to sweeten them and hand them to her one by one.

She won't think of Callie, won't think of the lack of air, even though she herself is suffocating now. The hospital is stuffy and smells like someone's dumped a container of cleaning fluid over the floor, and when she breathes in the odor stings her nostrils, burns them, lights them on fire.

Catey stayed by her side for a long time, bless her, watched them try the turbutaline pump until the baby's blood pressure started to drop, until they decided there was no other choice but to do an emergency C-section. Catey couldn't stay for that, of course, so she left her number with the hospital and went home to her own babies, at Amy's insistence. As she left she pulled a cross off her neck and latched it around Amy's. Amy doesn't go to church, quit believing in God a long time ago. But she believes in Catey, and the cross rests now on her collarbone, where once rested a blue Czech glass necklace, made by Amy herself. But those days are over, of course.

She glances down for a minute, but the big green curtain

means she can't see, and her eyes have gone all blurry anyway. She realizes she's crying, tears rolling down her cheeks, but she can't feel the place the anguish comes from, and she realizes suddenly that her big sobs always start in her uterus. She feels foolish for not figuring this out before, and imagines life beyond the curtain. They've sliced open her belly, yanked her half-full womb from her body and sliced it the other way, trying to pull out her baby, her little girl, her second chance.

The baby is lifted into the air, not much bigger than the doctor's hand, the tiniest baby Amy's ever seen, bright and red and not crying, gasping like a fish for air. *My daughter . . . My daughter . . . I have a daughter . . .* She's all skin stretched over bones, and right away they're hooking her up to a million monitors and wires, taping her here and there, attaching her to nasal tubes. In an instant she's in an incubator or an isolette or whatever that plastic box is called, and they wheel her toward the NICU and she's gone.

Her baby is gone.

Tears stream into Amy's hair, and where the hell are you, Scotty? And she can't heave those deep sobs that make her feel good, because her womb is her pit of tears, her source of everything. Someone says, 'You have a beautiful little girl. Don't worry, we'll take care of her. You can see her later.' Frustration oozes through her. She wants to get up from the operating table, run down to the NICU to see her baby, her little girl without a name, her little girl who was born the day after Scotty's birthday, her little girl who needs her, who's crying without her mommy. Amy's whole being aches with yearning for her child, the child who's been torn from her, the one who only moments before was a part of her. They need to be together; why don't the doctors understand that? She's going to jump up and bolt, but the problem is the only thing Amy can feel is that fucking hospital bracelet, the handcuff, so she's trapped.

They're mumbling something about stitching her up so the scar won't show. What the hell does Amy care about a goddamn scar? 'How much longer will this take? When can I see her?'

The doctor answers the first question but not the second. 'Well, the cutting's so quick but the stitching takes forever.'

That does not amuse her in the least, and now, *now* is when Scotty bursts into the room and stands over her. 'Amy, Amy, how did it happen?' It's like he's accusing her of something, of having lost the baby.

No, God, don't think that, you didn't lose the baby, not yet. How dare you think 'yet'?

She meets his eyes and in them what she's suspected for so long. In his widened pupils, the ones that suck her into the pit, the answer echoes back why he didn't come home for dinner, or for his fucking cake that's gathering dust now on the kitchen counter. He was with someone, and she's pretty sure she knows who. Suzy Petersen, that little brunette who's the receptionist at the Toyota dealership. Amy refuses even to ask him where he was or why he's so late. She won't admit she wished he'd been here. Let him feel goddamn guilty, let him feel like hell. All she can spit out is 'Catey drove me to the hospital. I bled all over her car. You should call and offer to have it detailed.'

Scotty just looks at her, his brown eyes filling up with something. *Don't you goddamn dare apologize, I don't want to talk to you.* He whispers, 'How is she? How's our baby?'

Someone must have told him it was a girl. She doesn't answer and lets the tears keep streaming into her hair. Scotty reaches out, strokes it. It feels comforting somehow, even though half of her hates his guts. She can't get up and bolt anyway, so she lets him rub her tangled hair. She drifts into sleep that's bumpy and wildridish, filled with pictures of *CallieHemmlerScottysnowbloodbloodblood*, and she doesn't sleep for more than a minute because when her eyes pop open, the curtain's still up. They're still making sure her scar doesn't show, and she feels very alone, here in this cold room with doctors and nurses and Scotty, and the world is cracking in two. The clock on the wall says it's early morning, and she hasn't slept at all. She closes her eyes again and groans at the neck ache that's suddenly seized up from her shoulder to her eyeballs. The spinal must be wearing off. She curves her thoughts around the neck ache and spins toward sleep again.

Scotty's hands move away from her hair, and she wishes she was dead, wishes she never had to wake up. In her dream babies are crying, fat cherubs with rosy cheeks and rattles and chubby tummies. A knife has sliced into her belly, but they'll sew it up so there's no scar at all.

Not even the tiniest little mark.

10
Rennie

March, 1988
Holland High School

I'm sitting in the second semicircle of desks in Drama class, legs crossed, staring at Mr Schafer, Rob, whoever the hell he is. Behind me are the makeup mirrors and the double doors that lead to the stage. I can't concentrate on what he's saying because I keep thinking of what happened there, in the great dark presence behind where I sit, a drowning bubble into another world, a pit.

It always hurts the first time, I remind myself.

You have to hurt if you want to feel anything at all.

I didn't say a word to Amy and Cherry. This is the first time I've kept something from them like this. Maybe I'm afraid they'll talk me out of it, because if I let myself think too much about it, the whole situation is vaguely terrifying. But I don't need their warnings. I know what I'm doing and it's fun and daring and all about the new me, and I'm going to keep doing it.

I'm staring at his face and he's conspicuously *not* looking at me. Instead he's directing his comments to Pammie McFadden, who couldn't care less about the Nurse's relationship with Juliet, who only took Drama because it's supposed to be an easy senior A. She's staring at him too, open-mouthed, lips wet, leaning waaay over to give him a peek down her top if he wants it.

And he takes it, what guy wouldn't? She crosses her arms on the table and leans forward even farther, and he gives her breasts the once-over. Fuck. Shit. My heart drums in my ears. Why does Pammie get to sit in the front row? It should be me.

God, yes, I'm sleeping with the sexy teacher, me me me. Boring Rennie Taylor is having an affair with a married man, and my breath catches in my throat. Before I know what's happening, my upper leg's rocking on my lower one, and I press my fingers to my temples. I have to get through sixth period French and the whole *Grease* rehearsal before I'll see him alone, and find out if he even wants to be with me again. I can stay out late again tonight, too, I'll tell him. Cherry's cutting school today, and she's meeting Amy later. I bet she'll ask us to sleep over, which is great because then I don't have to deal with Dad and Kelly and precious little Mallory howling for her 'binky'. Instead I can drown whatever ends up happening with me and Mr Schafer by firing up a great big old joint, blabbing with my friends, notebook scrawling. Of course I have the Bitch Goddess Notebook and haven't written a damn thing. I can't write about what I'm really thinking. I'll just have to tell them I'm too busy.

'Before the bells rings, I'm handing back your tests from last week.'

My heart thumps in my chest. Play practice has been eating into my study time, and I hadn't even read Act Three when I took the test. I'm a pretty good bullshitter, but I know I bombed that one.

His long fingers shuffle through the papers, slide them from the top, push them in front of other kids. Where's mine? More papers are handed out. Where?

He stops in front of my desk, and I'm eye level with the fly of his jeans. Despite myself I imagine reaching out, unsnapping the top, dragging down the zipper, the skritch like cicadas, and oh God, I'm staring, Rennie Taylor is staring at her teacher's fly. I glance around hoping no one's noticed, but of course Pammie's shooting me a sneer. I blush and cup my hand over my forehead as the paper slips onto my desk.

C-minus.

A C-minus? I don't get C-minuses. I don't even get B-minuses. A C-minus! My mind works over the grade, gnawing at it, trying to digest it, understand it, figure out how I'll align it with the real Rennie Taylor, the one who gets straight As, the one who's been accepted at Stanford, the one who's . . .

The one who's a virgin?

Tears sting my eyes, but I won't let them fall on the notebook paper and blur my ink words. I just turn the test over and stare at all the crossouts and question marks. At the bottom of the back Mr Schafer, Rob, whoever the hell he is, has written in clear even script: *See me after class about this, Rennie. R.*

'R.' Rob.

The bell rings, and everyone stuffs their test into their binders. I turn the paper back and forth on my desk, the front with the C-minus, the back with the R, letting the students around me stand up, start their chatting. Pammie hangs around awhile, flirting with Rob, leaning over, pressing her palm to his desk as he sits down. Won't she leave, won't she leave? He says something and she laughs, and he puts his hand on hers and leave it there just a little too long, and here I sit in the back of the classroom, folding and unfolding the edge of the test. Finally she pushes open the classroom door and we're alone.

'Rennie, thanks for staying.' He punches the lock button.

I push the test away and uncross my legs. 'The test. I · know I messed it up.'

His dark hair shimmers like an insect's wings, iridescent in the light, perfect. 'Come here, Rennie. I want to show you something.' He pats the chair next to his desk.

I grab my paper, pull my backpack up from under the desk, and join him, sliding my chair close to his; we are lovers, after all. 'I just didn't read it. I didn't read the section. I'm caught up now. I'm really sorry, Rob.' And I invoke his name, desperately hoping he'll forgive me. I care about drama and Shakespeare, I do, I do. Hell, it's not even the first time I've read *Romeo and Juliet*. 'I'll do better next time.'

He takes the test from me and puts it in a folder on top of his desk. 'This is what I wanted to show you.' He pulls open his gradebook and slides his finger along the marks for *Taylor, Rennie*. His fingernail's split, splotched with a snowflake. He lines it up with the Act Three test, and there it is, a bright red A.

'What? I didn't get an A.'

'You deserved one. I know you read the play, and I know you've been busy, and I know you're caught up now.' He reaches for my hair, pushes one of the long pieces over my ear. 'So, it's all right.'

All right?

'Isn't it?' Those dark glittering eyes pierce mine, open them, force their way in. 'You're special, Rennie. I just wanted to do you a favor.'

Special. I'm his special student. He could have any gorgeous girl in the senior class, but he picked *me*. Me!

'If it bothers you I'll change it back.'

Senior grades don't really matter. I mean, Stanford's already accepted me. But there's that perfect line after line of As on my report card, from freshman through senior year. It's some organized obsessive part of me, I know, but I don't want those As to be broken, especially not by my Drama class, the one I'm supposed to love, the one I . . .

'Thanks,' is the word that the air pulls from my mouth. I start to stand, but he rests his fingers on my arm and I keep sitting there.

'Rennie . . .'

And that's when I figure out why he locked the door.

It's kind of a sexy idea. In fact, the more I think of it the more excited I get, the sting of the air slapping my cheeks, my thighs, my nipples. I pull my chair closer and he reaches for my breasts, squeezes them gently, but hard enough so there's a good little hurt that makes me gasp. All I can think of is Madame DuBois, and I say, 'I have French class . . .'

He slides his hands under my sweater. 'This is my planning period. We have plenty of time.' He kisses my neck, and that stings too, the splash of a belly flop into the Holland Community Pool. The air buzzes around me, alive. 'I'll write you a pass.' Crickets are chirping, and at once it's perfectly natural to slip my top over my head and unhook my bra. My breasts tumble out and he reaches for them, but his fingers freeze mid-air like he's thinking about it.

I run my tongue over my lips and he breathes out a laugh, shakes his head, looks away. Putting my fingers over his, I pull them to my breasts and whisper, 'Juliet was only thirteen.'

His hands stay still.

I bite my lower lip, slowly, oh so slowly. 'It's too late anyway; you've already ruined me.'

Considering, his fingers skate over my bare nipples, and I link my fingers across his neck. 'You know you want to; don't pretend like you don't.' I'm breathless as I'm taunting him. Someone else must have put those words in my mouth, but I don't care, I want him. I pull him closer so his face is just a few inches from mine, brush the sexy tangle of hair away from his eyes. 'Just kiss me already, you foolish, foolish man.'

The magnet pulls our lips together and I let mine fall open, kissing him hard, hoping he'll bruise me. His tongue slides into every corner of my mouth and he breaks away for a moment, kisses my neck. He's mine and he knows it. He licks my earlobe and whispers, 'There's something else I want to show you . . .'

He shunts aside some papers and the gradebook and lifts me onto his desk, pushes up my skirt around my hips, slides off my underwear and drops them on the floor. I fill my head with the vodka of Amy's I drank on Friday, because now I'm a little nervous again, out of my territory. He pushes my legs apart and starts kissing my thighs, first the top, then the inside where the skin is smooth, and all at once he's kissing me *right there* – it's like nothing I've ever imagined, and his tongue moves along all the ridges and folds, and I close my eyes, dizzy, milky, I'm going to shatter into a million pieces, and he's lifted me up and placed me at the top of a mountain, and underneath I can see snowpeaks and buildings and people, and his tongue rolls around me, wriggles inside of me, and I stare at the sky and it's pure, stark white, oh, Jesus, I didn't know it was possible to feel so good, and I knot my fingers in his hair and pull him closer, closer, and his tongue dips into me again, and all at once I separate from myself and it's like there's another Rennie watching his face between my legs, and it's so good I know I'm going to die in a minute, oh I believe in fairies magic angels heaven God, I do, I do, and then my eyes squeeze closed and the Rennies crash together and a cry is pulled from my throat that doesn't even sound like me. Every cell in my body explodes and I can't breathe, and joy circles through me and squeezes out and finally the hum slows down. I open my eyes, and he licks my belly and draws a long line with his tongue up to my face and kisses my lips, salty, is that what I taste like? I'm sort of dreamy now; I could curl up and sleep right here on his desk.

'That you liked, didn't you?' He's hard against my belly and no, it's not over yet. He spreads me open with his fingers and pushes inside of me, and this time it doesn't hurt but I'm tired now, and I just sort of catch my breath as he presses inside of me. Now the tick of my thoughts start going, Lord, anyone could walk in here right now and figure out what we're doing, sure the door's locked, but if someone knocked and we had to finish quickly and let them in, there's sweat all over my face, there's a musty flowery odor all throughout the room and it seeps into my nostrils every time I breathe in, and Jesus, couldn't I get pregnant?

He pushes into me, deep, and I'm dizzy again, I've changed somehow, all I think of is sex, this isn't Rennie, isn't Rennie, isn't Rennie, and someone (not Rennie) makes an 'oh' sound and presses against him, and heat scurries across my arms. He's cast his spell, pulled me up to the top again, and I'm spun off a helicopter, tossed into the valley and I'm falling, falling . . .

And he comes and it's over. This time he kisses my lips before pulling away. I'm left buzzing all over, aching for more, but he hands me some tissues and we clean up, together, silently.

'I told you it would be better this time.'

A chill spins over my shoulders, and I realize I'm cold. I

snap on my bra, pull my sweater back over my head. I've turned into someone else, a character in a play, a slut, a whore, someone who's just not Rennie Taylor. I want to go home, but I look at the clock and there's thirty minutes left of French class. Already he's writing me a hall pass, glancing at his watch.

I try to turn off the thoughts in my head like turning off the spigot of a hose, then pick up my crumpled underwear and slide them on.

'Will I see you after school?'

I've changed; this isn't me. What would Dad think? Fuck Kelly, I don't care about her, fuck Mom too, I bet she did stuff like this. Who the hell is Rennie Taylor anyway?

Part of me doesn't care, just wants to be soared onto a cloud again by Rob Schafer, to feel his tongue working between my legs, to pull him inside me, to fall into outer space again. My throat thickens, and I can't swallow.

'Dawn's home at six thirty but I can cancel play practice. We'll go to a hotel, a nice one, out of town.' He puts a finger under my chin, lifts it, pulls me into the quicksand of his eyes. 'I'll bring some wine – would that be fun?'

I jump off his desk, and this time the trickle of his semen sliding out of me feels good, a reminder of our secret, our delicious and wonderful secret. Rob Schafer and I are in love, I'm in love, Rennie Taylor's in love. The delight at not being able to tell, I'll never tell, not anyone, not even my best friends, not telling is what makes it so wonderful. Oh my God, I'll never be able to look at that desk the same way again; he's married, I'm sleeping with a married man, I'm a homewrecker, a slut, and the realization thumps through my chest and makes my nipples hard again. Oh God, how am I going to get through French class? What is wrong with me?

He's still waiting for an answer about this afternoon and his eyes pull words out of my mouth like bunnies from hats. 'Count on it.'

I lift my backpack over my shoulders. Sliding the hall pass from between his fingers, I make a little kissy face at him but don't kiss him. Let him be tempted.

Will he think of me all through his planning period? Will he be unable to grade papers, with the smell of our heat still soaking up the room?

I'll do anything to feel that way again, anything, anything.

11
Cherry

Sitting in a chair in the lounge, Cherry breaks the seal on the envelope whose return address reads *Echo Magazine*. Her heart's skipping with the last remaining beats of anticipation she permits herself to feel anymore. After the fuck-this-fuck-that scene the other day with Michael, she can't afford to let herself feel much of anything. Feelings come too intensely. When they do, it's as though someone pulls a blindfold over her face, wraps her arms behind her back, pushes her off the cliff. But emotions seize up in her as she opens the flap, even though she can tell it's just a tiny, white square of paper.

Dear Ms Winters,

I'm not sure what you were thinking when you were submitting these, but your poems are far too bleak, grim, and unrefined for Echo. *Please, don't ever send us this type of writing again.*

HG-S.

Her hands shake as she covers HG-S's words with her palm to read the rest. Under it reads the Xeroxed message:

Dear Writer,

Although Echo *receives tens of thousands of submissions a year, less than five percent of those support our publication in any monetary sense. Won't you fill out the enclosed subscription card today?*

All best, Hattie Gibson-Smythe, Poetry Editor, Echo

A coil of hatred for Hattie Gibson-Smythe runs through her, unwinding along with the realization that perhaps Hattie's right. Perhaps her poetry is bleak and grim and unrefined. She guesses she wouldn't know. The poem she sent slips out of the envelope onto the floor, and she reads her words again:

Disoriented
My brain's compass
is demagnetized.
I can't steer my ship
in this swim of thoughts.
The needle spins
like a roulette wheel,
until East is West,
North is South.
In this Bermuda Triangle,
my ship sounds the SOS
before surrendering
to the deep.

A few years back, she read in a writer's monthly that her old friend Rennie Taylor had just published a novel, with Random House or Viking or some big deal publisher, the closest to which Cherry'll ever get would be running her fingers across a bookstore shelf, that is, assuming she ever gets out of this place. *Go Ahead, Embarrass Me* by Wren Taylor. Wren. That hippie name she complained about back in high school suits her just fine in California. Wren Taylor, Mill Valley novelist, Wren Taylor, Puck MacGregor's buddy, Wren Taylor, literary superstar. Thank God Rennie doesn't write to her anymore, she couldn't bear to read about success after success. Rennie Taylor, Stanford graduate, straight-A student in high school. Rennie Taylor, everything Cherry Winters could never be. She'll never buy that book. Hell, it's probably about her and Amy Linnet, dishing dirt, fictionalizing their drama, their whirlwind relationship, the Bitch Posse, the girls they once were. No thanks.

Cherry crumples the envelope and hurls it, a slip of crispy ice like the top layer of snow that she crish-crished through on her way to the Student Union all that winter, into the trash can that for some reason's always overflowing with snowballs of tissue.

At least her weaving project's going well, a jumble of triangles, bluegreenred, mountains in front of mountains in front of mountains. Cherry's half-afraid someone will steal it, or wreck it, so she takes it from the OT room each day and hides it under her bed, works on it sometimes before she goes to sleep. The therapist doesn't mind. Just another little quirk of the mental patient. The tortured weaver.

Writing's another story. She should just quit. Of course she should be happy for Rennie, her old friend. Who deserves success more than the smartest girl she ever knew? And of course she'll never stop loving Rennie, but the girl broke her heart, damn it. So Rennie's book reminds her of all she doesn't have, and never will. Obediently choking down meds, sitting through yet another round of useless group therapy as the Stanford grad spins stories while sipping coffee under the wings of that famous mountain in Marin County, what's it called?

Rennie, sobbing, at the clinic.

And, much later, at the Porter Place.

Those days are over. Their friendship, long over.

Than to give up his life for his friends.

She bites her lip, hard. As the blood blooms into her mouth, her anger falls away like ash from a cigarette. She senses a presence behind her and feels guilty suddenly. Being caught for biting her lip, imagine that. She bites harder and vows never to send out her poems again, never to make herself vulnerable again. Hattie Gibson-Smythe can go screw herself, and now the water springs to her eyes and she hates herself for crying. Are her poems really grim? Bleak? Worst of all, unrefined?

'Why try?' The words haul out of her mouth like boulders, rolling, heavy. But out of her pen, words dance like ants. Josie loves her poems. Writing opens her mind, frees her, sends her out of this place and into wherever she wants to go. Writing curls her inside herself, and she dives into the primordial ooze, pulling up fossils, dinosaur bones, pain, hurt, usually, but sometimes a diamond comes up too. Can she really give up writing?

She bites her lip again, and the breath at her ear is insistent now, smelling like milk and cigarettes. It's all she can do to restrain herself from yanking back her arm and slugging whoever it is, and she turns and it's Michael of the Mohawk, Michael of the Temper Tantrum, the Fuck You Michael, the one who reminds her of all her faults, the one who reminds her of Sam, Sam . . . Suddenly she's far too close to his glassy green eyes, and he's looking into her, way too deep inside. He sees the oozing pool, he knows, he *knows*, somehow she's sure of it. Energy seeps from his eyes into hers, and she's afraid suddenly, afraid she'll lose control like him, wreck her chances of ever getting out of here. Her hand shakes, trembles. It doesn't stop.

'What's that?'

She hefts across another brick of a word. 'What?'

'What you threw away. What is it?'

The old Cherry would've snapped back: *What do you care?* The new Cherry's tireder now, resigned. Too much effort even to answer.

He walks to the garbage and pulls out the letter. 'That's not bad, you know, Cherry?'

She just looks at him.

'If she really hated it she wouldn't have written a note.'

'No, she hated it all right.' She pulls the paper from his hand, crumples it up again, and puts it where it belongs.

'Just trying to be nice.'

'Why?'

His eyes harden into green Czech glass, like the beads on the necklace Amy made for her, way back when. She can see beyond the real skin of his flesh, and she watches anger creep into him, spread through his body. Josie, who's been sitting in the corner with the television all this time, turns up MTV probably in the hopes of avoiding another Michael tantrum, but his face webs over with fury. Cherry turns away, but not before Michael throws words at her. 'Fuck you.'

They hit her back like a whip. In a way it feels good to be insulted, to hear aloud the *Fuck You* Hattie Gibson-Smythe wrote her. The impulse spins through her head again, to pull out the pain through a slit in her arm. One slice across with a knife or razor blade and pain and hatred and self-loathing melt away, and oh, God, when she feels really bad she reminds herself Diana did this too, threw herself into a glass cabinet at Kensington Palace, slashed her chest and thighs in front of her Prince. He called her melodramatic, but how could he understand cutting if he never tried it?

And she will never write again never write again never write again and she's such a chickenshit for saying she will never write again. She sinks to her knees next to Josie and lights a cigarette and stares, stares, stares at MTV's *The Real World*. Laughter bubbles up in her. *The Real World*. Pretty funny.

74

12
Amy

March, 1988
Holland, Illinois

Me and Cherry are sitting on her bed, doing each other's toenails with funky polish Cherry got from her last excursion to The Alley in Chicago. She's already packed a bowl with primo weed from her mom's stash, but we're waiting till Rennie gets here to fire it up. While we wait we're chewing gobs of Juicy Fruit, which we're all of us addicted to. Patchouli incense burns next to the bed.

She's trying Rub My Petals, I'm being daring and going for Fuck Me Fuchsia. One of these days I'm going to get up the nerve to open the Manic Panic Atlantic hair dye I've had in my bathroom for a month and use it. Cherry insists blue hair would look great with my eyes. Like a lot of things (LSD, which me and Rennie are still fraidy-cats about), I need to close my eyes and just jump.

Cherry caps the Fuck Me Fuchsia polish and blows on my toenails. 'Looks great.' Later we'll watch the *DeGrassi Junior High* Cherry videotaped this afternoon. It's about eighth graders but we love it because the kids seem real. They watch porno movies, have sex, try drugs. I don't know why more shows aren't like this. Sitcoms are so phony and we all refuse to watch them. But sometimes *DeGrassi* freaks me out. Mr Colby looking down Lucy's top and groping her? Spike getting pregnant at fourteen? I don't even want to think about it.

Cherry Scotch-tapes another Diana picture onto her shrine by her mirror. I think we could safely call this an obsession. Forty million pictures of the gorgeous, perfect princess contradict the Sex Pistols poster that hangs next to the Diana Altar. I mean, in 'God Save the Queen' they pretty much call

75

Queen Elizabeth a Fascist, so what does that make Diana? But there she is, plastered to the wall, smiling up at Sid Vicious as if he's one of my most loyal subjects. Okay Cherry, whatever you say. But I'm drawn to Diana, too; we all are. I've never seen a more beautiful woman; she's not some manufactured model, she's like a rose, just real and breathed full of life. You get the feeling if you ran into her on the street she'd be really nice, would ask you if you were okay. You get the feeling, she'd actually give a damn.

Mom let me stay home from YMCA Day Camp to watch her wedding. I was eleven and of course Diana's set the stage for what my own wedding is going to be like, someday. Lady Diana Spencer stepping out of the glass coach, oh, my God. And the dress. The snowy satin ruffles, the crinoline, puff sleeves, sequins, jewels, and the train, oh, the train! Even the dress was only half as gorgeous as the new princess, a wide-eyed doe at the altar, positively scrumptious. The Arch-bishop of Canterbury said: *Here is the stuff of which fairy tales are made.* He was right. And since then Diana's only gotten more beautiful.

Cherry's fingers fall away from the photo. 'Why the hell'd she marry that dipshit?'

'Oh come on, don't tell me you wouldn't marry a prince if you could.'

She shudders. 'She's way too good for him. God, where's Princess Rennie? It's almost six.'

I wonder if Mom's passed out yet. It's a Hemmler week, and that means they start pouring the cocktails early, almost as soon as I get home. By dinnertime they're spilling spa-ghetti sauce, dropping bottles, there's an edge to their words. After dinner, Mom crashes for a couple hours on the sofa and Dad can start in on me. What I didn't do this week. The As I didn't get. All the million infinitesimal ways I've disappointed. Then Mom wakes up, pours some more vodka and orange juice, and the real drama begins: the Callie fight. I could write it all down, like a stage play, line by line. That's why I headed here straight after school. 'I don't know where Rennie is.'

One time I actually told Father O'Neill about Mom and Dad, figured he could talk to God for me or something. Seems stupid now. Know what he told me? *Pray, Amy.* So I did. That very night was the time Dad decided it was somehow my fault the Mustang got keyed, called me a brainless bitch, took my driver's license and scissored it up. That was the night Mom got so toasted she fell down the stairs and sprained her ankle. So, I guess there's static on Father O'Neill's direct phone line to God.

Sorry, that number is no longer in service.

You know it's gotten bad when the songs from Girl Scout Camp make more sense than stupid prayer. *A circle's round, it has no end, that's how long I want to be your friend . . .*

The only praying I really do anymore is *Hail Mary, full of grace, help me find a parking space.*

By the way Cherry chomps her gum I can tell she's itching for her dope, which is also why she's so impatient about Rennie getting here. 'If it's not rehearsal, it's studying,' she says. 'That girl needs to get her ass over here and get high so she can lighten up a bit.'

'She's not at rehearsal though. I wonder where she is.'

A strange expression crosses Cherry's face. 'She told me she had play practice today.'

'Well, she doesn't. Abby Green came running out of school this afternoon shrieking, all upset because the play's in a month and how dare Mr Schafer cancel practice?' Who else but Abby Green to play Sandy? If there's anyone more high-strung than Rennie, it's Abby, whose braids are wound as tight as her nerves.

Cherry starts to say something, then closes her mouth.

'What?' I ask.

She takes a deep breath, fingering the bowl. 'Why would she lie?'

Just then Rennie bursts in, all happy and breathless. Her cheeks are flushed like they are in PE when we run the mile, and she flings down her overnight bag and says 'What?' which is when I realize we're staring at her, both of us.

Cherry leans into Rennie and sniffs. 'You're drunk, you

bitch. What the hell are you doing drinking in the middle of the afternoon?' She shakes her head and I do too; something is definitely going on with our Rennie.

Rennie doesn't answer.

'Where were you?' asks Cherry.

'Play practice.' Her eyes shift from the ceiling to the bowl in Cherry's hand and she grabs it, foams the lighter over it, and takes a big long hit.

'You were not.' I stash my gum in the wrapper and take a hit myself. 'I saw Abby and she was freaking out because it was canceled. So what gives?'

The Bitch Goddess Notebook flops onto Cherry's quilt and Cherry reaches for it. Rennie's such a writer. Cherry's a little jealous, I think, but she always wants to read Rennie's stuff, says she wants to learn. 'Fess up, Rennie.' She flips through the pages quickly. 'You didn't even write this week.'

Rennie? Not writing?

'You've been acting weird all day.' Cherry tosses the notebook back down, takes a toke and passes the bowl to me. 'What's going on?'

'Nothing.' Rennie pretends to be very absorbed with arranging her hair. 'I just had a few things to go over with Mr Schafer.'

'A few things? Till six o'clock?' Cherry picks up the notebook again and sketches out the weekly questionnaire in a chart on a new page.

'What, have you been body-snatched and your brain replaced by Kelly's?' Rennie takes herself another hit, the bud glowing orange to red as she inhales. 'I have a mom,' she chokes out. 'I don't need you to step in.' She can't hold in the smoke anymore and lets it creep out.

Cherry and I exchange a glance. It's not like Rennie to be so defensive. 'All right, moving on,' says Cherry, dropping the subject. 'No poems, no stories, only empty pages to fill. Extra work for us all tonight.' She draws some flowers around the chart. 'So who got laid this weekend, let's see, Cherry did . . .' She spirals the pen around her name with a flourish. 'How about you, Aim?'

I sigh, not really wanting to share the fact that after Brandon and I drank most of the vodka I stole from home on Friday, he fell asleep on my shoulder. We just slept in my car in the parking lot for a few hours, my top off and my jeans half-unzipped, until I felt well enough to drive him home. Anyway, the true purpose of the evening was to blot out Callie from my head, which it did, despite a headache that lasted till Saturday afternoon. And now I'm thinking of Callie again, I'd rather just think of getting laid, and I pull in some more smoke and push her away from my mind. 'Put it this way, it's closer than we've gotten in a long time.'

Cherry gives a flat-lipped smile. 'That would be a "no" from the lovely Amy Linnet.' I poke her and she pokes me back; the pot's gotten into my head now and I can't help giggling. Leaning over to the stereo, I pick up a cassette by a new band called They Might Be Giants. Cherry says, *These guys are like the Beatles, they'll be around for years.* I fast-forward to my favorite song, 'She's an Angel', and hum along, since I'm following an angel too. I only need about one or two more tokes and I make this one nice and long. When I look up again Rennie and Cherry are giving each other a long, hard stare. 'So who's still the most beautiful virgin east of the Mississippi?' says Cherry as she does every week. We never give Rennie a hard time about being a virgin. I think we respect that she's waiting for someone special. Anyway, it's her body, hell, isn't that what abortion rights are all about?

Rennie doesn't answer and the music keeps playing in the background. Her cheeks are so flushed I can see the blood vessels, matching the tiny red glass beads of the necklace around her neck, the one I made for her that goes with my blue one and Cherry's green one. My Christmas gift for all of us.

'Rennie?' I take one last hit, and that's the one that gets me there. The air's breathing around me and, mesmerized by Rennie's glass beads that seem like they're on fire, for a minute I forget why I'm here and what we're talking about.

All I know is I'm in a room where I've been since the beginning of time, with my two girls, my best friends, the sisters I never had, for always. *A circle's round, it never ends . . .* I can read Rennie's mind, I really can; I'm about three thoughts ahead of her, and anyway, the truth is painted in her eyes.

'What, Aim?'

I can't remember what I was talking about. 'Crap.'

'Tell the truth, Rennie. You got laid, didn't you?' Cherry asks.

Rennie hates being questioned – her fingers fidget, her eyes float everywhere except to ours. I hate being questioned too; it's like Dad on one of his drunks, everything's up for debate: my clothes, my report card, even the way I'm looking at him. The most I can say is he's never laid a hand on me. He doesn't have to. He does it all with words.

So I know how Rennie feels, sitting under the burning naked lightbulb as you're the prisoner being questioned. Having your being poked and prodded, unfolded, like an origami project, revealing parts of yourself, the little white slips of paper you thought no one knew about. The nice thing about being drunk is that all that's blotted away. The nice part about being stoned is that it doesn't really seem to matter because all I care about is being here and now with my best friends in the world. But now Rennie's being unfolded by us, by Cherry specifically, and I don't want it to happen but at the same time I'm glad it's not me and so, despite myself I join in too. 'Virgin schmirgin.'

That of course makes us all laugh hysterically. Rennie blushes and she knows it's no good trying to deny anything. She throws herself on her back onto Cherry's bed and she's still howling, but it's so very obvious our Rennie has gotten herself laid.

'Who is he?' Cherry shrieks and jumps on top of Rennie, pulling her arms behind her head. 'I'm not letting go until you tell me.' And it's such a ridiculous scene, like Cherry and Rennie are in a slapstick comedy, that I burst into laughter again, and it's catching, Cherry's laughing too and

Rennie's shaking her head from side to side, tears coming out her eyes.

'Kent, maybe,' I say in a moment of making sense-ness (*God, where did words go?*) that's rare for me when I'm high. 'Friday, after me and Brandon disappeared with the vodka.'

But the answer in her eyes isn't yes. 'Maybe it's not a he at all,' says Cherry, 'maybe it's a she. Oh come on, don't look so scandalized,' she says to me, and now I blush, feeling unworldly. 'Open your horizons, Aim, it's 1988 after all.'

'It's not Kent, and it's not a woman, and that's all I'm saying.'

'Oh, just tell us, we're your best friends,' I beg. 'Is it someone at school?'

'Would I deign to fuck one of the lowlife jockstraps from the senior class? Are you serious?' The words are supposed to come out lightly, I'm sure, but Rennie's got a secret and she's not telling for a reason, and I decide to drop it.

'Listen, let's put on *DeGrassi*,' I say. Watching *DeGrassi* when we're high is the best because no one can stop laughing when Snake or Wheels or BLT calls somebody 'narbo' or 'broomhead' (what with the fucked-up names and wacky slang, Canada must be the Land o' Insanity, eh?), plus Joey Jeremiah's stupid fedora, and the band Zit Remedy with their one and only song. Oh God, I'm giggling just thinking about it.

But Cherry presses on. 'I'll bet he's married. That's why you're not telling us.' Rennie just gives a nod and Cherry lets her up. 'I knew it. I won't make you say who it is.'

Now I *am* scandalized, and the news almost kills my buzz: my best friend sleeping with a married man? What kind of married man would mess around with a high-school girl? I only hope she's not in too deep. Surely we can talk her out of this. 'Rennie, why? What would possess you to do something so . . .' I don't want to say *stupid* so I settle for, 'risky?'

'I don't want to talk about it, okay? Just—'

'Is that who you were drinking with? When you said you were at play practice?' demands Cherry. She's so lucid when she's stoned, so logical. I can't be that way; it's all I can do to follow the conversation. Yes we're talking about Rennie, yes she's no longer a virgin, yes she's sleeping with a married man, and my mind won't process any more.

Rennie nods and Cherry says, 'If you get pregnant I'll kill you.'

'He can't get me pregnant. He and his wife will probably have to adopt at some point.'

I can tell by her eyes that it really hurts to say 'his wife'. There'll be a bigger reaction from me in the morning when I try to change her mind, help her figure her way out. But right now Rennie just needs a hug. Her eyes are wide and kind of scared, and I fold her up in my arms and run my palms over her back. She seems to appreciate it, breathing out short little puffs. She *is* scared, like Alice falling down a rabbit hole, like a little fox cub who's had an adventure that's too grown up. I rub my knuckles over her hair, and I do have a lucid thought. *Please God help her through this, don't let this ruin her.* I meet Cherry's eyes over Rennie's shoulder and she says, 'Rennie, this has to stop right now.'

'Look, Cherry, I told you I don't need a mother. I can take care of myself.' The subject is most definitely closed, and the warm belly of the room has turned decidedly icy. Cherry takes a deep breath and swears as she realizes she's forgotten about the pot burning in the pipe, wasting away into nice-smelling smoke, and she pulls it to her lips and takes one last hit. But then she's choking, and she waves us off, tears squeezing out the corners of her eyes. Blood's trickling from her nose, dripping down her face, splashing onto her quilt, and Rennie grabs the tissue box. Cherry squeezes her nose as Rennie cleans her up, but the tears don't stop falling from Cherry's eyes. I'm compelled to ask, 'Are you okay?' feeling like a loser, the only one who hasn't had a crisis tonight, and Cherry waves me off again, fine fine, no problem, no problem at all.

But seeing Cherry cry breaks my heart. I pull her close, and even though I've escaped Dad's needling that sometimes comes when I've been talking to him for half an hour and one little remark makes me realize the conversation wasn't at all about what I thought it was, I feel my lips trembling too. I don't want to go to Hemmler on Friday; I love Callie but seeing her makes me depressed. I'll talk to her and read to her out of *The Very Hungry Caterpillar* again which, well I don't know if she loves it since she can't tell me, but which she always seems to pay a lot of attention to. Of course I can't read to her about things she can't understand – *Forever*, *The Grounding of Group Six*, or anything I like, I can't giggle with her about the *DeGrassi* episode, I don't have a sister, don't have a sister, don't have a sister and suddenly I'm crying too. God we must sound like a bunch of lunatics stoned and sobbing in Cherry's room, and it strikes me as funny all of a sudden so now my crying blends into another fit of the giggles.

As I run my fingers up Cherry's arm, my fingers trip over speed bumps, and I open my eyes and notice red scratches slicing across her left arm. I draw in my breath. 'Cherry!' Seeing your best friend's battle scars is the ultimate buzz kill, and in a second my high floats into nothingness and I'm my cold, dreary, depressed self again.

She pulls away and yanks her sleeve down, but I trade a glance with Rennie; she's seen too. 'Oh my God, what did you do? Did you try to . . . ?'

'Of course not. I wouldn't do that.'

I reach over and slide her sleeve up again. Long red stripes skate across the beautiful smooth unfreckled skin of her forearm. 'Why?'

She takes a deep breath and lights a cigarette.

'You're so beautiful, why would you hurt yourself?' asks Rennie.

'It's not like that.' She blows smoke over my head, and the strands tangle in Rennie's hair. I reach for a cigarette and light one too. 'Did you ever hurt so bad you just couldn't stand it, felt so bad inside that you thought you'd burst?'

God, I feel that way whenever I think of Callie and Mom and Dad. Emotions scratch themselves open inside me, gouges of pain that just expand and bleed and never get smaller. The only thing that helps is to drink, drink a lot, make my thoughts go away, turn myself into someone who doesn't think and just acts, impulsive, and I nod so Cherry knows I understand and Rennie's nodding too. I say, 'Cherry, we've all felt bad, but don't do stuff like that.'

'You haven't tried it. Look. You're not going to kill yourself. It's just taking the pain inside and putting it outside where it's real.' She opens the drawer next to her bed and pulls out a straight razor blade. Before I know what she's doing, she pulls it across her arm and beads of blood pop up, sparkle like glass. She holds up the razor blade in an invitation.

Rennie takes it and holds it in her palm for a moment, considering. Then she too closes her eyes, pushes the blade into her skin and slices across her arm. She opens her eyes as if shaken awake and her tears have stopped. She doesn't look afraid anymore. She just says, rubbing the drops of blood into her arm, 'Are you going to try it, Amy?'

It was like this when Cherry passed me a joint for the first time, when Pammie stole some beer from her parents' fridge in seventh grade. It's not like I'm going to Just Say No.

I reach for the blade and drag it across my arm. All I feel is a little pinch, and I look down. A white scratch zips across my skin; I haven't drawn blood. I'm just a wimp I guess, and I'm so pissed at myself I try it again. The blade chugs across my arm, slicing pretty deep, and the blood flows up to the surface, and goddamn, reality crashes into me like a world colliding against Amy Linnet, a ping of sensation. I'm struck like a tuning fork and vibrate with life; I *do* feel better. I feel alive and everything around me is crisper, cleaner, louder, more defined. The air rings with importance. I matter. I am. This is better than blanking out with vodka. And I know why Cherry's done this not just once but five or six or more times.

We're just a bunch of fucked-up chicks I guess. Before the wounds on our arms dry up all the way, Cherry decides we're all going to become blood sisters since we're sliced up anyway. We scratch open our valleys of blood, and Cherry presses hers on mine, then I press mine on Rennie's and

84

Rennie presses hers on Cherry's. Cherry says, 'The poet, some words from the poet.'

'I know,' says Rennie. 'We must all swear a solemn oath.'

How utterly fucking brilliant.

'First I'll say it, then the two of you.' She closes her eyes.

> 'We, the Bitch Posse girls,
> do solemnly swear
> to be undyingly faithful to each other,
> and to put no friends or lovers before one another,
> as long as the stars are fixed in the heavens
> and the fish sparkle in the sea.'

'Jesus, Rennie,' says Cherry. 'That's fucking beautiful.'

'Now you girls say it.'

Cherry seizes my hand and Rennie's and presses our fingers with abandon. Rennie reaches for my hand, so now we're a circle, a circle of three. 'We, the Bitch Posse girls,' we all say together, and our lips work in unison, we own the world, the whole motherfucking world, and the words come out so clean, like diamonds, sharp and hard, and our voices swell, we are better, stronger, more perfect than anyone else on this whole pathetic planet.

When we finish repeating the oath all of us are crying.

Rennie breaks the silence with a whisper, spinning her fingers along her red glass necklace. 'These beads that string us together shall never fall from our necks. Because "there is no friend like a sister."'

My fingers wander to my own necklace. When I was stringing all those beads I had no idea they'd mean so much to us.

'We should remember this moment.' Cherry rummages around her desk drawer for something and comes up with three little glass jars. 'Here.' We each squeeze some drops into the jars and I know that with the power of blood the three of us can do anything. We're stronger than anyone, stronger than Callie or Mom or Dad or Hemmler or married men. 'Diana's the Queen of Hearts,' Cherry tells us, 'you,

Amy, are the Queen of Diamonds, Rennie's the Queen of Spades and I'm the Queen of Clubs.' We are three queens and Diana's our fourth. We're all as strong as Cherry, who never seems to worry about anything.

Why the hell would Cherry need to cut herself?

As the last drops slip into the last jar and Cherry seals them, I feel so strong, stronger as three than one. Cherry whispers into my ear, 'Forever . . .' We lie back down on Cherry's bed and end up missing *DeGrassi* as we fall asleep in our clothes, tangled together, best friends.

13
Rennie

April 2003
Mill Valley, California

Rennie's running a brush through her hair, getting ready for Puck's book party. He's so famous, she can't believe she actually knows him as 'Puck'. Bay's not coming with her tonight. He shies away from parties, especially ones where Rennie's called 'Wren' and where her book inevitably comes under discussion. Lately it hasn't been *Go Ahead, Embarrass Me*, it's been the new novel, that beast she can't tame, the thing she's been working on for five years now. It's humiliating, this perpetually unfinished project people continually ask about and raise a brow when she says she's still working, like she's grown an extra nose. She hates thinking about her writing; it doesn't mean anything to her anymore. She doesn't read like she should, either. It requires too much thought, which is why sex is so great – you don't have to think about anything. She's grateful the attention'll be on Puck tonight, and his latest novel *Hayes*. Not her.

The party's at Beth Hartford's little rented house by the 2 A.M. Club in Mill Valley. Leave it to hanger-on Beth, the socialist socialite, to get The Puck MacGregor to her house for a party. Beth's place is a magnet for events of all types because she has the yard and the endless stash of pot and the big wolf-dog Bogie and the hot tub, of course – all the accessories of a successful Marin County get-together.

When Rennie parks her car and gets out, dusk is just drawing from Mount Tamalpais. Jasmine layered with nectar-seeking butterflies pours over Beth's fence, the heady odor floating in the air, making her drunk, happy, Marin County happy. Most people would kill to live here.

The occasional zoom of a car on Miller Avenue interrupts the silence but, mainly, it's Marin, where the air's ready to pop with the sound of a bird, perfection.

Beth's place is nothing fancy, a pink stucco bungalow that needs updating. Puck already had a big to-do in the city at the St Francis, the one that was written up in the *Chronicle* along with a glowing advance review of his book and a bunch of hype about the upcoming *Killing Butterflies* starring Angelina Jolie and Christian Slater. (Will Wren Taylor ever be reviewed in the *Chronicle* again?) This is the intimate affair, the one without Loretta Jacobs, the social scene columnist, without the reporters, just Puck and his agent and a few local writers. Puck knows everyone, and everyone loves him, the Golden Child, the Boy Wonder. He's like a magnet drawing famous people to him, and somehow, next to everyone, he seems even more important. Hell, Puck would make Queen Elizabeth look like a nobody.

Tonight Anne Lamott might show up, she heard, and Po Bronson, who's got a new book out, and Isabel Allende, and a bunch of other famous people. Beth even said that Amy Tan will try to drop by (well of course she'll drop by, it's Puck MacGregor after all), and Salinger's old girlfriend, who lives in Mill Valley too. Tonight Rennie will be among writers of such stature they're like fictional characters, writers so important that being in the same room with them will make her feel like a big fat zero.

Wren Taylor, of course, Wren Taylor the Mill Valley novelist, has been invited probably as an afterthought. As for Rennie Taylor the teacher at Tamalpais High, who's got an awful habit of fucking student teachers, well, that person hasn't been invited; that person doesn't even exist in these circles.

Funny how she keeps killing herself and getting resurrected as someone else. She'll never go back to Holland, not in a million years. She put all that behind her, froze out Amy right after it happened, stopped writing to Cherry too, because she couldn't bear to relive those terrible moments Cherry seemed so obsessed with confronting. That Rennie

Taylor is dead. Wren Taylor's the only one who really matters, the only respectable incarnation of herself she's been able to create thus far. Not the scared little girl at the Porter Place, God, no. Certainly not the slutty English teacher. No wonder Bay didn't want to come.

Rennie admits it, she's kind of glad he's not here, because she has a little crush on Puck, the ingénue who appeared from nowhere and took the literary world by storm fresh out of high school. She loved *Killing Butterflies* and his two story collections and was struck breathless, years ago, by his first novel *Dark Blooms* ('a provocative and elegant debut by a mesmerizing new talent', said the *New York Times*), which he wrote when he was seventeen. Some passages of that novel were so 'provocative' Rennie didn't just blush, she actually had to put the book down and mess around by herself for awhile. They've run into each other before, when she read at A Clean Well-Lighted Place for Books at Opera Plaza, back five years ago it is now. He came up to her, congratulated her, tiny but troubled twenty-seven-year-old with a debut novel, he, already famous at nineteen. Eight years her junior and decades her superior in the literary world.

Now, as she turns the doorknob, music spills out. Beth's big wolf-dog (why do people own those? Couldn't they go wild and attack someone?) jumps up on her and gets a muddy paw print on the front of her paisley skirt. Fortunately it's splashed with so many colors it doesn't matter. She laughs but is kind of pissed – why isn't Bogie in the garage? Beth's at the door smiling, Beth the perpetual wanna-be who's very good at cultivating relationships with writers, Beth of the red curls, long thin lips, Beth, who calls her 'Wren' and wants 'Wren' to call her 'Bee', Beth, whom Rennie's starting to think has a gigantic crush on her because her fingers always linger on Rennie's arm as they're doing now, a patchouli-scented kiss at that sensitive spot by her ear, a little too friendly-friendly ('Wren, it's so good to see you—' Beth's hand just happens to flutter across Rennie's breasts. '—it's been way too long!'). But that's okay, Beth's her ticket in to see Puck.

She spots him right away, standing near the stereo, a chunk of streaky brown hair hanging over his forehead as he holds a plastic glassful of Chardonnay. The skinny redhead next to him must be his agent, New York Uber-icon Pepper Perryman. Rumors have always buzzed around Puck and Pepper. Just like everyone else in the world, Rennie read the *Vanity Fair* article where the interviewer asked flat-out if he and Pepper were sleeping together. Puck pretended like she'd asked about the casting for *Killing Butterflies* and ran through the possibilities, role by role, in that way you avoid a question when the answer is yes but you don't want to say so.

Rennie's agent, New York Nobody Lisa Jenkins, has patiently accepted four drafts of the opening three chapters of her work-in-progress alternatively titled *Lori's Summer*, *The Narey Relatives* and *The Rest of Us*, and has patiently sent them back again. This past week, Lisa's ignored two e-mails and a phone call, and Rennie's starting to worry that even the Sara Kiernan Book Award that's plastered on *Go Ahead, Embarrass Me* is aging, five, six years old now. Crap, Puck MacGregor's staring at her, The Puck MacGregor. Does he remember her from the reading? Probably not; as famous writers go she's the least known here, ha ha ha.

She looks away from Puck and watches Amy Tan help herself to some crackers and Brie. Before Rennie knows it, Puck's crossed the room to her, and he smiles, chocolate eyes sparkling beneath that *touch-it-oh-go-ahead-mess-it-up-kiss-me-fuck-me* hair that hangs in his eyes. It evokes something in her, another chunk of hair falling into another handsome face, a kiss on a stage . . . She shuts down the thought. Her brain is half not working and all she can think to say is 'Congratulations.'

He laughs, takes a bottle of Chardonnay from somewhere near him, and fills a plastic cup for Rennie. 'Good to see you, Wren. Don't you love this kind of book party? The one no one knows about. No New York publishing people, no caterers, no evening gowns, just a bunch of friends getting together. Look, you're more dressed up than anyone.' She looks around and it's true; people are in blue jeans, shorts, T-shirts. One guy's even wearing some bizarre Mexican poncho, Birkenstocks, and seemingly nothing else, judging from the curly leg hair that escorts her eyes up ever higher, leaving little to the imagination.

Even the famous people look like they've just come back from a pick-up softball game. Po Bronson and Anne Lamott are helping themselves to hors d'oeuvres, he in a Stanford sweat-shirt, she in a solid green tank top. Amy Tan's sipping wine in the hallway, wearing a navy scoop-neck shirt and jeans. And there's Isabel Allende, talking to Beth by the screen door. Yeah, *that* Isabel Allende. If Rennie had the nerve she'd go up and start a chat about Chile, Pinochet, the coup, even Neruda. But she isn't up on politics anymore, and she'd probably come off like a loser. For her fashion selection this evening Isabel has chosen a plain black T-shirt and denim capris.

There is not one single other person here in a skirt.

Isabel has Beth in hysterics as she slides a chunk of French bread through the bowl of eggplant dip like she's at any ordinary friendly get-together. Rennie will never be so easy and relaxed, unless she has about ten drinks in her.

Amy Tan is eating a cracker not twenty feet away from Rennie. Yeah, *that* Amy Tan. Who won a little prize called the National Book Award. Anne Lamott's standing near the fireplace, adjusting the strap of her tank top. Yeah, *that* Anne Lamott, whose *Bird by Bird* owns a place of honor next to Rennie's computer. And Po Bronson's changing the CD in the stereo, yeah, *that* Po Bronson, whose new book about figuring out what the hell you're supposed to be doing with your life Rennie's afraid to read. All those famous people, in the same room as her. Looking like they're having a hell of a lot more fun.

Yeah, she would've fit in better if she'd come to the party naked.

Or not shown up at all.

'Hey. Wren.'

Heat rises to her cheeks as she realizes she's standing there like a fucking idiot saying nothing when Puck MacGregor, yeah, *that* Puck MacGregor, just asked her a question. 'Sorry. It's a great party; I love Marin,' she says stupidly and gulps the Chardonnay.

'Your novel was sensational.' He's staring into her eyes like she's the most fascinating person in the room. 'I still have the copy you signed to me.'

She nearly chokes on the wine. 'You do?' Oh shit, oh shit, oh shit. She got dead drunk that night after her reading, went for a drive with Puck and Beth and some others out to Fort Point, where they went walking to see the Golden Gate Bridge from below. Most of the night is blurred in her memory. She hates when she drinks so much she can't remember things, but she thinks, she's pretty sure, she might have kissed him. Maybe more. At the end of the evening she wrote some long, embarrassing, insipid thing in a book and gave it to him, maybe even something terrible like *To my idol, Puck MacGregor*, oh, crap.

He rests his hand on the bookcase behind her so if he bent his head just a little he'd be kissing her. 'You're working on something new, aren't you?'

Oh God. The dreaded question. Puck's a writer; he should know better. But then, he's had something in print almost every year since he was seventeen. Novels must fly through his window and present themselves at the bottom of his computer printer. 'Yeah, well, I'm reworking part of it.' As in, all of it. All three chapters of it. For the fifth time now.

'Let me know when you finish. I'll send it on to Pepper for you.'

Damned if he'll humiliate her with such condescension. She tilts the last swallow of Chardonnay into her mouth. 'I have an agent,' she says coldly.

But he just laughs again and pours some more wine into her glass. 'It's been too long, Wren. You should come down to Palo Alto sometime. We could get together.'

'Maybe.' What the hell did she do that night at Fort Point? 'I'm awfully busy up here with my teaching and stuff.'

'Oh, I didn't know you were teaching now. Where? Dominican?'

And of course he'd assume that; that's where someone successful would be teaching, where *he'd* be teaching, if he wasn't the Visiting Professor at the Stanford Writing Program. The program she couldn't even get into after she graduated, the reason she took a teacher credential at San Francisco State. 'I teach at Tam. I love working with young people – my kids are fantastic.' Teaching. She's just invited Rennie Taylor, teacher-slut, into the room, and she wishes she could uninvite her, immediately. She finishes almost all the wine in her glass, then looks at the swallow that's left and finishes it too.

Beth stands in the center of the living room and claps her hands. 'Who wants to soak in the hot tub?' Before Rennie can think straight, Beth's shed her top and shorts and is stark naked. About half the group, including the Mexican poncho guy, start whipping off their clothes and pour out onto the porch. The more respectable set gazes the other way and Pepper Perryman looks panicked.

The non-hot tub group drifts into the kitchen, and Rennie and Puck are left staring at each other halfway between the kitchen and the hot tub porch.

Behind them is Beth's bedroom where there's music playing for some reason, and Puck laughs and says softly, 'Want to disappear?'

No one even notices as Puck MacGregor, yeah, *that* Puck MacGregor, ditches his own party with Wren Taylor the writer, and closes the bedroom door behind them.

Almost before Rennie knows it she's taken off her top, then her bra, and he's touching her, kissing her face, her ears, her neck. 'Mmm, Wren, it's been *way* too long . . .' She's on her fifth or sixth wine now, and it's good to be drunk, not to care. The air hums in her ears, and she slips her tongue into his mouth, kicks off her underwear. He pushes up her skirt and they roll onto the bed, panting. 'You're such a cute little thing,' he says in between sharp kisses that he lands on her breasts. 'Are you sure you're not an elf?' She grabs him, pushing him into her, clinging, pressing her chest to his, pulling his power inside her, and if she fucks him hard enough she might even become him. Everything dissolves into kisses and ohs and wet noises and Rennie closes her eyes and spins into the darkness. But there's no way she can wrap her legs around him tight enough, and the question pounds through her: why does she always use sex to solve things? Until she erases it all in the rush of orgasm and it's over just like that, supersonic sex. It's all right though because she's too drunk or tired to want it to go on.

He kisses her and lights her cigarette, and they lie together quietly awhile, watching the smoke curl ghosts into the air as he rubs her belly under the elastic of the skirt, snuggles her under his arm, swats her on the hip a few times, just lightly, affectionately. She could fall asleep . . .

Then he sits up, drinks some wine and splashes some more into Rennie's glass. They make a little small talk as they trace circles over each other's backs, go on touching lazily and compliment each other's bodies, blab about the war (they're both against it but are fuzzy on the whys of it all, Puck thinks it all happened because of those misguided extremists who voted for Nader and Rennie's one of them so they shift the conversation), Beth's dog (Puck thinks Bogie's gorgeous, Rennie thinks Beth's crazy to own such a dangerous animal), the cost of housing (they agree it's outrageous, the only difference is that it doesn't matter to Puck). The conversation circles into writing and publishing, if *Hayes* is ever going to be made into a movie. Puck tells her Angelina – he's on a first name basis with her apparently – is interested in that one too. This is when Rennie hopes Pepper Perryman will come up again, but before that can happen, she runs the conversation into a wall by mentioning her old editor at Random House, Cath Zannini (shit, how was she supposed to know they'd been involved?).

Silence hangs between them like a ghost and anyway, Rennie suddenly wants to go home. Voices swell in the living room; the hot tub crowd seems to be coming inside already since it's a little chilly now that the sun's gone behind Mount Tam. She really doesn't want to be caught naked with Puck MacGregor in Beth's bedroom so she snaps on her bra, pulls on her top. He's already dressed and slips out, saying 'Call me' over his shoulder. But of course he doesn't leave his number, and she's so drunk she can barely wiggle her feet into her sandals. Glancing in Beth's mirror, she notices her mascara's run all over, her lipstick's smudged, and she borrows a brush to yank through her tangled hair. God, her face looks drawn and tired. *When you lose your looks there's not much else, not if you're a woman, anyway.* Emotion chokes her throat but she won't think about any of that now. She gulps the last drops of wine in her glass, straightens Beth's rumpled quilt, and slides out the door too.

Puck's already laughing with someone else – Ula, Rennie thinks her name might be, a tiny little blonde from the Stanford Writing Program, impish, ambitious. She thinks she hears Puck mutter something like 'Can't write worth a damn, but a lot of fun in bed,' and humiliation slices through her even though he may be talking about someone else.

Bay's face flashes into her head for the first time in this confused night, and oh crap, Rennie Taylor's screwed things up again.

14
Cherry

Hauled into the principal's office again; this is a pretty usual scene with me. If it's not for sassing a teacher or smoking at school, it's just because Mr Coldwell's bored with arranging paperclips or jerking off in his office or whatever the hell administrators do in their spare time. They called me out of Chemistry, the only good thing about it, and here I am, waiting my turn in the 'kid in trouble' chair.

The door swings open and Amy ducks into the office, small and scared and not at all perky like her usual self. 'Holy shit, what'd we do?'

'I have no fucking idea.' I never expected to see Amy here. As she's sinking into the chair next to me, the door opens again and in walks Rennie, looking confused, black hair fluttering around her face.

'Oh, my God.' She drops her backpack to the floor. 'Did you bring drugs to school?' she whispers.

It's insulting she'd think I'd be a) so stupid and b) so crass. 'I just told Amy I have no fucking idea.'

'I thought it was about Stanford. The school paper wants to do a feature on me.'

Sometimes, Rennie really annoys me. 'Apparently not.'

Mr Coldwell's door peals open and we step inside. There like a jury sit Marian, red hair sprayed to attention, so she can play the role of the normal mother; Amy's dad, squinting behind his glasses, and her mom, wearing her librarian outfit; and Rennie's dad, way too handsome for his own good (to me he looks just like Harrison Ford), and his attaché Kelly, with long brown hair.

96

Oh shit.

'Rennie. Amy. Cherry,' says Coldwell in his Adolf Hitler voice. 'Please, have a seat.'

They've spread out chairs all across the room so we can't be near each other. Now I notice Ms Phelan, the school guidance counselor, and a fat, bearded and glasses-wearing guy who looks suspiciously like a shrink, I can just tell.

'I wish you'd tell us what this is about.' Rennie's voice trembles. 'We honestly have no idea why you're all here.'

'I was just about to do that, Rennie.' He's such a disgusting Fascist. I'd love to smack him across his pig mouth. 'But perhaps your parents should start. Rennie, let's start with yours.' That must annoy the shit out of Rennie because she can't stand her dad and Kelly being referred to as her 'parents'.

Kelly clears her throat. 'I'll leave it to you, Ryan.'

And Rennie's dad stands up (stands up!) and says, 'Wren.' Oh God, the hippie name, Rennie can't stand that either. 'Wren. We've been really worried about you. You stay out late without calling. You lie to us.'

'What?' She cocks her head to the side. 'I don't.'

'Last month, you said you were staying late at school because of play practice. But we spoke to Abby Green's mother, and at least half the days you said you were at play practice there was no play practice. Now you say it's French Club. But Madame DuBois says you haven't been to a French Club meeting in months. Where do you go after school, Wren?'

Rennie just sputters and spits, and it's a question I couldn't have answered a month ago, but for some reason last week at my house she spilled the whole story. I'm determined to protect her; no one can find out about her and Mr Schafer. 'She's been at my house, Mr Taylor. Her grades have been sliding a little lately and I think she's been embarrassed to tell you.'

Rennie gives me a thank-you glance, but Marian of course decides to save the day. 'Amy's been at our house in the afternoons, but I don't see Rennie until about six o'clock or

97

so. I just assumed she was at her afterschool activities. Rennie's so smart she's always involved in something. As a matter of fact I was thrilled when Cherry started hanging around with Rennie, thought some of her good qualities would rub off on my daughter. But unfortunately, they're a poisonous mix it seems. I found this.' She pulls out a poem, *my poem*, where the hell did she get my poem? The best one I've ever written – yes it is that one, 'Graveyard'.

She reads it aloud:

> Stack bricks,
> scrape mortar
> across the wall.
> Build my tomb,
> protect my body
> from wild animals.
> Inside, I spin
> my sarcophagus
> of poetry,
> my death-shroud.

She widens her eyes at Coldwell and the other parents and they're shaking their heads: disturbed chick, crazy girl, sick, suicidal.

Coldwell clears his throat. 'Obviously that speaks for itself. And now I think it's time to hear from the Linnets.'

I glance at Amy. I know they've called her bitch, whore, worse names, names you should never call your own child. I want to smash that drunken asshole's face in, but he's lucid now, his words deliberate. 'As you know, our family's dealt with a special struggle over the years.' He frowns with the pinched face he probably makes as he stands over someone drilling out their teeth. 'Amy's given us very little trouble. There were signs early on, though, as she drifted away from her old crowd. We were concerned when she dropped cheerleading, and in such a dramatic fashion.' That's a lie, too. Amy told me they barely cared that she sliced up her cheer uniform. She came home halfway through practice, and they were both already drunk. It was a Hemmler week.

Mrs Linnet steps in. 'Then, we noticed this.' She leans over to Amy and pulls up her sleeve. Cuts and scars jag over her forearm, past her elbow and onto her upper arm too. God, she's been cutting herself a lot more than even I knew about. I cover my face with my hand and take three deep breaths, then look up.

The shrinkydink squints behind his glasses. 'This kind of maladaptive behavior is quite serious. When the Linnets called me, I told them we needed to do an intervention, right away. When we spoke with the school, we realized all three of these girls are in trouble.'

God, if they only knew. I vow to keep my mouth glued shut, and I try to psychically transmit this idea to the others by giving the tiniest, slightly Cherry-wink behind my hand. It's good we're here together. If they'd been smart they would've seen us all separately, tried to wear down the weak ones, and get the goods on all of us.

Mr Coldwell continues. 'We're going to nip this in the bud, before you girls get mixed up in even more frightening situations. Your teachers have been very concerned, particularly about you, Rennie. Madame DuBois tells me you're frequently late to class.'

'I always have a pass.' God, shut up, Rennie! The next question will be why you're always getting a pass from Mr Schafer, idiot.

I try to save her. 'I know just how she feels. Sixth period lots of times I just want to go home. Oh, what the heck, I'll admit it, sometimes Rennie and I'll have a cigarette in the bathroom by the orchestra room before sixth. That's why we're late. I'm late too. You can check.'

Fortunately that seems to throw them off track because the shrinkydink writes something down, the Taylors gasp (oh dear God! Cigarettes! Imagine!) and Rennie shoots me an evil look; I'll explain later.

'There have also been rumors,' continues Coldwell. 'Rumors brought to my attention by several other students.'

99

'What rumors?' *Please, God, not Mr Schafer, not that.*

'Many, many students have told me that the three of you are members of a cult. A cult flirting with lesbianism and witchcraft, that almost certainly involves drugs.'

What? 'Who the hell said that?' It has to be Pammie McFadden. That bitch hates us. If it weren't serious shit, I'd burst out laughing.

'I'm afraid I'm not at liberty to say.'

'Well, it's not true,' says Rennie. 'We're just friends. Best friends. I haven't had friends like these in my life.'

Her dad and Kelly exchange a worried look.

Marian steps in. 'Cherry, I've been dreadfully concerned.' Oh, really? Which coke-induced delusion prompted that? 'I know all the parents have. That's why we're here today.'

You know what's sick, they're blaming our problems on our friendship when that's the only good thing in any of our lives. 'Listen,' I say. 'This isn't true. Sure, we don't fit the mold. So we listen to different music and dress differently than other kids. So Rennie dyed her hair and cut half of it off. So Amy chopped up her cheerleading uniform. That doesn't mean we're bad or evil. Just that we don't play the game.' And I'm not sure I've helped anything either, because the Linnets just nod at each other; I apparently have confirmed their worst fears.

'The big concern for us,' says Coldwell, 'is the part of the rumor that suggests the three of you have a suicide pact.'

'What?' This crap is incredible! 'Look, none of us would commit suicide.'

'I'm Catholic,' Amy pipes in meekly. 'Suicides go to Hell.' Good Lord, Amy, shut up! They think we're witches; they probably think we want to be in Hell.

Coldwell goes on like he didn't even hear her. 'So, it's time for an intervention. The three of you are bad news for each other, and all the parents have agreed it's time to end the relationship. It's become too intense. Young girls have high emotions, and this friendship has gotten to be too much for you.'

Break up the Bitch Posse? No fucking way! But I shut up . . . for now.

Rennie looks like she's going to cry. 'No, please!'

'Wren. Madame DuBois is the National Honor Society advisor. She's brought to my attention the slipping grades, the chronic tardiness. Now we learn of lying to your parents, smoking.' Coldwell unfolds a paper. 'These are the tenets of the National Honor Society: scholarship, leadership, citizenship and character. Here, let me read something to you. 'The student of good character upholds principles of morality and ethics, is cooperative, demonstrates high standards of honesty and reliability, shows courtesy, concern, and respect for others, and generally maintains a good and clean lifestyle.'' Unfortunately, Wren, Madame DuBois no longer believes you represent those principles. Nor do I, nor do your parents.' Oh, poor Rennie, there's that word again. 'Madame and I had a long, tough conversation about this. But, in the end, we and your parents decided that it would be better to draw a line now than to allow you to throw yourself into more trouble. You'll be attending one of the toughest universities in the country next year, and you can't afford to slip up. It's for that reason that we've decided to revoke your membership in the National Honor Society.'

Rennie turns pale.

'It's just a club, Rennie,' Amy says, thinking she's being helpful. 'You never went to meetings anyway.'

'That's just the kind of attitude, Amy Linnet, that your parents, and all these parents, are concerned about.'

And shit, we're in deep this time, can't get much deeper. It's time to quit fucking around. 'So you've made your point, taken away something that's important to Rennie.' God knows why she cares about some boring club where people sit around being smart, but far be it from me to judge. 'What do you want from us? Do you want us to sign something that says we won't kill ourselves? Send the three of us into therapy?'

Coldwell sighs, drums his fingers on the desk. 'Yes, that'll definitely be a part of this.'

Dr Linnet smirks. 'We've been advised that it would be best to send Amy away for a while, to a hospital program that can take care of her. This cutting, it's serious stuff.'

They're sending Amy away?

'No, Dad, please,' says Amy. 'Please. I'll do anything, please.' Tears are running down her face now, splashing over her nose, dripping from her chin. 'I won't do it anymore. I had no idea you'd freak out like that. I'm not suicidal, really, I'm not. Ask Cherry, Rennie, ask anyone!'

Mrs Linnet crosses her arms. 'Amy, you're so frantic these days, you didn't even let your father finish. We were *advised* to do this. But you're so close to graduation, and we don't want to jeopardize Michigan for you. So after discussing this with several people, we've decided that intense therapy sessions, twice a week, will help you. Dr Whalen has found a wonderful psychiatrist for you, a woman who specializes in treating girls your age. But—'

'But,' interjects Marian, 'we've all agreed it's best that the three of you not see each other until further notice.'

They're ganging up on us when all we want to do is be friends. It's not fair!

'And Cherry, that awful piece of suicidal garbage you wrote?'

My poem?

'That's going in the fireplace, tonight. Along with the rest of that book you keep your poems in. They're evil, brooding things. If you ask me it's the same thing as Amy slicing up her arm.'

The shrink gives me a sympathetic look, but Marian's going to do what she wants. I glance furtively from Rennie to Amy and back again at Marian. Her eyes are steel. My poems, I have to save my poems. If I beat her home, I can throw them out the window, scoop them out of the shrubbery later. Oh God. My writing, she's going to burn up my writing? I picture smoke curling around the edges of my paisley-covered poem book, my words twisting into ash, puffing away in the little wood stove Marian calls a fireplace, up into the spring air, and that's not even the worst of it.

The worst is that we're not to see each other anymore.

Ever?

Amy's thinking the same thing. 'I don't have any other friends, Mom and Dad. I don't hang out with Pammie and them anymore, you know that. I—'

'Well, you'll just have to mend things, now won't you?' says Mrs Linnet.

And I'd laugh if it wasn't so sad. Amy's burned bridges with the popular girls from now till kingdom come. They'll never be friends again. Rennie could hang out with the drama kids again, maybe. The Honor Society smartie types don't like her anymore; they're afraid of her. They probably blackballed her at one of the meetings Rennie doesn't go to.

Me? I can take care of myself.

Fuck all that. No one breaks up the Bitch Posse, that's all there is to it. But dealing with the adults these days is only possible through resignation and that's what I do. 'We know you're concerned about our futures. I guess it's the end of a friendship, but we understand, it's all for the best.' And I put my head in my hands like I'm crying, but really what I do is give my two Bitch Posse girls my best Cherry-wink. Hell YES we'll see each other. Lying we're good at; we'll find a way.

15
Amy

April 2003
Sault Sainte Marie, Michigan

Amy stares into the isolette, her gaze trailing along the loops of tubes and cords attaching her daughter to the machines that are keeping her alive. Lucky's been in the hospital for almost eight weeks now. Amy's pumped breast milk religiously, has spent endless hours in the NICU doing 'kangaroo care'. Those she considers the most precious moments of her life, pressing Lucky's warm little body to her bare chest, Amy's fingers spinning among the wires that hook her daughter up to the cardiac monitor. Very premature babies often still have the lanugo hair covering them, and Lucky's no exception, but lately a little swirl of black hair's been growing on her head and she's even gained a little weight. Amy ran her fingers through that swirl endlessly it seemed. There's never been a better feeling than her daughter's hair brushing against her fingertips.

Twelve days ago, though, Lucky's breathing became compromised and they put her back on the ventilator. No more kangaroo care, not until she's stable on room air again. When Amy heard that she felt her heart would break. No more pressing her daughter to her chest and feeling their hearts beating together, the wonder of Lucky's vertebrae pressing against her fingers, her tiny arms. 'Soon,' she says aloud now, staring at her sleeping daughter. 'Soon, Lucky.'

That question her mother asked so long ago Amy can now answer: *Yes, I do know what it feels like, Mom. I do.*

But mostly she pushes away thoughts of her parents, because she has to concentrate on Lucky and not let herself get upset.

Of course, her life's been spun out of control. Her mornings are spent at the hospital, her lunches in the hospital cafeteria, her afternoons with Catey and her kids just to get her mind off things. Then it's back to see Lucky before dinner, and the dinners are the worst because that's when she sees Scotty.

This shit makes Baghdad look appealing. Most of the time she escapes dinner by staring at the war, or the pieces of it that are safe for ordinary people like Amy to see. To her it's as meaningless as one of those pep rallies where she used to do cartwheels and show off her legs beneath her little cheerleading skirt. The whole thing seems to call for a Holland High cheer: *Pass it catch it score for six, do it Americans, that's it!* The playing cards emblazoned with Saddam Hussein's cohorts remind her of Alice in Wonderland. Someone somewhere is painting white roses red, and she wonders if it isn't really the president and all his advisers who are just a pack of cards. The Americans, the good guys, captured the Queen of Diamonds a few days ago. *Take the ball, down that court, shoot for two and raise the score!*

Last night, the president asked the nation to pray for the troops and the rebuilding ahead.

Sorry, that number is no longer in service.

Right in the middle of the war on TV, Amy glanced at Scotty and laughed.

He didn't laugh back.

She poured another drink and switched the station to *Friends.*

Yeah, this whole thing has tried their relationship, severely, and Scotty's never admitted where he was the night of Lucky's birth, even though Amy sees the truth in his eyes. He's done nothing but deny, and it makes her lose respect for him. If he'd just admit he had an affair and say he was sorry, that'd be it. But instead he debases himself and her by saying, 'the roads, Amy, it was the roads . . .'

The watch, her birthday present to him, still sits wrapped in the bedroom closet. She's sick of all her things; none of them seem to matter now that Lucky's in such trouble. She should rent a barge, load it up, and drop all her stuff into Lake Superior. Drown all that crap, the 4Runner, the Ethan Allen bedroom suite, the Martha Stewart copper cookware, in that most amazing lake whose waves chop and roll with more power than even God can explain. Dump it, along with all that garbage that's loading down drawers in her kitchen. Her Parmesan grater, her julienne slicer. Her slotted fish turner and her butter curler. Her cocoa shaker, biscuit server, and spoon-type tea infuser. Top of the line from WMF Germany, 150 years of old-world craftsmanship; why should she settle for less?

What the hell, it's just a bunch of metal and plastic. It's not real.

Not like a baby, for example.

Nothing's real anymore.

Yeah, she'll drown all that useful useless shit.

Sink it.

Kill it.

When the white-crested waves crash over her clot of possessions, her heart attack waiting to happen, Amy will tremble at the terrible beauty of Lake Superior, 30 million times more amazing than anything a catalog copywriter could ever describe.

She'll keep the crib, though.

She needs that.

That fucking watch for her oh-so-fucking husband? She'll bury that in a watery grave too. That she can do without a barge; she'll just wing it into the water tomorrow.

Catey scraped the clock cake into the garbage while Amy was in the hospital recovering. Cleaned the whole kitchen. Dear God, blood must've been dripped over everything.

Blood. Dripped over everything.

Amy's stomach twists. The knife of her past scratches away chips of mortar, and they fall to the earth like flaming meteors.

Build it back up, one brick at a time. She sucks in fresh, sterile air. Don't drown in the past, the present's bad enough.

Who cares how much it's costing to keep Lucky alive? It's

just money, numbers, abstract things. You can't order a baby from a catalog. There's no free shipping or money-back guarantee. No exchanges or in-store merchandise credit if it didn't turn out just how you'd planned.

Nothing matters more than Lucky.

Amy bends down so the isolette is at eye level, sinks to her knees. She's so often like this here at the NICU. The nurses have all been incredible but the news hasn't been good. Two days after they put her back on the ventilator, Lucky needed an emergency heart operation, and they sawed her open. Amy gazes through the clear plastic, eyes burning as she follows the line of stitches zipping up her daughter's chest, such great big scars on such a little baby, just now barely three pounds. Lucky, the name Amy whispered out soon after her birth, the name that sealed her daughter's fate she hoped. Anyway, it's crossed her mind a few times since then that it's a crazy name, that middle school girls will pick on her daughter, and then the thought pops up that perhaps it won't matter, perhaps Lucky won't . . .

And that's the thought she has to squash down like a ball of paper into a wastebasket. If she thinks that way it'll affect Lucky somehow.

Scotty's at work, trying to be normal, he says, but he seems to sink himself in deeper and deeper these days. In her heart she has to believe the doctors, what they said, that Lucky has a chance if she makes it through the surgery. So now they're waiting, hoping there'll be no more bad news. They also brought up that there'd been (just as with Callie) so little oxygen at Lucky's birth that the chances of severe mental retardation were very high. Funny she feels, not close to her parents exactly, but a touch of empathy for them, even though she hasn't spoken to either of them in years. Dad's in Arizona, Mom's in Montana – they split up soon after graduation and Callie's death. Why they ever felt they had to keep up a charade of a marriage for Amy she'll never know. She sent them each a card to let them know she was pregnant, a cute little card with a horsie on it with a pink ribbon (Scotty hadn't caught that hint, or ignored it on purpose). She supposes eventually they'll write her and ask about the baby, but they don't know Lucky was born already, that she's here in the hospital. What's the point in telling them, really? Knowing Dad, he'll say something helpful like, *Weren't drinking during pregnancy, were you?* And Mom, well, she used to try to talk to Mom on the phone, during those first years in Ann Arbor. Amy would have to repeat major news on several separate occasions, had to tell her three times she was engaged before the information rested into Mom's memory. When she and Scotty moved to the Soo, Amy deliberately requested an unlisted number, so now all they have for her is an address, not the house number of Amy's refuge at the ends of the earth, but a simple PO Box she got just for this purpose.

She blinks out some tears knowing that she and Scotty may well just be spinning this situation out as far as possible without allowing it to reach its natural conclusion. Twenty years ago, ten even, they wouldn't have been able to save Lucky at all. And really, it's all they can do now to keep her breathing. Her daughter's little chest rises and falls, the tiniest preemie diaper wrapped around her. Her eyes are closed and puffy, and the scars down her chest are purplish and raised like rows of tilled earth. Lucky, little Lucky's breathing away, and she's a fighter, or is she? Lucky's been so listless in the last few days.

When Scotty gets home, they'll eat Chinese take-out from The Great Wall for the one millionth time since Lucky's birth because Amy hasn't pulled a pan from the cupboard since that horrible night in the kitchen. Amy'll open up the vodka and pour it with orange juice and stare at the war on television, not talking, just drinking and staring and drinking and staring, until the feelings are numbed and blotted out. That's what she'll do, that's just what she'll do, and not think about Lucky until tomorrow, not face the decision she knows is probably coming, not watch Scotty's face with the furrow that's suddenly appeared in his forehead, the slip of hair that clings to his neck that she used to lace her fingers through as she pulled him toward her. She can't look at him that way anymore, can't even bear to make small talk anymore.

Judy, the nurse with the cute little pigtail, touches her on the side of her arm. 'Please go home, sweetie,' she whispers. 'Get a decent night's rest for once.'

Amy tries to smile, makes a grateful mutter, and packs up to go. She glances over her shoulder to see Lucky one last time, the little creature attached to the ventilator, the IV drip, the cardiac monitor, still breathing inside her clear plastic box.

On the drive home, everything's still all frozen over. The hell with stopping for Chinese as usual; it takes too fucking long and she's not hungry anyway. She just wants to drink. There's some tortilla chips and salsa and that's all she wants. Scotty can fucking fend for himself – God knows she had to back in March. Why walk through blistering wind when she doesn't have to? Why go and order his fucking Emperor Chicken and Kung Pao Shrimp? It's not for her. She never eats much but the rice, so what's the point?

Up here it's a winter wasteland, and glancing down she notices the salt's stained her black coat. As she pulls up to the house there's another car backing out. It jerks out of the driveway and roars down the street and disappears.

'Oh!' That's what she gets for coming home a little early, is it?

She tears down the plowed path in her boots and she's for sure going to give him hell, because it's *her* car, she knows it. She'll make the biggest scene, make him pay for lying. She might even smash a few things and then get good and drunk and stony cold silent and maybe she'll hurt him, too.

16
Rennie

April, 1988
Hampton, Illinois

This is the suckiest birthday ever. It's my last fucking birthday in this shitty town, and I should be with my friends, getting drunk and stoned and laughing my head off at nothing. Instead me and Rob are lounging in bed at the Paradise Inn in Hampton, about twenty miles outside of Holland. I'm sulking and Rob's put on the TV. I pour myself the last little bit of Merlot that glimmers in the bottle he's brought. After all that shit went down in Mr Coldwell's office, I've been pretty depressed, even though Rob says that the National Honor Society doesn't matter, that I'm 'the best fucking writer and the most incredible fucking actress I've ever seen,' that high school doesn't matter either, that in just a few months I'm going to Stanford, one of the two or three best schools in the country. Which brings up the very awkward question of where our relationship is going, and you bet I'm gonna ask it.

I slide the last swallow of wine into my mouth. The acid clings to the inside of my cheeks, tasting of currants. Red wine's supposed to be blood, right, Communion? Well, this bottle of blood I'm sucking down should be labeled 'DRINK ME', because like Alice, I get smaller and smaller with each sip. Soon I'll be able to slip through the keyhole. Soon I'll be so tiny I won't be here at all anymore.

God, Rob Schafer really is driving me insane.

I pull the remote from his hand and mute out *Cheers*.

'Hey, I was watching that.'

I toss the remote to the end of the room, where it slams

into the mirror that hangs over the cheap coffeemaker. 'We need to talk.'

He misunderstands and tangles his fingers in my hair, covers my lips with his, reaches for my thigh.

I smack his hand away and break the kiss. 'Not that. Listen, we've been together almost two months. So where are we going? I mean I graduate in June, then the summer and then I'm in California.'

'You know I love you, Rennie.' And it's not the first time he's said this, but it still sends a chill down my back. I won't say it back to him, and that really, really bugs him for some reason.

I stroke my fingers over his chest, bring my lips to his. Squashing them with mine feels so good, and I pull in his sweet breath, *oh, please just make me real . . .*

When I feel him sliding his fingers up and down my back I pull away. He wants to make love again, but I'm going to pin him down. 'So, is this something you do every year? The senior fling?'

'Rennie, you know it's not. You know we're special.' He traces a finger along my lips. 'You're like no one else. You're magic, my fairy queen, I love you.'

I pull a cigarette from the rumpled pack on the nightstand. It drives him crazy that I smoke, even though he does himself. I light it and inhale, blow out smoke briskly, and don't offer him one. 'Just give it to me straight, Rob. Is there a chance you'll leave Dawn, come out West with me?'

He pulls his finger along my chin, bending toward me for a kiss, but I lift the cigarette to my lips and turn my head to the side. 'You're so young, Rennie. The world's waiting to unfold in front of you. I don't want to take that away from you. You deserve California. That's all yours.'

He's really pissing me off. My fingers shake as I bring my cigarette to my mouth, and looking down at the scar on my arm that's fading now, I'm reminded of how low I can get when I think about me and Rob. 'So, I guess that's a no. You're not coming with me.'

He sighs like I'm really stressing him out, slides a cigarette from the pack and lights it. 'Listen, Rennie. Do we have to decide all this now? It's months away.'

And I feel a sudden urge to hurt someone, to take the glowing end of the cigarette and press it into my skin or his, until it burns, blackens, hurts hurts hurts, like his words do. Even though I won't say it aloud I'm pretty sure I've fallen in love with him, and I do want him to come out West with me. I want to move in with him, and I'll go to Stanford and he can get a job teaching in California. Smoking harder, quicker, I tell him I've phoned the California Office on Teacher Credentialing and found out they have a reciprocity agreement with Illinois, that I read an article saying they really need teachers in San Jose, that there's a population explosion about an hour north and an hour south of San Francisco and, and, *and* . . .

'Rennie.' He puts a finger on my lips. 'Can't we enjoy what we have, live in the moment? Just relax . . .' He stares at the empty Merlot bottle. 'I've got another of these out in the car. I have something else for you too. Be right back.' He pulls on his jeans, no underwear, tucks his sweater over his head and is gone.

Here I am, alone in a hotel room with the smell of sex clinging to the Lysol-y spray. Alone alone alone. The room's getting smaller, the walls are closing in, and I lie on my back on the bed and smoke, the ceiling pressing down toward me, the little snowy patterns of paint ready to fold up inside themselves and send down flakes, freezing me, Rennie Taylor, ice princess, me, Rennie Taylor, Snow White in her coffin.

Today's Shakespeare's birthday too. *The course of true love never did run smooth* . . .

My hair's wet near my ears, and I realize I'm crying and turn my head to the side. I'm not even altogether sure why I'm crying, but sobs bubble up from a well deep inside me, and my guts spin. I feel so emotional, it's like my period is starting. But of course it's not, and the sobs tremble through me, my stomach, my uterus, everywhere inside me, and he'll be back any minute; damned if I'll let him see me cry.

I run my fingers over the red beaded necklace Amy made for me and take three deep breaths. *Give me strength, Bitch Posse.* As I sit up, the ceiling rises again, and I dry my eyes and cheeks with the back of my hand and pull in smoke real hard, scorching my lungs.

In a moment he slips in with some more Merlot and a box wrapped in silver paper embossed with white roses. Do I tell him? Do I tell him? I haven't told anybody, not even the Bitch Posse.

He doesn't even notice I've been crying and splashes some more wine into the little jewel-cut hotel glass, or really, if you want to call a spade a spade, the Paradise Inn's a motel. I'm not having a high class affair with a married man in a hotel, I'm just a slutty whore fucking someone in a seedy motel.

You have to hurt if you want to feel anything at all.

He hands me the box. 'Happy birthday.'

I tear off the paper and toss it in the floor. Nestling in the box is a thick silver bracelet, with flowers carved all over it.

'For my little pixie,' he says.

It's not really my style, but it's from him and it's pretty, so I say, 'I love it,' and put it on. The bracelet weighs down my wrist, making my arm look like a stick. Everyone says petite girls shouldn't wear big jewelry. In the end it's just another thing, a hunk of metal. It doesn't mean anything. It's not a promise.

I gulp some more wine, which actually clears my head, or at last makes it easier for me to talk. 'So, are you leaving Dawn, or not?' It's the first time I've come out and said that and thrown all my cards on the table, and I work real hard to keep the sobs boxed up inside me because I don't want him to think I really care. 'Because there's a guy at the college who really wants to hook up with me, and if you're not interested I think I'll give him a call.' And there, I've put him in the only corner I know how to, aside from the last trump card that I haven't played yet.

He stubs out his cigarette and rubs my cheeks with his thumbs, pulls me close. 'I told you. I love you, damn it, Rennie. I love you.'

'Those are just words.'

'You're a writer. You know the power of words.' He kisses me hard, squeezing me too tightly, nipping my neck for that good little hurt and pressing my back with his palms. I can't help it, I breathe out an 'oh' and the wind whistles outside, but I push him away.

'Am I just your little high-school fuck, or is this serious?' I turn away, grumpy.

'You know it's serious.' He licks his finger and runs it down my neck and back. 'Know what? If you want, we'll get married someday. After you've had your education, and time to grow.' He laces his fingers together over my chest and I lean back into him, as he brushes his lips across the top of my head, then lifts my hair to kiss the nape of my neck. The tingles send a real thought into my brain. Should I tell him? I don't even know what I'm planning to do about it yet. Should I invite him into the discussion?

The wine has all gone to my head and I'm a little giddy. I must have had at least four glasses, and anyway, he as much as said he's going to marry me, didn't he? Somehow my legs are opening again, and I'm falling back into the pillows, reaching for his ass, guiding him. I lock my feet around him let him pull me up, up, up in the hot air balloon, so I'm dizzy; and he shows me the view of the countryside, quilted with pastures and I'm dizzier; and he laughs and we jump out together and float, float, float like ashes of burned paper, down to the wet earth and I think, I think I'll tell him; and he moves against me one last time and gasps, and as he holds me for a moment against him, stroking my hair, I press my face against his earlobe and whisper my newest secret in his ear, the one that'll change everything, that'll get him off the dime about Dawn.

I tell him what I've been pretty sure of for a few weeks, what I confirmed this morning in the bathroom: that I'm pregnant.

17
Cherry

April, 2003
Freemont Psychiatric Hospital

Well, it's one of those days where Cherry doesn't want to get up in the morning. Lately things with Michael have gotten weird. Yesterday they got in another shouting match, but then he leaned over, right there in the lounge, and kissed her, and that was the last thing she'd expected. Half of her felt like breaking away and slugging him, and half of her wanted to lock her fingers around his neck, yank him toward her, and open her lips until everything heated to scorching. *Sam Sam Sam.* Josie, her roommate, pushed herself between them; but lately Josie's been acting strange too, asking Cherry if she remembers things like their kindergarten field trip to the pumpkin patch (which of course never happened). God, Josie can't help Cherry. The girl can't even help herself.

Last night Cherry dreamed about Michael beating her, lashing welts across her back, and what's weirder is that she woke up feeling like she'd had an orgasm. She got up and went to the bathroom and stared at that dumb red Emergency button next to the toilet. As if all emergencies occurred in bathrooms. So stupid! Like this whole stupid place.

She was still hot from her dream so she played around in the bathroom for a while, staring at that crazy red button, until she came and felt sleepy again and shuffled back to bed. Emergency. They wouldn't know one if it slapped them in the face. She pulled her half-finished tapestry from under her bed, curled up under her covers, and fell asleep clutching her mountains in front of mountains in front of mountains.

No, she hasn't dreamt like that for a long time, not since

she and Sam Sterling pushed things to the edge, way too long ago to even remember. The dream is surely the sign of some deep disturbance, something else to hide from Dr Anders.

Cherry rolls over, rubs her fingers over her eyes, and stashes the tapestry under her bed. 'Josie?' Josie's snoring softly in the bed next to hers – Josie, a little girl really, Josie who won't eat, hardly sleeps. 'Jos?'

Josie mumbles something and pulls the covers over her head.

Cherry decides to let her catch as many winks as she can, but in a few moments the morning nurse rouses them from their room with her usual robotic wake-up call. After they get dressed, run brushes through their hair, and have a quick smoke (with all that Michael stress Cherry's taken up the habit again), they walk together downstairs for the women's discussion group. It's a pale April day with fog high in the air and, Cherry supposes the daffodils may well be blooming outside, but she wouldn't know. She hasn't had a bench pass in several weeks, and anyway, it's been cold.

Josie and Cherry walk to the meeting room, and they all sit in a circle. Cherry's often thought that college would've been something like this, students in a circle of desks, discussing Shakespeare or Keats. Through the window it isn't such a pleasant spring day after all; the wind whips through the branches on the trees of the courtyard as Cherry slips into a desk near Josie.

The social worker, Leigh McLeod, pushes her brown hair back with a pencil. Leigh's like a needle; Cherry can't stand her. 'Patient Check In first. Relationships. Susan, you start.' This is as warm as Leigh gets. Her skin's vanilla ice-cream, frozen, pale, and Cherry snaps open her Zippy and lights a cigarette even though this isn't one of the smoking areas.

Susan gives her a glance and begins. 'As you all know, last weekend I had the opportunity to return to my home for a few days, to see my husband, my kids.' She takes a deep breath and explains that something very unusual happened there; she watched his face (Raymond's) and it was as though she could see into the future and all that was there was blackness, 'the memories of my months here hanging above him,' a book, Susan explains, that's forgotten how to be written. 'And so,' she says, with a deep breath, 'I've decided to ask him for a divorce.'

Cherry doesn't like Susan, who herself is an instigator, sliding subtle disapproval into conversations, stirring the pot. But she feels bad for her – this is obviously a wrenching decision – and she reaches for Susan's fingers that are tap-tapping in front of her on the desk.

'Cherry, would you please ex-tin-guish,' Leigh draws out the word like taffy, 'your cigarette.'

And there's not even an acknowledgment of Susan's divorce, just the needle, poking into flesh and pulling out again, again, again. Cherry breaks the rule about evaluating what others say and makes the effort to move words across her lips. 'I'm sorry, Susan.'

Leigh ratchets her nails across the desk. 'We need to bring the conversation back into the room. Susan, bring it back to Freemont. How are you feeling about others in this room, here, now?'

What she means by this is that the patients need to discuss their relationships with each other, because that's what this meeting is about, not Susan's divorce or Cherry's memories of Sam or any of that. So stupid. What's the point?

Susan's already talking. 'I'm feeling very upset that Cherry's still got her cigarette lit. I'm allergic, and she knows it's against the rules. There's a smoking lounge. Or she can smoke outside.'

Leigh's face settles into a thin smile, and Cherry stubs out the cigarette. She's going to lie her way out of here. These bureaucrats, these idiots, these needlers like Leigh, they can all just stuff it because Cherry's not going to take the bait. 'I'm sorry, Susan,' she says again and this time it's an acceptable response. Leigh smiles at what she must think is Cherry's shame.

It's Cherry's turn, and all she can think of is Michael. 'I'm feeling very confused by Michael because he continually screams at me and cusses me and yesterday he kissed me. I don't feel it's appropriate and it made me feel threatened.' She's spewed out a mouthful, thrown up what's been bothering her all day, and Josie tosses her a glance. After the Hattie Gibson-Smythe and *Echo* incident, Josie slid Cherry's 'Disoriented' out of the trash, smoothed it, left it on Cherry's pillow. She's a good friend, reminds her a little of Amy and Rennie, only she doesn't think of them anymore. Sure, Josie's a bit of a brownnoser with the staff, but that's Cherry's game too these days.

Of course, Cherry's comment is against the rules too. They're not to talk about someone who isn't here, and Leigh reminds her of this, click-clacking those nails again. 'Let's take it back to the room.' Cherry just stares at the long whitish nail tips. She hasn't felt like cutting for a while, but Leigh sure makes it tempting.

She can't think of anyone in the room she'd like to talk or complain about other than Leigh herself, and that wouldn't go over real well, so she says, 'I'm so happy Josie's my roommate. We're really getting along.'

That's just what Leigh doesn't want to hear. She tugs at a strand of brown hair that's escaped the bun at the nape of her neck and turns to Josie. 'How does that make you feel, Josie? The same?'

But Josie kind of scuffs her feet under her desk and says, 'I'm trying to keep thoughts out of my head these days. All I can think about is hurting myself.'

At this Cherry's blood freezes, chunks of ice floating down the river of her veins. Last night Josie said, 'I can't imagine being outside, on my own. Not without you.' Cherry thought it was a pass of some kind; she's used to that. It must be the red bob or her name or something, but women tend to be attracted to her – it's certainly not the first time. All Cherry said last night was, 'Don't worry about that now, Josie. Just think about getting through tomorrow, going to Group, seeing Dr Bowker, going to painting class, checking a book out of the library. You're safe here. That's why you're here.'

Soon after that Josie fell asleep, finally, the trembling girl who never sleeps, her hand extended across the space between their beds, their fingers laced together. Cherry feels good when she's taking care of someone, when she can help.

In an interview a little while before she died, her Diana said something that really stuck in Cherry's head. That the worst problem in the world was *the disease of people feeling unloved*. Like Diana, she'll do whatever she can to change that. Like she helped Amy Linnet and especially Rennie Taylor, so long ago. But thinking of Rennie, 'Wren' Taylor, shoots a realization into her. The Bitch Posse swore their allegiance for *as long as the stars are fixed in the heavens*. But Cherry doesn't get to see stars anymore, so that means it's all over and Rennie Taylor and Amy Linnet are just a dream. And of course Diana's a dream too, let Cherry down by dying. It was a lie: no one ever finds their way out of a fairy tale gone wrong, not even the strongest and most beautiful princess of all, Queen of Hearts, Queen of Blood.

The only one who matters is Josie, her friend, who's here and now.

This morning as they were brushing their hair, she told Josie, 'You think you're fucked up. Just look at me. You can get out of here anytime your mom decides to sign you out. I have to convince the shrinks here, then the shrinks from the county board, and finally a judge, that I'm okay. I've been through this whole routine before. What I did was unspeakable.' She was trying to make Josie feel better, feel normal or something. Josie just looked at her, deer eyes wide open, scared, and Cherry shouldn't have told her because it changed things. 'I wasn't the only one,' she said, to temper it somehow, but it only made the confession worse, more disturbing. Josie turned away, finished her cigarette in silence, terrified again, scared of her own shadow, scared of her impulses and she must think she can't trust Cherry anymore, that Cherry's dangerous. It was the wrong thing to tell her. She couldn't handle it.

Josie takes a breath and stares at the surface of her desk. 'It's not that I want to hurt myself. It's just that I can't stop thinking about it. I can't imagine what my life would be like outside of here, and I can't imagine living it. I don't want to deal with my mom. I'm getting better in here but she's still a flaming, untreated bipolar victim, and I can't live with her, ever again. Yesterday I stood near the window in our room trying to figure out how the locks worked, so I could jump.'

Cherry's heart pounds. Josie sounds so serious, but she's spilling stuff and that's usually good. Right now is when Leigh should get her into Dr Bowker's office, and maybe she can contract with him not to hurt herself. Maybe they can adjust her meds, even give her some Thorazine if that'd help, although Cherry hates Thorazine. They gave her some when she was here the first time but it made her sleepy and fat. Still, Thorazine can send you on an even keel for a while, just to get you through. And if Josie's really planning to kill herself, or even if she just wants attention, obviously she's asking for help. But instead Leigh says, 'Bring it back to the room, please. How much of this has to do with your relationship with Cherry?'

And that's just so cold, so fucking heartless, and in all likelihood completely unprofessional and against hospital guidelines. Shouldn't someone who talks about committing suicide be immediately sent to her doctor or at least a therapist or fellow or the psychopharmacologist? Josie's lip trembles, and Cherry stands up and puts her arms around her friend, this girl who could be her little sister, who's dealt with so much, a mom who gave her her first needleful of heroin, her own addictions, her mom's mental illness. It's all so familiar to Cherry, and the worst is that Josie bristles, shrinks away from her touch.

Cherry backs off and tightens her fingers into a fist. So she won't be permitted to help Josie after all. And now she knows she has to cut, to go back to her room and find the watch crystal inside her pillowcase, pull slices across her arm, the welts that make her sane, that keep her on an even tow, keep her from sinking into the depths. Maladaptive or not, it works, and she's lost Josie, her only friend in here. If Josie'd let her in she could help, but she's shut Cherry out completely.

Cherry unballs her fist, stares at Leigh. *Everyone needs to be valued. Everyone has the potential to give something back.* That's her princess talking. Maybe, just maybe, late tonight in their room, she can get Josie to open up, like the petals of a flower.

18
Amy

April 1988
Holland High School

I stand on the sidewalk outside the high school watching jocks and band kids and math brains get into their cars and drive away into their lives. Me, I'm the crazy girl, the cheerleader who lost her mind. Everyone's staring at Amy Linnet, the lesbian suicidal drug-addicted witch. May as well smoke dope right outside the school, make a porno movie with Rennie and Cherry, throw some spells in Pammie's direction, run my car into a tree. Everyone seems to expect it of me.

I just can't believe it: me, Amy Linnet, in therapy like some sort of mental loser who can't take it. The worst of it is I can't even skip; I have to drive myself to Mary Sue Gallagher's office every Tuesday and Thursday after school, and she wants to hear about my friends, why I cut, what my relationship with Mom and Dad is, and she's especially curious about Callie, nosy bitch. I tell a bunch of lies usually. Yesterday I told a whole big long story about me and Pammie in New Orleans over Mardi Gras last year, taking off our tops for beads and how traumatized I was. She was very interested, kept saying, oh, go on, go *on*! Probably, she went home and masturbated thinking about it. Of course the whole thing never happened; me and Pammie never went to New Orleans at all. Mary Sue is kind of stupid. She asked me how I got the latest set of cuts on my arm and I told her a cat scratched me and she believed me!

So today's the day after my jolly happy therapy session and we're on our pilgrimage to Hemmler. Oh, she gave me drugs too, a bunch of them. One is called Xanax, and it's a little white pill that's a miracle. One of them and all the panicky squashy feelings go away, but even better is two – you feel like nothing matters in the whole fucking world. That's why I took a couple right before sixth period today, so they'd kick in for the car ride and the trip to Hemmler, the endless horrible awful prison of the station wagon. The bottle says one as needed, so I figured I needed one, then I needed another one right after.

I'm feeling a little silly-giddy as the dentist-mobile pulls up, the green Volvo station wagon that's supposed to make us look like a nice normal family. Cherry disappears onto the school bus. She's been grounded from the truck and her mom remembers to enforce the rule about half the time. It's humiliating for a senior to ride the bus, but what's she gonna do? After the Coldwell meeting I slipped her a note in French class, and of course no one can break up the Bitch Posse. We already snuck out for coffee together once and this weekend we're gonna raise our usual hell, count on it.

The plan is that Rennie gets Abby Green to say she's inviting her over, I kiss ass with Pammie so she'll lie for me, or maybe I'll have to blackmail her about sex or drinking or oh, I'll think of something or else make something up. Cherry'll just say she's at Sam's. There's something going on with her and Sam, by the way, because the last couple times I've mentioned him she's given me this look. Whatever. We're going to meet up at the college like usual even if we all have to take fucking taxis.

I clatter open the door of the Good Ship Volvo-Pop and slide into the seat behind Mom, who's staring stonily at the dashboard. Apparently she got strong-armed into coming after last night's fight. I've been hung over before, and I have no clue how they can drink like they do every night and not spend every fucking day in bed. Yet here they are, stone cold sober. They stay sober for Callie; why can't they for me? But I push the thought away, tossing my backpack in the back and putting on my seatbelt.

'How was school, sweetie?' asks Mom like she's suddenly the nicest most normal parent in the universe.

'Great. Me and Pammie made up. It's all fine now.' Just a preview of the lies to come later tonight, when I say I'm going out with her.

'Oh, that's so wonderful!' breathes Mom. 'I like Pammie, I really do.'

The two Xanax have made me a little sleepy, and I rub my eyes. 'Long day at school; think I'll snooze on the drive up if it's all right.'

They give each other a relieved look like oh, marvels of modern medicine have made our little girl all right again. Fuck them. I can't help a yawn, and I lean against the car window and think about Rennie, because I really am worried about her. How the hell did she get wrapped up with Mr Schafer? And how the hell's she going to get out of it? Because she has to. It's so risky. He could go to jail for sleeping with her – yeah, she's eighteen now, but she wasn't when he started fucking her. And what the hell *he* is thinking I'll never know. What does a married thirty-five-year-old want with a high-school girl? Well, of course the answer is sex, but it must be more than that.

I'll admit the naughtiness of it all is kind of exciting. Hell, he is the sexiest teacher in school. I'll bet more than one girl goes to sleep thinking about him at night. Even I have a few times. Freshman year I had his class right before PE so thankfully I could run off some of the energy he pulled up in me. One night I got out of bed after playing with my fantasy Mr Schafer, and pressed my wet fingers to the essay I was turning in the next day. I don't know if he noticed, but I got an A.

Remembering that makes me tingle and so a tiny part of me is jealous of Rennie, but that's squashed by the part that's worried. It's a fantasy I'd never want to come to life, really, it's kind of spooky. If it was Coldwell or someone I'd be throwing up thinking about it. Even picturing Rennie in bed with the sexy teacher kind of spins my stomach. What's in his head? If you want to get legalistic about it, he's been raping her all this time. Not violently of course. I mean, I can't stop Rennie from messing around with him; she's one determined girl. But he's married – he should know better! I want to shake Rennie: what are you thinking? It can never go anywhere! But it was all Rennie could do to spill out the story at Cherry's house. I could tell by her pained face that the worst we could do would be to judge our Rennie, who'd confided in us. It seemed like she wanted to say more, but she stopped and I just rubbed her back. Then Cherry rolled us a big beautiful joint and we sat on her bed and got high and silly and nothing mattered.

It's supposedly springtime but it can't be more than forty degrees outside the car, and the sky is one big fog, one great big white Xanax pill. I twirl up into the atmosphere, make love to a cloud, dizzy spin around the dance floor. The Xanax blankets me into itself, wraps me up warmtightcozysnug and at once I'm asleep.

'We're here, Amy.' Mom's voice wakes me up. I check my watch and an hour's passed. Hemmler looms before us like a fancy bed and breakfast, two Greek-type columns, carved wooden door, brick entryway spilling with flowers. They have all kinds of ways to try to trick you into believing it's not a prison, but it is. Nausea tickles my stomach, which makes me feel like popping another Xanax, but that probably wouldn't be a good idea, would it, having just had two a couple of hours ago?

One as needed. Ah hell.

I rattle the pill bottle out of my backpack and swallow another one dry. Mom sees me and smiles. 'A little nervous?' She knows they're for panic attacks, but she doesn't know how many I've already taken. The sour Xanax residue dissolves in my mouth and the taste wakes me up. This is twice as good as cutting, bitter bitter Xanax on my tongue, my miracle in white.

'I'm okay. I want to walk with her today; is it all right?' I don't think I can bear to be inside Callie's room. It's freezing out but I think Callie'd like it. I can push her along the little path, brush her hair, talk to her.

'It's too cold.'

'I don't want to sit in The Box.' *The Box* is what I call Callie's room, precise corners, studied whiteness, like living in an ice cube, other than the little square of green and blue that is her window.

'Amy, I said it's too cold.'

'Your mother's right.'

'I hate it there.' Even the postcards and family photo Dad put up just emphasize the fact that they've penned her up like an animal. 'She does too, she just can't tell you.'

'I've had enough of your negativity.' Mom slides the door open. 'You don't have to see her at all; we can just drive you home.'

Fuck her. 'Dad? Listen, she hasn't seen me for two weeks and I miss her. It's not that cold; I'll put some throws on her lap. Don't you think it's all right?'

He looks from me to Mom. 'Barb, I think it'll be—'

Yes! 'Great, I'm taking her for a walk to see the ducks.' I quicken my pace to Callie's room. She'll be so happy when I tell her we're going outside.

I could swear behind me I hear the word *bitch* but when I turn around she's smiling. 'What a wonderful idea, Amy.' To Dad she said, 'Rich, we need to talk.'

After Mom and Dad do their hug-and-kiss ritual that smacks of phoniness, they disappear to talk to Callie's doctor. I tell Callie where we're going and pull some blankets over her. She smiles in that little slack-jawed way she has, the smile that can't quite hold itself on her face. Her eyes are so blue, her skin so smooth, her hair so curly. I take the soft brush and stroke it down the length of her hair, little strands coming off in my fingers. I wind them into a ball and put the ball in my pocket like I always do. Most people would think I'm loony, but I save her hair in a Ziploc I have in my drawer. If I can't have a sister at least I can look at the strands of hair, and imagine.

I push her all the way down to the lagoon at the end of the

property and talk about nothing. What could I possibly tell her that she would understand? Your little sister's fucked up, in therapy? Instead I point out the leaves popping out on the trees, the little patches of grass, and I'm so sad she can't walk anymore. For a while they were trying her in physical therapy, but it was hurting her legs so much she would cry, so they just decided to put her back in the chair. I pull the blanket up around her, and we stare at the ducks skimming over the lagoon. I'm certain there's a Hemmler duck family, the Hemmies I call them. Year after year they come back, and the babies grow up and have babies and then those babies come back. I wish I'd brought some bread because Callie likes to watch them dive for it. I wish she was at home with us. We could walk around the college instead of this little lagoon. She could live in a house and not a box with fluorescent bulbs burning onto her like she's a baby chick in an incubator.

I hate Mom and Dad.

I used to think I hated Callie for making all the problems, but it's not her fault. Sometimes I wish I was older and on my own, and I could just kidnap Callie, take her away from here.

My fingers slide over the blue beads of my necklace. I lean down, cross my arms around her neck and whisper, 'I love you, Callie. You're the most beautiful sister in the world.'

Inside my chest burns a rage I've never felt this intensely. I'm glad she can't see my eyes, not because I'm crying, but because they're hardened with anger, squinted, narrowed. I want to hurt someone. Anxiety pangs in my stomach, and I pull the bottle from my pocket and shake out two Xanax, and chew them down. When I stand up, I look across the lagoon, as the ducks drift away.

19
Rennie

On the kitchen table, Rennie leans against the wall and digs her heels into Bay's back, smiling. This has been the sixth or seventh in a streak of breathtaking Marin days, days when Mount Tamalpais rises over the high school like a lush, verdant goddess, days when Rennie feels the sleeping woman might really be her, rested relaxed and perfect, sure of who she is and what she is and at peace. As their rhythm speeds up, Bay kisses her on the neck. She relaxes into him, comes with a shiver and sigh, and blinks her eyes open; it's time to get ready for school.

She's breathed not a word of that night at Puck's book party, not because she doesn't feel guilty or it doesn't haunt her but because it hardly seems to matter. She'll never see him again, or if she does it'll be the same literary circles and he'll be easy to avoid. She don't want to see him again because he'll remind her of Wren Taylor, who should be writing instead of playing around with a student teacher, a fling that's probably already burned itself out. These relationships seem to have their built-in endings; they always graduate, move on, get jobs in Berkeley or Albany or change their minds like Seamus and head for art school.

Now that it's early May, her relationship with Bay is puttering to an end too. He's got applications in near Sacramento and Chico, won't stay here, smarter than she is, knows a teacher'll never buy a house in Marin. She reaches out and pulls a tangle of his hair toward her, laughing when it springs back to his face. It's been fun while it's lasted, and they've never said they loved each other; she thinks he knows the relationship is what it is and all it's ever going to be. He laughs too.

She missed a call while they were messing around on the kitchen table, but her hair's a disaster and she needs to brush it out in all of ten minutes. 'Pick up the message, would you, hon? It might be Mallory.' Her half-sister called last week and said she and her boyfriend Max and their little boy Caleb were going to be in town on their way to South America and could they stay with Rennie for a few days? Which of course is okay, but that means a few nights without Bay, because she doesn't care to explain her younger lover, the knife, the anything, to Mallory who's loaded down with her own problems.

Rennie rushes to the bathroom and plugs in the straightening iron. *Shit, I look like I've been fucking someone on my kitchen table. Imagine that.* She squirts some tangle spray into her rat's nest and brushes it out. As she pulls the straightening iron over her hair, she thinks of Mallory, perky little Mallory who's the mirror image of Kelly. Except, of course, Kelly's not running drugs over the border with her boyfriend, which is what Rennie's pretty sure Mallory and Max are up to. She slides the straightener over her hair once more and unplugs it, looking at her watch. Damn, she's running late already. How did this happen?

She hurries back to the kitchen. 'Did Mallory call? When's she showing up on my doorstep?'

But his face is hard and stony as he finishes listening to the message. When it's done, he presses a button. 'Listen.' The word shoves a great, immense distance between them, and hatred or something like it crackles in the air.

Rennie takes the phone and presses it to her ear. 'Wren.' It's a voice she can't place for a minute. 'Wren, hey, hey, Wren.' Oh God, it's Puck MacGregor. 'Got your number from Beth. Listen, I had a really, really, *really* nice time with you at my book party. Wren, you sweet little bird, Snow White's at my house for a visit. So get that pretty little ass down here to Palo Alto because I can't stop thinking about you. We'll have a little fun with the princess and here's what

129

else we can do . . .' He describes all the things he'll do with her and to her in great detail as Rennie feels her face getting hotter and hotter, particularly when he gets to 'sweep my tongue across your body from head to toe and every hot and spicy place in between, I'll bury my face between your legs, every part of you is so fucking gorgeous, Wren, you know it too . . .' And he finished with, 'Oh and by the way,' in a voice that means what he's about to say is definitely not just 'by the way' but perhaps the point of the entire phone call, 'your agent is obviously not doing her job, so I'm going to take your novel and go over it and send it on to Pepper. I was talking with her the other day and she's interested in you, Wren, really interested.' He gives out his cell phone number and his private e-mail address, the one that's not on his website. The message beeps at the end, and Rennie presses 'Save' as ideas spin through her head.

Bay's standing near the corner cupboard looking betrayed, and she sputters, 'It was just one time, a long time ago, before I even met you. I was drunk. I'm not calling him, so don't worry.' Of course, she's hardly sure of that. Puck is so sexy, and (she'll barely admit it to herself) an 'in' with Pepper Perryman is gold in the literary world. The cocaine worries her, though. At Beth's he asked if she still got high and she said yes, hating the 'still', which made her feel old. But coke was definitely not what she had in mind. Especially because of Cherry's mom. Damn, her past keeps popping out at her even though she's walled it over with stucco, her memories a toxic mold constantly returning to her house. Another thought stabs into her: is screwing Puck for an 'in' with Pepper Perryman edging a little close to prostitution?

Was fucking Rob Schafer for an A the same thing?

Oh God, shut up, Rennie! It wasn't about that!

You should pay for what you did . . .

'I'm really sorry,' she says, to slam out her stupid memories. She walks over to Bay; the air's grown less tense but maybe only because he's resigned. She pulls him to her for a kiss, but the passion's gone now, a bee that's lost its stinger, deflated. She half-heartedly works her mouth and tongue around his and closes her eyes and imagines Puck, but this time Rob Schafer's face pops into her head, the black wavy hair, his erection hard against her belly and Jesus, why, Rennie, that was so long ago!

She breaks the kiss, and Bay's smiling again, so *that's* all right, and she says, 'I'll never be ready in time. You go on ahead, get dressed.' He's got her first period class, but legally she's supposed to be there, responsible for her students. But she trusts Bay at this point and not just because she's fucking him. 'I've got a few things to take care of around here, anyway.'

She's going to open up her e-mail program and sit there with a blank message addressed to Puck MacGregor, and stare at the screen and think.

After school, one of her best seniors, Paul, stays after class. 'I wanted to tell you the great news.' He's breathless, his light brown hair buzzed around a front section that he spikes up with gel. 'Princeton gave me an academic scholarship!'

'Fantastic, Paul!' She's glad to have something to distract her from the blank e-mail to Puck that's puncturing holes in her brain. Paul's a cutie, a sweetheart. She had him as a freshman and again as a senior, and that ninth grade year was key for him. He was drifting, avoiding homework, probably smoking way too much dope and maybe, possibly, shooting heroin. Rennie's no saint herself but she saw him skating on the edge, a talented kid, directionless. She pulled him aside one day, told him how smart he was and how he'd never forgive himself if he, as she put it, fucked himself over. Apparently he appreciated the candor because at the end of the year he wrote her a thank-you card: 'You turned on the light bulb in my head.' He's put on some inches and muscles over the last three years and unlike freshman year, doesn't seem intimidated by his own good looks. Oh yeah, he's gotten laid and grown into himself, she can just tell. 'Good for you. But I'm not surprised.'

That e-mail to Puck still sits in her drafts folder. It's the first time she's considered saying no to sex. It's just too strange; that Pepper Perryman thing freaks her out, not to mention the cocaine. Sometimes she's grateful for these hours when she can be Ms Taylor, Teacher. Slutty or not, at least she's not someone who's supposed to have a second book out by now, Wren Taylor the has-been, someone so desperate for literary attention she'd sleep with Puck MacGregor for access to his agent.

'Sit down for a minute, Paul. I want to hear all about it.'

He sits and spills out the story, how they're paying half his tuition, how they might want him to play basketball too and that'd pay for the rest. She watches his brown eyes, his pale lips, studies the swell of his cheekbones under his skin, the tendons in his throat working as he talks. Before she knows quite what she's doing she reaches out, runs her fingers up the trembling hairs of his arm. 'Paul.'

He stops talking.

She slides her fingers back down to his wrist. 'Paul.' And he gives a nervous little smile. She's standing at the edge of the cliff again, looking down into the dizzying canyon.

And now, she's going to jump.

20
Cherry

May, 1988
Holland, Illinois

Before I threw a pizza in the oven, Marian rolled a joint for the two of us, and now we're sitting around the kitchen table blabbing it up like old friends. While it wouldn't be accurate to say I've forgiven her for burning up my poetry book (when the flames licked the sides of the pages, curled around from blue to red to yellow, and consumed my words, my thoughts, myself, she watched me as I cried, rubbed my back, thought she was helping me I guess), we've reached a sort of understanding and so we're chatting about friendships, giggling. The dope's gone to our heads and sometimes, during these good moments with her, I feel like her sister, not her daughter. I don't bring up what I found in the bathroom this afternoon because she's being nice and I don't want to spoil it. She's already opened up a little about her mom and dad, who we never, never see, and she told me how they kicked her out of their house when she got pregnant with me, how she worked two jobs until she delivered to save money so she'd have a few months with the baby – me – before she went back to waitressing.

'Tell me about my dad.' I pick up Bradbury, who's been crawling over the table, and drop him on the floor. 'What was he like?'

She shakes her head, holding smoke in her lungs and passing me the joint. This has always been forbidden territory.

I take a toke and pass it back to her across the table. 'Please tell me; I'm half him. I want to know.'

'There's not much to tell. We didn't really know each other.'

'Well, what was he? A doctor? A truck driver? A waiter?' I'll never have the man in my life, never even a photo of him, but if she's opening up she may give me a little piece of him.

'You're going to laugh.'

'I won't.' Bradbury jumps back on the table and I pull him off again, drop him in the living room and close the door.

'He was a cop.' She giggles and takes another hit. 'Imagine, me in bed with a cop.'

'What was his name?' I wonder if I could look him up, not to edge my way into his life but just to figure myself out, who I am, who he was.

'I never knew his name.' She shrugs. 'It was a casual thing. We were just doing each other a favor.'

Which means I'll never track him down. He probably doesn't even know he got her pregnant.

'I will say this, Cherry, you look more like him than me, your eyes, the shape of your nose.' She reaches over and strokes her finger over the bridge of my nose, and my heart swells with love for her. This is the same moment at the barbecue pushed forward eleven years, a carbon copy of the best moment I've ever had with my mother. Not Marian. My mother. 'This is him,' she says, her fingers brushing the cartilage near the top of my nose. 'This part of you is him.'

We both smell the pizza burning and I yell, 'Shit!' and rescue it. I pull a slice onto a napkin but now Marian's getting itchy for her coke. She shakes off the pizza, makes a bunch of excuses and takes off for the bathroom. That's when my worries burst into reality, worries so huge and intense they're monsters pressing their arms around me, choking, suffocating, sinking their teeth into my relaxed contentment, tearing off pieces and spitting them onto the ground next to me. My heart pumps the worries through my system until they've poisoned every part of me. No, no. It can never be simple with Marian, can it?

See, when I was touching up my makeup this afternoon I found the needle next to the sink. She didn't even rinse it

out, just left it on the counter with yellowish droplets clinging to the inside. Her little coke habit started about two years
ago, and I always hoped it wouldn't turn into this. I don't
know how long she's been shooting up, but I'm not going
to let her get away with it. Because the next step's
going to be heroin, and we aren't going there, we just
aren't, we can't.

After the clock spins out ten minutes that feel like twenty
hours I press my fingers to my green glass necklace for
strength. Then I walk to the bathroom and knock on the
door. 'Marian?'

'Just a minute.' Her voice is strained, thick.

I rattle the knob. 'Marian, don't give me that crap. What
are you up to?' I hate that I have to be the rational one, that I
have to click my mind away from my pot buzz so I can take
care of her. But I do it; it's easy to do if you know how to
shut off one part of your brain.

'Don't you dare talk to me that way.' Her voice flings
through the door, slices into me like a knife. 'I said just a
minute.' There's a little gasp, like the sounds that escape my
lips during sex with Sam. So of course she's mainlining right
now. The needle's sticking into the fleshy part of her inner
arm, and she's pressing the plunger in, letting the coke hit
her veins. God, I never thought Marian would sink this low.
I mean, snorting coke is one thing – that's even glamorous in
a sick, *Less than Zero* sort of way. But shooting up? That's
what junkies do.

I bang on the door. 'Marian?' Fear stabs me in the stomach.
I hate her fucking guts most of the time, but at the exact
same moment and from the exact same part of me, I love
her, and I'm worried. She's already fucked up anyway since
we smoked that dope together before dinner. What if there's
an air bubble in the syringe and it goes to her heart?
'Marian!'

She doesn't answer me, maybe didn't hear me.

'Marian!' I'm sure I've sent her into one of her rages, and
on coke it'll be even worse. But I need to know. With all my
strength, I pull back my combat boot and kick in the door.

Sure enough she's sitting next to the toilet, knees drawn to her chest. One of her belts and a glass of water and a spoon and her plastic bag half-full of coke and her little mirror and of course her goddamned needle all lie next to her on the floor. (*On the bathroom floor, Marian? It hasn't been scrubbed in weeks. I know I haven't done it and I'm sure you haven't.*) She's shaking a little, rocking back and forth, starting to cry. 'I didn't want you to see this, I didn't want you to know, it's the first time I've done it this way. I won't do it again, just leave me by myself for a while, go out with your friends . . .'

We've been in denial all along about her little habit. Hell, I don't talk about it to anyone, not even my best friends, certainly not to Marian herself. So basically what she's done is given a confession, and the reason she wants me to leave is so she can chase her cocaine high, keep doing it till it's gone, only this time she's injecting it. I'm not going to let her.

I grab her wrist and pull her to her feet. Needle marks trace all up and down her arm, and my stomach turns. How long has she been doing it like this? Who showed her how to do this? 'Marian, don't lie. It's not the first time. Look, who made these?' I hear my own voice, but it's like I'm disconnected from myself and I almost don't know who's talking. I sound sure of myself, but I have no idea what the hell to do. She should be in treatment or something, but what do I, how can I . . . ?

Just then her knees crumple under her and she falls to the floor. 'Marian!' Her eyes roll back in her head, fall closed.

Jesus, she's not dead, is she? I slip my fingers next to her neck, and her pulse is pounding like machine-gun fire so no, she's not dead, but she's gone all stiff and wired up. 'Marian, wake up!' Her knees move back and forth and her arms flail about like a newborn baby's. What do I do? Jesus, what do I do? I press her wrists to the floor to stop her from hitting herself. Her knee lands in my stomach. Is my mother dying right in front of me? Tears blur my vision, but I sniff them back where they came from. 'Marian!' I should call 911, but can I leave her? The seizure stops as quickly as it began, and I pull her to a sitting position and lean her against the wall. Her head dips down, like she's a kid who's fallen asleep in the car, and the knot in my stomach tightens. I need to get her to the hospital.

I stand, holding her hands, and lift her to her feet. But she's still not awake and her skin is burning. I run cold water in the sink, soak a washcloth and press it to her face, her neck, her chest, and thank God, (thank *God*) her eyes blink open. Her glance flitters from left to right and fuck, I'm still taking her to the hospital. 'Marian . . .'

' 'Sfine,' she slurs and narrows her eyes to slits. 'Th' wall . . .' She leans against it like she's too dizzy to stand.

I push myself into some other universe so I can be Just the Facts Ma'am. 'You had a seizure. Maybe you hit an artery. Are you okay? Do you know where you are?'

She's sweating now, her red hair tangled at her neck. An image flashes into my mind, my best memory, a barbecue on a hot summer day when I was little, six maybe, and Marian (back then, I called her Mama) laughing, flipping some hot dogs on the grill, music swelling in the air, I was singing along too the best I could. And she knew every word: it was 'The Times They Are A-Changin' ' by Bob Dylan.

I loved the song then, but let's be honest, it's a bunch of bullshit. I'd really like someone to explain to me what was so great about the Sixties, because kids like me got fucked over and half those flower children are now wearing suits and thinking up ways to make money by ruining the environment and screwing over children in third world countries.

Or else drinking up the world, fucking teenagers, rigging coke in their bathrooms.

Mama's hair was clumped in just that way, the way it is now, in the hundred-degree weather, when she pressed me to her hip (so long ago!) and said, 'My sweetums, my Cherry Pie.' The air was thick and sweet with marijuana and love and hugs and kisses but where did it all go? When did all those hippies turn into cokeheads, drunks, child molesters? How can we believe in their dream of peace and freedom when it's turned into shit right before our eyes?

I reach out and smooth her tangled hair. I'll never believe in anything. All those big houses in the subdivisions are filled with former hippies who said Make Love Not War and Never Trust Anyone Over Thirty. My anger at an entire generation could consume me, swallow me whole. But I have to focus on the here and now and not fly into a philosophical rage. So I bite my lip hard, anchoring my thoughts in reality. 'You're here at home. Do you know who I am?'

I concentrate on Marian's eyes and she makes eye contact, a glimmer of recognition glints in them, and she says, 'Course, Cherry. Don't worry. 'Sfine.'

She's talking like she's drunk and I have to wonder if she lost oxygen. What if there was brain damage with the seizure? 'We should take you to the ER. I'll drive the truck. Can you walk?' I take her by the hand and start to lead her to the bathroom door, but she freezes.

'No.'

I tug her arm. 'Yes.'

'No. No one can know.' The words are coming out better now, and she knows it and pulls a smile over her lips. 'See? I'm fine.'

I feel sorry for her, for Marian and her whole spoiled generation, who can't think of anyone but themselves and can't even keep their own shit together. Like a bunch of babies. No wonder kids like us fall for the spun-sugar dreams of Princess Diana (once in a while her smile drops from her face and I'm certain she's hiding something), or dumb sitcoms that solve problems in half an hour. Because there's nothing else to believe in. Nothing real.

'Let me look at your wrist.' The little pop of fresh blood marks what looks like an artery, and a big purplish bruise spreads in a teardrop shape around the needle hole, and I'm pretty sure my mother almost died just now. 'You're not fine, Marian. Let me take you to the hospital.'

Her eyes harden, and she's starting to get paranoid and

weird because she says, 'You're ruining the whole thing for me, Cherry. Run some more water, it sounds so beautiful.'

I ignore her. 'Come on. We'll take the truck, I'll drive.'

'You're not taking me to the hospital. Not if you want to be alive in the morning.'

I whistle out a deep breath. 'You need help. Don't you see that? Look at yourself.' I pick up the needle from the floor, clatter it onto the counter. 'Look at your arms; they're a mess! You criticize Amy for slicing her arm – well this is self-mutilation if I've ever seen it! You're killing yourself. You. Are. Killing yourself!'

'Fuck you.' Somewhere in those angry eyes is a little girl, a little seventeen-year-old girl with a baby. 'What's that you always say to me? It's *my* life.' Didn't all those flower children want to be like the Lost Boys in *Peter Pan*? Never gonna grow up. Now *that* was a brilliant idea.

Peace, and freedom, and the rest of that hippie bullshit can lick my fucking ass. Rennie still believes, but she's been sold a bill of goods.

She pushes me away, hard. 'Get out of here, get out of this room, get out of this house, leave me alone!'

'I'm not leaving you like this, Marian.' If I leave her she'll just shoot up again, and again, and again, until it's gone. This is my mother, my mother, my mother. All pale and chalky and marked up with tracks on her arm, eyes webbed through with blood and sweat all along her face.

This is my mother.

Her lips curl into anger. That Mama at the barbecue is dead, has been for a long time.

She balls up her fist and takes a swing at me. But I'm not as fucked up as she is, and I duck.

I can't help her.

I turn away and leave her there with her syringe and her buzz. If she wants to rig coke, I guess I can't stop her. I don't say goodbye, just imagine the smack of her fist into my cheek and walk toward the door. I'm going to Sam's. And even though I'm not supposed to see Rennie or Amy, I'll damn well find them. I may even spill my guts tonight. *Cherry*

Winters isn't as strong as you all thought. I slide the keys to the truck off the hook in the kitchen and slam the door.

She can die for all I care.

21
Amy

May, 2003
Sault Sainte Marie, Michigan

Amy presses her hands to her aching breasts. Time to pump her milk. She needs to be a lot more careful about how much she drinks because alcohol can get into breast milk, but she pushes that thought away. Scotty's in Lucky's bedroom hammering and banging and clanging away at what he insists is going to be a dollhouse. A dollhouse. Imagine. Lucky isn't even home yet, and the thing will be a hazard until she's at least four or five. Just something to get hurt on. But Amy knows better than to criticize. The air is thick with tension, and she's been taking long walks along the Soo lately, watching the boats go up and down, making themselves useful, unlike Amy, drifting along.

She plugs in the breast pump and attaches the bottles. Things were going so well for Lucky for a while after the heart operation. It seemed she'd gotten past a big hurdle; she'd had a nasty chest infection and her lungs were secreting something, but they put her on antibiotics and soon after lowered her respirator rate to eighteen breaths per minute. She put on weight and was almost three and a half pounds.

Then the reflux started, and Lucky'd stop breathing for minutes at a time to try to keep the milk from getting into her lungs, Amy's milk, the milk that's now flowing through the clear tubing into the bottles. A wave of sadness washes through her. She knows it's physical, the let-down reflex that's swooshing the milk from her nipples. But it feels phony, like eating a picture of a sandwich instead of a sandwich. Her baby should be attached to her, nursing, gulping down milk, tiny streams rolling from the corner of her mouth. Instead Amy's attached to a machine, not unlike the ones that are attached to her daughter. This communion of machines, this sad force of connection, these wires are all that unite them.

Upstairs, Scotty bangs the hammer. 'Shit.' They rarely speak, except to exchange news about Lucky. Now that Amy can't stay the long days anymore, they get most of the news at the same time.

The reflux stopped for a while, but Lucky got sick with another lung infection and they had to put ventilator tubes in her chest. The doctors gave her a medication to keep her from moving around and using up her energy, and that's when it became painful to see her, because it was like she was paralyzed. When the tubes didn't seem to be enough, they attached the high frequency ventilator. The thing pumped in breaths so fast it sounded like a helicopter flying over fucking Baghdad.

The pulmonary specialist told her and Scotty that Lucky, if she made it through the lung infection and made it home (the 'if' was the specialist's, not Amy's – she still believes, she does, she does), she'd probably be on a ventilator until she's three years old.

And somehow, she can't even imagine still being married to Scotty three years from now. Maybe if Lucky gets better it will change things. For now, the valley between them has opened up so wide and deep no bridge can ever make it across.

The pump has emptied her breasts and she switches it off, caps the milk bottles, walks to the refrigerator and puts them in. Tomorrow morning she'll bring them to the hospital and drop them off. She's not allowed to visit Lucky anymore because she's in an isolation room to cut down on outside noises that may stimulate and upset her, wasting her energy. Energy seeps out of her baby like a battery gradually going dead, and the word drops into her mind, just like that.

She slams the refrigerator door, and Scotty's swearing again at the damn dollhouse. What is there to do but drink? She's pumped out the clean milk for Lucky, and it doesn't matter now. So she opens the refrigerator again and pulls out the old orange juice. (*God, I'm like Mom despite myself*), grabs the vodka from the liquor cabinet and pours herself a good stiff one. Just then the phone rings and Scotty shouts, 'Get it, will you, Amy?'

And no she doesn't want to get the phone because it might be news about Lucky, but she picks it up anyway. The 'really sorry' and 'cardiac arrest' and 'resuscitate' of Judy, the nurse, hardly register with her. The last thing she hears is, 'down to say goodbye to your daughter.'

She drops the phone and yells for Scotty, just like she did that night back in March, and he runs into the kitchen and picks up the phone from where it dangles against the wall and is banging, banging against the beadboard. Amy just wants to blot everything away, so she chugs her screwdriver and pours another. Goodbye to Lucky? Did she really say that?

Scotty presses his fist to the curls that fall across his face. 'Yes. I understand.' He hangs up the phone and says without a trace of emotion, 'Come on, Amy. Get your coat.' Noticing the full drink in her hand, he says, 'What the hell are you doing?' He grabs the tumbler and hurls it across the room, where it smashes against the tile above the stove. Pieces of glass fall in slow motion inside the vent of the Viking range – *that'll be a bitch to clean* – and the orange juice trails down the wall. It's so not appropriate, but Amy begins to laugh hysterically. Goddamn it, Scotty won't stop her from drinking. She uncaps the vodka and swallows some right from the bottle, and it burns her throat, lights the fire in her stomach.

He seizes her hand. 'Amy. Get a hold of yourself. Stop it. *Stop it.*'

She still doesn't stop laughing, and his open palm smacks across her face like a splash of cold water. The laughter stops and she's calm again but pissed. 'What the hell'd you do that for?'

'This is it, Amy.' His face is steady. 'You can't drink it away. Come on. Lucky needs us.'

143

He gets her coat, slides her arms into it, and in a strange moment of affection presses his arms around her chest from behind. She leans into him, wishing he'd kiss her ear like he used to; he hasn't kissed her anywhere in months. But he doesn't, and she pulls away.

He offers his hand, but she won't take it. On her own she follows him out the door.

The chaplain's at the hospital even though Amy didn't request it, along with the nurses who've taken care of Lucky all this time. They link hands around Lucky's incubator and pray and Amy's prayer is this: *If You are real, God, I hate You for doing this to me, to Scotty, to Lucky. Just go fuck Yourself and anything You ever created.*

God doesn't answer, of course.

Sorry, that number is no longer in service.

She clings so tightly to the hands of Scotty and Judy the nurse that Scotty gives her an evil look and Judy shakes her hand when Amy lets it go.

They've resuscitated Lucky, so now she's attached to the ventilator again. But they did an EEG, and the results said Lucky's brain activity showed low voltage, and the doctors told Amy and Scotty she'd never recover from it. So when it comes down to it, if they took off the ventilator Lucky'd just stop breathing. She might move for a few minutes and then she'd slip away. They know they can only suggest that to her, they can't make her do it. What they decide to do is to give her and Scotty 'some time alone'.

'Amy,' says Scotty when the room's empty.

She won't answer him.

'Amy, I just think we have to get into reality.'

'Fuck reality.'

He grasps her face and turns it toward him and she's drowning in his eyes – they're full of heartbreak and she knows he's hurting too. 'I love you, Amy. I won't do anything you don't want to.'

The machines, the machines hum, breathe in, breathe out, the rhythm's driving her mad and words come out of her mouth from somewhere. 'Don't you dare say you love me because I'll never believe you.'

'Amy—'

'But you love *Lucky*, I'll buy that. I do too.'

'Amy—' Heartbreak's poured onto his face, his lips are tight, his skin pale, and his eyes, those eyes, so searching, so beaten down . . .

Emotion pulls itself up from a place so deep inside her she didn't even know it existed, and pushes words out of her mouth. 'Oh, God, Scotty, why, *why*?'

And now, now is when she falls into his arms.

They have a conversation without words and without tears (they've been driven so deep they'll never come out). At the end of it all he brushes his lips over her hair and pushes the button to call in the doctors. Scotty's the one who tells them that they want Lucky to be comfortable before she . . . And he can't say that last word but fortunately the doctor lets him trail off into, 'We've decided it's best for Lucky if we remove the ventilator.'

Scotty gets to hold Lucky one last time, run his fingers through her hair, a bittersweet smile on his face, and then it's Amy's turn. He turns to her, stricken. 'I can't, Amy. I can't stay here when they do it. I can't watch her . . .' He won't say the word, the final final word.

So he's left it all on her, but that's par for the course. Amy says sweetly, 'That's all right, Scotty,' because she can't bear any more conflict, any more energy floating in the air.

It's so, so dark outside, dark as only the Upper Peninsula can get. The overcast night is a warm blanket of death. A choke of sadness seizes up in her, but she knows the real tears will come later. Now is surviving, getting through it.

Scotty leaves the room, and the doctor removes the ventilator, and she holds Lucky and rocks her in the rocker. It doesn't take long for the life to slip out of her little body, and after she's gone, the staff leave the room, Judy touching Amy's shoulder before she goes.

Amy holds her baby and rocks her for even longer, rubbing her back. She loses track of time and stares into the night, pressing her eyes into the blackness so they become one. *This night will never leave my eyes.*

Finally Judy comes back, and Amy hands Lucky's body to her. Judy takes scissors and cuts a little piece of Lucky's hair for her. Amy's numb now, number than vodka ever makes her, number than the Xanax ever made her, and all within her is the black night of outside.

Scotty returns, and she sees the heartbreak in his eyes and falls into his arms, not because they're warm and welcoming but out of sheer exhaustion. It's three a.m. now, she somehow registers, and Lucky, their Lucky . . . This is the first day starting without Lucky.

They drive home in silence. Inside, Amy leaves the glass and orange juice mess and just pours herself another one. Scotty pours one for himself too, and they sit like that in the kitchen, drinking and pouring and drinking and pouring until the sun rises over the Soo. Scotty tries his voice and says, 'I'm calling my folks. Then I'm going to bed.'

The dollhouse flits into her head and it's the saddest damn thing in the world. She whispers, 'Lucky would have really liked the dollhouse.'

And he bites his lip. It was the wrong thing to say. Tears burst out of his eyes, and it's like the spigot has opened, but when Amy goes to hold him he pushes her away. 'You call my folks. I can't do it.'

On his way to their room, he closes the door to Lucky's nursery. Amy shoots up the stairs after him, but he closes the door to the master bedroom too, so she goes back down to the kitchen and pours one big last drink and finishes half of it in the living room before passing out on the sofa.

She dreams of blackness, of nothing, of emptiness.

22
Rennie

May, 1988
Westville, Illinois

I'm chomping on an enormous wad of Juicy Fruit, my teeth smashing in and pulling up and over and over. The rhythm and fake fruit smell calm me somehow as rain crashes onto the windshield, and I don't have to think. Cherry's truck bumps down the road, and Amy says next to me, 'No, you missed it, turn around.' Cherry U-s it, and we turn into the parking lot and pull up to the red brick building, Westville Women's Health Center.

Cherry turns off the engine. 'Are you sure this is what you want to do?'

I'm not sure at all. Part of me even hoped the weather would cause us to have an enormous wreck and I'd be injured and it'd all happen on its own, so it wouldn't be my fault. But of course, since that didn't happen, there's no other way out. I just tell myself, *I'm Liz in a* DeGrassi *episode. This is TV, not my life.* 'Sure as I'll ever be.'

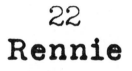

The three of us are cutting school to do this. We usually cut to do fun things, head into Chicago à la Ferris Bueller, get stoned at the Porter Place. This time?

Let's just say it won't be so fun.

When I told Rob the first words out of his mouth were, 'How much money do you need?' They were a slap in the face. I mean, he just assumed I was going to do this. Then, when I told him I wanted to have the baby, to marry him, a hard look crept into his eyes. He gave me a big talk about

Stanford, my writing, my future. He talked not one bit about himself, but it sure makes things easy for him, now, doesn't it? Nothing to explain to Dawn. No nasty little rumors about the high-school girl he got pregnant.

I can't help resenting him, but I also know he's right. Who would take care of a baby while I went to classes? So over the last couple weeks I've convinced myself it's better this way, that the baby wouldn't have a very good life. Adoption, well, then everyone would find out about me and Rob, and it would mean his job, plus he could go to jail for sleeping with a teenager. Besides, I don't want to have a baby and then give it up. Mom I rarely hear from and I'm sure she wouldn't give a shit, but Dad would flip if I gave away his grandchild. Anyway, I don't want to get huge and fat and start at Stanford as the slutty cheap pregnant girl, have a baby by myself around New Year. I don't want to face Dad and Kelly, who'll be absolutely self-righteous about it and who I'm sure will pull her precious Mallory close and whisper to Dad that all my character flaws came from Mom. No thanks.

Since I had no idea, I told Rob I needed five hundred dollars. Months ago, the Bitch Posse started an Abortion Fund and whenever one of us had money, we'd throw a few bucks at it, just in case one of us got in this situation.

No one ever thought I'd be the one.

There's less than a hundred bucks in the Abortion Fund anyway, and if Rob Schafer's not going to take responsibility and marry me and move to California with me and help take care of our baby, well, then, the least he can do is pay for my sorry abortion.

We're still just sitting in the truck in the parking lot, and I reach over Amy and flick open the door. 'I just want it to be over.'

The craziest part is that after I agreed to this whole thing, we've gone on with our relationship like nothing's changed at all. I mean, we're still meeting once a week at the Paradise Inn. Drinking it up since it doesn't matter that I'm pregnant if I'm getting an abortion anyway. I even brought over some weed a couple of times, and we've gotten high, him reading aloud the play I'm working on (it's about three sisters who coincidentally share a lot of personality traits with the three of us), starting a list of competitions to submit it to, even laughing sometimes and then having our sweet pretty sex, just as drawn out and spinningly amazing as usual.

To me, though, it feels forced. I don't think he understands that things changed when he got so matter-of-fact about my abortion. Like I'm getting a haircut or something.

Cherry squeezes my hand. 'It's all right, no one will find out. They don't make you tell your parents if you're not using insurance. Which we aren't.'

And I'm grateful for the 'we'. It makes me feel not quite as alone. Amy hops out of the truck and I follow her.

Rob gave me the five hundred dollars in cash, and I'm carrying it, ten fifty-dollar bills, in my purse. He decided not to come here. I asked him to, but he said it was too risky; someone might see him. Instead he wants me to come by after school so we can 'talk'. I wonder where he got the money, how he'll explain the five-hundred dollar deficit when he and Dawn pay the bills this month. I wonder if he cares if anyone sees *me* at the clinic, or if he's just concerned about his own reputation.

I didn't ask.

Outside the clinic ten or so people are marching up and down shouting stuff. One of them's carrying a gigantic picture of a fetus. It's bad enough coming here without dealing with this, and Cherry grabs me by the waist and so does Amy. Cherry leans to my ear and whispers, 'I love you, Rennie. *As long as the stars are fixed in the heavens and the fish sparkle in the sea.*' And I'm flooded with warmth; this is survivable.

Shouts zoom through the air and pelt me on the back and yeah, it'll be bad. 'Thou shalt not kill!' *Oh shit, fuck, please God just strike me dead now.* 'It's not a choice, it's a child!'

Amy mutters, 'Keep your head down. You don't have to talk to them.' At least I'm not alone; I have the Bitch Posse's strength behind me.

'They aren't allowed to touch you,' says Cherry loudly as we walk by. 'You don't have to take their flyers.'

One man gets right in my face and says, 'I'm praying for you and your baby. Please don't kill your baby!' and a woman behind him shouts, 'I'll take your baby, give it to me! I can't have a baby.' Flyers are pressed in front of me, with graphic bloody pictures I can't even make out because my eyes somehow aren't processing images. The only word that really makes sense is 'baby'. What's inside me couldn't be a baby – it's only been six weeks since I missed my period. But the word 'baby' makes me sad, and I wonder for an instant, how will I remember this day? Maybe I can forget it, blank it out in my memory. But I don't want to think about that just now. *Stay focused, Rennie, think of Stanford, think of how relieved you'll be when this is all over.*

Amy pulls open the glass door, and the protesters' shouts dim away behind me. It's a great comfort to be in here, in the clinic. And it's surprisingly pretty, the waiting room done in shades of rose and lavender and a big flower arrangement at the center of one of the tables.

I go up to the desk. 'Wren Taylor.' I hate my real name so much, but I have to use it. When I made the appointment I had to give all my contact information in case of an emergency, but I'm still kind of freaked out about it. It'd be easy for them to call Dad and Kelly if they wanted to.

I'm starving because I wasn't supposed to eat anything last night, and the receptionist looks suspiciously at my gum, but gum's okay I think. She hands me a bunch of forms, medical history, consent to surgery, and shows me where to sign. I take them back to a chair with a clipboard, and Amy and Cherry sit on either side of me as I fill them out, wordless support.

'Don't put in the insurance info,' says Cherry like she knows. 'Unless you know for sure what their confidentiality issues are.'

'But then—'

'That's why you have the cash, Rennie.'

I take the forms back to the desk and slide them at the

receptionist. She glances over them and says, 'These look good. We'll just give you a follow up pregnancy test then?'

Like the results are going to magically change. 'Whatever.'

'Are you friends waiting for you? Do they know how long it'll be?'

On the phone the woman said two to three hours. Amy's brought homework and Cherry's brought her new poetry book, the one she hides between her mattress and box spring, after what Marian did to her old one. 'They know.'

'They need to stay here so they can drive you home. You're not to drive.'

'Yeah, okay.'

'We ask you to pay in advance for the medical procedure. You can file a claim with insurance later, or give us a card now. Do you have a referral authorization for your insurance?'

'No.'

'And how are you paying? Money order, Visa, Master-Card, Discover . . .'

'Cash.' I open my purse with all the fifties inside and she asks me for two hundred and eighty dollars. I hand over six fifties and put the others and the two tens she hands me back into my purse. Then, Rob Schafer's face washes over my mind, and I pull all the money out and bring it back to my friends, handing them each two fifties and a ten. 'Here.'

Amy looks at it. 'Aren't you bringing this back to Mr Schafer?'

Anger cycles through me, pulls up in a spiral through my chest and comes out in my words. 'Fuck that. I'm not bringing him change from my abortion.'

Cherry hands the money back to me. 'You keep it then. He owes you that and more.'

I snap it back into her hands. 'I don't want his abortion money, I just don't. It's yours. Buy something great with it.'

Someone's at the door and says, 'Wren Taylor?'

I stand up, and the woman leads me down the hall to a locker. 'You can put all your stuff here and change into a gown. You need to take off all your jewelry including any piercings.'

I change and unlatch the red glass necklace Amy made for me, unlace my sisters from my neck. God, I feel naked. Alone at my most important moment.

In the exam room I'm joined by a nurse, who asks a bunch of medical history questions that I already answered on the form, takes my blood pressure, and draws some blood. Then a hundred-year-old male doctor comes in and does a pelvic exam, which is more humiliating than anything I could have ever imagined. I stare at the ceiling as he probes into me, examining parts so hidden and secret I'm amazed anyone would even care about them. Should I explain how it happened? It all feels so impersonal. 'The guy who . . . He said he'd marry me but his wife—'

The nurse curls a frown and interrupts me. 'We don't want any of those details. Your boyfriend doesn't matter. This is between you and the doctor.' She was so cold before, but now a pleasant stream of chat floods from her mouth as if the words can't pour out quickly enough. 'I see girls like you all the time. You're making the right choice, the responsible choice. Are you scared?'

I nod.

'I bet you didn't know the whole procedure takes about five minutes. We put you under general anesthesia and you won't remember a thing.' She smiles. 'Follow me. We'll go into the surgical suite.'

Thoughts are jumbled up in my head right now, but I do know one thing: I am not going to be pregnant anymore after today. Hopefully all my awful feelings about Rob and myself will be gone along with this pregnancy, be washed away, taken from me. A tense of anticipation wriggles through me, like being at the top of a Ferris Wheel. A voice creeps into my head: *Are you sure, Rennie? This is your last chance . . .* but I banish it. I'm here, my friends have driven me into the outskirts of Chicago and cut school to help me do this, this is the right thing right thing right thing. Having a baby fucks up my life and Rob's life and just about the entire world around me. Having an abortion just fucks up my own, and only (I hope) for a little while, and then I can forget about it and move on.

In the surgical suite, soft cheerful music is playing. Barry Manilow, I think, something I'd never listen to in front of anyone, but it calms me down in a ridiculous sort of way. The nurse puts my legs up in stirrups, and looking around the room I notice a table with a bunch of tools, including a long slender clear tube that I guess they use to do the abortion, pull stuff out of me with.

That's when my stomach starts to turn over in itself, and it's a good thing they're going to put me under because I'm pretty sure if they didn't, I'd faint. They attach a drip IV to me (*this is the anesthetic, Wren, you should feel it in just a minute or two*) and I'm thinking about the Bitch Posse and the night we swore our solemn oath.

> *We, the Bitch Posse girls,*
> *do solemnly swear*
> *to be undyingly faithful to each other,*
> *and to put no friends or lovers before one another . . .*

The scene shimmers in front of me and I'm asleep.

The next thing I know I'm in the recovery room. A twang shivers out of me almost like an orgasm, and my body feels empty for the first time in weeks. I know it's relief that the burden of my pregnancy's been taken away. Then, a feeling of darkness sinks into me and that's what fills me now. It's like a real cloud entering my body, and I feel very, very alone and afraid and too young to be mixed up in all of this.

The nurse is here. 'Are you all right? It went fast. Come on, let's get you dressed.' She leaves a Kotex on the table. 'Use these, don't use a tampon. The bleeding'll stop in a couple of weeks. No sexual intercourse for two weeks, until your follow-up visit. Otherwise, you risk infection and another pregnancy. A counselor'll be by in a minute to go over the whole post-op sheet with you and to talk about birth control options.' She touches my arm. 'It's okay, you did great. It's good you didn't wait very long. The longer you wait, the more complicated the procedure.'

She lets me dress, which I do very robotically, and then comes back to sit with me for a while. The counselor comes in and she tells me a bunch of stuff, no aspirin only Tylenol, and no sex for two weeks (guess that'll surprise Rob; he probably didn't know about the bleeding either – I sure didn't). She hands me a sheet of instructions and tells me I need to stay here until I've 'stabilized'.

I blank myself out because it's so boring waiting, and try to remember *A Midsummer Night's Dream*, scene by scene. Act I, Scene 1. Hermia and Lysander are in love, but her father wants her to marry Demetrius. *'The course of true love never did run smooth.'* Hermia's friend Helena's nuts over Demetrius, but Demetrius is nuts over Hermia. Hermia and Lysander plan to run away to the woods.

The nurse takes my blood pressure every now and then. Why can't I go home? Act I, Scene 2. The players, Peter Quince, Snug, Flute, and Bottom practice their play. The tragic love story of Pyramus and Thisbe.

For some reason that tube falls into my mind. Are they washing it now? Is it full of blood, or skin, or . . . My stomach turns.

Concentrate, Rennie, concentrate. Act II, Scene 1. Puck, Robin Goodfellow, flirts with a fairy before Oberon and Titania, rulers of the fairies, arrive. Oberon tells Puck to play a trick on Titania by squeezing the magic flower juice onto her eyelids . . .

My head's hurting. I feel an itch to smoke some dope and forget everything. This day is endless.

Finally the nurse says, 'Come on, let's have a snack.' My red beads wink from the counter, and I lace them around my neck and fasten the clasp. She leads me to another room where a couple other girls are sitting at a table. One's a Pammie McFadden look-alike with a ton of makeup, the other looks about twelve, with a Dorothy Hamill pixie cut. They look at me dispassionately. We sit and eat our donuts and drink a little orange juice. No one talks. I don't feel like eating. Funny, I was so hungry earlier.

I look at the clock and already it's almost noon. Cherry and Amy must be starving. I stand and grab the little paper bag with the Tylenol samples and a month's worth of the Pill, which they've decided to put me on, and walk like a zombie out to the waiting room.

Amy slides her notebook to the floor, and Cherry puts her poetry book on her chair. They both rush over to me, and I'm suddenly so exhausted I could sleep for a year. My friends open their arms and we hug and tears flip out of my eyes, but they will never understand me anymore. No one will understand me anymore. I've changed; I'm someone else. At once I realize I will never forget this day; you just don't forget moments when your life path changes forever. Tears swell to the surface as I try not to think of babies, sweet warm good-smelling babies.

I will have a baby someday. I'm not ready for a baby. It was the best thing.

But it makes my stomach swim to think like this. Squashing down my inner voice, I call a thank-you to the receptionist, who reminds me of my two-week appointment. But once we're outside, my thoughts pop up at me like weeds.

When I see Rob at the motel today after school, I'm going to tell him how I bled. How I'm cramping now despite the two Tylenol I just took. The tube, I'll tell him all about the tube and force him to hear me speculate about what the stuff they sucked out of me looked like. I'm going to give him as many details as I can remember, except of course giving his change to Amy and Cherry.

I'm going to make him feel like hell.

Make him feel just as bad as I do.

23
Cherry

May, 2003
Freemont Psychiatric Hospital

Cherry studies the sleeping shoulders of her roommate Josie, breaths pulling her chest up and down, blonde hair curving around her face. She's so skinny, like a bird. She reminds her of Rennie Taylor in a way, and at that thought Cherry's disappointment with the poetry crests through her. Yesterday she took that poem that Josie saved for her, the one rejected from *Echo*, and over an ashtray lit the corner of it, watched flames lick across it, until the edges curled up like the wings of a bird and the black ash dropped into the tray. Following that she got a reprimand from the social worker, Leigh, for 'lighting fires'. Oh Lord, if Leigh only knew the fires she wants to light. Though Cherry can't help the chuckle that presses out of her chest, she suppresses it, not wanting to waken Josie.

Cherry's having trouble catching up to the elusive bird of sleep; seems she's chasing the days so hard it's impossible to drift off and forget. Since Josie's remark at the women's group meeting Cherry's made it her quest to look out for this girl, protect her, make sure stuff doesn't happen. She's told Josie too much about herself and shoved a wall between the two of them, but the wall is climbable, the wall can be broken down. There's no one else to save the girl, surely not Leigh, surely not Dr Bowker, whom Josie calls 'The Wanker'. The only one she's ever trusted is Cherry. She wants to tell Josie about Diana, what Diana said: *I understand people's suffering, people's pain, more than you will ever know yourself.*

Josie moans. Through the dim moonlight streaming in the

window Cherry slides to her friend's bed and sits at the foot. Josie yanks at the covers, and Cherry lifts herself up for a moment so Josie can grab them; but Josie's rubbing her eyes and mutters, 'Fuck.' She shoots her gaze around the room, and the bones in her neck seem fluid. Moonlight dips into the hollows formed by her collarbone, and she looks even frailer.

'Can't sleep either,' says Cherry. 'Maybe it's the moon.' The moon is full and wide and wild and sparkling. Light dances through the window and encompasses both of them, and despite the setting Cherry feels hopeful. 'Did you have a dream?'

Josie slides a cigarette from the pack on the table and lights it, staring at the wall. 'It was weird. I was in my car driving to school and I felt this presence behind me. I don't know what it was, but it was something huge and dark, and it reached down and grabbed the car and crushed it, and I got smaller and smaller until I fell out through the keyhole, and then I started spinning toward earth and . . . I don't remember any more.' She extends the pack to Cherry. 'I wonder what it means. I used to have this dream book but I didn't get to take that here with me. My mom thought it was Satanic.'

That reminds Cherry of the day the Bitch Posse landed in the principal's office faced with flurries of accusations, soon before the world unhitched and she swung into the universe, unfettered. Dreams are just another kind of lie, something else keeping people solid and sane and under wraps. Diana's dream turned into a nightmare. So did Cherry's. Josie's mom shoots heroin, she knows that. The two of them are cut from the same cloth, raw edges matching up. If you pulled a thread on either of them they'd fall apart.

She pulls a cigarette out and lights it, even though she knows smoking will wake her up and according to the clock on the wall it's only three a.m. She blows out smoke. 'I dream about rivers. Dark rivers that stop flowing and just sit there still like a lake. I don't know what the fuck that means either. But I talk about it in therapy sessions; seems to keep the doctors entertained.' She wonders if she should ask about Josie's suicidal ideation, or if doing that would just remind her she felt that way. No, better not. She settles for 'Leigh was a bitch in women's group yesterday. She didn't even listen to you.' She's opened up the conversation, drawn a doorway if Josie wants to step through.

Josie just smokes in silence.

Cherry pulls her bare feet up onto the bed and crosses her legs. *Criss-cross applesauce*, Marian used to say, back when she was Mama, back before the cocaine and the shooting up and all that followed. 'I'll be honest, Josie. I'm a little worried.'

'About what?'

'About you.' And there, it's said, she's grabbed the risk out of the air and seized it and it's wriggling in her fingers and she looks hard into Josie's eyes, waiting.

Josie's hand shakes as she pulls the cigarette to her lips. The orange glow reddens as she inhales, softens as she blows out. 'You don't need to be.' And it's very sudden the way it happens, but in an instant Josie's face falls apart, sobs howl through her and she drops the cigarette onto the bed. Cherry grabs it and rests it in the ashtray, then takes Josie's hand and strokes it. But Josie shakes her away, pulls her knees to her chest, buries her face in her knees, and the sobs are softer now because she's hidden her face. Cherry wants to comfort her but doesn't know how and so she just waits.

It's a full three or four minutes that Josie cries and there's a break and then the sobs peal out of her again and strike the air in the room. Cherry shouldn't have pushed it, no no she shouldn't have asked, she'd make a lousy therapist, probably that was why she put herself here in the first place and damn, damn, damn she feels the urge to lift the cigarette from the ashtray and press it to her flesh until the skin reddens and then blackens and she's done it all wrong.

Finally the sobs slow down and Josie quiets but she won't look up from her knees, won't unwrap the arms that cling to her calves, interlaced with each other. Into the silence Cherry whispers, 'I'm sorry . . .'

Josie mumbles something.

'I'm sorry,' Cherry says again, 'I didn't hear you.'

Josie lifts her face from her knees for a moment to say, 'It's okay. This has been inside me for the last week; it's probably good for me to cry.' She drops her head to her knees again and begins to rock back and forth on the bed. Cherry scoots up to the headboard and slings an arm across her back, and this time Josie doesn't push her away. Cherry rubs her friend's back like she would if she was a little kid, and finally Josie lifts her head again and looks around and finds her cigarette half burned up in the ashtray. She grabs it and starts smoking again.

'Do you want to talk about it? Is it about being here?'

'I got taken away from all my friends to come here. I'm not even supposed to associate with them when I get out, if I ever get out. So what happens when I get out of here? They'll throw me back into the house with my mom and the same old shit's going to start again. The people here don't care if I get better anyway. They just want the money from my insurance. But if I stay here I'm damned between these walls that are caving in, crushing me. We're so wrapped up in here, the world's spun inside itself. If we weren't warped before we got in here, the experience of being here will warp us. It's like being in prison. I can't even go buy a pack of smokes myself, it's . . .'

And all the doubts Cherry had about coming here wash over her again. She came here because she was going out of control, because of that thing at Marshall Field's. She doesn't remember much beyond holding a knife to a cashier's throat, shouting, *Take her, God, take this whole motherfucking world!* Even though she didn't hurt anybody, obviously her past was creeping up inside her, following her, and now it's happening again. It's like Josie's monster; she can't outrun it. A shiver creeps over her skin, and for a moment her hand trembles on Josie's back. But she has to be strong, for Josie.

'There's no way out for me.' Josie's cigarette hovers over her wrist, and a hot ash flakes down and winks out against her skin. 'Getting out of here is worse than staying in.'

Cherry tries to say something helpful. 'Then maybe you still need to be here. I mean, isn't that why you're here? Because you can't handle things outside? That's why I'm here.'

She turns to face Cherry. 'Do you really think that being here's helping you?' Her pupils are so wide that only slender green crescents encircle them; it's the dark room but she looks like she's messed up on drugs.

Josie's is a question Cherry can't answer. The question almost doesn't matter for Cherry because for her it *is* about getting out, making it, landing on her feet, and she's determined but Josie's flailing. All Cherry can say is, 'You're better now than you were outside.'

'Do you know what happened that got my mom scared enough to send me here?'

Cherry shakes her head.

'I took a bunch of pills and woke up in the hospital. After I got well, on the outside I mean, she sent me here.'

Do you think you might do it again? Cherry wants to ask but doesn't. This is the safest place for Josie; here she can't get at much that will hurt her – Cherry doesn't think so anyway. 'A lot of people really care about you, Josie. I'm sorry you're feeling bad. Can I help at all?'

Josie leans her head on Cherry's shoulder. 'I wish someone could. But it's all over for me; the road's at an end. That's all right.'

Cherry doesn't like the way she's talking. Maybe if she talked to Josie's doctors . . . She needs to help this girl; she's so young and sounds so desperate.

If she can save Josie, she can save herself.

And she pulls Josie into her hug and says, 'Don't ever feel like it's the end of the road. You're just turning a corner.'

It sounds so stupid, she should write for fucking Hallmark. But Josie doesn't seem to care. She grabs Cherry's hand and squeezes it so tightly it hurts. They sit like that for a very long while, smoking, wisps drifting up toward the ceiling.

24
Amy

May, 1988
Holland High School

God, what if I'm an addict? floats across my mind as I'm chewing my sixth or seventh Xanax of the day. But that's stupid, only old ladies get addicted to prescription drugs. I'm chewing my little white miracles now because they hit me waaaay faster that way, but man, they taste awful. I pull my hair up from my neck and suck down some drinking-fountain water before the bell rings.

When I lift my head from the drinking fountain Rennie's standing there. 'Hey.'

'Hey.' I glance around to see if there are any teachers or student spies, but mostly it's quiet near the Ag Wing, which is why we meet here. When I look at Rennie these days I take some extra time because I know she's depressed about her abortion. I wouldn't judge her but the Pope says it's murder. Rennie's not Catholic or anything, but I wonder if that ever crosses her mind. Then again, what does some old Polish guy know about Amy Linnet, Rennie Taylor, Cherry Winters? I've got secrets I'll never tell Father O'Neill, secrets I keep even from my friends. For example, no one knows how much Xanax I'm taking, and what I'm thinking now is that I'm running through it so fast I'll ask Mary Sue for a bigger dose and then maybe I'll go see my regular doctor and ask him for a prescription too. I could work like that, alternating scripts, and then I'd have enough.

Rennie, like Mom and Dad and Mary Sue, thinks I'm taking Xanax when I'm feeling the urge to cut, what Mary Sue calls a 'panic attack'. They shouldn't put drugs like

Xanax in the hands of people like me. God, I love the stuff. Xanax is keeping me Amy Linnet these days. When I feel like I'm spinning near the edge I chew one or two and feel just fine, better than fine. So are my best friends still my best friends if they don't know that?

When I think about that too much it makes me realize that none of us really knows what's going on behind each other's eyes. Even when you think you're best friends with someone there's stuff you can never know.

Rennie's eyes today are blank, not sparkling, just kind of empty. But that's better than the hollow darkness I've seen most of this week. 'How was Paradise?' That's all I'll say in reference to Mr Schafer because we are at school, after all: loose lips sink ships.

'All right.'

'Is he okay with things?'

She shrugs.

I uncap my bottle. 'Do you want one? Calm you down.'

She shakes her head. 'I'm really sleepy these days. If I took one of those I'd probably collapse.'

Two or three Xanax in the morning on the way to school make me feel so relaxed and happy, almost drunk. Not blotto drunk where I forget everything (which has its appeal too) but just giddy, high. Best of all my relationship with Xanax is totally legal, even encouraged. I take a few more during the day and at least three when I'm on my way home to face Mom and Dad.

'Are we getting together tonight?' One thing I'd like to try is Xanax and vodka. Both are so great separately I can only imagine how numbing they'd be together. 'The liquor cabinet is stocked and open for business.'

'Sure.' She glances over her shoulder. 'McFadden sighting, better go.' And in a breath she's gone.

Damn, she has good eyesight. That *is* Pammie McFadden coming down the hall.

'Well, Amy Linnet, how *are* you?' breathes Pammie in a super-phony voice. She's pissed off at me because I told her if she didn't act like she was my friend in front of people and let me use her as an excuse, I'd spill the beans about the night last year when she got so drunk she fucked six guys from Sigma Nu the same night, one after the other. Something only I know about, something she trusts me with. I don't like Pammie anymore, but it would hurt me to do that to her. I don't think it was really her fault. Well, it was her fault for getting drunk but . . .

But nasty's the only way to go with Pammie and if she pushes me, I'll go there. 'I'm great, Pammie, looking forward to *going out to the movies* with you tonight. My mom may call.'

She wrinkles her nose. 'No problem, but I have better things to do and if she shows up at the movies I'm not gonna be there.'

'She won't.'

Her eyes narrow. 'So what's up with Rennie Taylor these days?'

'Who wants to know?'

'No one. I've just heard some stuff.'

My heart stops. Mr Schafer? 'What'd you hear?'

She smirks. 'That she can't lift weights for PE because she had *a medical procedure.*'

Oh shit, oh no. 'Where'd you . . . ?'

'Miss Miller has a really loud voice. Don't worry, though. I was the only one who heard.' She spreads her hands. 'Wish her the best, won't you? Oh, and don't expect any more favors after tonight. We're even now. I take it none of it will go any further than this.'

She's gone in a breath of perfume. God, should I tell Rennie she knows? My hand shakes as I open my pill bottle and slowly, deliberately, chew another Xanax.

The air hums alive and the evening's cresting. Lately the Xanax makes it kind of hard to drive because I keep getting sleepy and drifting toward the center line. It's a miracle I made it here at all. My ever-loving vodka's tucked away in my backpack and maybe Cherry'll bring some weed and I can do all kinds of messing around.

I think I'm getting better with the Xanax. I hardly ever feel like cutting anymore. Once I caught myself starting it and I just chewed up a couple Xanax and ran the hot water over my arm and I felt better. Tonight'll be fun. I love experimenting.

Oh, I'm not stupid. I know mixing alcohol and pills can fuck you up. That's why I haven't taken any Xanax since the one I chewed outside the Ag Wing after talking to Pammie. And I'm going to drink very slowly, no more than two per hour. I'll buy a bunch of orange juice out of the vending machine so I can mix up the vodka a little bit and drink it slower.

I don't think I'll tell the girls I'm trying this. Why worry them? Rennie's been through enough shit lately and something's bugging Cherry too. Or maybe she's just like me, way stressed out over Rennie and dealing with her own problems. God was I glad to leave our house tonight. When I left it wasn't even six and already Mom was nodding like it's hard to keep her neck straight, asking me questions that I've heard a million times before and answer patiently. (Did you study for finals? *I already took them.* When can we shop for your Prom dress? *Brandon's not into it, I'm probably not going.*) By tomorrow she'll have forgotten both her questions and my answers.

I pull open the door of the Student Union, shove some quarters in the vending machine and buy three orange juices, which I tuck into my bag. Just before I walk into the cafeteria I chew up four Xanax, wince, and slurp down some water from the drinking fountain.

Maybe Brandon and I will actually get it together tonight. We always seem to get too messed up to do anything. 'Hey guys!' I wave and walk over to them. Cherry's tucked up next to Sam but looks sad. Rennie's smoking a cigarette,

Kent's hand pressing hers on her lap. He's not a bad guy, kinda boring to me, but really smart, probably her type. I don't know why she doesn't tell Mr Schafer to take a hike and hook up with Kent instead.

I light a cigarette from the open pack on the table. 'Without further ado the alcohol has arrived. What did you bring, Cherry?'

She heaves a big sigh. 'Marian and I aren't getting along these days. She cut me off, trying to teach me a lesson I guess.'

And that's a real surprise because Cherry and Marian totally get along. I can't imagine a cooler mom than her; how great would it be to have a mom you could sit down and smoke a fatty with? But Cherry's gaze says not to pursue it, so I just say, 'Let us begone to the basement of the Psych Building, forsooth. Oh, don't look at me like that, Rennie, that was Shakespeare.'

She gives a flat smile and what *is* it with the Bitch Posse tonight? We're positively blah. Then I realize what I've said. Shakespeare reminds her of Rob Schafer.

Damn, we should all just get really fucked up tonight. 'Come on already.'

We pack up our stuff and head across the courtyard to the Psych Building where we'll all get drunk before we go our separate ways and hope to get laid. Well, all except Rennie. She's 'faithful' to her faithless Mr Schafer and she's not even supposed to have sex anyway for two weeks. I'm dying to ask her what he said about that. I sidle up to her as we're walking and whisper, 'How'd he take it? The no sex thing, the bleeding?'

She stares at me icily and says through clenched teeth, 'I don't want to talk about it.'

We all definitely need to get drunk. I wish I had more than just a fifth of vodka.

When we get there I gulp a little OJ from the top of the first bottle and dump in some Smirnoff. 'Amy Linnet mixing drinks? What, are you reformed now?' says Cherry.

I'm still not going to mention the Xanax. It doesn't take me long to swallow down what I would consider a double or maybe a triple vodka and I open up another juice. No one blinks, hee hee, they think I'm being *good* tonight, responsible Amy, hee hee. I mix my second screwdriver and slurp it down. In an instant warm water's rushing over my skin, and I feel amazingly, incredibly, unbe-fucking-lievably high and happy. I've never felt so good, not even on pot which is just a more relaxed and giggly what-the-hell-*ever!* kind of feeling.

Rennie's giving me a funny look. 'Amy. You're all red. What's up with that?'

I burst out laughing because she doesn't know, ha ha, I'm giddy and warm and happy and my knees have turned into jelly, this is great. 'I took some Xanax before I started drinking and oh, damn I feel good!'

Cherry and Rennie exchange a worried glance. Cherry says, 'How much, Amy? How many did you take?'

I burst out laughing.

Kent says, 'Get the booze away from her, now.'

And I'm feeling very silly and I pull the vodka and OJ away from his reaching hand and it splashes all over, wrecking my high, so I gulp down some more and the warm rush goes through my body again. 'I know what I'm doing, I'm drinking slow!' I'm slurring now, I can hear it, and everything, the air, my blood, my body's humming like crickets.

Rennie grabs my arm and Cherry grabs the other and Kent finally gets the OJ away from me. I'm pissed off but totally sleepy all of a sudden. Rennie and Cherry drag me against the wall and Rennie says, 'Damn it, Amy, what are you thinking? Where is your head?' Cherry whispers something to Rennie and she says, 'I don't know, I think so.'

Sam sits down beside me and lights a cigarette for me. 'Smoke, it'll kill some of the buzz.' I take a few smokes, but I'm awfully sleepy and everything's blurry and I can't hold onto the cigarette and it falls to the floor where someone takes it away and does something with it, I don't care. I lean against Sam.

His heart's beating into my back. Mmm, he's so cozy and warm, no wonder Cherry likes him so much.

I drift off into blackness.

25
Rennie

May, 2003
Highway 280, San Mateo County

Rennie's cheeks are burning, but she's zooming the green
Beetle toward Palo Alto anyway. The cookie-cutter stucco
homes of San Francisco's 19th Avenue streak by, and then
the mountains tower over Highway 280, a golden haze
suspended in the air over the city she's leaving behind.

As she passes the enormous statue of Father Junipero
Serra, guilt or something like it bounces through her. *This
is so fucked up, Rennie. What are you doing?* She squashes
down the thought, and anyway, she knows what she's doing
and why. To erase what happened with Paul and the message
she picked up from the San Francisco State professor, to erase
everything, all her shit.

This is what you might call a 'coping strategy'.

She's drunk with something even though she's stone cold
sober, weaving in and out of traffic, passing cars on the
right. The odometer's reading ninety and is pressing toward
ninety-five and Paul, Paul, she's maybe messed him up for
life.

But it's such a yummy memory, she'll let herself savor it
again, just for a second. She ran her fingers up and down his
arms, lifted her head to his, tucked her fingers behind his
neck, closed her eyes and pulled him toward her. His lips
brushed hers *right there in her classroom* and the danger and
sheer stupidity of it sent rushes of passion through her
and a panic of thoughts, *oh touch me, won't you touch me?*
And she clasped his fingers, pressed them to her breast, and
he squeezed her nipple, drawing it to a point for one perfect,
fantastic, amazing moment . . .

168

But then he stiffened and pushed her away. 'Ms Taylor, we can't, this is wrong, I can't, I'm sorry.' He turned and walked away and this is where the memory sours. He'll never, never speak to her again, and all the good work she's done for him, it's all nothing because he can never trust her again, never see her the same way. She'll have to face him in senior lit day after day after day until graduation, and she'll never be able to look at him the same way either.

At that moment she felt so fucking embarrassed and high, coasting on anxiety, she couldn't get out of her classroom fast enough. Of course she was going to solve it how she always does. As she backed out of the school parking lot, she picked up her cell phone, punched in his number and said, 'It's Wren. I'm coming.' And Puck said, 'When you get here I'll be coming too. I can hardly wait; I'll chill some wine.'

Of course it's more than wine waiting for her there. She knows she'll be doing cocaine with him too and somehow it doesn't seem to matter. She just wants to blot everything out and erase Rennie Taylor the teacher-whore, the student-abusing rapist teacher-slut, and while Wren Taylor the coke-snorting washed-up writer doesn't sound much better, at least it's someone else. She'll get laid and messed up and then she'll feel better.

Maybe she's regressing or something. Back at Stanford she couldn't go through guys fast enough, and when she got rejected from the writing program, that's when she opted for the teaching credential at San Francisco State. Then she started edging toward naughtiness, pushing it farther, sex with student teachers, sex in random, public places, the Town Square in Mill Valley, the football field at Tam, under the Golden Gate Bridge at Fort Point, half-hoping to get caught. That was when all the knife stuff started, too.

Someone whales on the horn as she drives past the San Mateo Bridge exit. The haze thickens. *Rennie, you're thirty-two years old, too old to be acting this way.* Man, she's spiraling; how long has it been since she felt this low?

She knows when.

To press down the thought she turns on the alternative

music station. Something sad's happened to 'alternative' music since she was in high school. It all sounds the same now. She misses the old stuff, like The Pixies' 'Doolittle', one of the greatest albums ever made. No one makes stuff like that nowadays. But of course thinking that way just proves she's an old woman.

From the speakers bursts another one of those songs that's played so much it can hardly be called 'alternative' anymore. 'Bubblegum Punk', Bay calls it. As she zooms past a VW bus it comes to her with a thud. A good portion of the kids who are listening to this music weren't even *born* when all her high-school shit happened.

And the grown-ups they don't ever want to be like, are people like *her*.

At once she feels dreadfully, horribly, terribly old and she snaps off the music.

She speeds up more and in an instant she's pulling off in Palo Alto, driving past the Stanford campus (her old haunt – she spent many long nights there crying over Rob; the only thing that burned away his memory was sex with someone else. She hadn't made many friends and of course she wasn't in touch with Amy and Cherry by then, but she did get laid a whole bunch of times, and graduated with honors). A few more turns and she pulls onto Puck's street. He must be making a shitload of money off his books to afford to live here because the housing market's even worse than it is in Marin. In Palo Alto, especially the nicer parts like this street, shacks on postage-stamp lots are going for a million and up.

She pulls her Beetle into the driveway. In front of her windshield floats a swallowtail butterfly. It hovers for a moment, then like a knife blade cuts upward and out of sight.

Rennie slides out of her car and a magnet pulls her up the brick walk. Puck's house is a sweet yellow bungalow, the one she wishes she had. Hard little green fruits weigh down the branches of a plum tree that bends over a big front porch, and pale pink climbing roses cling to the freshly painted white columns. Obviously Puck has a hired gardener.

A black, speckled bird with a few spikes on its head perches on the porch rail. It's not a wren; those are brown. A sparrow? No. It's a starling. *I talk in a daze, I walk in a maze, I cannot get out, said the starling . . .*

Where the hell is that from? She searches her memory banks for books, plays, poems. Shakespeare, maybe? Rossetti? Who else are her favorites? Shit. Her mind is a blotto, blacked-out blank.

The starling flies away.

It doesn't matter. Nothing does.

She walks up the porch steps and presses the bell and for the first time she's thinking this might have been a mistake. But then Puck answers the door, and he's not even wearing a shirt, and his hair's falling across his face in that little fuck-me way he has about him, and she forgets everything she was thinking about. 'Wren, Wren, I thought you'd never be here. What made you change your mind?'

She slips inside and doesn't answer. The house is dark and smells of cigarettes. Two glasses of white wine sparkle on the dining room table, on either side of a crystal vase spilling with purplish roses. He says, 'You brought your book, I hope?'

There is no book, Rennie thinks but doesn't say. 'Actually, no, I was hoping we'd just have some fun.'

And this is the old Rennie, the saucy cheeky spicy sexy Rennie. She gives him a wink and he says, 'Girl after my own heart,' and hands her one of the glasses. 'Russian River Chardonnay, the best.' They clink and the wine disappears as they stare at each other over the rims. When they're finished, he goes to a drawer in the sideboard and pulls out a small beveled mirror, a couple of crisp fifty-dollar bills, and a razor. It clicks – that's why there were so many razors around Cherry's house: they were for her mom . . .

She feels like screaming at herself, *All that's behind you, Rennie! It's over!* And she hopes cocaine makes you forget stuff because she needs to forget her whole awful day, smash down her curiosity about whatever happened to Amy Linnet and Cherry Winters, her fuck-up with Paul, the voice mail from the San Francisco State professor: *Bayuni Henares has brought up some things to me that are very concerning . . .* Not only is it all over with her and Bay but now she's not a Master Teacher anymore.

Oh Lord and praise Jesus, he's gotten the cocaine from somewhere and is cutting lines. Rennie picks up one of the fifties and watches him do his first because she's never actually tried cocaine, mainly because of Marian and shit — there it is, her past popping out at her again, no matter how hard she's tried to tie it down. Puck closes his eyes and takes a long, slow draw, the sharp inhale piercing the silence. The powder disappears up the shaft of the rolled-up bill as he slides it along the mirror, and Rennie tries to memorize the process, step by step. When he looks up a tear blinks at the side of his eye and he rubs it away. 'Your turn, Wren.'

She leans over and snorts a line into each nostril. The texture's rougher than she expected, finely ground glass spiking her nasal passages in a million different spots. Her nostrils burn, the flames sear into her sinuses, *how strange, my nose is on fire*, but it's that good kind of hurt, the kind that quickens her heartbeat, forbidden glamour, gritty naughtiness, it's so unspeakably great, like a knife slicing across her belly, and a thrill twangs between her legs, *oh, I'm being so bad*. She holds her nose for a minute while her eyes tear up, then she swallows. *Jesus, it tastes like crap.*

The air sizzles and an ocean roars in her ears. She spins up into the sky like Dorothy in her funnel cloud, and just like that she's in Oz. Is it possible to feel your own pupils dilating? Everything's brighter, the roses are a million shades of purple, shades that have no names, subtleties of color no one knows about but her. The walls are breathing, Puck's chandelier glows with neon light, every part of her is ready to burst. Everything tingles, her arms her legs her neck her scalp, oh God, she has never felt this good. She can't wait to get her clothes off and jump into bed with him, and her hands are doing stuff she's not aware of apparently because she's already unbuttoned her blouse. He whistles. 'Man, Wren, you want it bad . . .'

The words are a slap but she ignores it. Instead she pulls him to her, kisses him, opens her mouth almost immediately. She's dizzy, in a racecar that's about to spin out, and something braces in her like panic, but she pushes it aside so she can speed into oblivion. The only thing that matters now is getting him into bed with her. She whispers in his ear, 'Bring the wine.'

Puck takes the bottle and the glasses from the table, leading her upstairs, the shiny crisp hardwood floors, the saturation of color on the walls, here plum, here beige, here green, and the bedroom's sea blue, perfect. He sets down the wine and grabs her ass in both hands, kissing her hard. As he leans her over the bed, he's peeling her blouse off her, swaying her, weighing her down until she falls onto the mattress. He seizes her wrists and presses them together over her head, landing a bite on her neck, an odd sort of bite that lingers long after his teeth leave her skin. She laughs, fights her wrists free and unhooks her bra. He envelops her breasts with his hands, skimming over them in intricate patterns he must have learned from somewhere because it's absolutely perfect. Even when he's moved his fingers away he's still touching her, phantom caresses that linger, intensify, bloom with heat. 'Oh . . .' she breathes. He presses his lips to her nipples and so strange, the kisses radiate outward from the spots he's touched until warmth has spread over each of her breasts.

'I told you we'd have fun . . .'

He slides off her pants, and the cool air on her skin shocks her, sending a ping of sensation through her whole body. Then he pulls off his own jeans and suggests a blow job, which is a little disappointing since he's not offering to reciprocate, but that's okay, it'll still be fun.

She gives him an extra nice one, slow until he wants it fast, with lots of lips and tongue. Heat radiates from the swirl of hair blossoming from his crotch and she's sweating in a jungle; rainforest insects buzz in the shadows. As she's speeding up and slamming down on him again and again and again, her nose starts to run and it's the most annoying thing you could imagine, this tiny drop clinging to her nostril, damn, fuck, damn, what to do, it's not like you can sniff it back when you're giving a blow job, so she just lets the drop fall onto him but he doesn't seem to care, pushing harder and faster and groaning, and she wraps her tongue around him and sucks even harder and more urgently, and everything doesn't matter at all anymore because it's all a haze of perceptions that are way too magnified, the inside of her mouth for example feels like someone's scrubbed it with a wire brush, and *hurry up, Puck, hurry up, this is getting boring, come on, I don't have many more tricks left,* and finally he comes with a shudder and whispers 'Aah, Wren, perfect.'

She swallows and runs a hand over her mouth. 'You're welcome.' She spreads her legs and he licks her belly and thighs and his tongue skates across her pussy, yes, oh please! She raises her hips and moans, closing her eyes as desire rips holes in her flesh. His mouth's leaving tracers of sensation everywhere and this is going to be so goddamn great, the best ever, yes, yes, God, yes! His tongue swirls everywhere, even places where it's not, she can't wait, she's in a dream, she's going to cry it's so good, oh this won't take long at all, not at all . . .

All of a sudden he stops, resting his head on her thigh.

She opens her eyes. 'What?'

'Wren, I'm so burned out. Let's just take a break and do this later.' Now she's annoyed. *This is what I came down here for?* And the coke makes it even worse because it's like she's standing at the wall behind the orgasm, and she wonders if she snorted more something great would happen. Who the fuck cares. 'Fine then, I'll be right back. She goes downstairs and sucks in some more cocaine, and yeah, she does feel better. But unfortunately when she comes up he's asleep, so she just downs the wine, turns on MTV, and pours herself another. It's too much, this wired feeling; she needs to be drunk.

Energy patters through her and it's very urgent that she walk all of a sudden, so she paces up and down the length of the bed. It's too goddamn hot in here. She opens a window and the cool evening breeze shuffles in, but that's even worse – she feels naked and fat and like a raw chicken with goosebumps all over her skin. When he wakes up stuff'll be better, when he wakes up he'll make her come.

She closes the window.

It's still too goddamn hot in here. She finishes her wine, watches the blur of images on MTV, and lets the music fuse into her body like hot lead.

She doesn't know how long she's like this, in his bed. They do fuck a few times although he never goes down on her as promised, and she walks by the refrigerator numerous times but doesn't eat, and day washes into night washes into day, and she's wired, high, cresting on the top for so long she's barely aware of what she's doing and how much time has passed, and once in a while he reaches for her nose and lets her sniff a bump right from his fingernail – he must have it stashed all over the house apparently – and again, again she spreads her legs, again, again he fucks her, then they sleep fitfully, and he presses some more cocaine into her nostrils from the web between his thumb and forefinger, grabs her head and inches it down his belly and she blows him again, she's dizzy, she's lost track of how many times, he comes and shudders and pulls away and rolls over and says nothing, and it doesn't matter that he won't eat her out, she'll feel better if she just has some more cocaine.

Where is it? Where? Where did he get it from? The bedside table is clean and neat and empty and out of the pages of *Architectural Fucking Digest*. Damn, shit, fuck. Not a grain of coke in sight. Of course Puck's sleeping now and damn it, there must be more downstairs, she needs some or she'll fall into a pit, she needs some more cocaine, now, downstairs, *right now*, downstairs, *as in this very minute*.

She floats into the dining room and cuts lines and sucks them in, rubs her nostrils shut like an expert. Then she walks back upstairs and since he's spent or asleep or passed out or in some kind of a stupor maybe she'll just get herself off, and after she goes to the bathroom she tries to make herself come but she can't break through the wall, damn, she is on the crest of orgasm all the time, it's fucking insane, and she glances in the mirror.

Her eyes are webbed with red. Blood trickles from her left nostril and dries to a crusty smear on her lips. Her sinuses are screaming like the worst infection she's ever had, and her eyes feel like someone's thrown gasoline in them. Bees have crawled inside her nose and are stinging away, and her hair's tangled, clotted, sticky. It's the middle of the fucking afternoon and she doesn't even know what fucking afternoon it is, and Rennie Taylor is wired on cocaine and just gave the millionth blow job of the weekend to a younger man she barely knows. She touches the stain on her lips. *I'm bleeding? Me?* And maybe she's fucked up her nostrils forever, maybe she'll have to go see her doctor, maybe she'll never breathe right again, maybe she's picked up some disease from him, maybe the burn and the stinging and the pain will never, never, never go away. *Oh my God.* A good old sobbing jag wells up deep inside her, but she's so dry and brittle that tears can't fight their way to the surface. *I'm so fucked up I can't even cry?*

Suddenly she's just so sick of herself. She walks back into the bedroom and says, 'Puck, I have to go.'

'What? No, stay.' He pushes her thighs apart, and hmm, *now* he's interested in pleasing her, but she just won't have any more of this, won't sink so low.

She pulls on the rest of her clothes. 'I'm sorry, Puck. I'm leaving.'

His eyes widen into a quizzical and hurt look, like a bassett hound's.

She won't fall for it and doesn't feel like explaining. 'E-mail me if you want. You have my address.'

'Your chapters, what about your chapters?'

'Fuck my chapters.' There are no chapters, Lisa hates them and now so does she. She should just quit writing; it's too fucking humiliating.

'Wren, what did I do?'

'Nothing.' She turns and won't look back or her whole world will turn into salt. She walks down the stairs to the living room and hurries by the mirror streaked with dusty residue, the crumpled bills still sitting out on the table. She pushes the door open and steps out into the afternoon sun.

Somehow California's too bright for someone like her. The sky's way too blue, and she's sure she'll go blind until several blinks send her vision back to normal. A warm breeze is blowing, and a bird's singing somewhere.

The only way she figures out it's Sunday is the fat newspaper sitting on his driveway. Dirty names for herself float through her head, and she's not altogether clear where she's headed, but she's getting the hell out of Palo Alto, that's for sure.

It's Half Moon Bay where she ends up, vaguely unfamiliar, perfect, someplace where nobody knows her. She kicks off her shoes and skates her feet through the white sand. The bay's like a crescent; of course the word 'Bay' upsets her but she won't think about that.

Almost no one is here: a family with an umbrella, a curly-haired woman with a dog, an older couple holding hands. It's the perfect peaceful place. She scoops up some sand and flings it into the water, watching it crash and disintegrate in the foam. The surfers are out, but the waves suck. They suck at surfing, too, because they keep missing the waves and getting caught under, and suddenly Rennie feels like tearing off all her clothes and swimming out in the freezing water until she's caught in a riptide and pulled out to sea.

But instead she decides to hunt for beach glass. She picks up green pebbles and blue pebbles and brown ones, bottle pieces worn smooth by the waves, and she hardly knows what she's after but she keeps picking them up and putting them in her pocket. She picks up a sharp one and starts to throw it back into the water so it can get worn down for someone else, but for some reason she pulls her arm back. As she studies the green shard in her palm an urge comes to her.

She sits on the wet sand and pulls the sharp glass over her skin until it hurts, does it again until petals of blood bubble up against the scratch she's made. She closes her eyes. Everything feels so clear; the horrible self-hating feelings are gone. The salt that must be clinging to the piece of glass stings into her wound as the sun hazes the sky over the Pacific. She cuts again in the glowing yellow dusk, as a wave rolls to shore and drops foam on the sand in front of her.

As long as the stars are fixed in the heavens and the fish sparkle in the sea. She was so strong then and so weak now; it doesn't make sense. Her eyes fall closed and she pictures her old friends, Amy and Cherry, just for a minute. And odd, she doesn't feel like crying anymore, doesn't feel quite so desperate anymore, feels at peace, just for now. Abruptly a thought falls into her head from nowhere and her eyes pop open.

Mallory!

Mallory and Max and Caleb, their two-year-old, are taking a taxi from the airport to Rennie's house in Mill Valley today. Rennie offered to pick them up but Mallory insisted – she likes to throw money around. Her flight was getting in at three, and Rennie told her sister she'd be at home when she got there, and they'd maybe walk to dinner at D'Angelo's because they like kids there and and and . . .

Oh, what a fuck-up she is. The door'll be locked and they'll bang on Beverly's, her landlady's door and that'll piss her off. She thinks Rennie's trouble, she probably wishes she hadn't rented her guest cottage to someone so fucked up, Beverly who trades stocks in the city and damn, Rennie, what are you doing?

She becomes aware of the blood smearing across her forearm, and it turns her stomach now. What the hell was she thinking? She's too smart, too old to act this way. She's acting like a teenager and fuck, why does she always do this? Cutting was over long ago, why start again? Why pull out those feelings again? And now that she remembers how good it is she'll never be able to stop. *Oh, please, let me stop* . . .

She throws the beach glass into the ocean and rubs the blood into her skin, shame flooding her. She walks back to where her sandals are, and cursing herself, jogs back to her car, opening the wound with her fingers and letting the hurt pulse through her.

You have to hurt if you want to feel anything at all . . .

26
Cherry

May, 1988
Holland, Illinois

Well, ladies and gentlemen, this is your morning anchor
Cherry Winters reporting on another frighteningly fucked-
up crack of dawn in Holland, Illinois. Wretchedly humid
with the thermometer already inching toward ninety and
the heat index way beyond that. At this very moment, the
Valedictorian of Holland High School, Miss Rennie Taylor, is
screwing our married Drama teacher. Homecoming Queen
Amy Linnet's spent a night fucked up on Xanax and vodka
and is now out cold on Sam Sterling's sofa. Juvenile Delin-
quent Cherry Winters is the only one who's responsible
these days and yes, she feels vaguely superior about that.

Last time I checked her, Amy was snoring happily, no
problem. But she scared me, damn it. After Sam and I drag-
ged her in here and dumped her on the sofa, I pulled his old
Army blanket over her and slid a pillow under her head.
Then I called her mom and dad and pretended to be
Pammie's mom, explaining that Amy was spending the
night. Fortunately Mrs Linnet seemed pretty wasted herself
so she didn't recognize my voice.

I pushed aside my anger at Sam in favor of some pretty
noisy sex and Amy didn't even stir. Guess that Xanax
knocks you out. It was one of those really delicious nights
where every time I woke up he woke up and we'd reach for
each other and we've just had sex for the third time. Now,
Sam's climbing off me and zipping over to get a smoke. Oh it
was perfect beautiful sex. Well, sure he slapped me around a
little bit, but just the way I like it. We haven't revisited that
thing with him punching me and it will never, never happen

again. He curls back into the pillow (the boring bed, I have come to realize, has its advantages, easy to fall asleep right after, no splinters in my bum), slides a cigarette into my mouth, and holds his under mine to light it.

And now is when I will deal with the shit that went on after Amy's drama. I inhale and blow out a flat stream. 'So, what was the deal with you and Amy last night?'

'What do you mean?' He whistles out some smoke. 'She was all fucked up.'

'Yeah, but grabbing your crotch. What was that all about?' I know she was fucked up but once she collapsed next to Sam, he tucked his arms around her (like a friend, I thought at the time), and Amy slid her fingers up his leg and grabbed him. And he pulled her jacket over his lap and just let her do it.

This is one of those times when I question why I'm with Sam at all, why I put up with his bullshit, and the only answer I have is that it's better than being alone. Which makes me so fucking pathetic and un-Bitch Posse-ish that I can't let that thought tug me any farther. Anyway, maybe he'll change. He could, people change, don't they?

'I don't think she even knew what she was doing.' He kisses my neck. 'I doubt she'll remember it.'

For now, he's the same old bad old Sam. He's totally talking sideways, missed the point completely. 'Why'd you pull her jacket over your lap?'

'I didn't, she did.'

Liar. 'You let her give you a hand job.' I smoke faster, angrier. 'She's my best friend. Why'd you let her do that?' And why, why did *I* let him do it? I'm such a fucking wimp.

He laughs. 'What are you talking about?'

'You know how fucked up she was. She'd never do that sober. I'm surprised Brandon didn't say something.' And why didn't I say something? Or Rennie? It was almost like we were in a dream-world; I couldn't believe it was happening. And, though I will never admit it, a tiny part of me is afraid of Sam's reactions. 'You should have moved her hand away instead of let her feel you up.'

He slides some more smoke from his mouth. 'You're making a big deal of nothing, Cherry. She was messed up, she won't remember it, who cares?'

Me. He's supposed to be my boyfriend. Amy's got an excuse; she was fucked up on pills and vodka. I pulled the prescription bottle out of her purse and read it while she was passed out. There was a whole shitload of warnings about drinking with Xanax, and I'm pretty sure she's setting herself up for some major trouble. 'She was totally off her face, Sam. You just don't do that shit to someone who's fucked up like that, especially when your girlfriend's sitting right there.' I hear my own words and realize they sound pretty dumb. 'Hell, Sam, you don't do that shit any time, under any circumstances.' A draft pulls up goosebumps on my arms, and I gather my clothes from the floor and start putting them on because this is as far as this conversation will go. I've made my point and we'll go on from here like we always do, because the relationship fits me like an old pair of shoes, and anyway, I wouldn't know how to act with someone who didn't need fixing.

'What're you so controlling for?'

'I'm not controlling.'

'Fuck you are.'

Where the hell's that come from? 'Fuck I'm not. Just drop it, Sam. Don't pull that shit anymore.'

I've just slipped my shirt over my head when he grabs my wrists, and his nails bite into my skin, hard. I shake him away, but next thing I know he pulls my hands behind my back and slams me into the wall. Lightning bolts shoot through my entire face. I yell, 'What the fuck?' and he smashes my face into the wall again. Blood trickles down and my mind turns off somehow.

I sniff in blood, and fuck, did he totally fucking fuck up my face? He grabs my hair and yanks. My scalp burns – he may very well pull all my hair out. Shit, Cherry Winters is getting the shit kicked out of her and shit, this just doesn't happen. Cherry Winters is as tough as nails.

I gather all my strength and twist my hands free. As I turn

around I can feel my lips bleeding. 'This is bullshit, Sam.' Are those tears streaming down my face? Cherry Winters doesn't cry. 'Fuck you.' And Amy, Amy, doesn't she hear? I knee him in the balls before he can think about it and he howls and doubles over. I dart under his arm and into the living room, where Amy's sitting up groggily. I know she doesn't know where she is or half of what happened last night. When she sees me, she goes, 'Cherry, oh my God . . .'

I grab her arm. 'Come on, Amy, now.' I pull her to her feet as Sam tears into the room. I hurl open the door to the hallway and drag Amy along.

'What, what happened, Cherry?' We're outside in the thick humid morning and she's rubbing her eyes. 'God, I feel like crap.' Then, she looks into my face. 'Cherry! Oh, my God. It looks even worse in the light. What'd he do?'

I'm humiliated that Amy sees me this way. 'Forget it, Amy. Come on, let's go.' And shit, my purse is in there in the bedroom and Amy's too. Fortunately my keys are in my pocket so I'll just leave my goddamn purse and drive without my license.

We jump into my truck. I start the engine and we pull out of the parking lot. I don't know where the hell we're going, but damned if I'm going home to Marian like this. I check myself in the rearview. It's not as bad as it felt at the time. My left eye's blackening and there's some blood by my nose that's already starting to clot over, but other than that I look okay. My nose still has its shape, and I can cover all this with makeup.

Amy's still annoyingly worried next to me. 'He fucking beat you up. I'll fucking kill him. Cherry, you should go to the police.'

'No, no, I don't deal with cops.' They're unreliable, absent, don't even know I exist.

You could say that cops are not a part of my life.

'I'm fine.' Despite my efforts to push them down, sobs tear out of me, blurring the road. I have to pull over, and fall into Amy's arms. I'm not usually like this; I don't need people.

She runs her fingers down my back and traces circles on my T-shirt. 'Cherry, be reasonable. Go to the cops.'

'No.'

She sighs, a breath fluttering against me, then lets me go and sits back. 'I can't make you.'

'My purse. And yours. They're back there.'

She shrugs. 'I'll get Brandon to get them. Drive without a license for a while. I can't drive anywhere but Mary Sue's anyway. I'll just say it was stolen at the movies which is where I was supposed to be with Pammie . . .' Then she realizes. 'Pammie! I was supposed to be home by one.'

'Don't worry, I called. I pretended to be Pammie's mom.'

She runs her finger over the bridge of my nose and gives a low whistle. 'First things first, let's take care of you. Come on, there's a Shell on the corner. I'll walk over and get some paper towels wet from the bathroom.'

She hops out of the truck and leaves me alone for a minute and funny, the tears have all sighed themselves out of me. I feel like an empty bottle. Why the fuck did Sam do that? What did I do? What did I say that was wrong?

Amy swings open the restroom door across the street.

No way can I go home after this. Marian is more fucked up than ever these days. Coke always made her paranoid and angry, but now that she's shooting it it's a harder high, harder for her to come down from without the shakes. Even buckets of pot don't help her. We're at a stage now where she's either begging me to do coke with her, or screaming at me and pulling down all the window shades and locking and bolting the door in the middle of the afternoon, on our little street. If she was beating me up or raping me I could report her to Child Protective Services, but what do I do about a cocaine habit when I can hardly function without drugs myself? And anyway, if I reported Marian, I'd lose her entirely, and then I'd have no one.

Amy returns with paper towels and a tube of makeup. 'No purse, I figured you'd want this. Palmed it on my way out.'

She's so smart, and her thoughtfulness touches me. 'Thanks, Aim.'

She washes my face with the towels, slow even strokes. 'Now, that looks a lot better.'

I look in the mirror and she's right. The blood's all come from one cut about half an inch long near the bridge of my nose. She hands me the makeup tube and I squirt some out and fix myself up. Not bad, not bad at all. 'I'm fine now. What about you – are you way hung over or what?'

'It was strange.' A worried expression crosses her face. 'I was having all this fun and then several hours are just blank. I have no idea how I got to Sam's, I don't remember anything beyond Kent taking away the second orange juice.'

Oh, here it comes. 'I was pretty sure you wouldn't remember all of it.'

'All of what? Fuck, Cherry, what did I do?'

Should I tell her? Ah, we're about nothing if not honesty. I draw in a long breath. 'You grabbed Sam's crotch. Then he pulled your jacket over his lap and I'm not sure what happened, but he let you do it. That's why I was pissed off at him, and that's where our fight started.'

Her expression's gone from worry to panic and she says, 'Oh, jeez Cherry, God, I'm sorry.'

'You had nothing to do with it. It's okay.'

'It's scary to be so fucked up you can't remember things.' She lowers her voice. 'It's not like us getting high together, that's like social. You just smoke a certain amount and then you don't feel like smoking anymore. Getting high's like having a few beers . . .'

And Amy never has just 'a few beers', she usually has half a bottle of vodka, but I won't mention that for now. 'You don't have to justify getting stoned to me.'

'. . . but the Xanax, I do this alone and I do more and more each time. I'm only supposed to take them once or twice a day but I take five, six at a time. Once I took ten. They make me feel so happy and relaxed. It's better than drinking, it is—'

Shit shit shit. 'So take the bottle and flush it all down the toilet.'

'Then I'll start cutting again. I'm sure I will.'

'Isn't there something else you can take? Tell your shrink they're not working?'

'So she can give me something stronger?' Tears roll down her cheek. 'What's that going to do? Please don't tell anyone, Cherry. It's embarrassing. Old ladies get hooked on prescription drugs. Anyway, I don't think I'm really hooked. Just forget what I told you, forget the whole thing. I'll stop doing it. I will.'

But it's stuck in my mind now, and I wonder if I wrote her shrink a letter telling her I'm worried, would the shrink blab to the Linnets that Amy and I are still seeing each other? 'Amy, if you can't give them up totally, at least promise me you'll stop drinking with them. I read your script bottle when you were passed out. You can die from doing what you did. Just don't do it anymore, Aim.'

'I feel dumber than Rennie,' Amy says. 'I could've told her months ago that Schafer was nothing but trouble.' Funny isn't it, we can see each other's problems so clearly. But she can't see herself jumping off the cliff.

Maybe I'm jumping off cliffs too. Guess I wouldn't know. One thing's for sure. I will never, never, never see Sam Sterling again. Unless he calls and offers me a big-ass apology, which he won't.

Fuck. I'm so sickeningly weak and disgusting.

I glance at Amy's hollow, tired eyes, and my heart aches with love for her. We both just need to escape. 'Let's go to the Porter Place. I'm not going home.'

The Porter Place is an abandoned farm on Route 12. The farmhouse burned down long ago, but the barn's still there, weathered red, with a hayloft, and a giant swing hanging from the ceiling. Kids have parties there and stuff. Once in a while kids will go there to have sex if they don't have anywhere else to go. But no one's ever there during the day, and it's the perfect place to hang. 'Too bad Rennie's not here,' says Amy. 'Did she go home last night?'

I nod. 'Wish I could call her, but her dad and Kelly are sharp. They'd know right away it was me, or you. Anyway, she's probably busy banging Rob Schafer today. His wife's out of town at an attorneys' convention.'

Amy rolls her eyes. 'I don't think she can do that yet; she must be blowing him instead.'

Ugh, that's nothing I want to picture.

'I thought after the clinic it'd fall apart on its own.'

I thought so too. Rennie's eyes are so sad and hollow and she's still kind of distant when she talks, like half her head is somewhere else. I want my friend back. I want Rob Schafer to give me my best friend back. 'Let's just us go then. I wish we had some stuff to get messed up with.'

And I reach into my pocket and slide out a blunt that I snagged off Sam's dresser last night. I normally don't steal drugs from my boyfriend, but I refuse to take the risk of buying myself, and besides, I'm flat broke. I just popped it into my pocket. 'Courtesy of Sam Sterling,' and I laugh. 'He owes me that at least.'

'You are ballsy, sister. Let's save it till we get there – oh, you're so great!'

I start the truck again and we head for freedom.

27
Amy

Amy flings a sweater into her suitcase. This is the worst packing job she's ever done. The suitcase is a mess of jeans and flannel shirts that are the uniform of the Soo but won't look right wherever she's going. She's thrown in her hiking boots and sunscreen and shampoo and a couple of chick-lit novels she ordered from Amazon a few weeks back, the second Bridget Jones that she hasn't yet stumbled through, something else with a woman with bright red lips and a great big beautiful martini on the cover. Lately she's found it hard to pay attention to these kinds of books – she guesses they're just an escape like so much else in her life. Some things she's taken along for no reason: chunky jewelry she never wears, her collection of smooth rocks from the beaches of Lake Superior. All swirls in a massive pool in the bottom of her suitcase, a pool that beckons, *Drown yourself, Amy, in the sea of your life.* She slides in her laptop, too, and rumples some clothes around it.

At the very top of all her stuff she places The Bitch Goddess Notebook.

Scotty's in full support of her decision. It's no surprise to him; she thinks he's seen it coming. He didn't want to be here for the packing and the actual leaving, and she supposes that once she gets to wherever she's going she'll give him a call and find out if the house has sold. They'll go through the paperwork of the divorce very peaceably – she doesn't hate him and doesn't want to hurt him. She just needs to make a shift in her life and she knows he does too. When she told him, he looked a little sad but resigned and said simply, 'I'm so sorry, Amy, I wish . . .' At that moment he probably figured nothing he could say would changes her mind and he interrupted himself. 'I understand. I hope we can do this with a minimum of conflict.'

It was at that instant that her heart split in two. She wanted to sink into his arms and have him comfort her, run his hands over her hair like he used to do, way back in college when she felt sad. But this is the one thing they can't comfort each other about. They've both taken so many steps back they can never be that close again. Divorce, even when peaceful like hers and Scotty's, is a lonely endeavor.

She zips the suitcase and glances in the mirror. There's a crease in her forehead that wasn't there before Lucky, the wrinkles around her eyes are etched deep, and heavy lines frame her mouth. Dark circles shadow her eyes. Scotty's face, too, is lately so much furrowed with worry and regret he looks much older than thirty-five. Streaks of gray are even appearing near his temples. She feels an affection for him like the page of a picture book she had when she was little, something she's outgrown but knows is still beautiful. When she feels best about it, she thinks that maybe this new start for him will show him a doorway to happiness. They'll never find it with each other, but as their wounds heal perhaps they'll both find someone, be able to put the puzzle pieces of their lives together in a different way.

When she feels worst about it, Scotty's affair smacks her in the face, and she aches to tear his heart out and stomp on it, and she wonders if it wasn't something she did, or didn't do.

And that's when anger boils up in her and threatens to overflow into a great big old crying jag, but she can't afford that, not now, so she gulps and pinches her cheeks, hard, until she feels cold and hard and indifferent again, and that's the only way to feel, anyway.

Now there's nothing left to do except grab the keys to the 4Runner, which Scotty said was hers to take. But a pang of guilt winds through her, and she stops at the chalkboard they used to use for copying out Neruda poems to each other, scrawling 'ScottyandAmy,' drawing little hearts and birds.

Dear Scotty,
I'm sorry it all ended this way. 'Puedo escribir los versos más tristes esta noche. Tonight I can write the saddest lines.' I don't think I have to tell you where that's from. Please know I want only the best for you. I did love you, more than you'll ever know.
Amy.

If she didn't feel so old she'd sob like a baby. She touches the locket around her neck. It clicks against the cross she tried to give back to Catey, and annoyance flashes through her. Prayer doesn't work, see, Catey?

Sorry, that number is no longer in service.

But Catey's such a sweetheart Amy'd never question her. She only said thank you and kept the chain around her neck. Catey insisted several times that Amy write to her when she gets to wherever she's going, to call, even, while she's on the road. Inside the locket curls a swatch of Lucky's chocolate brown hair, woven together with some of Callie's that she's kept in her dresser drawer since she was a teenager. Scotty keeps his in a leather box on his bureau. She supposes they'll both hold onto those things forever; it's just not something you ever get rid of. So no matter where they are they'll be linked by these few strands of hair.

Amy knows she's thinking too much. When she gets this way she usually opens up some vodka but she can't today, she has a long, long drive in front of her. She walks past the liquor cabinet and out the front door one last time, closes it one last time. The For Sale sign swings in the Soo spring breeze, and amazingly, a monarch butterfly dances around it, a flame burning like a miracle into a time and place too early and chilly to contain it. She'll hate to leave this lovely town teetering on the edge of Canada, this simple place without illusions, the river, the locks, the rocks from the beaches, the granite, the white quartz, even the ugly awkward roller coaster of the International Bridge. Amy's own Sault Sainte Marie, the place no one knows about, her refuge.

She'll miss it.

And though she knows it's best, she'll miss Scotty too, more than any of the rest of it; and now she's getting maudlin again.

She hurls the suitcase into the back of the 4Runner and gets in and starts up the engine. As she shifts into reverse, she throws in a Siouxsie and the Banshees CD that Scotty always hated because she can't bear to listen to anything they listened to together. 'Peek-a-Boo' shrieks through the speakers so loud that her ears tingle, and she lets the music stab into her. Nothing means anything at all.

She tears out of the driveway with a recklessness that surprises her and she doesn't know where she'll end up, but it won't be here.

Hours later she finds herself on Highway 80-West, that great stretch of asphalt that bisects the country. She's curled her way through Michigan and down toward Toledo, where she picked up 80. At that point she didn't need her map anymore and she unrolled the window, flung it outside, and laughed as it whipped behind her in the rearview to land on the side of the highway.

Now evening's fallen and she's heading through Illinois of all godforsaken places. The state makes her paranoid – the flatness that goes on forever, the dizzying cornfields that stretch on and on, the way you can see the horizon miles away and it all looks just the same as what you left. She rolls down the windows for a moment, but it's ugly and humid and the air is barely breathable, thick, wet. These are the days she hated in Holland, and she must get out of here, quickly.

She floors it, zipping by cars. Out of the blue she feels like smoking a cigarette, even though she gave that up in college. Shit makes no sense anymore, may as well try for lung cancer. At least it'd be interesting, and maybe she'd even learn something from it, who the hell knows? She needs to join the fucking Bitch Posse again. Jesus, why is everyone in her life so fucking distant these days? Where'd she fuck up to make that happen? She'll never have real friends again but if she smokes maybe she'll pull back some of that old strength, that old certainty. Maybe she'll be the Uber-Bitch-Goddess again, the Amy who can tackle the world, oh yeah.

She pulls off at a rest stop, buys herself a pack of Marlboros, and gets back in the car. She lights up as she merges into traffic, and as the smoke creeps into her lungs she starts to cough, oh God, it's like the first time she ever smoked. The nicotine rushes to her head, and she feels a little nauseated. God, it's been years, and that word echoes in her head: *years*.

And unfortunately even though she's hundreds of miles away from the Soo she can't get Lucky out of her mind. It was stupid to think she could ever make things better, and she's beginning to think there was no way out after all. Staying with Scotty would've been torture, day after day having to look into each other's eyes and remember the baby they lost. But this doesn't feel like freedom, she just feels alone. She smokes the rest of the cigarette quickly, stubs it out in the ashtray and speeds up again. As she approaches a green highway sign, she realizes she needs to stop and sleep somewhere. But goddamn if she'll stop in Illinois. *Des Moines, 205 Miles.*

Des Moines, Iowa. Perhaps that's where she'll end up. She can't imagine a more desolate place. The Midwest is so flat and empty and lonely, just like Amy herself. Why the hell didn't she go the other direction, towards New York, Manhattan, where she could be anonymous in the massive clot of people? New York City, the center of the goddamn fucking universe. New York City, the only place that really fucking matters.

If Amy lived there, maybe she'd matter too.

Or not.

It's all so crazy. Why is she in the Midwest again? Why? Why? Why? All that's here in Illinois is death; her past is like a sore that won't ever heal, memories are spurting at her like blood and she can't close the wound. Cutting, cutting, cutting – she hasn't thought for a long time of how good that feels.

Her vision blurs, and she veers into the next lane by mistake. A car blasts on its horn and she looks in the rear-view to notice an old VW bug swerving onto the shoulder to avoid rear-ending her. *Shit, shit Amy, that was close.* Her heart's pounding now and she's adrenaline-pumped. She's either got to drive really fast or pull off and buy some vodka and down it and sleep that way.

Barely conscious of what she's doing, she moves one hand off the steering wheel and onto the soft skin of her forearm. Her nails pop through easily, and in an instant lucidity spins into her and she feels calm again, centered, herself. She takes some deep breaths, lets up on the gas a little, reads the highway sign. Beyond Des Moines is a place called Omaha, Nebraska, and she'll find her way somewhere. *It's all right, Amy.* She presses her hand to her locket. *It'll all be all right. You did the right thing.*

28
Rennie

May, 1988
Hampton, Illinois

Whispers of smoke curl through the air in the motel room —
yeah, I've resigned myself to the fact that's it's a motel. Rob
decided we had to come here instead of his house, even
though Dawn's out of town, because the neighbors might
talk and that wouldn't be good. So once again I don't get to
see the beautiful sleigh bed he talks about fucking me for
afternoons at a time on, once again I don't get to have him
cook me a meal in his granite-tiled gourmet kitchen Dawn's
salary paid for, no, none of that for Rennie Taylor.

We got Chinese take-out for dinner, something with
shrimp and another thing with shiny pink pork and
clumpy rice. It's all cold and we're eating right out of the
containers. Well, Rob is. I'm done. I couldn't eat much, and
that's my cigarette the smoke is tumbling from. It's funny
how we talk so little now — it's all about the sex. Our charming little conversations from early on, the philosophical
discussions (Do you think we knew each other in a past
life? Do you believe in God?) have tripped into nothingness.
Kind of freaky, being in a relationship that's all about getting
laid. Like being on a boat going nowhere, with no oars, no
compass.

I can't think about it much.

The pork glistens from the end of the plastic fork on its
way to Rob's mouth and he opens it and shoves in the food
and closes it and chews. Eating is a disgusting act when you
think about it. Ingesting. Destroying. Digesting. Ugh. All I
could force down was a few spoonfuls of soggy rice. Lately I

seem to be getting most of my calories from wine. I just can't eat.

We've blocked out this Saturday to be together. Rob told Dawn he was in Springfield at a teacher training institute. I got out of babysitting Little Miss Mallory by telling Dad and Kelly I was going to a day of lectures and workshops at the college on People and Politics in the Post-Reagan Era. It sounded just like something the old Rennie would do and they bought it, hook line and sinker. Last night Amy got way fucked up, and Cherry took her to sleep over at Sam's. I'm pretty worried about Amy, to tell you the God's honest truth. She popped a handful of pills and sucked down some vodka and before she passed out with her hand in Sam's crotch (and Cherry, smart-assed Cherry said *nothing*) she promised she was never going to do that again. But I know she probably will. One thing about Amy, she's not good at hiding things, and it was soooo obvious she was rattling her pill bottle all night. Two vodkas later she was toasted. Now if you knew how much it usually takes to get Amy drunk you'd know something was up. I have to wonder if she's not coasting to the edge on purpose, seeing how far she can go without totally losing control of things. Such as her life.

Rob's packing up the Chinese food. Is he planning to take it home tonight, warm it up in the microwave, eat it in front of the TV with Dawn? How's he going to explain boxes of Chinese food coming from a teacher training in Springfield? He folds the lids down neatly and places the boxes on the dresser. Smiling, he shows me two bottles of wine. 'Cabernet, or Pinot Noir?'

Like it really makes a fucking difference. 'You pick.'

He chooses one and opens it. He's made a fuss for some reason; from his briefcase he pulls two wine glasses and pours us each a glass. 'Cheers.'

It's two weeks to the day since I've had my abortion and I know he's been keeping track of it because he says, 'Today's the day, right, your self-imposed celibacy can end?'

I swallow some of the wine. 'Doctor-imposed.'

The word 'doctor' seems to throw him and he drinks

faster, his Adam's apple bobbing in his throat. His jaw line is a little bristly with those hairs so dark they're almost blue. He notices my empty glass and pours some more, red liquid sparkling like a jewel. I'm glad he's brought two bottles because I'm feeling down and I'll probably want to drink them.

He puts on the radio to a boring station that's playing John Cougar Mellencamp, the closest thing to decent music we get out here. But I can't stand hearing about how great the Midwest is when I know it's one big lie. 'I hate shit that makes living in a small town sound like the greatest thing on earth.' The heartland, what a joke. There's no heart in the heartland. She's been raped and had the life sucked out of her; she's become a bitter old woman.

He laughs. 'Do you really think it's different anywhere else?'

And Mellencamp sings endlessly about his fucking small town in that fucking Midwestern twang that I'll do anything to get out of my voice, for-fucking-ever.

My throat gets thick. Damn it, I'll drive to San Francisco and jump off the Golden Gate Bridge before I die here. 'Maybe you weren't listening. This is shit music, can we put on something else?'

'I thought you liked Mellencamp.'

And I do and I don't. It's some kind of masochism probably, but Rob's pissing me off and I don't feel like explaining. 'Get real. The Bible Belt's not going to save my soul or yours or anyone else's.' I twist the dial around for something else and of course, there is nothing else, why would there be? We're in the middle of a fucking cornfield, nothing here but country and western and crappy top forty hits. I wish we had a boom box or something because I twirl and twirl and twirl the dial and every station's playing the same damn song. I snap the radio off and we stare at each other in the silence.

Things have gotten so uncomfortable, and we drink and smoke and finally start kissing. He pulls my Cure T-shirt over my head and runs his fingers up my belly. Last time since I couldn't have sex all we did was drink and watch 9 ½ *Weeks* on the motel cable (goodness there's a lot about sex I didn't know before), and he talked me into giving him a blow job, which like a lot of things I can now say I have done.

Blow job. Sex. Abortion.

Racking up experiences.

He hasn't seen me naked for a while, and he breaks the silence with, 'You're still so beautiful.'

Still? 'Post-abortion, you mean? You thought I'd look different maybe? My hair would turn to snakes? I'd have 666 written across my tits?' I'm trying to be funny but it comes out as sarcasm.

He blushes. 'I didn't mean that. I don't know what I meant.' His fingers skate over my hips, tracing figure eights, over and over, the same figure eight each time, the same pattern. 'You've lost weight, haven't you?'

It's true, I've dropped about five pounds in the last two weeks. Ninety pounds is what the scale said this morning, and on my five-foot frame I know it shows. But I like being skinny, the long whalebones of my ribs showing. If I press I can see the shape of my liver, my stomach, my ovaries. I like being so thin I could break. 'Just a few pounds, not on purpose.' I'm not anorexic or anything. It's just that I can't eat anymore, and I remind myself to drink more wine just to send some calories to my body.

He runs his fingers along my ribs. It tickles and I laugh and that breaks the tension. As he presses his lips on mine it all feels good again. Maybe we are in love after all, maybe something can come of this; he's said he loves me. And he breathes it into my ear again, 'Rennie, I love you, I love you, I love you . . .'

I wonder if I should tell him I love him too and stop playing the stoic, the strong one, like Cherry. Whenever I'm not sure of myself I think of what Cherry would do. Now he's biting my earlobe, slipping his hands down my pants and pulling them off, and it's that fast hot passion I can't control. I pull off his clothes too and suddenly it's those sticky sweet sounds, those kisses and tugs and little moans. Rolling over, I press him onto the pillows and draw my tongue down the hair that runs along his breastbone and past his navel and all of a sudden I'm doing things I wouldn't have imagined I'd do just a few months ago. I cup the plums of his balls, slide my lips over him. I want to suck the very life out of him, drain him, strengthen myself and forget all the stupid shit about the real world. As I'm blowing my married Drama teacher who got me pregnant and threw money at me to get an abortion (*shut up Rennie, just shut up, shut up*) my favorite poet Christina Rossetti bursts into my mind. I fill my head with her words to blank out my own stupid thoughts. A few lines from 'Goblin Market' echo in my brain as Rob's fingers shift through my hair, pulling me toward his warmth, for him, for him, for him, oh, I'll do anything to keep him, anything.

> *Then suck'd their fruit globes fair or red:*
> *Sweeter than honey from the rock,*
> *Stronger than man-rejoicing wine,*
> *Clearer than water flow'd that juice;*
> *She never tasted such before,*
> *How should it cloy with length of use?*

I'll do whatever he wants me to. I just want to forget, forget the reality of our relationship, Dawn and Stanford and the baby I'm not going to have and all that shit. I press those thoughts away, all thoughts away, with my tongue and teeth and lips that work around him.

> *She suck'd and suck'd and suck'd the more,*
> *Fruits which that unknown orchard bore,*
> *She suck'd until her lips were sore . . .*

Oh God, did Christina know what she was writing? The body's a remarkable anesthetic – my mind numbs out and all I can think of is Christina in her long black dress stalking to the center of the room to defend poetry, saying *I am Christina Rossetti.*

I am, I am, I am, I am, Christina Rossetti.

He arches toward me and trembles and comes and I drink, drink, but at the end I'm still so thirsty, and I climb back up and start kissing his face but he says, 'Rennie, I have nothing left, you've taken it all.' So I grab his fingers and push them inside of me and rock against him, and that's it, I don't have to think, just to feel. In a moment electricity flashes through my body and I'm enchanted.

I press my face into his sweaty salty neck and he holds me there. We lie that way for a while and then I slide off him and nestle into the brush of hair under his right arm, the little secret Rob spot that smells of animals and sex and danger. I feel like crying, and I'm still so thirsty. I'm going to say it, it's the last thing I can do because I want him want him want him, he's mine, and I say, 'I love you.'

He squeezes my shoulder for a minute, a little too hard. Then he turns his face to the side and says, 'Goddamn it.'

It's not the answer I expected and I sit up, pull a cigarette from the table. 'Did you hear me? So, you love me, I love you, we're in love.'

He sits up too but won't look at me, runs his fingers through his hair. 'Oh, Rennie, it's gotten so complicated. I hoped you wouldn't get wrapped up this way.'

'What? You told me you loved me. I can't tell you?' I'm panicking now, my guts are spinning through me, curling inside themselves. Maybe I'll even be sick.

He snaps a cigarette from the pack and lights it. 'I guess now's as good a time as any to tell you.'

'Tell me what?'

He whistles out some smoke. It streams from his mouth in one perfect line, a knife blade. 'Dawn's pregnant.'

She's going to have a baby?

That was supposed to be *my* baby.

'So we're going to have to stop seeing each other.'

'But . . .' But we're in love. You said we'd get married

someday, after Stanford and I had time to grow. Tears spring to my eyes.

'I need to pull things together, Rennie. It's been a good time, and I think you've enjoyed it too. I'm sorry to see it end, but it's just not in the cards.'

My tears coil up inside my eyes and harden and I will never let them slip out again. 'Why'd you let me give you a blow job before telling me that? Were you going to tell me this all along?'

He won't look at me, still.

I have never felt this much anger, bubbling steaming like a pool of blood inside me. I feel betrayed at a spiritual level. 'And you said you loved me? Didn't you have any compunction about whispering that in my ear knowing full well you were going to dump me?'

'Don't say it like that.' He reaches for my arm but I shake his hand away. He sighs. 'You know I love you, but things have gotten too complicated. You've gotten too involved emotionally and it's dangerous, Rennie. I can't lose Dawn now that she's going to have our baby.'

Our baby.

I hope she has a miscarriage.

I pull on my clothes, tears clinging just behind my eyes. I will not cry in front of him. I should slap his fucking face.

He just stares into nowhere. The two glasses of Pinot Noir or whatever he poured are glaring at me from the table. I stub out my cigarette, pick them up, one in each hand, and throw them into the wall. Ten million shards crash to the floor, and the wine trickles down the wallpaper, red red red.

I wish they were pieces of his heart. I hate him. I will never hate anyone as much as I hate him right here and right now.

'Rennie . . . I'm so sorry . . .'

I grab my purse and keys. 'Fuck you.'

He stands up, tries to follow me.

I slam the door in his face. I want something, anything to

fill the emptiness inside me, the hunger I can't indulge, the big lonely spot that's growing ever larger. Christina's words tumble through me:

> *When I am dead, my dearest,*
> *Sing no sad songs for me.*

I start the car and I have no the fuck idea where I'm headed.

29
Cherry

May, 2003
Freemont Psychiatric Hospital
Freemont, Illinois

Cherry lights a cigarette and blows out the smoke, alone in her and Josie's room, where she's retreated for the afternoon to try to write some poetry. If the poetry doesn't work out there's always the tapestry. Her project's coming to an end, and now she's filling in the red, green, and blue triangles with a royal purple background, a special yarn with some silver and gold mixed in. It's going to be terrific, but today she'd rather write.

Josie's gotten permission to walk around the grounds of the hospital, a bench pass they call it, and even though her mom's stood her up, Josie's taking advantage of the ticket out. Her mom sounds more and more like Marian all the time. It was almost a relief when Ms Mainliner OD'd. Just as Cherry had predicted, rigging coke turned into shooting smack turned into a death sentence in a motel room in Las Vegas. The news stabbed Cherry in the stomach two years ago, and maybe she should be sadder about it, but mostly she's pissed. Anyway, she was an orphan all along, wasn't she?

Josie's so lucky to have that bench pass. There are lovely grounds here, several acres, and woods. A pang of loneliness shoots through Cherry, even though it's good for Josie to get out.

She felt a stammer of hesitation knowing of Josie's recent suicidal thoughts, but she put a bug in the ear of every hospital person she could think of, and Josie, when Cherry asked her last night, said vaguely, 'No, I don't think of that anymore. I'm doing just fine.'

I always was good at therapy. Cherry presses open her spiralbound notebook. What is there to do here but write, smoke, complain? She'll write a poem for Josie, give it to her tonight after dinner, after Josie's enjoyed her nature wanderings and hopefully been healed by the environment. Cherry's had a few bench passes lately even though no one visits her either, and it's fun to follow the twisting winding paths through the woods, listen to the birds chirp, smell the flowers, touch the tree bark and just be amazed that all of this was created somehow, brought to earth and living. And to realize she's living too, part of it all, and all that surrounds her is beautiful so that means she is beautiful too. That thought makes her happy even in the memory, and she reminds herself to work extra hard for a bench pass.

She doesn't think about publishing her work anymore, sending it out, competing with the stellar Wren Taylor, only now she catches herself thinking about it and says aloud, 'Fuck the publishing industry.' Her stuff's not about that, anyway, getting attention or positive pats from people, six-figure advances, literary awards. No, Cherry Winters' stuff is just for her, just to work shit out, real stuff. She uncaps her pen.

In the Forest's Pale Light
For Josie

Your smile
gleams fresh as a fern
growing tall in shade.

Strong stalk, backbone
supports fronds. Like feathers
on a bird's wing, your leaves shelter
toadstools. In this damp forest,
your green light
shines like elfin hair.

Damn. She still can't get rid of that nagging suspicion that something isn't right with Josie. She flips her notebook over.

An envelope's taped to the back, something she never noticed before. She opened her notebook just this morning so the envelope's definitely new. On it's written CHERRY.

In Josie's writing.

Her heart thumps, and she sets down her cigarette and tears open the envelope with shaking fingers.

Hey Cherry,
    You're a fantastic woman and you've taught me a lot over these last few months. I'm getting rid of a few things cuz I don't have enough space in my dresser and I want you to have this.
    Love you,
    Your Josie.

So it's not a suicide note or anything horrible like that, thank God. Josie's face is fixed in her mind, hair a seashell swirl, chin resting on her clasped hands, small smile with the sad eyes of a doe. With that pale sequined dress, she would have been Diana.

Cherry reaches into the envelope and pulls out a small Ziploc. Inside the plastic sparkles Josie's diamond tennis bracelet, the one her mom gave her when she turned thirteen, which as Cherry knows is the year Josie started shooting junk.

Oh . . . she can't really mean for Cherry to have this. Surely it's worth at least several hundred dollars. It's a nice gesture but an erratic one, completely typical of Josie. When she comes back from her walk Cherry'll set her straight, hand the thing back to her, and if Josie really insists, she'll let her give her something else, something small.

Cherry slips the bracelet back inside the plastic bag and for some reason the terror feelings gnaw at her again. Then it hits her.

Yeah, Josie's erratic, but you don't get rid of a diamond tennis bracelet if you're trying to clear out your dresser. A sweater maybe, even a leather jacket. But a bracelet?

Takes up hardly any room at all.

'Shit.' She drops everything onto the bed and pulls on her coat.

Downstairs, she burst into the hallway and past the lobby to the front door. 'Let me outside!' she screams.

Leigh, who's appeared from somewhere, holds her, grasps her wrist, twists it.

'Goddamn it, let me outside!'

'Cherry Winters. This is completely against protocol, as you well know.' She clicks her tongue. 'And you were doing so well, too. A shame.'

Anger swells in Cherry. 'Josie Chapman is out there!'

'Of course, Josie's earned a bench pass. Something you, sadly, are far away from.' Leigh's still holding her wrist. 'Now are we ready to calm down, or do we need to take measures?'

And measures are things like what happened to Michael back in March, being put into the quiet room by yourself. Cherry's been there a few times, a green room with a teensy little mattress and some bullshit mural of rolling hills and still waters and nothing in there but yourself and your thoughts. She shakes off Leigh's fingers. 'She's going to hurt herself, I know she is!'

Leigh raises an impossible eyebrow. 'Just what makes you think that?'

'She gave me a diamond tennis bracelet. Said she was cleaning stuff out.' The frustration is a suction valve around her heart. Goddamn it, the staff are insane; that's why this place is so bad. If she and Josie and Michael and Susan ran the place it'd make sense. At least there'd be people in charge who understood hurting, who didn't assume that friendships and love and high emotion were bad things, to be numbed, drugged away.

'Josie's been doing quite well over time. She's on some of the latest meds. Her doctor wouldn't have approved the pass if he didn't feel she was safe. Anyway, what's there for her to get into trouble with? Just the woods and the clean outside air.' Leigh's upper lip beads with sweat. 'I wouldn't worry.'

'Aren't you listening? She's been talking about how much she hurts for so long! Are you people stupid?'

'Cherry, that kind of attitude won't get you anywhere. I think it's time for a little break for you.'

No, no. She won't let them put her in a room because they don't want to hear what she's saying. 'She is in all likelihood out there trying to kill herself. And you, all you can do is scold me for my attitude. *Listen to me*. She wrote me a note.'

'Let me see it.'

'I don't have it with me.'

'What did it say?'

'That she was cleaning out her drawer because she was running out of room.'

Leigh shrugs. 'It sounds perfectly natural to me. Cherry, I think you're overreacting. You're not getting good sleep. Have you been taking your Carbitral? Or hiding them?'

And that's a stab – Leigh knows that Cherry hates taking downers, especially after Amy, though Carbitral's been pre-scribed and insisted on so Cherry can get 'a good night's sleep'. The fucking stuff's probably why she has such fucked-up dreams. She just shifts back to the real subject. 'A diamond bracelet takes up hardly any room. She wouldn't have given it away, she would've given away something that took up a lot of space. Damn it, listen!'

Leigh sighs. 'It's highly irregular and we don't normally respond to this kind of coercion from patients. But we'll send someone to look for her.'

That's the best Cherry can do. She sinks into a chair until Leigh leads her to the lounge and she stares, catatonic, at MTV forever, and hardly notices Michael rubbing circles on her back.

She leans into him; there isn't anyone else. At least he understands what it is to be *here* and if she wasn't so worried about Josie she might try to understand him. But for now she just lets him trace patterns on her back, light her cigarette, lift it from her lips for her, nestling his goatee bearded chin into her hair.

He whispers 'I'm worried too . . .' and she turns and sees tears in his eyes and of course, of course he's in love with her Josie. She's seen the little signs for so long, and her heart feels it's going to burst. She tucks herself away into his arms and they just sit there as show after show comes on. The more minutes that tick away, the worse Cherry feels. The news can't be good – they're just deciding how to tell the patients. When the cigarette's done she just lets it melt the plastic foam filter. She presses her fingertips to the end and pinches it to extinguish it, and the pain helps somehow. She blinks awake and stares at Michael's empty eyes.

At last, at long last, Leigh shows up at the doorway and says, 'We're having a patient meeting, now, in the main lounge.'

30
Amy

May, 1988
The Porter Place

Walking into the barn I breathe in the haystack spiderweb dusty air and sigh. I love it in the Porter Barn, the way the sunlight slants inside, the way you're no longer in the real world but in somewhere from a long time ago, back when things made sense. You can almost believe that ghosts of chickens, horses, cows are here among the very real barn swallows that have built their nests in the rafters.

You feel, in a way, that you're Laura Ingalls Wilder. That your ma and pa love you more than anything in the world. That you pa's about to call you his little half-pint of cider half-drunk up. That the worst you have to worry about is that your family'll be eaten by bears. That it'll all turn out okay in the end because Michael Landon believes in God.

Inside here, you can think that way for a minute or so.

I'm not altogether sure of why we've come here except we can't go home. I can't face Mom and Dad today. I'm sick of their drinking – they're so fucking weak and pathetic, and such assholes, Jesus. And Cherry? Where does she have to go?

The cut on her nose has come open again, and a few drops of blood soak through the smear of cover-up. Seeing her like this, my strong friend, makes me want to cry.

But the magic of this place is that once we've passed through the opening of the barn, we've walked into free-dom, into somewhere where nothing matters. This is the place where you can believe your life'll end up like a John Hughes movie. That you'll be Molly Ringwald dancing with Andrew McCarthy at the Prom. That the soundtrack of your life will be the Psychedelic Furs and OMD. That everyone will love you, even if you're a misfit. That you'll be Pretty in Pink.

This place just does that to you.

'Let's hang out and smoke,' I say. And it's so Cherry-like to have thought to nab the joint off Sam's dresser as she was leaving; why can't I be so spontaneous and perfect?

But she shakes her head. 'Let's wait a little. I have a feeling Rennie's going to show up later.'

'She's at Rob's.'

She shakes her head again. 'I just have a feeling.' Her lips flatten, then she smiles. 'Want to swing?'

We climb up into the hayloft. Even though it's empty a few shafts of golden straw catch the light, and Cherry unhooks the swing from the wall. I wonder who used to swing here. What little girls grabbed this swing and flung out into the outside? Are they old women now? Dead? Or just moved on in life, went to college out of state, got married? 'You first,' she says.

'No, you. You deserve it.'

She holds the swing out to me, listening. And so I wrap my legs around the rope, creep to the edge of the hayloft, hang on for dear life and take a leap.

The swing floats out and there's that creak as the rope strains with my weight, and there, there's that moment when the swing flings me out through the barn door into the daylight, and it's just then that if the rope broke I'd be flung about twelve feet in the air before landing on the ground. I'd break bones for sure, oh yeah.

The swing sucks me back into the barn, and then the world rushes back up at me as I fly outside again. I swing back and forth, a little less each time, until I hop off and toss the rope up to Cherry for her turn.

As she jumps I light a cigarette and watch her sail through the air, her red bob streaming out behind her. For a moment she looks like a little girl, eleven years old maybe, like Megan Follows playing *Anne of Green Gables*. I'd love to paint her like this, a blur of red and pale lemon and the black of her sweater and skirt. She's swimming by so fast I can't even see her bruises and blood; she's just a palette of colors, the reds the yellows the blacks, the hair the blood the skin, the bruises the sweater the eye, and none of it matters because for that one pure moment she just is. It's not even like she's Cherry, she just is beauty and colors and the swipe of a painter's brush across the sky. Slowly the rhythm relaxes, and she jumps off the swing and sits next to me on the ground.

'Don't you love to swing?' she asks.

'I haven't felt so good since I was a little girl and I still believed that every flower had a fairy living inside it.' I burst into laughter, but it doesn't feel real. There's more shit I used to believe: the tooth fairy, Santa Claus, that Callie would get well, that my parents were normal, that Jesus was keeping track of whether I got laid this weekend, that God cared if I gave Father O'Neill the full fucking report.

'That's why you should swallow your fears and drop acid with me sometime. You would see fairies inside flowers again.' She's remembering something now and shakes her head. 'Who's that artist who does those paintings, it's a flower but not really a flower, you look at it close and it's a—'

And she's going to say 'cunt' and I hate that word so I interrupt. 'Georgia O'Keeffe.' She's right of course, *Black Iris*, my favorite one of hers, the folds of petals, well let's just say I am intimately familiar with them. Maybe she didn't know what she was painting, but yeah, that's what she was painting.

'Your stuff's as good as hers, I swear. Someday you'll be a famous painter and I can say I knew you when.'

Someday. If I can survive senior year.

'Speaking of pussy pictures . . .'

Oh, thanks, Cherry. But I don't say anything. Some of her fuck-the-world, say-anything attitude must be because of the shit she just went through. I wonder how much of Cherry is just an outer shell, armor?

It never even crossed my mind before.

I watch her talking, her lips moving. Funny, I think in a

way I've idolized Cherry, and it's strange not to see her perfect. It's like an answer on the SAT, one of those analogy questions. Amy is to Cherry as Cherry is to Diana. 'I read or heard somewhere that all those years we were innocent little girls drawing hearts all over everything, each heart we made was actually a—'

She's going to say 'cunt' again and I love Cherry but I can't take it anymore so I say, 'Did you ever feel so angry you felt like if you didn't hurt something you were going to go up in a cloud of smoke?'

She stops talking and rests her fingers on my wrist. 'Who are you angry at, Aim?'

I look at the clear crisp blue sky, the sweat of the morning clinging to my arms. 'I don't even know, all the stuff with Callie, my parents, Mr Schafer, Sam, the world I guess.' There's no way to express it so I settle on, 'Mostly I'm angry about Callie.'

The words fall hollow; that's not quite it. As if by putting words to my anger I could define it, when it's so prismatic that any way I could describe it would be only one of a million facets. It feels good to try to explain though; anyway it's better than holding it in. 'I'm eighteen. I should just get an apartment and take her home with me.'

Cherry blows a smoke ring and shakes her head. 'It's not so easy, Aim. You'd have to go to court. And aren't you going to Michigan?'

Michigan. It seemed like such a good idea at the time. Big Ten school, I can major in art and study something else too, something practical. And Ann Arbor, what a great place. They have a Hash Bash every April supposedly. Supposedly, everyone gets high in the streets and the cops take a day off. Supposedly, I got accepted to the University of Michigan and I will receive a wonderful education and my life will be perfect.

Supposedly.

Michigan's for smarties, Rennie-types. Lots of kids I know would kill to get in there. I should be happy. But now, it seems awfully far away. Which I guess was the point, but my ties, the ties with Callie, with Cherry who's going to community college, especially with Rennie who's headed out West, will be stretched so thin, like a wad of Juicy Fruit pulled out from my mouth. Eventually all my ties will break, I know that. 'I don't want to think about Michigan.'

Abruptly she says, 'You know you can't stop them from drinking. They're going to do what they're going to do.' She flings out a tunnel of smoke. 'I finally figured that out. If people want to destroy themselves you can't stop them.' She stubs out her cigarette and puts it into her pocket. Cherry hates it when kids litter at the Porter Place.

'I don't get what that has to do with Michigan.'

'Just don't sink your dreams on someone else's ship. You know?' She touches her nose. 'I should talk. I can't even have a fucking relationship.'

'He's a dickhead. That was his fault.'

'But I picked him . . . why?' And this is the first time I've seen tears glint in Cherry's eyes. Bizarre. She always seems so strong . . . so sure of herself.

I stub out my cigarette too, slink my arms around her and float my fingers over her hair. Poor Cherry . . . poor Cherry. Her tears don't fall.

Before I know what I'm doing I lean over and brush her lips with mine. I twine my fingers through the short hair at the nape of her neck and she's kissing me back. My lips fall open. This is so different from kissing Brandon or any of the Sigma Nu guys, different from kissing anyone. Something sharp skates through me and I'm spinning a figure eight across the ice. My hand runs over her breast. Her nipple tightens under my fingers and I'm dizzy, I'm in love, and my other hand slips under her skirt and stumbles up her thigh.

And oh God, it's then that I open my eyes and it's my best friend I'm kissing, I didn't mean to, I didn't . . .

I break the kiss, pull my fingers away, retreat from her lap. She's not looking at me and that's bad. 'Cherry, I'm sorry. I'm not . . .' How could I have fucked up like that? I've totally messed up our friendship; she thinks I want some kind of relationship with her, she thinks . . . 'You know I'm dating Brandon. I don't . . . I just . . .'

She turns to meet my eyes and gives a little smile. 'It's okay, Amy. I love you too.' She stands up and brushes off her skirt.

As I stand up apologies start flooding out of my mouth again.

She interrupts. 'I'm not reading anything into it if that's what you're thinking. It's fine. Let's swing some more.' We walk back into the barn and she slings an arm over my shoulders and gives me a best-friend squeeze and at once I know it *is* fine. 'We're friends, best friends.'

'I've never had friends like you and Rennie,' I say.

Suddenly, I know why it felt so good to kiss her.

It's because I was kissing someone who gives a damn.

'We'll just forget it happened, it's totally fine.'

I don't want to forget it happened because it's the first kiss I've ever had that's meant something. But I know what she means. She means we won't be talking about it after this and I think that's a good idea. 'Okay.'

Something rustles, clip-clops outside. We exchange a glance and walk back into the sunshine. There it is: a doe, soft-eyed, furry, close enough to touch. There are woods all around the Porter Place and it must have wandered away. 'Oh, it's beautiful,' I say.

'It must be lost. I hope it doesn't run into the highway.'

And just then there's the spin of tires coming up the gravel road from the back way, by the silo and shed, and it's Rennie's Beetle. Damn, Cherry has some good instinct. 'You were right,' I say. The Beetle frightens the deer; it trots the other direction around the skeleton of the farmhouse and toward the woods. Rennie parks the car, flings open the door, and stalks toward us looking like she's ready to explode. Thank God Cherry brought that blunt because in a matter of minutes Rennie unloads an amazing but predictable story of Rob Sorry-Ass Schafer, and the deer trots away, farther into the distance. It'll either run straight into

Route 12 or into the woods, and I hope it heads for the woods where it's safe.

And despite all the shit at least the Bitch Posse's together again, together, together forever.

31
Rennie

May, 2003
Mill Valley, California

Rennie's pretty beaten up when she pulls in front of her Sunnyside Avenue cottage. She curses herself. What was she thinking? A three-day coke binge and Mallory's in town? Shit, shit, shit.

She walks up the sidewalk and pushes open the little gate. Caleb's playing in the yard, alone. Damn it, Mallory, leaving him outside by himself? He's discovered Beverly's golden poppies, because three have been pulled by their roots and hang from his grubby hand. His diaper sags on his bottom, the tape holding on by a thread, and mud streaks across his full, candy-ribbon lips; he's been eating it. Her heart soars. Her little nephew's adorable. How long has it been? Six months?

He sees her and points. 'Intide! Wanna go intide!'

Beverly must have let Mallory and Max inside and they're having coffee or more likely smoking a joint while the baby plays outside ready to get kidnapped or eat a poisonous plant. How irresponsible.

Rennie laughs out loud. Who is she to judge?

She takes Caleb's hand and squats next to him, pulling his fingers away from Beverley's sweetpeas that crawl over the fence. 'Hi, Caleb, remember me, Aunt Rennie?' She makes to give him a kiss. He turns away, pouting, but not before she sees laughter sparkling in his blue eyes. His blond curls tangle down past his shoulders, her little elf-boy.

Rennie puts her hands under his arms and lifts him up, and the vanilla smell of baby pours into her nostrils, warming her. She feels so good now, so happy, keying into some deep hurt that's being smoothed over by Caleb, even though he's got no idea she's hurting. She gives him a squeeze. *I hope they're staying a while.*

She walks up to the house, brushes a cobweb away from the doorframe, and turns the knob. Locked. Shifting Caleb to her hip, she knocks on the door. 'Mallory? Max?'

No answer.

She leans over to the window and peers inside. Nothing, it's dark. Where did they go? Ran an errand? Went for coffee and let Caleb stay in the yard? 'This is beyond irresponsible, Mallory,' she says aloud.

Caleb sticks his dirty thumb in his mouth. 'Malla-wee.'

Swearing, she digs through her purse for her keys and unlocks the door. She turns on the lights and drops Caleb to the floor. In a moment a puddle pools over the hardwood, and Rennie registers for the first time that his diaper's soaked. 'Shit!' She tosses her cotton throw blanket onto the puddle.

'Shit!' Caleb laughs.

'Listen, Caleb. Did Mommy leave a diaper bag?'

'Mommy leaved.' Chunks of mud pepper his nose. After she takes care of the diaper she'll give him a bath.

'I know Mommy left. Did she leave some diapers?' She tugs at Caleb's. 'These?'

Caleb tears open the tape and the soaked diaper falls to the floor. A moth flutters by him and lands somewhere Rennie'll never find, and he shrugs off his T-shirt. 'Caleb nudie!' He struts around, waving his penis like Rennie's supposed to be really impressed.

Great, great. Boys must have this fixation from birth. Rennie scoops him up, tosses the wet diaper in the trash, and draws some bath water.

The bath is complicated by the fact that Rennie has no boats and no duckie, plus her shampoo is the eye-stinging kind. She's never bathed a baby before and, absurdly, wants to get him clean without touching him. But there's no way around that and she finishes, a little embarrassed. She wraps

Caleb in a warm dry towel. Mallory and Max should be here any minute.

What about the diapers? Could just let him run around without one for a while. She remembers the puddle in the living room. No, not such a great idea. She pulls a hand towel out of the closet and wraps it around him, hmm, maybe with some safety pins . . .

It falls to the floor in disgrace.

Mallory, where the hell are you?

'Diapies out dare.' He points.

'In the yard? Where we were?'

Caleb nods. 'Outtide, Ann Wennie.'

And that's who she is now, with Caleb, Ann Wennie. She sucks in a breath. That's so much better than Wren Taylor, failed writer, Rennie Taylor, teacher-whore.

Ann Wennie.

It's perfect.

She buries her face in his clean hair. God, they're cute when they're little. It's when the hormones hit that they're trouble. She's in love in a way she's never been since the Bitch Posse broke up, in love with this little cherub who calls her Ann Wennie. If only she could be Ann Wennie forever.

Someone loves her, anyway.

They head out to the garden together, Caleb still 'nudie'. There's no way Rennie's putting on that T-shirt again, it's filthy. On the bench sits the diaper bag where she should have seen it before. Maybe there's extra clothes in the bag too; if not, well, it's pretty warm out, she'll just let him run around in his diaper until Mallory gets back.

She sits down to open the bag and finds a fresh diaper and a red T-shirt, which she slips onto Caleb. She's pretty sure she got the diaper on the right way, but if not she'll find out soon. Caleb walks toward the flower bed. 'Look, don't touch, sweetie, okay?'

She zips up the diaper bag and a note slips out of the pocket. *What . . . ?*

As she unfolds it, something hits her: there was no luggage in the living room.

She reads the note but she doesn't have to; she knows what it says.

Dear Rennie,

I'm so sorry to do this to you but there's no other way. We have to go down to Bogotá, and it's no place for kids, not where we're going anyway. I'll be back for him. I don't know when, but I really will try to make it sooner rather than later. Here's some money for diapers and babysitting and stuff. Call Dad and my mom if you need something.

Mal.

Inside the note is a small stack of fifty-dollar bills.

The world slams into Rennie and explodes, and she tucks her knees to her chest. *Oh shit oh shit oh shit, I can't deal with this. I have to be at school tomorrow. Oh shit, Mallory, what the fuck are you thinking?* She balls up her fists and presses them to her closed eyes, but she won't scream and scare Caleb. When she opens her eyes he's picked the tops off three of Beverly's tulips that are just closing for the evening.

'Come on, Caleb. Let's go back inside.' She leads him into the living room.

Toys. Why the fuck doesn't she have any toys? 'Sorry, I . . .' But it doesn't matter because Caleb's mesmerized by the cardboard box her curriculum materials came in, that and today's paper, so she sets him up with that stuff and shifts to the kitchen to make some calls.

Her father and Kelly aren't answering the phone, but she leaves a long, detailed, pissed-off message and very calmly requests that Kelly fly out here right away to help her deal with Caleb and figure out who's going to take care of him since God knows when Mallory's coming back, if ever. As she hangs up she realizes she'd better call in for her messages, and also, she needs to call for a sub for tomorrow. Finding a sub at the last minute for a Monday's a bitch, plus Tam's principal Josef Stalin (it's really Joe Stoland, but it's her private joke) will think she's just extending her weekend because she's been known to do that from time to time.

She phones the sub line and explains that family stuff has come up, no she doesn't have a lesson plan but the movie of *The Crucible* is in her closet and no, they haven't finished the play yet but oh well. She thumbs through the yellow pages and leaves messages at Simply Au Pair and North Bay Nannies, not like she has money to pay any of these people. (That little stack of fifties? Good one, Mal, ha, ha.) But someone needs to fill the gaps so she can make it back to school, hopefully by Wednesday.

All of a sudden Rennie's feeling very dizzy, and she realizes she hasn't eaten anything all day. When she was doing line after line of coke she wasn't thinking at all about eating; she probably hasn't had any food for two days, maybe more. Caleb must be hungry too.

She opens the fridge. Not very promising: a jar of cocktail onions, a squeeze bottle of mustard, some skim milk, take-out Chinese from a week ago that she immediately throws into the garbage along with the onions, which she has no idea why she has since she hates them. Left over from a party maybe. Does Caleb need baby food? No, no, he's two, he must eat regular food. Doesn't he?

God, she knows nothing about babies. She needs a tutor or something.

She needs to go out anyway, stop at Safeways, buy diapers and kid type food and maybe even run to Mervyn's or somewhere cheap for some clothes since Mallory's just left the one outfit.

She walks back into the living room. 'Caleb? Do you like burritos?'

Caleb abandons his forty million shreds of now-ruined newspaper and squeals with delight. 'Breetos!'

Great. Okay. My afternoon's cut out for me. Time to worry later about Puck, her book, Paul and whether he's told anyone what happened in the classroom. Her heart closes up just to think of all the crap she's got to deal with. It'll be blissfully normal and respectable to walk into Joe's Taco Lounge and order a kiddie meal. Hell, she might just order one for herself.

She runs a hand through her hair (*God, I must look like utter hell*) and grabs her purse. 'Let's go, sweetie.'

The phone rings. Rennie hardly wants to answer it, but thinking it might be Kelly or one of the nanny services, she picks it up. 'Hello?'

'Wren?' His voice is dark, sexy, a blackberry dripping juices. 'It's Puck. I can't stand being without you. Come back, come back, come back.'

Her heart thuds to her stomach. If he only knew how much she wants to. It's not just the sex, not just the cocaine; it's more the danger, the allure of being so close to the edge. 'Oh . . .' is all she breathes out, like the sounds she makes when he touches her.

32
Cherry

May, 1988
Holland, Illinois

It's so good to have the girls back at my place, and we have it all to ourselves. Marian's off somewhere doing some shit that I've made myself stop caring about, because all my caring's not going to change her, so fuck that shit. One nice thing coke's done for her is made her careless about hiding and keeping track of her pot, so it's been very easy for all three of us to help ourselves. Oh and I finally did tell the girls about Marian's little hobby. Why work so hard to hide something when we're all of us so fucked up and really I'm the only liar in the bunch? And it's funny, telling them helped me let go of a little of the shame. Of course, I told it like it was a joke and like I don't care; that's the only way to tell it.

Rennie's a wreck. Watching L'Affaire Rob Schafer's been painful enough, but now that it's slammed into the wall I knew it'd hit sooner or later, she's an emotional disaster. It doesn't take a genius to figure out she's been slicing her arm – that's why she's wearing a sloppy White Sox sweatshirt (and again, that is *so* not Rennie) on an eighty-degree day. Every time you say something to her she answers really quickly and then goes all silent and brooding and staring at the wall like she's doing now, over there on the edge of my bed, distant-like, turned away from me and Amy.

'We should go after his fucking credential,' Amy says.

Rennie just shrugs and kicks the wall. Fuck. Nothing's ever going to make her better. Bastard. How dare he?

Amy's on the right track, but her idea is seriously stupid.

221

'Fuck that, Aim. You really think Coldwell and the shitheads who booted Rennie out of the honor society are gonna help us?' Even if we went to a school run by rational people, it'd take a million years to push something through the asshole fucked system that tried to break up the Bitch Posse.

'So it's a dumb idea. Forget it then.'

'No, but you're right. He needs to pay.' What he needs is a good scare. This calls for some careful planning. 'I'll come up with something better.' I always do.

Rennie leans into my arms. 'Can we just drop the fucking subject?' Her voice is shot through with tears and *shit, Rennie, I'm sorry*. But she wraps her fingers around my forearms and I know she forgives me and I don't have to say a word.

Amy scoots over to the stereo and puts on that Sisters of Mercy song I can't bear to hear. Well of course, it's goth music, we're supposed to be depressed when we listen. But that's not the reason. No, by some unbearable coincidence the song is called 'Marian'.

It's very hard to figure out the lyrics to this one because Andrew Eldritch's voice is so slow. But Amy's done me a real favor, listened to it tons of times and written everything down, except the chorus in German of course, that's beyond her. 'Listen, Cherry.' And she chants on and on with Andrew about the ship of fools and drowning and graves. Great, oh so happy. 'Isn't that hilarious, there's this song about your mom?'

Hilarious is not the word that comes to mind. I tap my cigarette ash and take another puff, trying not to listen.

Amy keeps singing about fatal waves and death and my mother until I'm about to implode. Finally the words blessedly drift into German and she stops.

I reach over and snap on the fast-forward. 'Let's skip it.' I pop out the tape. 'Better yet, let's put on something else.' What will make me not think of Sam, Rob Schafer, Dr Linnet, Coldwell and his cronies, the whole stupid fucking world, everyone we hate? I put in the Violent Femmes and listen for a while and smoke. Then my favorite song, 'Kiss Off', comes on, and I crank the volume.

Anger surges through the room and it feels good, empowering. Amy straightens up and says, 'Know what? That bruise is so light, I bet it'll be almost gone by tomorrow morning. No one at school will even know.' She runs a finger over the cut on my nose. 'This too, it looks good.'

As she touches the marks Sam's made on my body, I feel that yawn of pain again. It's not so much that he hurt me, it's the sting of betrayal from someone I trusted, someone I let my guard down with, someone I thought mattered, and I shared *everything* with him. The first time I dropped acid was with him. I told him the story of Marian, my hopes for the future, my jealousy (that's what it is, I admit it) of my friends who despite their problems really do have their shit together. Rennie's going to fucking Stanford, Amy to Michigan, they have a future. What do I have but an associate's degree and a waitress job to look forward to?

Amy's fingers float over my face and the memory of her kiss presses into my mind. It's not the first time a woman's kissed me. One of Marian's friends who doesn't come around anymore (I guess now that she's shooting up she's disgusted even her fellow cokeheads) and I used to make out, oh no big deal, just smooching, just for fun, when Marian was in the other room. But that was more my do-whatever-the-hell-I-want-to-because-Cherry-Winters-tries-everything phase.

No way was it anything close to what I felt with Amy.

Oh, I'm sure Amy and me will never turn into anything else.

Probably.

That's okay, though. I'll always have the memory.

You know why kissing her was so great? It was because it was Amy, someone who cares what happens to me. Someone who loves me. I haven't felt loved for a long time, not since Mama pulled me to her hip at the barbecue and called me the Cherry Pie I'm not anymore.

I'm getting sentimental so I know it's time to crank the music. All of us know this one by heart and we belt out the rest, especially the part about our 'permanent records'. Even Rennie's singing along, her eyes bright for the first time in months. I think we all know how much power the Bitch Posse holds together, and as the song finishes we collapse into laughter and somehow all three of us decide it's a great time for a walk.

There are these beautiful woods behind my place that I guess belong to the city or something. We trudge through Marian's neglected garden, sagging excuses for tomato plants choked with weeds, a watering can that's been there all winter. Smoking our cigarettes, we drift onto one of the winding paths, a bowl and some weed tucked into my jacket. We'll stop in the clearing and get high there, back to nature.

Amy's decided we can make some wreaths from the heather and other stuff that grows here, which sounds fine to me; it'll be fun to do a little-girly-girl art project when we're stoned. So we've brought our great big kitchen shears too, which of course Marian never uses, because Marian never cooks, because Marian is Marian.

I hate Marian, too, for taking my mother away.

I stomp my rage onto the path, snapping sticks, imagining I'm breaking bones.

We round a bend and there, two feet in front of us, limps a doe. One of her back legs is broken, and she's dragging it behind her. A splash of red floats over the top of her back like she's been grazed with an arrow. I don't know if it's hunting season or not, but obviously someone's shot her. It's so sad, this soft innocent animal, hurt this way, why?

She's trembling. And she's absolutely beautiful.

She stumbles and lands on the ground. 'Oh, it's so sad,' says Amy.

From the way she's lying down, I can see another arrow hole near her chest, a spray of blood over her snowy fur. A little rhyme goes through my head for no reason, something Marian used to read to me (back when she cared): *I, said the sparrow, with my bow and arrow* . . .

'A hunter,' says Rennie. 'Poor helpless thing.'

'We should call the Humane Society,' says Amy.

Which is crazy. We'd spend twenty minutes walking back to my place and the Humane Society'd take at least an hour to get here. By then the doe will be dead, the blood trickling out of her like blackberry jam, life flowing out. I tell the girls this, and Amy lifts a hand to her lips and goes pale. Rennie just shrugs, looking resigned.

'So what do we do?' asks Amy. 'Just leave her here?'

The doe's glassy eyes stare up at me. I gaze into them, fall into the pool. Her eyes are enchantment itself. Through her eyes she's talking to me. *Please, free me from this body . . .*

Diana, Goddess of the Hunt.

'What we should do,' I say, 'is put her out of her misery.'

'If we had a gun, it'd be easy.' Amy shudders. 'Oh, the poor thing. I can't believe I'm even talking like this.'

An odd expression crosses Rennie's face, and she slips the kitchen shears out of her bag. She knows what I'm thinking.

Amy sucks in her breath. 'Rennie!'

'It's die now or suffer for an hour. If you were the deer what would you want?'

The doe's chest rises and falls, shuddery breathing. The eyes tremble open. *Help me . . .*

I slide the scissors from Rennie's hand. 'Now's not the time to be squeamish.' My heart thumps as I sink the shears into the doe's neck. The doe makes a raspy noise, and the scissors pop through the skin and the softness inside. Blood pours over the blade onto my hand.

My eyes fall shut and I imagine Marian's blood, Sam's, steaming over my arms. The metallic warm smell fills my nostrils as I bring my fingers to my face and open my eyes, let the blade slide across my neck, the tiniest wisp of a hurt, just a scratch.

'Oh . . .' Amy covers her eyes, but I press the shears into her hand.

'Come on, Amy. Help the creature out.'

She shakes her head and Rennie snatches the shears from her. 'Honestly, Amy. Look at her.' The doe's choking out breaths, but my stab hasn't killed her; there's an artery I didn't hit or something.

Rennie plunges the scissors into another part of the animal's neck, and she must have hit it closer because the pressure forces blood into the air in droplets, and Rennie's sprayed by it, blood spattering her face in little dots.

Is she sick like me and thinking of violence? Or maybe she's just feeling she's freeing an animal from pain. Guess I'll never know. That'll be one of the things the three of us always keep from each other. Her expression reveals little as her eyes shift into distance again. It's funny how you can see life ebb out of something, a magnet pulling it into the sky, a spirit (do animals have a spirit?) shifting from a warm live body into the lifeless air.

The doe's holding on by a thread. It's up to Amy.

Rennie presses the shears into her palm.

Amy closes her eyes and (who knows what's going through her mind?) raises the scissors and slams them into the bloody stained fur of the doe. She cuts so deep and so hard that her fingers disappear into the doe's body, and blood soaks over the whole white section of fur. The doe's eyes go silent and still, and tears fall from Amy's. My own vision's blurred too, and I know Rennie's crying, but aloud I say, 'We had to do this, girls, we had to do this. It was the only way.'

In that moment of consciousness we stare at each other. The enchanted hunters. Blood streaks across Rennie's face, pours over Amy's fingers and mine.

'We should go back to your place,' says Amy. 'Take showers.'

'What about the doe?' asks Rennie.

'Leave her here,' I say. 'Back to nature.'

Have we all changed somehow, shifted? I feel a sense of steadiness I didn't before, my anger at Sam and Marian defused. As we walk back to my house in silence I sense peace in Amy and Rennie as well, Amy's steps solid and sure, Rennie's head held high.

Funny.

How hurting something seems to have put us back together again.

33
Amy

May, 2003
I-80 West

It feels a lot better to be behind the wheel of this sporty red Mustang than the 4Runner she and Scotty owned together, the one she pictured using to drive Lucky to ballet lessons and soccer practice and fucking school. Of course, the SUV came in handy when she was driving through the moonscape of Wyoming and over the Rockies, where it was snowing, snowing in May!

Later, just outside of Reno, she made a quick trade. No problem because they love seeing SUVs in the mountains, and she paid for the rest with a check, cleaning out her and Scotty's account, probably. Someone had to do it. She's glad she swapped though; the Mustang handles so nice on the highway.

A little while back, she stopped at Donner Memorial State Park and read about the doomed pioneers while she ate a sandwich, because it makes her feel superior to think of people who had it worse than she does. Now, as she's flying toward the coast, she savors the details of the Donner Party, compelling in a sick way, like so much else in Amy's life.

They drew straws to see who'd be the human sacrifice. Patrick Dolan got the smallest, but no one could bear to kill him. That was before stuff got really bad, of course.

Dolan died anyway. Then the pioneers realized they had no other options.

You might say they had run out of luck.

One woman had to eat her own husband. Yeah, that one begs for a dirty joke. But seriously. What else are you going to do?

At the end of it all one of the survivors opened a restaurant.

When life gives you lemons, make lemonade.

It all makes Amy feel so blessedly normal, just for a second. The highway spins by her and nothing really matters, not anymore, nothing means anything, not really.

Even Donner Pass is just a tourist spot, like everywhere else in America.

She grips the steering wheel of the Mustang, the leather rippling under her fingers, the pedal so light, she's flying. Zipping in and out of traffic, she spends about fifteen minutes thinking about how she'll make it on her own. Scotty's alimony will last a while, and then she'll have to figure out what to do with her life. What the hell can she do with an art degree? Teach, that's a joke; she's the last person who should be teaching anyone anything. Maybe she'll become a stripper, or a hooker. That sounds appropriate. Anyway, who cares about the future? It's just a dream, imaginary, something you make up in your head.

She makes herself stop thinking.

After she speeds through Sacramento she stops in some little town and buys a bottle of Belvedere at a Safeway near the highway, the good stuff. (Goddamn it, she deserves the good stuff, doesn't she?) It is now hidden under the passenger seat, and she bends down and takes a swig every now and then. The booze has given her this incredible high, and it must be a third of the bottle she's drunk, but funny she doesn't feel plastered or silly. She feels sharp, sharp sharp sharp sharp sharp, buzzed. It's as if she herself is a razor blade, ready to slice thin little pieces of pain off herself and ditch them here on 80.

The sign *Oakland 35 Miles* comes up, and shit, wasn't this where she always wanted to be? Back when they were the Bitch Posse Goddesses? They were all going to head out West together. Rennie would already be here with her ticket to Stanford, Cherry'd finish her associate's degree and transfer to San Francisco State, and after Amy was done with her undergrad at Michigan she'd head for the Academy of Art, and it didn't work out that way did it? She fell in love and Cherry got in trouble, and really it was that night at the Porter Place that screwed them all.

To blot all that out, she pulls the Belvedere from under the seat and takes a swig. Straight's the way she likes her booze now, and it burns her throat going down. She makes an 'ah' and caps it, and *goddamn, these people are driving slow! What the hell, they're in the fast lane and going seventy! What the fuck's with that?*

Amy turns on the radio, and for some amazing reason she runs across a station that's playing 'Please Please Please Let Me Get What I Want' by The Smiths. Now there's a blast from the past. Scotty hates The Smiths and most of the music from her old days, says it's depressing.

So she cranks it. God, that *Pretty in Pink* soundtrack was good. All those songs still hold up. She belts the words out by heart and as the last notes fade her throat's knotted up, but damned if she's going to fucking cry.

She cuts all the way to the right lane and the odometer rails to eighty-five, ninety even, and she cuts back in just a smidge before rear-ending some slow-ass in the right lane and there, there, nothing but open road in front of her, sweet goddamn, it feels good to be so free.

The odometer curls toward ninety-five, and now the booze hits her head. Some other song's playing now, some hideous brand new song that repeats the same three lines over and over again. So fucking irritating. What's happened to music these days? 'Damn,' she says aloud, *'everything's dying.'* She snaps the radio off.

Giddy, she reaches with one hand for the bottle and swigs more. She tosses it on the passenger seat, not even bothering to hide it. Who the fuck cares, she's flying away, leaving it all behind, no more memories of Lucky or Scotty or her parents or the Bitch Posse or any of that, she's just a star falling through space and the road blurs ahead of her . . .

Suddenly (all of a sudden! This never happens!) there's two of everything, and she leans into the left-hand vision of the road and wobbles back into her right-eye vision of the road, and a little voice in her head says, *Pull over, pull over, Amy.*

But aloud she says, 'Fuck that shit,' and keeps on flying and the car spins out and the world crashes to an end with glass breaking and metal tearing and the squall of tires and Amy laughs just moments before everything dims in front of her, and the shades fall down on her eyes.

Her eyes pull open and even that hurts. Her body yawns with pain, and sitting at the foot of her bed (*bed? What?*) is a man with a Winnie-the-Pooh tie and a clipboard and a stethoscope around his neck. Her right leg's jammed in a gigantic cast and hoisted up in traction while her left arm is covered with gauze from her wrist to her elbow. 'Where am I?'

And of course it's obvious: she's in the hospital. Shards of the wreck pierce into her. Someone yelling about an IV. Faces swimming above her. Then blackness.

'Summit Hospital, in Oakland. How much do you remember?' asks the doctor, he must be a doctor.

The IV tube's still attached to her arm. 'What's in the IV?'

'Some pain medication and heparin. We need to prevent clotting; you won't be moving for a while. Do you remember the accident?'

'Not much, just a spinout and a couple moments in the ambulance.'

'You're lucky you didn't hurt someone else.' He gives a flat smile, as in, *What a fuck-up you are.* 'You may be here for a couple of months.'

A headache washes over her. The Belvedere, oh good God, the pain throbs in the front of her forehead. 'Months?' A couple months in Oakland in a hospital? 'Will I walk?'

'Your right hip was shattered. Your femur's broken too but the hip's what'll take the most time. We had to replace it. Those burns on your arm are from the airbag.'

She hates it when people don't answer straight out. 'Will I walk?'

He whistles out a sigh. 'You'll be doing some physical therapy. Yeah, you should walk. I wouldn't suggest you run a marathon, but if everything goes according to plan, you'll walk.'

The Belvedere, the Belvedere, oh shit, what a fucking idiot! 'Were the cops there?'

'Paramedics, and police, sure, they filed an accident report. They used the Jaws of Life to cut you out of the wreck.' He flips through the pages on his clipboard and stands up. 'You were lucky. I'll be in tomorrow.'

With that he's gone.

Gone?

God, I need a drink.

At that moment she realizes that they surely took a blood sample and found out she'd been drinking which means she'll be getting a nice horrible drunk-driving citation when this is all over.

The pretty, older Chinese woman in the next bed's in traction too, but she's sleeping, her hair curled about her pillow, framing her face.

God, she wishes she could sleep. Her suitcase is gone, no books, no clothes, no laptop.

And now the Bitch Goddess Notebook is gone forever too.

Scotty.

Has anyone called Scotty?

Does it matter?

He must be listed as next of kin on her hospital record. Her Soo address was on the driver's license. They figured it out.

Of course, up till now, she hasn't been in shape to deal with any of that hospital stuff, and she guesses that the next time a nurse comes in she'll be filling it out, giving insurance information, all that crap.

Did I almost die?

Holy shit.

I don't even know anyone around here. Except . . .

Would Rennie Taylor really want to see her? It was so long ago. And the memories, the last ones, are so, so bad . . .

Assuming she could even find Rennie in the first place. Does she lives in San Francisco? 'No, no,' she says aloud. 'It's somewhere else.'

Her book. It has to be in the back of her book. Amy always knew Rennie'd make it big with her writing, and sure enough she won some literary award a while back. Amy picked up a copy of the thing, small-town-girl-goes-to-the-big-city, not demanding, just a fun, quick read. But in the midst of the move from little Soo house to the big one it somehow got lost. Amy's sure it said on the back something like, *Wren Taylor makes her home in . . .*

And of course, she can't remember the 'in'.

Crap.

Does it matter? Why dig up the past, scrape out old wounds?

Because that's the way they'll heal?

She sure can't hurt any worse than she does now, be fucked up any worse than she is here with a shattered hip and a broken femur and a barbecued arm. What the hell. She leans over to the telephone and dials for an outside line and information. She gets the Barnes and Noble in Jack London Square in Oakland and asks for 'that book by Wren Taylor. W-R-E-N.'

'Not in our computer,' says the young, perky girl. 'Is it out of print maybe?'

Double crap. 'I really need that book. I just need someone to read me the stuff on the author flap, that's all.'

'It's out of print. We don't have it.' The girl sounds like she's about to hang up.

'Listen,' Amy says. 'I'm in traction in a hospital bed at Summit, and Wren Taylor's an old friend of mine. Please, please tell me where she lives. Just the town.'

The girl's voice softens. 'I could take a minute to look it up on the Internet. Can I call you back?'

'Yes, yes, you're wonderful!' Of course she has no idea what the phone number here is. The pain stabs into her face again. *Maybe I can get Rennie to bring me something to drink when she comes, she'll come, oh God please let me find her so*

I'm not here all alone. 'Just look up Summit and ask for Amy Dionne's room.'

The girl agrees, and now begins the long wait. With her right arm, Amy reaches for the TV changer and turns it on. Exactly three stations come in: Judge Judy, local news that means nothing to her, and Jenny Jones. Amy turns it off in disgust, then turns it on again because she can't bear to be alone with her thoughts, and Judge Judy Justice will put the world in order again, problems solved!

A nurse walks in, a stunning black woman with an accent Amy can't place. Her nametag reads Dalila, and she tells Amy she's from Kenya.

'Kenya.' Amy pictures tigers, elephants, stretches of grassy savannah. 'I hear that's a beautiful country.'

She nods. 'I hated to leave, but I had to.'

Being a fellow runner-awayer (*God, where did my words go? I can't even think*) Amy can't help asking, 'Why?'

'They used to do terrible things to women in my country. In some places they still do.'

Now she wishes she hadn't asked because it must be female mutilation or something horrible like that. Now there is nothing to say.

Dalila takes some blood samples and her vitals and swaps out her IV for a new one. Then she takes down the hospital information Amy's finally coherent enough to give, Next of Kin *Scott Dionne*, Religion *Roman Catholic*. The answers feel like lies even though they're as close to the truth as Amy gets, and Dalila writes them down and smiles. God, that smile was a gift.

Amy notices all the monitoring going on around her. Shit, she doesn't even want to think about what a close one this really was. Just as Dalila's leaving the phone rings, and Amy struggles to reach for the receiver across her body with her right hand.

Dalila picks it up and hands it to her.

'Thanks,' mouths Amy. Sure enough, it's the bookstore woman, who's not only looked up Rennie on the Internet but has found out she's living in Mill Valley, just north of San

Francisco. She's even gone ahead and called information. She reads Amy the phone number, which Amy takes down in sloppy writing on an old napkin that's been left from the lunch she didn't eat and didn't know about and wouldn't have eaten if she had known about it. 'Thanks, you don't know what this means . . .' Hanging up, Amy realizes she doesn't know what it means, either. The last time she saw Rennie she was a skinny, tiny teenager. Has she changed?

Has Amy? Amy nods despite herself. Of course she's changed; she's lost a child.

Lucky, Lucky. Tears sting her eyes. The curl of brown hair, the swatch of rosy lips, the tiny twig fingers. She'll never lose Lucky. Lucky will always be a part of her.

Amy's not convinced that's a good thing.

She pushes Lucky out of her mind and stares at the number for a while. Good-idea-bad-idea bounce around in her mind.

Her roommate mutters in her sleep, 'Show me the way . . .'

The way. Amy thought she knew the way when she was speeding down Highway 80. Obviously she was wrong, as usual. A pang gnaws through her for the Soo, but happiness isn't about a place. Amy knows that. Or does she? She's not sure of anything anymore. Impulses. That's all she has left, really.

She closes her eyes and waits for an impulse to come.

When it does, she picks up the phone and dials Rennie's number.

34
Rennie

I'm sitting here in Drama class letting Rob Fuckhead Schafer's words float around me. They are empty noises, meaningless, and his lips work around them, vomiting them out. My eyes glaze over as I separate from the room, and my pen rests idle in my fingers when I'm normally scribbling down notes as fast as I can take them. I vaguely hear him mention 'test' but I couldn't give a fuck. Sick of watching his yawning gaping dead face, I drop my eyes to my notebook.

Instead of taking notes on whatever the fuck play we're supposed to be reading, I curl the pen into meaningless squiggles of ink, following it whatever direction it takes me and filling the page until it's a maze of enormous proportions, endless twists and turns.

I wish there was some way to make him leave town in a sea of humiliation. *Hate hate hate hate hate.* Make him lose his job and never get to teach anywhere again. *Hate hate hate hate hate.* Not that the fucking school would ever help us. *Hate, hate, and more hate.* My pen's stabbing the paper so deep it's making a hole. *Double hate, triple hate, quadruple hate.* In the center of my maze I draw a girl, a skinny little girl, cross-legged smoking a cigarette. If I was Amy the thing'd turn out decent, but the legs seem too short, so I cover them with a black blanket of ink. That's better. I'm just going over the blanket making it darker when the bell shrieks. I blow on the page to make the ink dry and finally close the notebook and slide it into my backpack. Just as I'm leaving this dead gray hollow place I feel a touch on my arm.

His touch.

I shake it away.

'Rennie?' He puts his hands on my shoulders and turns me to face him. Around me students are packing up, laughing, filing out.

'I have to go,' I say coldly. I blur his face in my vision and look beyond him at a fly buzzing around the makeup mirrors.

'I've missed you at play practice lately.'

I've cut all week since he pulled his scene at the motel. Dawn's pregnant. Who the fuck cares? 'Yeah, well. I've been busy.' I lean against the table that faces the back wall, refusing to look at him.

Behind me, the door clicks shut as the last stragglers make it out of class. 'Listen, Rennie,' he says under his breath. 'I'm sorry. You know that.' He presses his fingertips to my shoulders. 'Look at me.'

'I push him away. 'I have to go. I'll be late.'

I start down the aisle but he stands in front of me, blocking my way. 'Don't think I can't see what this is doing to you. And don't think it doesn't make me feel like hell. This has been so hard for me, Rennie.'

Hard? For *you*?

He reaches for my chin, cups it in his right hand, and strokes my skin from my ear to my lips, where he rests his fingers. 'Goddamn, what I'd give to be able to kiss you right now.' Almost like I've changed into another person my lips fall open, my fingers slide up his arms, and I'm drunk with him, about to pull him down to kiss me when he says, 'Stop it, Rennie. You have to stop it.'

Stop it? *I* should stop it? I push my palms against his shoulders and shove him away. 'Listen, Mr Schafer.' He winces. You *bet* I hope that stings. 'After what happened last weekend I'm just another senior. So treat me that way and let's not get personal, ever again.'

He heaves a great, heavy sigh. 'I'm so sorry.'

'Sorry?' Sorry is when you bump into someone in line by mistake. Sorry is not when you fuck up someone's whole fucking life. 'You're sorry. Huh.'

'Sorry it had to end this way.'

I make the mistake of looking at his face. His eyes are so brown, so soft, so bright. My tongue slips over my dry lips. 'I'm sorry it ended this way too.'

He seizes me under my arms, lifts me onto the table. Before I know it he's kissing me hard, casting his spell. He wiggles my lips open with his tongue, and breathless, I kiss him back. My thighs are trembling, just a kiss, just a kiss, how can just a kiss get me so hot? And it's just like it used to be only things have changed and evolved so much; I'll never be as innocent as I was that first day on the stage.

I pull away, but he chases me with his lips and lands a few more kisses. 'We could be together again if you want . . .' he whispers into my ear, his breath fluttering my hair. 'No strings attached though . . .'

I reach up with my free hand and slap him across the face.

He blinks, touches the spot with his fingers.

Oh, the anger's pounding through me now. I want to slash his throat. I hate him so, so much. 'You're a fucking lunatic,' I force out. My throat's closing up. 'What the hell is wrong with you?'

'Rennie . . .' He lands a hand on my arm. 'Calm down.'

'Me? What about you?' I'm blazing on now, not caring. 'You're the one who can't keep it in his pants. You're the one who lies and says he wants it to be over, when what you want is things the way they used to be, with no commitment, nothing for you to be scared of. What you want is a cheap little fuck, a cheap little high-school fuck who gets you hot because she's so tiny and innocent and weak. Well, keep looking. I'm not it.' The tears are streaming down my cheeks now, but I'm not sad, just pissed, and although my voice is shaking and my hands are too, inside I'm so steady and I don't care who hears me. 'And another thing. I think Mr Coldwell would be very, very interested to know what you do with students in your spare time.' Sure, going through the school bureaucracy's a bullshit idea, Cherry convinced me of that. But he doesn't know I think it's bullshit, and his eyes mist over with fear.

'You wouldn't, Rennie.'

'Try me.'

'You started this, you know. You begged for it. *Corrupt me*, you said.'

'What kind of pervert gets off on teenagers who look even younger than they are? Don't put this on me; you're the grown-up.'

'You're not a baby, Rennie. You made your own choices, just don't forget that. What do you want? Money?'

So he thinks I'm not just the regular kind of slut, but a mind-slut too, a whore for cash. My stomach turns. He makes me sick. 'No.'

'Then what?' His skin is pasty, chalky.

I want him out of my life. I don't want to see him every day at school. I don't want him to fuck over anyone else the way he fucked me over.

Ever.

Yeah, it'd feel good to shove a pair of scissors in his throat, like I did with the deer. Yank them through his flesh, stab him over and over and over, and picturing that sets me apart from the scene again; I don't feel real.

And I'm not that evil anyway. I couldn't do it.

I don't think.

Since I've gone a while without answering he says, 'I doubt you'd want this relationship out in the open yourself, Rennie. People might find out about your abortion. What would your parents think?'

My abortion. Like I really wanted to think about *that* on top of everything! He's right, of course, but he's such a cold, insensitive, boorish asshole! And he referred to Dad and Kelly as my 'parents'. He doesn't fucking know me at all.

'Go ahead and leave, I don't care. What makes you think you're so special?' A smirk creeps across his lips. 'I could make a list a mile long of girls who'd like to be in your position. Pammie McFadden . . . Abby Green . . . So—'

'So just go fuck yourself!' I don't care who hears me. *HATE. HATE. HATE. HATE. HATE.* The word pounds in my head, threatening to overwhelm me. 'You're a fucking cocksucking fuckhead and I hate your fucking guts and I always will!' I pull the silver cuff bracelet he gave me off my wrist and hurl it at the makeup mirrors. One shatters. The jagged pieces hang in their frame for a split second, then fall to the floor.

'And know what else I figured out? Life is not a mother-fucking Broadway musical. So guess what? I quit the god-damn play. Find yourself someone else to learn Rizzo's part in a week. I don't want it.'

I don't even look at his expression as I stalk past him and out the door beyond the orchestra room. I hate his fucking face. I want to smash it, destroy it, destroy him, like he's des-troyed me.

The orchestra kids are doing some shit with the Madrigal Singers for the Spring Concert, and they're playing so damn loud no one heard our fight. I guess that's good, though I'm kind of disappointed because a big scene, a huge drama, would play real well about now. What drifts past me is some English or Scottish folk song, slow music, mournful almost, probably what they always sing, *hey nonny nonny* or some crap like that but it's kind of compelling:

> *Oh where are you going said Milder to Moulder*
> *Oh we may not tell you said Festel to Fose*

I slam my hand into the wall as I walk past, my bookbag hitting my hip, hard. The pain wakes me up, makes me feel alive, strong.

> *We're off to the woods said John the Red Nose*
> *We're off to the woods said John the Red Nose*

The woods sound mighty appealing about now. Cherry and Amy and I should just run away from everything, secede from the world, start a commune of three.

> *And what will you do there said Milder to Moulder*
> *Oh we may not tell you said Festel to Fose*

Maybe I'll find a way to hurt him. If I hurt him I don't have to hurt me. As I push open the door to the main hallway the last thing I hear is

We'll shoot the Cutty Wren said John the Red Nose

Then it all hits me and my stomach heaves. I duck into the girls' room, run for the toilet, and throw up. As my tears drip into the water, the lyrics echo through the walls of the orchestra room to the hallway and into the bathroom itself.

We'll shoot the Cutty Wren . . .
. . . said John the Red Nose.

35
Cherry

Josie, her little princess, her second chance, is dead.

It's that stun she felt when she saw the BBC announcement, via CNN. *A short while ago Buckingham Palace confirmed the death of Diana, Princess of Wales. The princess died following a car accident in Paris. She was thirty-six.* The gulp in the stomach, the world shifted off its bearings. Her Queen of Hearts, dead. Killed by the media giant, eaten by the vultures of prime time and supermarket tabloids.

Josie's death is an echo of it all over again.

Cherry presses her face into her pillow, clasps her hands behind her head and pulls them against each other, unlacing, unlocking, falling to the floor. She drags her fingertips across the wooden headboard. The tears aren't anywhere near to coming; she's not even sure she has any left.

Josie was supposed to be her second chance. Her opportunity for redemption. Getting something right for a change. She was so close . . .

Or maybe she wasn't nearly as close as she thought she was.

The second death she's responsible for. Taking someone's hand (just about, it was just about that), leading them toward the black-cloaked figure, pushing them into Death's arms, into Nothing, into blackness.

The emptiness inside is so vast that not even self-hatred can fill it.

It was the oak tree, the oak tree and her long winter scarf. The red one.

Anyone determined to kill herself will find a way. Marian taught her that.

Josie's mother came by yesterday to pick up her things. A thin, drawn face. Gaunt, her arms needled with track marks that belied her real-estate broker job, a heroin junkie as Josie had said, a functional one; there were probably more out there than you thought.

Cherry rolls onto her back, presses the balls of her thumbs into her closed eyelids, the blackness breaking with red and purple spiderweb patterns, and a dull ache throbs into them. She sits up and opens her eyes. The diamond tennis bracelet from Josie sparkles on her wrist. When Josie's mother stopped by, Cherry hid the bracelet in her own drawer, so she'd get to keep it. It's not that she covets the thing for what it's worth (she'll never sell it, never), but for the fact that Josie gave it to her. Later she fastened the double clasp again and here it rests, on her wrist, the scars from years of cutting faintly visible.

Anyone determined to kill herself will find a way.

She's been palming her medications for a while now, even before the Josie thing happened. It's pretty easy to pretend to drop a pill into your mouth, gulp down the water with one hand as you slip the pill into your jeans with the other.

Not that she's planning to.

It's just in case.

Another set of poems came back from *Echo*. Michael convinced her the personal note from Hattie Gibson-Smythe had meant something so she wrote a cover letter saying 'Thank you for your encouragement.'

This time Hattie wrote back with: *Please don't misconstrue my personal note as encouragement. Take some writing classes. Lose the sentimentality. Don't submit here for at least five years.*

That set of poems went out with the trash yesterday. Josie wasn't there to pull them from the wastebasket, smooth them out.

The spiral is sucking her down farther into the vortex, the spin where she's lost control. She can't even weave anymore,

243

she's getting so careless. This morning she was trimming the tail off a finished green triangle and almost cut the warp thread too. Who knows how she'll fuck up next?

She remembers what it's like to function when she feels this bad and it doesn't take long to get used to. The crash at the bottom's what she looks forward to because then it'll all be over.

She's really only hit the bottom once before. That night at the Porter Place. The scene at Marshall Field's with the knife – the *Take her, God, take this whole motherfucking world!* – that wasn't really a bottom. That was an excuse to come here so she could get well so she wouldn't crash and burn like she did at age seventeen, ever again.

Until, maybe, now.

Funny. Cherry slides a cigarette from the pack on the nightstand she doesn't share with Josie anymore and lights it, slipping smoke from her lips, thinking. She came here to get well. Only it didn't work. Somehow, she's sliding toward the bottom, again.

This time, though, she won't hurt anyone else. She sets her cigarette in the ashtray, slides open the drawer of the nightstand, and counts nine Carbitral. Sleeping pills: that's one of the easiest ways to do it – shouldn't take much. Nine? Will that be enough?

A knock comes on her door and Dr Anders walks in without a word. Cherry slams the drawer shut, shaking, and picks up her cigarette.

'How are you doing, Cherry?' Her voice is gentle, kind.

Cherry won't meet her eyes. 'Fine.'

'Good. Listen. The staff and I have done some talking about you.'

About me? Oh crap. Someone's seen her hiding the pills. Cherry says nothing, blows out more smoke.

'You showed a clear head. It's unfortunate it turned out how it did, but you showed real leadership, determination. You've been progressing well for several weeks, in fact. Your therapy's going well, individual and group. We'd like to recommend to the county board that you go outpatient.'

244

Outpatient? 'Me?' Cherry can't help it and her lips curl into laughter. She giggles silently, tears squeezing from her eyes. 'I just don't think I'm ready for that.'

She rests a hand on Cherry's arm. 'The important thing to know is *we* think you're ready. All of us. We're all behind you, Cherry. And you'll still be coming here to our Partial Hospitalization Program, five days a week.' She taps Cherry on the shoulder and flashes a wide smile, the first one Cherry's ever seen Dr Anders give. 'You think about it.'

'Yeah,' says Cherry. 'I will.'

Later, at dinner, she sits next to Michael and whispers the news to him. They've attached somehow since Josie's suicide, have even, for some odd reason, been walking around holding hands. Relationships among patients are against regulations, but theirs is a friendship. On their walk back to the lounge, he asks her what happened with *Echo* and she tells him and he's pissed she threw her poems away. 'Don't do that again without telling me, Cherry.'

As they're walking back to their rooms, he leans down and kisses her. There's no violence, no forcefulness, nothing like that. Just a warm, sweet kiss. He's twelve years younger than her, but it could work, it could work, couldn't it? She opens her mouth and kisses him back. Then she sinks into his arms, and he holds her for a long time.

I'm not ready to leave. Not without him.

His eyes are so green, green like grass, green like hills. *I can't leave him, I love him . . .*

You're so fucking pathetic, Cherry! A man. She'd fuck herself over for a man? The Bitch Posse would never forgive her.

But they're not real anyway; they've left her forever. She breaks away, turns without saying a word.

'Cherry?'

She doesn't turn around and walks back toward her room.

'Damn it, Cherry, what the hell did I do?'

I could never explain it. Only a woman could understand.

'Fine,' he calls after her. 'Fuck you then.'

The words slap her, and maybe he doesn't care after all. She pushed him away and he's pushed back. The Fuck You was likely deserved, but something impels her to spin around and say, 'I love you. So fuck you too.'

As soon as the words – not the Fuck You, the other words – float out of her mouth she regrets them. *Damn you, Cherry. You're too strong for this bullshit!* She closes her eyes. The tiny pieces of her friends that are still in her heart jigsaw together, and each grasps one of Cherry's hands. 'Fuck you is all I meant.'

Heat drains from her face. She whirls around and runs back to her room and opens up the drawer. On her pillow she lines up the nine Carbitral, lights a cigarette, and stares at them, thinking, pondering, deciding.

36
Amy

May, 1988
Holland, Illinois

Well, the shit is officially coming down because Mom went through my backpack and found the Bitch Goddess Notebook. Now not only does she know about the fact that we've been seeing each other all this time, but I'm standing here in the kitchen watching her read every word about me and Brandon, as Dad stares over her shoulder, skimming it too. Thank God (THANK GOD) we never used anything but initials, because for all they know the R.S. Rennie's been fucking (yeah, we used that word, stupid I know, believe me I've been beating myself up over the whole fucking thing) is Ron Stapleton the math genius. But it doesn't really matter, because Dad's face is turning red and his hands shake as he reaches for his Scotch and soda. Oh damn, he's pissed.

Mom belts down some of her screwdriver and keeps reading, not looking at me. I want to disappear into the floor.

Finally she finishes. She slams the book shut and her eyes narrow. Then, like she's thinking or something, they widen. 'Amy?'

God, that screwdriver looks good. It's a Friday night and I already know I'm grounded which means no going out with the girls and getting drunk and/or stoned. At least I have my Xanax, and my razorblade, ha ha ha. 'Yeah, Mom?'

She sucks in a breath. 'This is so far beneath you. Rich? What should we do?'

Dad slams his drink down on the counter.

Mom passed out earlier as usual and then woke up again to start in on her second round of drinking. So I know any

247

conversation is going to be tangled like a blood clot and I'll never say anything right. 'We made a lot of that stuff up,' I say, 'just stuff we saw in movies and—' It sounds like the bullshit it is.

'Liar.' Dad unscrews the bottle and splashes some into the glass, straight. 'We counted on you, Amy. Do you know how hard this has been?'

'Listen, it's been hard for me too. I don't have any friends now. That's why I've been seeing my old friends.'

Mom walks toward me and stumbles on the perfectly flat floor as she reaches for my face. 'Amy . . .' She rubs a thumb down my cheek. Then she starts to cry.

Oh, crap, I hate seeing her cry. Her face squints up like a baby's and then goes limp. She gasps out a sob, and a thin stream of snot drips from her nose. 'How could you, Amy?' She pulls in her tears for a minute. 'Do you have any idea how hard it is for us to see you do this to yourself?'

Do you have any idea what it's like to have parents who are plastered after school, whose moods are unpredictable, and change on a heartbeat? But I don't say that. I'm dying to get out of the room so I can at least go upstairs and chew some Xanax because my heart's racing in my ears. I'm bursting with anger, not the least bit sorry.

Dad's already finished his straight Scotch and pours another. 'You're missing the point, Barb. Amy here is screwing anything that moves and not only has she disobeyed us but she's done it flagrantly,' and that last word trips him up a bit, but he finally gets his lips around it.

'Well, you know what? You don't have to like my friends, but it's my life. I should be able to see them and I will anyway whatever you say so—'

Mom interrupts. 'Amy, do you have any idea what it's like to be the parents of a handicapped child?'

And of course my answer is no, how could I? So I just stare, but she pushes. 'Do you?'

I flatten my lips, shake my head.

She seizes my shoulders. 'Then why the hell do you make it even fucking harder?' And she won't stop shaking me.

I look to Dad for help but he just says, 'You're hurting your mother, Amy. Can't you see that?'

And I burst out with, 'You should take her home, take her home, why lock her in a box miles away?'

Oh God. Did I really say that?

That's when she slaps me across the face, not once, but twice. 'You little bitch.'

I won't cry in front of them I won't cry in front of them I won't I won't I won't.

'She's going to die, Amy,' says Dad in the background. The Scotch tumbles into his glass, tickticktick. 'You need to face that.'

Did I hear right? 'Die?'

Mom traces her fingers in a pool of orange juice from the drink she knocked over when she was smacking me. 'They don't expect her to last more than another year. Her heart's always been small. Now that she's an adult her body just can't take it. We knew this would happen, eventually.'

Then why didn't they ever clue me in? Now I do start crying, hard, but they just stare at me from across the kitchen. I grab Mom's fresh drink and although it's so tempting to just down it, I take a step forward and fling it into the wall. The glass shatters and hangs there for a moment before the pieces fall to the floor and the orange juice trickles down the paint.

'Amy!' Mom grabs my wrists and bends them backward. 'How did I raise such an impossible slut?'

I glance at Dad again and he coughs and says, 'Barb.'

She lets go. 'Go to your room.' She spits out the words, as if with a great effort, and doesn't make a move to clean up the spoiled drink.

'You heard your mother.' Dad's voice is slurry now, coming from far away.

'It's my life, it's my body, what do you care?' I want to fly out the window, drift into outer space, float anywhere but here. 'I can sleep with whoever I want and you can't stop me.'

'Maybe if we keep you home you won't act like such a

little cunt.' The word trips out of Dad's mouth and shoots into my heart, piercing it.

I feel dead.

'Your room, now.'

'Gladly.' Shaking, I stalk upstairs. There've been scenes with them before but none like this. Mom's never hurt me like that. Dad's never called me *cunt*.

You know what's even worse, they won't remember a word of this tomorrow. Or they'll pretend they don't.

Upstairs I slam the door. My Smiths poster shakes with the vibration and falls to the floor, but I don't pick it up. I throw a cassette, any cassette, into my stereo and turn it way up. It happens to be The Talking Heads, that get-up-and-dance song 'And She Was', but I just hurl myself onto the bed. It's a song that should make me happy but I can't do anything but cry. My sobs smother David Byrne's voice as he sings about the magical woman taking off her dress and rising above the earth. Damn, why can't that be me? I want out of here, now now now.

At least they can't hear me, fuck them, fuck everyone, everything. I pull my Xanax bottle from my nightstand and spill them onto my quilt. How many? I count them in fives: ten, fifteen, twenty, twenty-four. It wouldn't be hard to swallow them. What would twenty-four Xanax do? Would that be enough or would I end up in the hospital in deeper shit, hating myself even more for fucking up yet again?

If I took them all and went downstairs while they're passed out, and grabbed a fifth of vodka and drank it, I bet that'd do it.

I pull out five from the pile and shove them into my mouth, chew them while I think about it.

My beautiful sister – could it be true what they said? Then the sobs start again. I have no family. Even God probably hates me. I don't have anyone, really, who accepts me no matter what. The Bitch Posse's the closest I'll ever get.

Goddamn it, they are not going to ruin my Friday. Fuck them.

I turn down the music, pick up the phone and get a clear

dial tone. So, they're too drunk to imagine I might try and call somebody. There's always a benefit to their drinking, one of which is the cluelessness that allows me to steal booze right in front of them on my way out the door. They might even forget they grounded me within the next hour, but it's not worth the risk. I'm sneaking out. First I have to call though, because I'd better not take Dad's Mustang tonight. *Fuck you, fuck you, fuck you*, I mutter as I drop my Xanax into the bottle one by one.

The phone rings three times and Rennie picks up. 'Yeah.'

She sounds so listless and depressed, but she can't feel worse than me. 'Listen, it's Amy. For the last ten minutes I've been staring at nineteen Xanax ready to gulp them all and it's really hard not to take them right about now . . .'

She slides out a whistle. 'Shit, Amy, your parents?'

'Who else? I don't want to talk about it.'

'I'll be over in ten minutes. Don't do a thing, okay?'

'I have to climb through my window. Meet you in the alley?'

'I'll call Cherry. I'll pick you up, then her. We'll all go there together.'

'Where?'

'The Porter Place.'

It makes sense really; there's nowhere else to go, and we agree. I hang up and fix my makeup, stuff my pillows under my quilt and turn up the music super-loud. Then I slip out the window and drop to the pavement, jog to the alley, and wait.

In a few minutes she's there in her Beetle, and she rolls down the window and hands me a smoke. She's talked to Cherry, I can tell, because she's smiling like a girl who is most definitely not depressed. Thank God. She'll cheer me up.

When I get in, she laughs and shifts the car into gear. 'You are beautiful, my darlin', beautiful.'

'What are we gonna do tonight?'

'Listen, we need to talk. We're all feeling a little angry, aren't we?'

251

God, I know I am. Even the Xanax hasn't blunted it yet; the anger's like a knife in my hands. I hate my mother for hitting me, I hate my father for standing by. I hate them both for their words and for fucking me over just so they can get drunk and feel sorry for themselves. They're so fucking self-righteous about having a 'handicapped child' but they don't stop to think about what it does to someone to grow up with fucked-up parents, what about that, huh, huh, huh?

My finger drifts too close to the cigarette and it burns my flesh, but I feel good, alive, alive. 'You don't have to ask that, Rennie. You know I'm angry.'

Her eyes are glassy, excited. 'Me too.'

'So are we gonna get wasted? Stoned? Drop acid together like Cherry always says we should do?'

The car jerks along. She doesn't normally drive so fast. 'You want to know now, or wait till the moment?' Her face betrays nothing.

'What moment? What do you mean?'

Her expression doesn't change. 'Cherry and I talked. We've got it all figured out. The only way to do something is to do it right the first time, and not fuck around with half-assed solutions.'

'What?'

'We're gonna really kick some ass tonight, scare the shit out of someone. The Bitch Posse, the avenging three. But you don't have to be in if you don't want to.'

' "In" ? What the hell are you talking about?'

She signals left onto Cherry's street. 'Before we head to the Porter Place, the three of us are taking a little drive.' She blows out some smoke. 'And when we get there, we'll have our revenge.'

My heart drops to my knees. 'What do you mean?'

'No one fucks with the Bitch Posse.' She reaches over and squeezes my shoulder. 'We're gonna teach someone a lesson, that's all.'

'You're scaring me, Rennie.' I roll down the window and throw the cigarette into the street. I don't want it anymore. 'You're not making any sense.'

'I already said, if you want out, you're out, no problem, I'll drive you back home. But listen to me first. Then decide.'

37
Rennie

May, 2003
Mill Valley, California

Rennie walks Caleb in from the car and picks up the envelope that's been slid under her door. As he toddles around the porch, she lugs in the gigantic pack of diapers and the groceries from Safeway. She leads him inside and tosses everything on the counter. Maybe the babysitting service called. Maybe Kelly called. Or Puck again, begging for sex, even though she put him off with vague promises about 'next week'. Good Lord.

She slides a Guinness out of one of the Safeway bags, pops the top, and pours it into a tall glass. A drink is surely the last thing she needs after several days without having eaten anything except the veggie burrito that's turned into a rock in her stomach, but the smooth head rolls over her tongue, and the dark brew tastes so good going down. Caleb's already torn open the little cars she picked up at the store and is rolling them across the floor. Messages first or the envelope? She slips open the envelope and it's a quick note:

Ms Taylor,
What happened in your classroom, I don't know why it happened but you really need to take a step back from whatever's going on in your life. Listen, you told me once not to fuck myself over. I'm telling you the same. I'm worried about you – you seem run down and strange and well, just don't fuck up. You're not a bad person. Sorry for all the swearing but I know you understand.
Paul.

She smiles, well *that's* okay then. Then she frowns, humiliation pouring over her like blood. It's not really. She still has to face him day after day, still has to relive the embarrassment of him walking away after she made the most overt pass she's ever been guilty of making. God, did she really grab his hands and shove them on her tits? Did a seventeen-year-old kid, who should be desperate for any sex he can get, really turn her down?

Did a seventeen-year-old kid, who shouldn't know anything about anything, really tell her she needs to take a step back from her life because she's acting run down and strange and might fuck herself over?

She's so fucking evil. A fucking child-molesting psychopath. God should just take her sorry ass. *Kill me now, God! Come get me!*

Eyes burning, she picks up the phone and checks for messages. Four. The first is from North Bay Nannies. All their nannies are European educated and bonded. They can have someone starting on Tuesday but they ask for a finder's fee up front of $10,000. Nannies are paid at a salary of five hundred dollars a week.

Rennie bursts out laughing. 'Fuck that shit,' she says aloud and glances at Caleb, who's barreling cars into the wall. Fortunately the little echo didn't hear her this time. She erases the message and hopes the next one is from the other nanny place. But it's Kelly, explaining that she and Dad are in the Virgin Islands (oh nice!) and will be back in a week. In the meantime they're glad to send some money for a sitter (wonder who'll sign that $10,000 check?) and try to find Mallory with the contact information she left.

The third call is a familiar voice she can almost place, but can't. Amy Dionne? She doesn't know an Amy Dionne. The voice corrects herself. 'Amy Linnet.'

Rennie almost drops the Guinness and listens to Amy tell her that she got in a car crash on Highway 80, that she's in the hospital in Oakland, that Rennie crossed her mind and she just felt she should call; would she mind coming for a visit?

Rennie's head swims as she presses 'save'. *Speak, memory* . . .

She needs those girls now, maybe more than she knows. Where did they go? If she could just go back in time, back to that moment in the circle when they swore their solemn oath.

> *as long as the stars are fixed in the heavens*
> *and the fish sparkle in the sea.*

Oh, God . . . A sob rips through her and her heart splits in half all over again and she throws her face in her hands so Caleb won't see and tears flood out like waves, all over her fingers. She can't see Amy. She can't take it. She just can't.

She takes a deep breath, dries her tears and listens to the final message, from Lisa, her agent. 'Wren, I'm so sorry. I just can't get through these rewrites. It's too heavy, there's no love story. I can't imagine who the audience would be.' She sighs. 'Let me know when you make it through another project, okay? Try some chick-lit – I can sell that. And I want to be the first to see whatever you come up with. But I don't see that this back-and-forth on something we both know is just not working is doing either of us any good.' She hangs up without saying goodbye.

She feels like crying, like hitting the wall, like breaking something, hurting herself, hurting someone else. She runs her fingers over the Guinness glass. It'd be so easy to throw it to the floor, slide her fingers over the shards, splinter one under her skin . . . Phone Puck back, beg him to come over with plenty of coke, put Caleb to bed early and . . .

Something hits her foot.

She looks down. It's a little purple car.

Caleb laughs. 'It's a zoom zoom go car.'

A zoom zoom go car. Someone's telling her something.

Face things.

Face things.

Face things.

She throws the rest of the groceries into the fridge without even taking them out of the white plastic bags. 'Back in the carseat, Caleb. We're going for a drive.'

Caleb clutches the pink teddy bear he bought in the gift shop, and Rennie puts on a cheerful voice as she walks into the room. 'Hey, Amy!'

She looks like she's been in a fight. She looks awful, really; bruises molt over her face, a five-inch cut skates across her upper lip, she's in traction and her whole left arm is bandaged. But when Rennie looks at her closely, she's still the same old Amy; there are a few wrinkles near her eyes (Rennie's got them too), and she's put on five or ten pounds (so has Rennie), but she's still adorable. Her freckles are a little lighter, but her hair's that same washy blonde, cut in a shag. 'Rennie,' she whispers, 'good to see you.'

How do I look to her? Are my nostrils red? Can she tell I've been in a coke haze for the last few days?

Is it really Amy? My Amy?

'Who's the little guy, yours? What a sweetie!'

Rennie laughs. 'Mallory's. Remember Mallory?'

'She was just about his age when I saw her last.'

'Well, she's all grown up and irresponsible. Long story.'

They chat like that for a while. But it's odd the years have put distance between them; Rennie's not quite comfortable talking to her. Frustration aches inside her – why can't they just pick up where they left off? Go out and raise some hell?

That's so stupid. We've both changed so much.

But all of a sudden Amy spills out some major stuff, just like that. The reason she got in the crash. All her drinking. And her marriage ending. Rennie's shocked to learn that Amy's lost a child, doesn't quite know what to say, how to feel.

She bites her lip. 'I'm so sorry, Aim,' and the comfortable old name slips out. 'I just wish I . . . Listen, if you must know I'm not the nicest person in the world myself. I've been fucking myself over, as one of my students would say, since that night, you know, the night.' She pours out her own story: Puck, Paul, her cocaine binge, the endless sex – God, it's good to talk. 'I just don't know where I am anymore.'

'Neither do I.'

They study each other for a minute. *What's going on in those angel-blue eyes?* 'Does Scotty know?' asks Rennie. 'I mean, the whole thing?' Even as she's saying it, she's pushing it down, *bitch bitch bitch bitch bitch*, hating herself, wanting it all to go away. A delicious image of her and Puck in bed for endless hours presses into her brain and she closed her eyes for a moment, swallows the pretty picture whole, yum. Maybe she'll call him when she gets home.

Amy shakes her head. 'No one knows. Just you and Cherry. I haven't heard from her since, well, you know. I always thought it was better that way, always thought we shouldn't see each other again. Maybe calling you was a mistake but . . .' She shrugs. 'I don't know, at least you understand.'

It gets Rennie thinking, maybe it's better to spill things out, instead of pretending you're someone you're not. But then Caleb tugs her arm and says 'I don't wanna . . .'

'Don't want to what?'

He points at the bear, then at Amy.

Rennie still doesn't get it.

Amy laughs. 'He changed his mind about giving me the bear. That's okay, sweetie. You don't have to. It's yours.'

Caleb holds the bear close, wipes his nose with the back of his hand. 'I'm tired,' he announces and of course he is, it's almost eight o'clock. Rennie leans over, hugs Amy, and says, 'Call anytime.'

'I might.'

Rennie's eyes catch Amy's, and just like that the Amy of 1988 appears in front of her again, the girl almost a woman, her best friend, forever. Rennie smiles, and a smile creeps across Amy's face too. *Hello, friend.* Unspoken between them is the Bitch Posse oath, the words that will always bind them: *As long as the stars are fixed in the heavens and the fish sparkle in the sea.*

Sure, it's over, Rennie knows that. Amy'll never call. Probably. But that's okay. They'll always have their Posse, and their memories, and that's enough. 'If you see Scotty again, if he comes here . . .'

Amy's eyes well up with tears. 'He'll come. It's over with us, but he'll come see me.'

'Just tell him the truth.' *Don't pretend you're someone you're not. You're no angel, my sweet Amy, but you're no devil either.*

That thought feels like it's about to spin out into another one, but Rennie's in a hurry and the whole visit's been so intense, she's got to go.

They hug quickly and Amy whispers, 'Bye, Rennie,' brushing her hand over her collarbone.

I love you, Amy, she can't bring herself to say aloud. Amy's thinking it too, maybe, but words don't need to strike the air to be real. 'Bye, Aim,' she says instead and watches her best friend's fingers slip between the locket and the cross she never thought she'd see Amy wearing.

The trip over the Richmond Bridge is speedy, dark, clear, like driving through a tunnel into the light.

When she pulls into her driveway, Caleb's asleep in his carseat. She turns off the engine, carries him inside to the bedroom, and rests him in the middle of the bed so he won't fall out. 'I'll take care of you, sweetpea,' she murmurs, and it's the best feeling in the world to know she means it. His little chest rises and falls. As she strokes his pale curls for a moment, he rolls away from her and she whispers a little nursery rhyme from Christina Rossetti.

Angels at the foot,
And angels at the head,
And like a curly little lamb,
My pretty babe in bed.

259

It brings to her an inhale of Mom, back when she did stuff like read nursery rhymes, back before she took off for Texas and drifted out of Rennie's life. She rests her palm on his back, his breath nudging her hand as he sleeps. For a moment she feels so sweet, so great, maybe Caleb should stay here, even after Kelly and Dad get back . . .

Crazy.

She lands a kiss in his curls, and warmth spreads through her heart, melting whatever's been frozen around it all this time.

Or not so crazy at all.

She returns to the living room and the horrible feelings clot back up in her, the hating, the self-loathing, all her trouble, Paul, Bay, the goddamn book and Lisa's fucking message.

'Chick-lit,' she says aloud. 'I don't even know what it fucking is.' She lands a punch on the edge of the sofa, the part where the skeleton meets the fabric, and it hurts like hell, leaves a bruise. Good.

Something in her wants to blot away, push away, fuck away the pain, the roots Amy's dug up by her very presence in Rennie's life. She pulls the Guinness out of the fridge and throws some whiskey into the glass along with it. Then she dials Puck's number by heart, yes yes yes yes, he'll come over with the cocaine and his hot young body and they'll fuck on the sofa, push Amy's face out of her life. She'll change her number so Amy can never call her again, and her breath catches in her throat as she waits for Puck to answer, the phone humming in her ear.

It flashes in Rennie's head, the painful cold clear memory of that night, one piece, unshattered, whole, perfect in its intensity, gorgeous in its passion, and the ending, the swallow of guilt in her, the constant pushing it down, fighting it back, fucking it away. Her thought from the hospital echoes in her mind: *Don't pretend you're someone you're not.*

Her fingers tremble as she curls the phone cord.

Sexy, dripping, crushed blackberries ooze through the receiver. 'Hello?'

'Hi, it's Wren . . .' But before she can say any more, that thought that she had in the hospital finally finishes itself up. *Fucking isn't love, and it's a pretty shitty replacement for facing yourself.*

Without explaining anything, she clicks down the phone. She tucks her laptop under her arm, walks to her room, and slides into bed next to Caleb. His little face is bathed in moonlight as he sleeps; he looks as if he might be out of a dream.

She loves him like she hasn't loved anyone in years.

Screw chick-lit.

She opens her laptop, starts a blank file, and stares and stares and stares.

Caleb rolls over and sighs like the most beautiful symphony Rennie's ever heard.

She closes her eyes and in a second she's back in Cherry's room, the girls in a circle. *We, the Bitch Posse girls, do solemnly swear to be undyingly faithful to each other, and to put no friends or lovers before one another, as long as the stars are fixed in the heavens and the fish sparkle in the sea.*

I love you, Amy.

I love you, Cherry.

The girls press their wounds together. Three into one.

Tears are loosened behind her eyes. She might just have a heart after all.

I'm not evil. God doesn't hate me.

She's not ready to write anything, not now. But that's okay. She will, someday. She closes up her file and switches off the laptop.

The phone rings.

It's him, that hot sexy powerful famous writer from Palo Alto. That really famous and important novelist who posed half-naked in the *New Yorker* last winter. That stupid pathetic little snail of a person she's been fucking in order to run away from something she should never have tried to escape at all.

Rennie listens to the phone ring a couple more times, then unplugs it.

She doesn't need anyone else to make her real. She knew it when she was in the Bitch Posse, but the years made her forget. No matter. The next thing she writes will be something real, something that means something. *Something Real* by Wren Taylor. Wren. Not a bad little name, that.

The poor wren, the most diminutive of birds, will fight, her young ones in her nest, against the owl.

Wren. Small and plain, but she sure can sing.

'My name is Wren,' she says aloud. 'Wren Grace Taylor.'

She tangles her fingers in Caleb's hair and switches off the light. Two ghosts of girls crawl into bed next to her, cross their arms over her back. She sobs into her pillow for a while, but it's the good kind of crying, and it doesn't take her long to fall asleep.

38
Cherry

Just before Rennie heads to his door, she leans into me and prsses her forehead against mine for luck. 'Guess what popped into my head in the middle of the night?'

'What?'

'A nursery rhyme.' She reaches into the back seat for Amy's hand, then mine, and we're in a ring-around-the-rosy circle as she recites:

> *Who killed Cock Robin?*
> *'I,' said Jenny Wren.*
> *'With my poison pen,*
> *I killed Cock Robin.'*

Then she bursts into laughter.

'That's pretty good,' I say. But that's not how I remember the poem. Didn't Jenny Wren and Cock Robin get married? And there was no poison pen in the rhyme at all. I certainly won't point it out to her though. Hell, for all I know, Jenny Wren really did kill Cock Robin and the whole Sparrow thing was a set-up.

Amy giggles too, a little gulp that sounds like half a sob. She *is* scared. Shit. I hope she gets her nerve before it's time. She will. The Bitch Posse girls don't take shit from anyone.

Rennie slides out of the front seat and blows us a kiss as she walks to his doorstep. Amy and I wait in silence.

It doesn't take long.

They walk down the driveway, arm-in-arm. She's a study in pale skin and dark hair, black dress clinging to her tiny body, black silk scarf flying out from her neck. A cat, elegant, graceful, perfect.

I slide into the driver's seat so she and Schafer and Amy can play it out in the back. This is how it's planned. After Rennie and I hung up from each other, she called him and said she wanted him back, suggested a little fun with all four of us, tonight at the Porter Place. With all those rumors about our being in a lesbian drug cult, he bought it, no problem.

Fuck his credential and all that. The Bitch Posse's going to kick some ass and draw some blood, and that's just how it has to be. He brought it on himself. We're going to fuck up his head, scare him good. And when we're through with him he'll be so fucking humiliated he'll never touch another girl.

I glance at Amy in the rearview. Her eyes are glass, but I don't think she's afraid anymore. I don't know. Sometimes it's hard to tell with Amy.

Right now I can't let myself feel my hate. I can't let the flash of the day of Rennie's abortion, and all the pain and tears about Rob Schafer pick their way into my head. I can't let him see that stuff because there are appearances that must be kept up. So I breathe in and out, pushing away thoughts.

He'll be so sorry he fucked with us. And if things get messed up for some reason, well, let's just say I have it all planned out.

It's all scripted. Every. Fucking. Word.

Rennie whispers something in his ear, and he laughs and squeezes her close. She opens the back door. They tumble in, first Schafer, then Rennie, kissing. When I shoulder check to back out of the driveway, I catch Amy in my gaze and narrow my eyes. *Come on, you know your part.*

He's sliding his fingers up her thigh already anyway, and I have to turn around and drive. Behind me he says, 'Rennie filled me in on everything, and I can't wait. I always knew good things come in threes . . .'

I glance in the mirror in time to see Amy rest her head on Schafer's lap, her hands working on his zipper as he starts unbuttoning Rennie's sweater. 'Amy. Amy Linnet. Freshman year, third period, second row from the front. Why'd you ever quit cheerleading? You looked so cute in that little skirt.' He sucks in his breath at whatever she's doing. 'Oh, Amy,' he whispers, 'we'll have to get together more often.' Then Rennie, I guess it's Rennie because Amy's otherwise engaged, shuts him up with a kiss. He breaks away for a minute to lean up to me, his breath hot in my ear. 'You have a beautiful name, Cherry, want me to break you . . . ?' and I fight so hard not to shrink away from him.

As warmly as I can manage I mutter, 'That won't be necessary.'

He lands a kiss on my neck and Rennie, protective, says, 'Let her drive, Rob.' God, I'm glad I don't have to be there in the back with them. My heart's breaking for Rennie — how can she do this with how much she hates him? And Amy, I hope she doesn't end up blowing him before we get there. But this is the only way.

So I pop my new Jesus and Mary Chain tape into the player and turn up 'Kill Surf City' really loud so I don't have to hear the smacks of kisses, the moans. This song is about hate hate hate, and it's just perfect. I step on the gas and light a cigarette and get us there quick.

A light rain pitters on the roof of Rennie's car, and I pull in close to the barn, turn off the engine, and leave the keys in the ignition. All part of my plan of course.

Schafer doesn't notice a thing. He's practically in a drunken swoon, lipstick all over his face and neck, unzipped pants ready to fall down off his ass. Amy and Rennie each take a hand and lead him from the car into the barn, laughing. They're both doing such a good job.

I rummage through the glove compartment for one last thing. He turns around, tosses words at me. 'You coming, Cherry?'

My hand freezes. Does he see?

'Coming?' I say. 'You bet I am, more than once I hope.'

265

He laughs. 'I knew you weren't named Cherry for nothing.'
Oh, he is a sick, sick slob.

'Come on, Rob,' calls Amy, tugging his arm. 'I hope I can call you that now.'

'Call me whatever you want, Amy, you gorgeous thing.'

Their voices disappear into the barn.

I get the knife out of the glove compartment and tuck it into my long black coat. The cold rain sprays over me, spitting on my face. I stand there for a minute, alone against the sky. We could go further, if we wanted to. We could jump over the edge and go spinning into the valley below.

It's more tempting than you'd think. Really, what's to stop me? What's to stop *us*? It's all empty anyway. The sky goes on forever above me. If I closed my eyes I'd be swallowed up in the blackness, be part of it, just be Nothing. I try it for a minute.

My consciousness slips back into me. *Goddamn it, Cherry, stay focused.* I slide my finger along the knife, the little slit of a cut waking me up, making me real.

Tonight the Bitch Posse's going to mess with his head so much he'll end up in a fucking mental institution. We're going to fuck him up so bad even his wife won't want him. *Guess what, God? I don't feel one bit bad about it.*

I walk into the barn.

The girls have lit the candles that are scattered around the place, and Amy's unscrewing the vodka bottle, as planned. I try to send her a psychic message: *Don't get drunk.* I give her credit; she presses the bottle to her closed lips and passes it to him. He lifts his hand from between her legs and grabs the vodka, takes a hearty swig, and gestures at me with it. 'Cherry, join us!'

I pull my coat close, sit cross-legged in the circle, and shake my head when he offers the vodka. 'I took three hits of acid an hour ago.' A bold-faced lie. 'Booze doesn't do a thing for me when I'm tripping.'

'Tripping, huh?' His eyes are marbles in the candlelight. 'God, that takes me back. I used to be pretty wild, back in the day.'

Back in the day. All that hippie bullshit, peace love and happiness, is a big fat lie. Just what has he become? He leans across the circle and smashes against me in a kiss.

I can't let him feel the knife that's pressing against my side, so I pull away.

He locks his fingers in the hair near my ears. 'Not as wild as you girls, though.' And he laughs as if he's said something terrifically funny. His skin is like wax, like something in a museum. Not real.

Not real.

I glance at Rennie. Beads of sweat spring onto her upper lip.

A barn swallow screams past us and swoops to the opposite rafter. He stiffens, checks from left to right. Rennie laughs, a low, husky laugh. 'It's just a bird.'

'So where's Dawn?' I ask.

He lets go of my hair, swallows more vodka. 'She's working late at the firm. I left her a note that I decided to take in a movie, alone. I do that sometimes.'

Yeah, I just *bet* you do.

'Come closer, Cherry.' He reaches for Amy's breasts with one hand and Rennie's with the other, his mouth hanging open like a dog's. He's not a person, not really. He's a bundle of hormones and impulses, a great big cock on legs. He slides his tongue over his lips as he runs his fingers over my friends' breasts, and my heart aches for them; I've seen about enough. 'Come *here*, Cherry,' he says insistently. 'I want *all* of you near me.'

I nestle up behind him, lift the wavy hair at the nape of his neck, and slide my tongue along his skin. Moaning, he squeezes my friends, and I give them a Cherry-wink. 'Put your hands behind your back.'

'What?'

Amy lands a bite on his earlobe. 'If you want to play our games, Rob, you have to follow our rules.'

Smiling, he lets Amy pull his fists together behind him, and Rennie unwinds the rope. 'Just a little extra fun,' Rennie says, tightening the knot around his wrists and scooting around to the front to kiss him. She laces her fingers in his hair and tugs him closer, gazing at him extra long before glancing at me. Her brown eyes are open wide as a doe's, and then slowly, deliberately, she returns my wink.

I slide the knife from my coat, give him a choke hold, and press the blade to his throat.

He stiffens. 'Rennie? What's this about?'

'Yeah, Rennie,' I say, sliding the blade gently along the skin.

Her face is stony.

Love swells in my chest. I will give my friend this gift, her sweet revenge. 'Rennie, darling, you explain.' Every word is scripted, every movement choreographed, and my darling Rennie'd better draw up some courage.

'Tonight . . .' She pauses.

Fuck up his head, get him good. I close my eyes, sending her my strength, and mouth the words '*Bitch Posse . . .*'

When I open them, she's smiling. 'Tonight, Cock Robin . . .'

She knots her fingers in his hair and yanks hard.

'We're gonna slit your fucking throat.'

39
Amy

After Rennie and her nephew leave, Amy watches TV and then drifts off to sleep. She dreams a wobbly dream, with black and white lines going up and down her sightline in lightning jags. She's walking through a grassy field, all alone. High fog clings to the sky, and a clot, that's what it looks like, a clot of blood high above, sinks toward her, picking up momentum. As the clot nears Amy, it separates, grainy, a million red dots. Closer still, she sees the dots are birds, birds? They zoom closer, suffocating her. No, not birds.

Bats.

Red bats fill the sky, every inch of it as they swarm about five feet above. The Dream-Amy screams and falls to the ground, covering her ears and head with her hands. The bats scream too as they draw nearer. Something or someone puts a hand under her, turns her over like she's a baby, holds her eyes open and makes her look as the red bats dart and shriek, mice-birds, as red as dried blood. One flies near her face. She tries to scream again and the bat flies into her mouth, and next to her stands a girl, tall, with blonde curly hair holding a baby . . .

She awakens in a cold sweat. The Chinese woman next to her is talking to a visitor. 'Yes, yes, but you are lucky her doctor is so smart, you should listen.' She is full of advice, Shu-Qing, always. They've chatted a little, and Shu-Qing's given Amy all sorts of tips, from taking up painting again to letting her parents back into her life. Amy agrees with some of it, not all, never all. She notices Amy awake next to her and says, 'You were dreaming, Amy?'

269

'Yes.'

'I heard you muttering, that's how I know. You pay attention to your dreams, Amy. Shouldn't she pay attention to her dreams, Stephen?'

And the tall Chinese man with the long nose, the nut-brown eyes, the bow lips, smiles.

'This is my son, Stephen.'

Cherry's lips were shaped just like his.

Cherry.

She's what's missing from this whole equation. *Where are you, Cherry? Come back, come back, oh please don't leave me.*

'Handsome, yes?'

Heat blooms in Amy's cheeks.

'Stephen is very lucky. His wife is diagnosed with cancer, breast cancer.'

Oh my God.

'But she will get well. This cancer they can treat. What first seems unlucky is actually lucky. Mothers know these things.'

'What was your dream?' Stephen asks.

Amy tells them. They exchange a glance. 'You pay attention to your dreams, Amy,' Shu-Qing says again.

'What, does it mean something?'

'You're lucky you can remember your dreams. Stephen hardly ever remembers,' Shu-Qing says. As usual no one will answer her straight out.

'Amy? Amy Dionne?' And it's him, him, he's here, he's here, maybe that's what the dream was about, seeing Scotty.

'Amy, you have a visitor, and very *handsome*,' Shu-Qing emphasizes and Stephen laughs.

When he walks around the curtain Amy's stunned. The Scotty in her memory has been breathed full of life, and he comes closer, hair dipping into his face, eyes full of concern, flowers, he brought her flowers, white roses. She never thought he'd bring her flowers again. Her eyes fill with tears. *Scotty . . .*

'Hi,' she whispers, emotion catching in her throat. *It's over, it's over, he's just being nice, don't let yourself care.*

'Hi.' He sets down the roses, reaches out, shakes her hand. (Shakes her hand!) Then he sits in the chair opposite the bed. They stare at each other for a moment, uncertainty tripping between them like gnats. Stephen and Shu-Qing keep talking about Stephen's wife and their chatter fills the air. Funny a Chinese woman would name her son after a Catholic saint. But she'll never go back to church – it's all a lie.

Scotty and Amy keep staring.

She finally thinks of something. 'How was your flight?'

'Fine, good.' His fingers rub against each other in his lap, and he notices her empty pitcher. 'Want some water?'

She forces a smile. Her face hurts so bad. 'Thanks.'

He gets up and fills the pitcher from the tap of the bathroom. When he comes back they still keep staring. He points to her cross. 'Where'd that come from?'

'Catey gave it to me before I left. I hardly remembered I was wearing it, then I crashed and I really shouldn't have pulled through. I can't take it off now.' So embarrassing, atheist Amy walks around with a cross for the rest of her life. But it can't be helped.

'That and your locket.'

She fingers it. 'Yeah. Well, that'll never come off.'

That's as close as they've come since it happened to discussing Lucky, and she whispers, 'God, Scotty, I don't know what I was thinking. I can't tell you how fast I was driving, and I'd had so much to drink. What the hell was I doing?'

And the answer falls into Amy's mind, *I guess I was trying to kill myself.*

The realization thuds her in the stomach.

She tries to make a joke. 'Guess this is an enforced drying-out period,' she says and laughs, but Scotty doesn't. He looks as if he wants to say something, but instead he pulls a couple of books from a paper bag.

They're two Neruda paperbacks, his *Memoirs* and a book called *Passions and Impressions*. 'I'll read if you want.'

'That'd be nice.' She remembers what Rennie said. *Just tell him the truth.* 'But first listen.'

'I've been listening,' he says, a little testily.

271

'That's not what I mean. Come here.' She beckons him to the bed. 'I need to tell you something about me. I've needed to tell you for a long time.'

Uncertainly he approaches her and sits near her. Cupping her good hand as he bends close, she whispers to him the entire untold story. She's told him bits and pieces before but certainly not what they ended up doing, and now she tells the whole long story of the Porter Place and Rob Schafer and her two best friends in the world, and it takes a long time to spill it all out (she includes everything – her emotions her friends the drugs Rennie's abortion, her parents, kissing Cherry, everything) and he keeps nodding, nodding, and at the end of it all he bends away and says, 'Wow. I'm not sure I can deal with that.'

It's so anticlimactic somehow; she's pictured his look of shock and horror, names thrown at her.

'I guess,' he says, 'in some way, I sensed it all along.'

'Does it change things?'

'Amy, there's nothing left for it to change.'

And that realization, that it's all gone away, leaves her numb.

'I have something to tell you, too.' He recounts the details of his affair with Suzy Petersen, much more actually than Amy would have preferred to know, but like Scotty it's what she's suspected for a long time. As he winds down the story he just says, 'I'm sorry,' and his eyes are wide and brown and soft.

But she can't forgive that, fucking someone else, that's just not fair, and when she was pregnant too, and she says, 'I'm not sure I can deal with that either.' She doesn't blame him for not forgiving her – she is, after all, an unconvicted criminal, and again they stare, the wall between them invisible but six feet wide. She wishes somehow she could break through all the shit, reach for him, kiss him, but that won't happen again, maybe never, maybe not with anyone.

Take me back, Scotty . . . Please take me back . . .

Words fall into her head. *Be strong, Amy! He fed you shit. Are you going to ask for seconds? Be strong! You don't need him!*

She knows who it is. Her very best friend in the whole wide world. Cherry Diana Winters.

Take me back, Bitch Posse . . . Please take me back . . .

The same voice speaks in her head. *We never let you go, silly! You are the Uber-Bitch Goddess, now and forever!*

And so she just looks at him instead of apologizing again like she was about to do.

She puts her good hand to her locket and her cross. She's not sure she believes in God, hell, she's been let down so many times . . . But she wishes she could believe in something. Maybe she could believe, or just pretend to believe, in Luck, in things unfolding in a certain way for a reason.

And he stands up and returns to the chair and pulls the book onto his lap and asks again, 'Want me to read?'

'Yes, read, please, Scotty. I'd like that.' Escape into words, dive into someone else's emotions – that is about all she can deal with right now.

He opens *Passions and Impressions* and Neruda's words float around her softly: *'This woman fits in my hands. She is fair and blond, and I would carry her in my hands like a basket of magnolias. This woman fits in my eyes . . .'*

Oh, God, her heart's breaking. Scotty feels it too, because he trails off, watching Amy's face.

No. She won't allow herself to be manipulated by words again, won't let him try to rekindle the flame that's long since burned away. 'Read something else.' *You don't need him. You don't need anyone. You can stand on your own.*

He doesn't fight her and opens up the *Memoirs* instead. *'In these memoirs or recollections there are gaps here and there, and sometimes they are also forgetful, because life is like that.'*

Sounds a bit like Amy's memories. She wishes she could remember every moment with her beautiful Bitch Posse girls, the girls who saved her so many times.

'Intervals of dreaming help us to stand up under days of work. Many of the things I remember have blurred as I recalled them, they have crumbled to dust, like irreparably shattered glass . . .'

What they did was wrong, worse than wrong. It was evil. But even the worst evil is forgivable.

273

Scotty can fight his own demons. That's his business. She'll take hers head-on, thank you very much.

'. . . *Perhaps I didn't just live in my self, perhaps I lived the lives of others . . .*'

The sentences fall into words and the words break into letters and the letters drop onto Amy and scatter and build up into a blanket that's tucked over her shoulders by her two best friends on earth.

'*From what I have left in writing on these pages there will always fall – as in the autumn grove or during the harvesting of vineyards – yellow leaves on their way to death, and grapes that will find new life in the sacred wine.*'

And this moment is perfect, scripted, not anything like what she expected, not out of a fairy tale or a feelgood movie or a paperback novel, but all right. The only way, really, that this chapter of her life could have ended.

'*My life is a life put together from all those lives: the lives of the poet.*'

Scotty weaves the tale of Neruda's childhood in a Chile that's so far removed from this hospital, her life, their marriage. She smiles, just a little, and lets the words fall onto her, Scotty's voice warm and red and true and all right. This isn't love, not anymore, but it's something kind and comforting, and she lets his words cover her until she's asleep again. This time she dreams only of a warm summer night, a clear white moon, and silence.

40
Rennie

May, 1988
The Porter Place

As soon as the words are out of my mouth I'm terrified. I can't do this, I can't, I can't.

But for some reason he doesn't sense my hesitation. As a matter of fact he looks like he's scared shitless, and pleasure washes through me. *Yeah, I've got you now, shoe's on the other foot . . .*

Still, I'm feeling kind of chickenshit; after all I've never hurt anyone but myself before, and I wonder if this wasn't a mistake.

Cherry reads my mind. 'He's not a someone, Rennie. Think of what he did to you.'

'I'm not—' Rob starts.

She goes on like she's not listening. 'What he did to Dawn. All his lies.'

'Leave Dawn out of this.'

'Shut up, Schafer.'

And that helps, the last name. Not Rob, not even Mr Schafer our teacher. Schafer, I can deal with that.

I run my fingers through my hair. The chunky bits slide over my fingers like snakes, and words spill into my head, dripping from the pen of the greatest writer who ever lived:

If you prick us, do we not bleed? If you tickle us, do we not laugh? If you poison us, do we not die? And if you wrong us, shall we not revenge?

Yeah.

Yeah.

Yeah.

You bet we shall.

It also helps that Cherry slides the knife over his throat, breaking the skin, blood popping up like butterflies on either side of the cut. I don't have to be the first one. He doesn't scream but he squints, he's shaking, it hurts, good, good! 'If you're lucky we might not kill you,' says Cherry. 'If you're lucky we might just give you a few scars of your own, instead. What do you think, Rennie? Should we let the little motherfucker have his little motherfucking stinking life?'

My cue. *'What's fair is foul, and foul is fair. Hover through the fog and filthy air.'* A puzzled look crosses his face and I say, 'Don't act like you don't know where that's from, you asshole.' Can he really be so stupid?

'Up to you, Rennie,' says Amy. 'Does he live or die?'

'He's an asshole and a pig and an animal . . .' We're playing Good-Cop-Bad-Cop, surely he knows this, but the important thing is *I hold his life in my hands.* '. . . but no one deserves to die.'

He's glancing from me to Cherry to Amy and back again, and the stark terror in his eyes sends a rush of power through me. 'All right then,' says Cherry. She hands the knife to Amy and the three of us just look at each other.

A swallow of hesitation trembles in my throat and I whisper, 'What'll become of us . . .'

'The power is ours,' says Cherry loudly. 'Fuck consequences.'

'Anyway,' says Amy. 'Hang us, Schafer, you hang yourself.' She rips open his shirt from the front and slides the knife from his chest to his stomach, not too hard, but deep enough to leave a mark. She scrapes a channel through his skin, like the ones I've scraped on myself so many times, but this is so much more empowering. She draws it out and makes an angle, then returns to the starting point and smoothes it over as he moans until it's a gorgeous letter D.

Then, she passes the knife to me.

The handle feels smooth against my fingers, an object, lifeless, the object. The object the object the object. One object meets another, that's all this is. I carve out an A, digging deep, making channels, furrows, and blood bursts to the surface just like it does when I cut myself. 'That's *my* A,' I say aloud. 'I earned it.'

And he's sobbing, words are falling from his mouth that aren't even making any sense except it sounds like he's begging for his life. I'm so happy, he sounds terrified, and I don't even care that we're hurting him. He's hurt me so goddamn much, maybe other girls too, his wife for sure.

Cherry makes the W, working fast, slashing down and up and down and up and it's very raw, her W, very sharp and edgy and dangerous, just like my very best friend in the world.

My head feels foggy, and I shake it to wake it up. Funny, I don't feel evil at all. I feel righteous and justified and higher than I've ever been in my life. And Cherry passes me the knife. I get an extra turn because it's me he fucked over, and very carefully and deliberately and slowly I make the N. I take my time and make it excruciating and horrible and neverending, because that's just how he did it to me.

And now it's done. D-A-W-N.

'So you'll remember who you belong to,' I toss at him. 'Not that she'd want you if she knew what you really are.'

Beads of sweat roll down his face, his hair is damp, and he looks so fucking terrified. 'Please . . . I'm sorry . . . Please don't hurt me anymore.'

Hmm, interesting how he suddenly cares about someone hurting.

'Don't kill me.' *No one's going to kill you, asshole*, I want to say, but don't. This is the ultimate mind-fuck after all. 'Please, I'll do anything. Money, grades, anything.'

'Why?' says Cherry. 'You're a sick, abusing, cheating, manipulating rapist. Give one good reason why you deserve to live.'

He's begging for his life. We hold his life. The knife. The knife could end his life.

'Shut up, Schafer.' And now I'm doing it, too.

Cherry pulls the blade out of my hands. 'Really, girls,' and she's speaking like he's not even there, 'why not end it now, just take his fucking life, reduce him to the object he is? Why let his sorry soul stay trapped in his body any longer? He doesn't deserve it, doesn't deserve to see to hear to feel to anything.' She grabs my hand and Amy's and slips them over hers on the knife. We press the blade to his throat. 'Come on, girls. Are you with me?'

'Please. Please . . .'

And this is part of our script too. We're going to make him face death, taste death, touch death, just for a minute. We're going to drag him right to the edge and then pull him back to life, and once he's seen his end he won't fuck with anyone else, ever again.

'Please . . .'

We trace the knife over his neck. 'We might let you live,' spits Cherry. 'If you promise to never touch another girl. We'll let *you* figure out how to explain your little tattoo work to your wife. Since you're so good at lying.'

His eyes are darting back and forth and he's trembling, good, good! And I get to say the next part, my line. 'The woman who made the mistake of marrying you would be standing right next to us if she knew what an evil, heartless, soulless prick you are.'

His blood-soaked shirt clings to his chest, letters etched in his skin, and I ball up my scarf and shove it in his mouth. There's just one thing left to do, one last mind-fuck to pull, and Cherry's the one who brings it up. 'Get him undressed.'

I yank his pants and jockey shorts the rest of the way off him (how many times have I done this before?) and it's all lifeless, the parts of him that used to make me crazy, mindless, that mesmerized me, put me under a spell and made me an electric current of impulses I couldn't say no to. God, what was wrong with me?

Cherry's got the knife now, and she draws it along his balls, pulling up blood as she cuts the skin. Thank God there's my scarf in his mouth because I don't want to hear any screams. 'So, Schafer. You can choose. Your cock, or your life.'

He shakes his head, his eyes pleading.

I close my own. I can't look, I can't be drawn in, he's

becoming a person to me again. I've fallen for him so many times before . . .

Cherry senses my weakness. She grabs my hand, presses it under hers on the knife handle. 'You, too, Amy.' Amy slips her hand under Cherry's. 'Look, the sorry little dog's terrified. A creature like you,' she spits, 'can't function without sex. That's the reality, isn't it? You can't say no. You'd even fuck a teenager. You'd even get her pregnant and then try to wash it away with money and an abortion and then pass it off as a little fling and then try to seduce her best friends. I pity you. But most of all I pity your poor wife. She deserves better.' Hatred pushes the words from her lips. 'You're pathetic.' Our hands follow Cherry's as she moves the knife to his throat again. 'Maybe it *would* be better all around if we just kill you. You're nothing without your testosterone, and well, that's the choice we're left with, isn't it? You surely can't be allowed to go around following your impulses, now can you? You've done enough damage. And you'd rather be dead than look at a world without fucking whatever looks pretty to you at the moment.' She sighs. 'Like I said, no one fucks with the Bitch Posse. Want to die? We aren't afraid to go there. Be a man, Schafer, be a man and take it. Maybe then your wife'll have the chance to find a decent person. Notice, two words. Decent. Person.'

And this'll be our last mark, an underline below our beautiful red word. His eyes widen, he shakes his head. *Now you'll learn your lesson.* Cherry's hands guide ours and we slide the blade across his skin, and I close my eyes.

Words push their way into my head. *Awake, ye powers of hell! The wandering ghost that once was Clytemnestra calls — Arise!* and my heart catches in my chest and our hands are all melted together, it's one hand that's doing this, and more words, I love words, I would breathe words, eat words, wordswordswords scream into my head, *Seize, seize, seize, seize-mark, yonder!* and I don't care, I don't care, I don't care, *Of justice are we ministers* . . . I don't even know where the words are from, *We wear and waste him; blood atones for blood,* but it doesn't matter because life buzzes in my ears,

279

our ears, *Queens are we and mindful of our solemn vengeance*, and I am alive again, I am me again, me me me me me!

I open my eyes. Our line slashes jaggedly under the four letters that drip into it, and we hold the tip of the blade right under the N. Our final mark. Everything's perfect.

A cry escapes his throat, and his body goes into some kind of spasm, jerks toward the knife. At once the blade sinks into his flesh, presses deeper, and blood splashes into the air, sprays against my face, and, and, and . . .

What?

So much blood, so much blood. Flowing over the knife handle and our fingers. Our arms. The barn floor.

What just happened?

A scream presses into my mouth, but fear claps her hand over my lips. Blood, blood everywhere, still pouring from him as he's twitching, trembling, gurgling. Words scramble up and drop themselves into my head at random; they aren't quite right. *Yet dear Rennie Taylor, who would have thought your lover had so much blood in him?*

Shut up!

And so I am empty of words, except for those simple ones that drum in my head, in this odd and blackened silence: *Oh God oh God oh God . . .*

All we can do is watch; and I can now put into words just how eyes change when the soul slips out of them, when a living being becomes just another object. In one moment his eyes sparkle with pain, fear, emotion, life; and in the next they are empty. My heart sinks to my toes and nausea creeps into my throat. The three of us back away, holding hands, and the knife drops to the floor. I'm numb.

Oh, my God.

We've just killed someone.

I want the universe to swallow me up into it, my head's going to explode, my heart is an empty balloon.

I *am* evil. Truly, truly evil. I didn't think I had it in me, but I was wrong.

I study the girls' eyes and I can't even imagine what's going through their heads. It wasn't supposed to end like this.

It was an accident.

An accident an accident an accident.

A murder.

I don't even know what the words mean anymore. They may as well be synonyms.

Words. We are in a place now where they can't exist and so in silence we walk together to the barn door.

That's when we see the headlights approaching from the highway.

41
Cherry

May, 2003
Freemont Psychiatric Hospital

A spring rain is falling and Cherry's awake, watching it sob down the dark windows, the spatters crystalline against the glass, the moon casting a shaft of light across the empty bed next to her. Tomorrow they will tell her she's ready to go outpatient. She's not so sure.

Michael's slipped from her grasp. She's pushed him away, or he's pushed her away. Last night, after they told each other to fuck off, he stole into her room (how he snuck out she doesn't know) and said, 'This may be goodbye, Cherry, so let's make it a good one.' Before she knew what was happening they were in bed together, sheets tangled around their legs, but it was less like making love and more like fucking, Sam Sterling all over again, hot and sweaty and *slap-yes slap-yes slap-yes* and in the end just messy. The condom discarded in her wastebasket is still shiny and sad-looking, a wrinkled lump of what could have been, and he left without kissing her and what the hell did *that* mean?

Another 'fuck off', most likely.

She's so fucking weak and pathetic. Why does she let men walk all over her?

It hurts too much to try to help people, anyway. You set yourself up for disaster and you end up not even being able to save yourself. She fingers the quilt on the plain wooden bed, the bed she may be leaving. The diamond tennis bracelet of Josie's still sparkles from her wrist; a bunch of rocks and some metal is all it really is, but it's a reminder of what she almost accomplished, the redemption she almost made. Anyway, she tried.

They don't build empires on 'tried'.

She takes a deep breath, wanting a smoke. But the pack on the table between the beds is empty, so she sucks in pure white air instead. It clears her head and she stares out the window into the rain-soaked night. *I always had a hunch there was no God . . . now I know there is no Goddess, no Buddha, no Vishnu, no Mohammed, no Diana, no nothing.* Every single time she thought she'd found The Answer, she turned out to be wrong. There's really no one out there listening, no one at all, just this wide vast expanse of Nothing. Nobody looks out for you, not really. You have to look after yourself.

So I will pray to the God of Nothing, Nothing above, Nothing before, Nothing beyond.

The only real Goddesses are the ones who were in the Bitch Posse.

She pulls the tapestry out from under the bed. Almost done, now. She knots a few more stitches and taps everything into place. Then she uses her safety scissors to cut the threads and pulls the weaving from the loom.

Lacing the first two warp threads together, she knots them, then ties together the second and third. She works quickly along the top edge of the design, slides in that last yarn tail, and does the same along the bottom edge.

She holds the weaving up in the air. A million mountains in red, green, and blue, with a night-sky deep-sea background of richest purple. The little silver and gold threads blink like stars in the sky and fish in the sea. It's perfect. Complete. Like nothing else she's ever done.

Well. Like one other thing she did. A pair, the best moment of her life and her greatest creative work.

She closes her eyes and lets the girls sit next to her for a minute and gives them each a hug and a kiss. *I love you. See ya later.* Then she spreads the tapestry over her pillow, lights an imaginary cigarette and pretends to smoke it. The phantom scorch of heat in her lungs is twice as hot as the real thing. She always thinks deep when she smokes, and sure enough something else comes to her now.

What awaits her outside is just another Institution. Fewer rules and more ways to fuck yourself over but another Institution nonetheless, with Someone Else in charge. Oddly enough the realization sobers her, and the nine Carbitral in her dresser flicker into her palm again. She licks her finger and presses it to one of the tablets, then licks it again, thinking

Amy Linnet. Whatever happened to her? What did she do with the freedom Cherry gave her? Did she keep pounding down pills and vodka and turn into her parents despite herself? Or did she make something good of her life?

And Rennie, 'Wren' Taylor. What made her embrace the name she hated, the person she hated? Did killing purge her of all the anger she felt? Or did it just fuck her up even more?

The answers might be interesting, but they don't really matter. Her Bitch Posse girls aren't part of her story anymore, but she'll always love them and they know that.

It all makes sense in a weird sort of way. Because the Fates and the Furies were sisters, children of Mother Night. Straight Ds in senior English but she remembers that little tidbit.

The windows on the second floor don't open, of course, but she presses her face to the glass, imagining the rain soaking her face, wetting her hair. She will never know what happened to her friends, not unless she goes on some big Internet search for them and looks them up and calls them out of the blue: *Hey, you probably don't remember me, but . . .* and that, well, that's just not the kind of thing Cherry Winters does. Cherry's too strong for that. Right?

Right?

She's just a pinprick of light in an enormous roll of butcher paper; she will drown in the sea of the world. If she could turn invisible and float through the glass without being cut, and be outside in the rain, pelted by cold water, soaking, real . . . would that make her strong? Strong enough?

Diana used to listen to her little brother crying in the night, calling for their absent mother, while Diana lay frozen in bed, terrified.

When the princess threw herself down a flight of stairs, her prince ignored her and went out horseback riding.

Next to her on the bed breathes a princess, diamond-tiaraed, a spray of pink roses in her arms, that pale sequined dress. She's a half a ghost, as real as anything else in this fucked-up world, and Cherry laces her fingers through hers.

And Diana says: *If I was perfect, I wouldn't be dead.*

And Diana says: *I was never as beautiful as the media made me.*

And Diana says: *It's too hard to be your queen. Can I just be your friend?*

And the princess takes the crown from her own head and places it on Cherry's.

Happily ever after.

Jagged images flash into Cherry's head of car crashes, drug parties, buying everything in sight, spreading legs and sucking in the world to fill some emptiness that yawns and aches and is never satisfied.

Thank God I'm here.

God? Is that what went through her mind just now?

Sorry. I don't believe in You. I forgot.

Tomorrow they will come in and tell her she is ready to go outpatient. Their little rules and regulations and phony women's therapy sessions are shams, fake, useless. Cherry hates being watched, accounted for, checked in and out with charts and bench passes. She should just go. *I don't want help, I don't need help, I won't take help, from anyone. And that's the goddamn truth, God help me.*

Outside the world is so big no one could keep track of her. They don't know she's fucked up in love and in hate with Michael. That probably, she'd let him beat her up if that's what he wanted to do, might even goad him into it, for some fucked-up reason she can't figure out.

They don't know that she sits here with nine Carbitral in her palm.

Marian is long gone now but words of hers echo in Cherry's head: *Do you want to be like me?*

Cherry pounds her fists on her perfect tapestry, her mountains of triangles, her creation. Tears that aren't tears bleed out of her eyes. *I'm not like this, I'm not weak, I'm strong!* She wants out, out of this goddamn place. There's no one to help here. The one person she tried to help said sayonara to life.

Josie's tennis bracelet comes unclasped, flies cross the room, jangles to the floor. And another moment of clarity hits her. There are corners of the outside Institution where people are more fucked up than Cherry herself. When Cherry makes her way out of this little Institution into the bigger one, she will find those places, help those people.

Maybe she will look up her old friends, after she has her own shit together.

But not yet. Right now, she has a bottom to hit. A fate to fulfill.

Cherry reaches into the corner, picks up the bracelet, strings it back onto her wrist.

The air shimmers with a princess-girl's smile. And the princess-girl whispers: *Whoever is in distress can call on me. I will come running, wherever they are.*

Cherry tucks her weaving under her arm. She walks into the bathroom, gazes in the mirror one last time, and spreads her tapestry on the floor. Kneeling on it, arms outstretched, she prays to Someone.

As long as the stars are fixed in the heavens and the fish sparkle in the sea.

With her right hand, she presses the handful of pills to her mouth.

God . . .

She reaches for the red Emergency button.

Help me . . .

The pills slip between her fingers, scatter like beads across the floor.

She pushes the button and closes her eyes.

Rain patters on the window.

42
Amy

May, 1988
The Porter Place

My consciousness returns to my body as the headlights flash from the highway. 'A cop?' I look down at myself, hands trembling. I'm covered with blood; it's drying already, cooling off. Who knew blood was so hot?

Blood?

What have I done?

My two best friends are covered with blood too. There's a body on the barn floor, four letters carved in its chest. My lips are sticky. I lick them and taste iron.

Oh, my God.

He's dead?

Sobs choke my throat and rock through me, my stomach my heart my ears, ohmyGodohmyGodohmyGod, *oh my God* . . .

A smack burns my face and Cherry's palm flies by me like a bird. 'Damn it, Amy, get a hold of yourself. Listen. There isn't much time.' She picks up the knife, wipes the handle against her shirt, presses her fingers around it, and throws it down again.

'Is it a cop?' I ask again. No other thought will pass through my brain. I feel dumb, like I can't process anything.

'No, no, it's kids, it's an old boat-of-car, you still have time.'

'My car, quick!' Rennie fumbles for her keys.

'Keys are in the ignition. You two go.'

'Us two?' repeats Rennie.

'Just you and Amy, hurry up!'

'You're crazy.' Rennie grabs Cherry's arm. 'You come too!'

'Listen. In a couple minutes those kids'll be up here and they'll find the body and call the cops and who the hell do you think will be under suspicion?'

'We won't let you take the blame. We're staying with you,' says Rennie.

She's right, we've been sisters all along; we face everything together.

'No,' Cherry says. 'It isn't gonna happen this way.' She pushes a sticky strand of hair behind her ears. 'Amy, Rennie, you guys are eighteen – you could go to jail. You have your futures to think—'

Rennie cuts in. 'Fuck Stanford! It's just another fucking school.'

Cherry takes a deep breath. 'Rennie Taylor, you're the smartest girl I've ever known, and you're going to be writing some important books, and I'm not going to let you screw that up.'

'Fuck books! You'll write them too. You're as smart as I am and don't you ever forget it!' She seizes Cherry's arm. 'Now come on already!'

Cherry shakes Rennie's fingers away. 'You and Amy deserve the most beautiful things in the world.'

All I can say is 'Cherry . . .'

'You know I'm right. It was my fault anyway. I let it get out of control. I pulled you over the edge.'

'Fuck that, Cherry,' says Rennie. 'You're fucking crazy. Get in the fucking car!'

She shakes her head. 'No one in the Bitch Posse's going to fucking jail. I'll confess to everything; no one will ever know you were here. The worst I'll get is juvie for a while. I can take that.'

'Cherry . . .' I squeak out again, like an idiot.

'This is the best way, the only way, this can end! Stop wasting fucking time. Just jump in Rennie's car. Go!'

Rennie tugs her hand. 'No way, let's all go, come on!'

'It's gonna hang on someone, Rennie. A bloody body, blood all over your car, all over our clothes? Look, it's better that it's just me.'

Finally I find words. 'I won't let you do that!' *Has this really happened? Have we really* . . . I won't think it.

'I said to myself earlier that if it ended up like this, this was how it'd have to be.' The headlights swing to the left; they're almost here. 'You two have more at stake than I do. Just let me do this!'

'No!' I yell, stomping my foot like a little girl. 'Come with us, or else let's all hang together!'

Tears creep down her nose. 'Damn it Amy, Rennie, why won't you let me save you?' She wipes her eyes, and blood comes away from her fingers, streaks her face.

'Because you're acting fucking crazy!' Rennie chokes out, her chest heaving with sobs.

Cherry smacks her across the face and Rennie's hand flies to her cheek. 'Listen to me, you bitch. You always said you believe in Fate. All those Greek tragedies and shit. Not even the gods could mess with the Fates.'

'Fuck Fate!' screams Rennie, still pressing her hand to her face. 'Just fuck Fate!'

Cherry slaps her other cheek and Rennie shuts up. 'Listen, girls. This is my moment, the best fucking moment I can create. I won't let you take it from me.'

Rennie seizes her arm again. 'Just get in the fucking car!'

Cherry unpeels Rennie's fingers and slaps her a third time. 'You bitch, you bitch, don't betray me like this!' Her tears come in sheets. 'This is my chance to be somebody, to make a difference. Don't you understand I love you two girls more than anything in the world?' She leans forward and with each hand grasps our Czech glass necklaces, the ones I made for us for Christmas.

'Why . . . ?' Rennie starts.

Cherry yanks them, hard, and before I know it my blue beads and Rennie's red ones pop off, float like teardrops through the air, and go rolling across the dirt. Then she seizes her own and tugs, and green beads fly like lightning bugs, scatter into the grass. 'It's over.' She pulls open the car door and pushes me and Rennie inside. 'Go.' She slams the door behind us and I can read her lips. 'Go!'

Rennie's sobs slow to hiccups as she starts the car. Hundreds of beads wink in the headlights. The tires spin and we drive out the back way, past the shed and the silo. Rain trickles over the windshield, and when we hit the highway I start to cry again.

'She shouldn't have done that.' Someone's tied a rope around my neck and is squeezing, squeezing, squeezing, and tears pull themselves up from my heart and burst into the air. 'Rennie . . .' Words don't come, my best friend, *my best friend* . . . She saved our asses and put her own on the line. Oh, *Jesus* . . .

My heart splits down the middle and I'm not even a person any longer. I wipe my eyes with the back of my hand. 'Why, why'd she do that?'

Rennie sighs, a deep, aching sigh that's edged with pain. 'She told you why.'

Fate. Fate. Fate.

Fuck fate.

But it's too late for that.

Something big pushes into my head and threatens to consume me, and I know what it is: it's the enormity of what we've done. I'm suddenly dizzy and I'm glad I'm not driving. 'We all took part. We're all to blame.' And when I say it that way, it really does seem awful.

Rennie's eyes are hollow. 'Blame, shit. He motherfucking deserved everything we gave him, and don't you forget it, Amy.'

But her words don't ring true. She's playing tough and I make up my mind to do the same, for the rest of my life or as long as it takes me to forget this night.

And in an odd sort of way it was the most amazing thing I've ever done, swimmingly exciting, hypnotic, satisfying . . .

What am I?

A killer.

I'm not I'm not I'm not. I reach into my purse and grab my Xanax bottle, pull out five and chew them. Wordlessly, I pass the bottle to Rennie. She takes a few and tosses them into her mouth. What's going through her head? No matter how close you are to someone, you don't really know them at all.

I concentrate on the routines I know are ahead of me. Slipping early morning into my house because my folks'll be too passed out to notice. Grabbing clothes for me and Rennie. Taking our old ones to the landfill in a giant trash bag. Scrubbing her Beetle at the car wash, with none of the sudsy water fights we've had in the past. All without words. I don't have any.

That'll all be for later.

The Xanax has pulled away some of my feelings, but there's a big hole in my heart, a hole where Cherry should be. She's ripped herself out of our lives, rewoven the pattern so that her freedom buys ours. What happened in the barn was an accident, a terrible and stark mistake, but she's done her best to patch it over, even if it means destroying herself. Would I have done the same?

Of course I would have. We all would have.

She's already sunk away, a stone flung into water, nothing left but the circles rippling around the splash. But is she gone forever?

Impossible.

She'll always be in my head, passing me a joint and laughing about nothing, rubbing my back as I cry in her bedroom, closing her eyes as I lean toward her for the first best kiss of my life. She'll always be taking care of every living thing that crosses her path, will always be screaming through the car window as she seals her fate.

My heart stops beating for a second.

The excitement and power and unity and love of our circle of three will never never never be unbraided, no matter what happens to any of us. And the three of us will always be woven back into the tangle that was and is and will forever be The Bitch Posse.

Rennie'll feel the exact same thing, Cherry too, wherever she ends up. Only we'll never talk about it.

How can we? Our bond is stronger than any words we could use to describe it.

This was the only way our story could have ended. *Killing is wrong killing is wrong killing is wrong* but events fell together this way for a reason, this was the way everything was meant to unfold. And Dawn, I don't know her; perhaps she will find happiness, but she'll never thank us for it, that's for sure.

God?

Give me a break.

You think God's looking out for me? After all the shit that's happened?

That's one of those questions that answer themselves.

Anyway, I'll never go back to St Sebastian's, and I'll never again pretend my parents have their shit together.

And Michigan and all that, I can't see that far ahead, but I suppose if Brandon and I don't fall apart before summer's over, it'll end when I head to Ann Arbor.

I'll meet someone new.

He will make me happy.

And then?

Then my vision stops.

Will things work out for me in the end? Can I have a normal life, in the end, in the far far away end that isn't anywhere close to being visible?

Can any of us?

I mean, the end is when you're dead, isn't it? And I have no clue what a normal life would be.

So fuck that shit.

For now, for this moment, all Rennie and I have is each other . . . and I lean into her shoulder, and she curves an arm around me. The night is lifting, and the road forks in front of us. Pink and purple bands of color streak across the sky, as the sun emerges from the horizon, as this tomorrow dawns.

Bitch Goddess Notebook

Final Entry (for now)
For all our Posse, everywhere

A circle's round, it has no end;
That's how long I want to be your friend.

Tear off the mask and stop pretending. Your Posse knows the truth.

Want to put the puzzle together?

Your weakness is your strength.

Lose your mind to find your heart.

Through rage, make peace.

Dig deep. Make it hurt. Make it bleed.

We fucking dare you!

Greater love hath no woman than this, that she lay down her life for her friends.

A boy's not going to save you.

A baby's not going to save you.

A book's not going to save you.

God's not going to save you.

But you'll always have your Posse, and don't you ever forget it.

As long as the stars are fixed in the heavens, and the fish sparkle in the sea.

Don't worry, princess. Your Posse will forgive you if you leave us for a boy.

We'll forgive you if you shoot for the stars and forget about us on earth.

If we never see you again, that's okay. We'll always have our memories.

But be honest. Scratch the surface and see a glimmer of yourself. Gouge deeper and harder until it hurts so bad you want to die.

This is my blood.

And now we're all broken,

and now we're all alone,

and now we're all sad and small and not making much sense.

But you'll never get found if you don't get lost.

Now we see through a glass darkly, but then we shall see face to face.

Take a long hard look:

Objects in mirror are closer than they appear.